OLIVERO'S OUTRAGEOUS PROPOSAL

OLIVERO'S OUTRAGEOUS PROPOSAL

BY

KATE WALKER

First published in Great Britain 2015
by Mills & Boon, an imprint of Harlequin (UK) Limited,
Large Print edition 2015
Eton House, 18-24 Paradise Road,
Richmond, Surrey, TW9 1SR

ISBN: 978-0-263-25664-2

Harlequin (UK) Limited's policy is to use papers that are natural, renewable and recyclable products and made from wood grown in sustainable forests. The logging and manufacturing processes conform to the legal environmental regulations of the country of origin.

Printed and bound in Great Britain
by CPI Antony Rowe, Chippenham, Wiltshire

For my dear friend Pat
1949–2014
Good friends are like stars…
You don't always see them,
but you know they are always there.

CHAPTER ONE

ALYSE HAD ALMOST given up on her plan, and was on the verge of deciding that the whole thing was a crazy, downright dangerous idea, when she saw him. She was actually thinking about leaving before this dazzling charity ball had really got started, suffering second and even third thoughts about the wild scheme she had come up with when the crowd before her parted slightly, forming a pathway that led straight from her to the tall, dark male on the opposite side of the room.

Her breath caught, and she knew that her eyes had widened even as she pushed back a fall of golden-blonde hair so as to see him better. He was…

'Perfect…'

The word slipped past her lips, escaping her control and actually whispering into the overheated air.

The man on the far side of the room looked so different, alien almost. He stood out as vividly as a big black eagle in the middle of a bunch of glorious, sparkling peacocks. Of the same species but somehow totally unlike everyone else.

And that difference was what caught her eyes and held them, finding it impossible to look away. She even froze with her champagne flute halfway to her lips, unable to complete the movement.

He was stunning. There was no other word for it. Tall and strong with a lean, powerful physique encased in the sleek sophistication of formal clothes in a way that somehow made him look dangerously untamed in contrast to the elegant silk suit, the pristine white of his shirt. His tie had been tugged loose at some point by impatient, restless hands, and it now dangled limply around his throat where the top button of his shirt had been wrenched open too, as if he needed space to breathe. The fall of his black hair was worn longer than any other man's there, like the mane of a powerful lion. High slashing cheekbones were etched above the lean stretch of his cheeks, long dark lashes concealing the burn of his eyes as he stared out across the room, the faint smile on his sensual mouth one of cold derision rather than any real sign of warmth.

And it was that that made him perfect. The faint but obvious sign that, like her, he didn't quite belong here. Of course, she doubted that he'd been pushed out into the public world as she had. Her father had insisted that she come here tonight, when she'd much rather have stayed at home.

'You need to get out after spending your days stuck in that poky little art gallery,' he'd said.

'I like my days in the gallery!' Alyse had protested. It might not be the job in fine art she'd hoped for, but she earned her own money and, if nothing else, it gave her a break from the stresses at home when the demands of her mother's illness seemed to throw a black cloud over everything.

'But you'll never meet anyone unless you socialise more.'

For 'anyone' read Marcus Kavanaugh, Alyse thought wryly. The man who had made her life hell recently with his unwanted attentions, his persistent visits and determination to persuade her to marry him. He'd even started turning up at the 'poky little' art gallery so that she had no peace from him. Then just recently, for some reason, Alyse's father seemed to have decided that the marriage would be a match made in heaven.

'He might be your boss's son and heir, but he's just not my type!' she'd protested, but it was obvious that her father wasn't listening. He wasn't actually pressing her to accept Marcus's proposal but, all the same, it was plain that he thought it was unlikely that she'd do better with anyone else.

In the end, exhausted by feeling harassed and oppressed, she'd resolved to come to the ball tonight and use the event as a way to break out of the predicament in which she found herself. Which was where the stranger across the room came in.

Of course, this man obviously wasn't slightly out of his depth like her. His height, stature and the fine cut of his clothes were the match of anyone here, and his expression showed that he wouldn't give a damn what anyone thought of him. Which gave him an added advantage as the necessary partner in what she had hoped for tonight.

Her partner in crime, as it were.

It was as that thought crossed her mind that it seemed it had reached out and touched the man opposite. Because he stirred as if something had alerted him. That leonine head swung round, and his eyes clashed with hers.

It seemed that in the moment her eyes met his the world suddenly tilted, lurching dizzily, so that she actually reached out a hand to press against the wall beside her and keep herself upright.

Danger.

The word seemed to flash wildly inside her head, making her bite her lip in a sort of a panic, but one that was mixed with excitement too. She'd wanted a way to put an end to Marcus's over-persistent pursuit; it would be great if she could have a little fun as she did so. If *fun* was the way to describe the fizz this man put into her body.

She'd started slightly in that moment of fierce contact, jerking her glass so that drops of the pale sparkling liquid splashed out of it, landing on the rich blue silk of her dress and marking it with damp, spreading patches.

'Oh, no!'

She had a tissue in her tiny silver clutch, but reaching for it with one hand while trying to balance the glass with the other only made things so much worse. The delicate stem of her glass flute was clutched between her fingers, the bag almost tumbling to the floor. Her desperate grab to stop it escaping made it slip dangerously in her grasp, slopping more wine onto the tops of her breasts exposed by the scooped neckline of her dress.

'Allow me.'

It was a cool voice, calm and smooth as silk, powerfully soothing. Alyse had barely enough time to recognise that it was deep, masculine and beautifully accented before a pair of hands—long, strong, bronze-skinned—reached out and took the vulnerable glass, the silver clutch from her, depositing them on a nearby table. Then he snagged up an immaculate white napkin and shook it loose before pressing it against her waist, padding at the spill that stained her dress.

'Th-thank you.'

The foolish weakness in her legs was still afflicting her, so she fought for the control she needed. But, in spite of her efforts, she still swayed awkwardly on the ridiculously high heels she was unused to wearing.

'Steady.'

That voice was closer, almost in her ear. Or perhaps that had something to do with the way he had stopped mopping her dry and now that powerful hand had closed around her own, holding her upright.

'Thank you.'

To her relief, her voice was stronger now, firmer, and she felt her balance return. She could stand upright at last, bring her head up, look him in the eye…

And almost lost all that hard-won stability when she looked up into the bluest eyes she had ever seen, deep and clear and bright as a Mediterranean ocean in the sun at the height of the day.

The man who had been on the opposite side of the room now stood at her side, big and dark and disturbing. His tall frame blocked out the light, the sight of everyone else in the ballroom. The heat of his body seemed to reach out to enclose her, and the scent of his skin, mixed with some tangy cologne, was like a warm enchantment all around her so that inhaling it made her head spin in sensuous intoxication.

'You.'

This time she had enough thought left to twist her hand from under his and grab at the strong arm that was near to her. She felt the hardness of bone, the power of muscles bunch and tighten under the silk suit and knew a rush of heat and flame that seared along her nerves, threatening to melt her strength away in the same moment that she rediscovered it.

'Me...' he confirmed, the uneven smile that accompanied the single word strangely ambiguous.

He took the napkin from the hand that still held hers, freeing it for use again.

'Better get this dried off fast,' he murmured, 'before it ruins your dress completely.'

'I—yes...'

What else was there to say? And who else to say it to? It seemed that they existed in a private, closed off bubble, a world of their own while the buzz of conversation went on around her unabated.

That proud dark head was bent, the brush of his waving hair soft against her cheek as he concentrated on the task of cleaning up the mess of wine. He was so close that she felt he must hear the unexpected thunder of her heart, see the way her breathing had sped up, bringing a rush of colour to her skin. That napkin was now moving over the edge of her neckline, crossing the point where blue silk met creamy flushed skin, stroking over the sheen of wine on the tops of her breasts.

It was soft, delicate almost, but in the same second it felt like an invasion, far too intimate for the moment and their surroundings. Too intimate from *him.*

'I think that will do...'

She wanted to spin away, knocking his hands aside, so shaken by the effect his touch was having on her even through the folds of that starched linen napkin. But at the same time she wanted *more* of it. More of that touch and closer, nearer to skin.

So she pushed the response from her mouth, afraid that if she wasn't careful she would replace the words with others. Ones that her primitive female instincts wanted her to throw at him, the words *more* and *please* hovering dangerously close to her tongue.

'I'm fine now—thank you.'

'Yes, I think you are.'

He was still so close that his warm breath stirred the blonde tendrils of her hair where they curled over her ear. But at least his hand had stopped that slow, caressing movement, and he had lifted it from her skin, bundling the napkin into a ball before dropping it back on to the table beside them.

'So perhaps now we can start again.'

The beautifully accented voice had a smile in it, one that was echoed in the curve of his lips. But those deep blue eyes had a cooler, assessing expression in them that made her feel uncomfortably like some specimen laid out on a microscope slide.

'Or, rather, *start*.'

He straightened up fully and it was only then that she realised just how tall he was, the way he had bent to his task disguising the long, lean frame that was approaching three inches taller than hers, even in the four-inch heels.

'My name is Dario Olivero,' he said, holding out a hand in a formal greeting that seemed ridiculous after that enclosed moment of heightened intimacy they had just shared. His voice sounded strangely rough, as if he was speaking from a dry throat.

'Alyse Gregory…'

She followed his lead, her voice almost failing her as she slicked her tongue over suddenly parched lips in an attempt to moisten them, and watched his intent blue gaze drop to watch the betraying movement. She could have sworn that the corners of that beautifully shaped mouth curled up slightly in response and it seemed to her that it was the sort of smile that might appear on the face of a tiger when it realised that the deer it had its sights on was tremblingly aware of its presence.

But even that thought fled from her mind when he took her hand in his and held it, strong and warm and shockingly exciting. It was as if no one had ever held her hand before. At least not with this sizzling burn of contact, the shockwaves of heat that seemed to spread out from every tiny point of contact, burning along her nerves straight to the most feminine centre of her body. The sensations, the thoughts this created felt positively licentious, indecent in such a public place and with someone she had only just met.

They were also the sort of sensations she had never felt before. Never this fast, this strong, for a man who was almost a complete stranger.

But at least now she knew his name. And she'd heard of Dario Olivero of course. Who hadn't? His vineyards and the superb award-winning wines they created were known the world over.

'Alyse…' he said, and his tone made her name into a very new and very sensual sound, curling the two syllables around his tongue and making them seem almost like a caress. But the look in his eyes still seemed to contradict the soothing sound. The clear dark blue had sharpened, focused strangely just for a moment, then his face relaxed again and he turned on a brief blinding smile.

Alyse Gregory. The name echoed round inside Dario's head. So *this* was Lady Alyse Gregory. He had been told that she was to be at the ball—it was the only reason he had endured the boredom of the evening so far, though it had amused him to watch the other guests, see their false smiles, the air kisses that made no contact, meant nothing at all.

Way back, he would not even have been able to cross the threshold here, let alone mix with this titled and moneyed crowd. If he'd tried, he had no doubt that he would have been shown the door. The back door. A door he'd had plenty of experience of when he'd been in charge of deliveries for the Coretti winery, the place that had given him his first job and set him on the road to success.

Perhaps once he might have been given entry as Henry Kavanaugh's bastard son, if his father had ever acknowledged him. Just the thought brought a sour taste into his mouth. If he had ever hoped for that then tonight the hope was completely erased from his mind. Tonight he was here, accepted, welcomed as himself. As Dario Olivero, owner of the hugely successful vineyards in Tuscany, exporter of the wines that the wealthy and powerful fought to have on their tables at events like this…

A man who had made his own fortune. And of course money talked.

But that wasn't what had brought him here tonight. Instead he'd wanted to meet one woman—this woman.

'Hello, Alyse Gregory.' It took an effort to iron out the note in his voice that revealed the blend of satisfaction and surprise that flooded through him.

He'd expected her to be beautiful. Marcus certainly wouldn't be seen at a huge social event like this with anyone who was less than supermodel material, even if she did have the title that both the Kavanaughs, father and son—legitimate son—believed to be so important.

But this Alyse Gregory was nothing like Marcus's usual run of women. She was tall, blonde, beautiful—that much was true. But there was also something different about her. Something unexpected.

She was far less artificial than the sort of painted sticks Marcus liked to be photographed with. She had curves too—real curves, not the silicone-enhanced bosoms flaunted by Marcus's last but one model of the year. Those moments spent mopping the wine from the creamy skin exposed by her neckline had set his pulse thundering, his trousers feeling uncomfortably tight. The scent of her body, blended with a richly floral perfume, had risen from her skin to enclose him in a scented cloud that made his senses spin. And the moment that a small, glistening drop had slid down into the shadowed valley between her breasts had dried his mouth to parchment so that he had had to swallow hard before he could give her his name.

He was on the verge of making a complete fool of himself, holding on to her fine, long-boned hand for so long. The smile that had come to her lips was wavering, and he could feel the tension in her fingers as if they were hovering on the edge of being snatched away.

'Forgive me…'

'Hello, Dario…'

The two sentences clashed in mid-air between them, and the sudden release of tension made them laugh, even if a little edgily. When he released her hand he was surprised to see that she still held it up just for a moment, suspended between them, not quite breaking the contact.

But a second later she had dropped it to her side again, looking round for the bag he had placed on the table moments before.

'Thank you for coming to my aid.'

'I was coming towards you before that.' He couldn't hold back the truth.

'You were?' Her blonde head went back slightly, green eyes looking up into his face, a small, puzzled frown creasing the smoothness of her brow.

'But of course…'

The smile he gave her now was much more natural, so that he could feel the spark of awareness in her before her own lips curved in response.

'And you knew it.'

'Did I?'

She was going to back away from it; the sharpness of the question told him that. That, and the sudden lift of her chin in defiance, the firming of that full, sensual mouth. She was going to deny that stunning, fiery spark of awareness that had flashed across the width of the huge room in the moment that their eyes had met. An awareness that had pushed him into action, moving towards her before he had even recognised what was happening or stopped to think, in a way that was totally out of character. He was not the sort of man who acted on impulse; he never made a rash move. Everything was thought out, the last detail finalised—'i's dotted, 't's crossed. He was known for it. It was what he'd built his reputation—and his fortune—on: that total focus, the white-hot attention to detail.

And yet here he was, standing before a woman he had seen from across the room, simply because he had been unable to do anything else.

He didn't even have the excuse that she was the woman he'd come here looking for. When he'd taken those first steps to her side he'd had no idea that she was Alyse Gregory.

That feeling had been in her too. He had seen it in her face, in the way she had choked on her wine as she'd tried to swallow it. He had been so totally sure…

'Did I?' she challenged again.

Those green eyes dropped from his, glancing swiftly to her right, to the huge archway where, even this late in the evening, a steady stream of new arrivals were making their way into the overcrowded ballroom. She must be looking for a way of escape, and irritation at the thought that her cowardice would make her deny the truth started to prickle over his skin.

But then, unexpectedly, she paused, turned back, lifted her head again.

'Yes, I did,' she said, strong and firm and almost bold. 'And if you hadn't, then I would certainly have come to you.'

It was such a turnaround that he felt almost as if the world tilted on its axis and something happened so that the woman he had first seen had disappeared and been replaced by another one. Identical in appearance but so very, very different.

'So come on then,' she teased, a new light in her eyes. 'What were you heading towards me for?'

Good question. And one that he was damned if he could answer, with his brain suddenly turned to mud, while the more basic response of his body threatened to scramble his thoughts.

It was just his damned luck that the Alyse Gregory he had come here looking for was the sex kitten who had looked at him across a crowded room, their eyes connecting in an instant lightning strike, calling to him wordlessly with a come-hither glance. And now that he was here…

At that moment, out of the corner of his eye, he saw a movement on the stairs, a sleek blond head he recognised instantly. Marcus had finally made his appearance. Reminding him that the whole point of this had been to make sure that Marcus's scheme to present his father with a titled daughter-in-law came off the rails before the night was over. Time to go back to plan A. Though, if he was lucky, he could put the new plan B into action at the same time.

'I wanted to ask you to dance.'

Now, which woman would answer him? Which Alyse Gregory would give him a response—and in what sort of mood?

'Of course.'

It was another Alyse entirely—a brand new one and one that was totally disconcerting. That smile would have lit up rooms, rivalling the huge glittering chandeliers in the high ceilings of the ballroom. And yet there was something odd about it, something that did not quite ring true. It was *too* bright, *too* blinding.

Too much.

But if that was what she was going to offer then he was going to take it. It fitted with what he had planned. Hell, it fitted with what he *wanted*, and he was having a hard time remembering what he'd planned when what he wanted was beating at the inside of his head like a pounding headache.

'I'd love to dance.'

She held her hand up towards him, and what could he do but take it? They turned towards the dance floor, made their way into an open space. They had just a few moments of the lighthearted waltz that was being played. Enough time to take up the correct position, his arm at her waist, and, as soon as they had, the dance came to a halt, the music stopped.

'Well…'

Alyse laughed, slanting an amused glance at their still linked hands, the careful positioning of their arms. But she didn't make any move to turn away, to break his hold. Instead she stayed where she was, eyes the bright green of purest emeralds as she looked up into his face.

'I still want to dance…'

Dario didn't give a damn about the dancing. But if it meant that she stayed here like this, hands touching, close to him, so that he could see the rise and fall of her breasts as she breathed, watch the colour come and go in her cheeks, inhale the warm soft scent of her body as it came up to him with his head bent down towards hers, then he wasn't going to be the first to break away. So he stayed where he was and waited.

Luckily the next dance was another waltz and, after a couple of seconds counting the beat, Alyse launched into the steps, swaying sensuously, taking him with her. She was incredibly light-footed, barely seeming to touch the floor as she drifted over it.

I still want to dance…

Her own words echoed inside Alyse's head, but she hardly recognised them for what they were. In that moment she had felt as if her mind was suddenly assailed by a multitude of sensations, buzzing and fizzing through her thoughts.

She hadn't just wanted to dance. She had been overwhelmed by an uncontrollable hunger to dance with this man. To feel his hand in hers, his arms around her. And it had nothing to do with the idea that had been in her mind when she had first seen him. The wild plan to find someone who would help her put Marcus off. Who would—hopefully—stop his intent pursuit of her when nothing else had worked.

But this had nothing to do with that. It had only and everything to do with Dario Olivero and the man he was. The man who had knocked her off balance from the moment she had first seen him and from then it felt as if her mind was not her own.

'Dario…' She tried out his name, feeling it as strange on her tongue, catching on her lips. But it was swallowed up in the melody they were dancing to. 'Dario…' she tried again, louder this time.

The dark head bent, blue eyes connecting with hers, searing off a protective layer of skin so that she felt everything—every touch, every movement, the warmth of his breath as it stirred her hair with a new and shocking intensity. She didn't know how she moved her feet, only managing to keep to the steps of the dance by pure instinct as her gaze locked with his.

'You dance very well…' she managed, a tumble of words over a tongue that was thickened with tension and awareness. 'More than well,' she added and felt rather than heard the rumble of laughter in his chest so close to her ear.

'It's a bit late to realise that,' he teased softly. 'What if I had two left feet and trampled you underfoot from the moment we started?'

I wouldn't have minded. She had to clamp her lips shut fast to stop the words escaping from her unguarded mouth. She didn't feel as if her feet belonged to her anyway. She could almost have been hovering six inches above the floor, her steps so light and beyond her control.

'Then relax.'

'I am relaxed.'

He didn't respond—at least not verbally but the slow lifting of one dark brow to question her comment made her heart kick in stunned reaction. Her mind might be whirling in sensation, but her body was holding itself straight and upright as she had been taught in the dance classes her mother had insisted on at the exclusive school she'd attended. The distance between their bodies was tiny—barely there.

But then she looked up into those stunning blue eyes and her heart skipped a beat. There was so much less of that blue there now, the enlarged black of his pupils swallowing up all the colour until his gaze was like a lake of black glass in which she could see herself reflected, small and so very vulnerable. She lost time for a moment, and almost stumbled. She might have tripped if it hadn't been for the strength of the arms supporting her, the width and power of the broad shoulder under her hand.

But it wasn't vulnerability that made her heart kick so hard under the blue silk of her dress that she had to catch her breath on a hasty gasp. It was a realisation that made her head spin, her pulse race.

He felt it too.

She could hardly believe it but there could be little doubt it was true. Dario Olivero, the dark, dangerous-looking pirate who just minutes before had been a total stranger, was now in the grip of the same heated response that was burning her up like a bush fire. He was as aroused as she was, and she was close to swooning with need, weakened by the sort of sensual hunger that she had never known before.

'Dario…'

This time his name was just a croak, the dryness of her mouth, her throat making it almost impossible to speak. But he caught it and a strange flicker of a smile curled the corners of his sensual mouth before he bent his head again and let his cheek rest against the side of her head, his lips brushing her hair as he whispered one word again.

'Relax…'

Gently but irresistibly he drew her towards him, the pressure of one powerful hand tight against her back, the heat of his palm burning the exposed skin over her spine.

'Relax…' he repeated, the softly accented voice entrancing her.

She melted against him, her body curving against his, loose and pliant. Her head was against his chest so that she could hear the heavy, strong beat of his heart under her ear. The scent of him enclosed her, the sway of her body matching his, and she gave herself up to sensation, to an awareness and sensitivity that swept aside the possibility of any other feeling. The heavy pressure of his arousal against her stomach awoke an answering hunger deep inside, an ache of need that was both pleasure and a yearning that demanded to be assuaged.

But not yet. Not until she had enjoyed this sensation of closeness, this connection for a while longer, and taken from it all she could get.

He had a nerve, Dario told himself, telling her to relax, when all the time his whole body felt as if it was in the grip of a raging fever that threatened to burn him up, reducing any chance of control into a pile of ashes blowing round his head. The fact that she had obeyed him only added to the tautness of every nerve that stung with tension every time she moved.

The whisper of her soft soles on the floor, the swirl of the bright blue dress around her slender legs all worked on his senses with hypnotic effect. Every sense, every part of him, his whole concentration was on the woman he held in his arms—the feel of her, the scent, the touch of her against his hands, skin against skin. But it was not enough. He wanted more and yet he was not prepared to stop this, to have it end. Not yet, even if it was to move on to something more viscerally satisfying. Something that every cell in his body was starting to demand with hungry determination.

This wasn't what he had planned on, what he had expected to happen. But right now he was more than prepared to let it go its own way. Any thought of thwarting Marcus's plans had been relegated to the hazy part of his mind. He would let this play out as it was for now…

He drew in a sharp, controlling breath just as one song came to an end and the band began another one. A slow dance. The sort of dance that encouraged a man to take a woman in his arms and hold her close.

So had he made the move or had Alyse stepped closer, moving into his arms without hesitation? She was so close, curved against him, the arch of her body pressed against his at breast and waist and hip so that it was impossible that she couldn't feel the heat and hardness of the hunger he was unable to disguise. She must feel it and yet she showed no sign at all of objecting. If anything, she slid a little closer, making him curse silently at the pleasure that was so close to pain that burned through him as a result.

'Alyse...'

It was just a groan, a note of warning. A public gathering, an elegant ballroom, was not the place for a response like this—so hard, so hot, so strong. This was a sensation that belonged in the bedroom, with his clothes flung wildly aside, the blue silk ripped from her body. It was all he could do to rein his raging senses in, hold himself upright...

'Oh, hell...'

It was impossible. Couldn't be done.

With an acknowledgement of defeat, he dropped his head down low, brushing his lips against the golden silk of her hair, feeling the delicate strands slide under his mouth. She murmured something softly and moved just a little closer, angling her head against the support of his chest so that the fine skin of her cheek, her neck, were exposed, offered to him for the kiss, the caress he knew he could not hold back from taking.

The taste of her flesh was like a drug, intoxicating, seducing him. He couldn't wait any longer.

'Alyse…' His voice was rough and thickened with passion against the delicate curve of her ear. 'I want… Let's…'

'Let's go somewhere else.' Her voice blended with his, the words exactly the same. The same note of hungry need blurring the sound so that they swirled and spun inside his head. 'Somewhere more private.'

When she disengaged herself from his grasp and her hand slid into his, curving soft and warm around his fingers, Dario had no idea whether he was the one who took them from the dance floor or if in fact it was Alyse who led the way.

He only knew that this had been inevitable from the moment their eyes had first met. It was written into their fates, and no one and nothing was going to stop this now.

CHAPTER TWO

THE HALL BEYOND the ballroom was silent, strangely unoccupied after the crowds that had packed the other room. A buffet supper was being served as part of the event, and many people were already queuing there, waiting to be served. As a result, the almost empty hallway seemed unexpectedly cold and uncomfortable, making Alyse shiver in shock at the sudden change of temperature.

'I need my coat…'

She fumbled in her clutch bag, looking for the cloakroom ticket. She had just found it when Dario reached over and took the slip of paper from her hand with a sharp tug.

'Wait here.'

A gesture of courtesy—or taking control? Alyse couldn't help wondering as she watched him stride across the marble floor to where the cloakroom attendant stood on duty. She didn't know and she didn't want to stop and consider the question. *Control* was a word she associated with her father—or with the sort of behaviour Marcus had been trying to force onto her—and she didn't want to think of either of them right now.

Just two minutes out of the ballroom—two minutes away from the warm and intimate closeness of their dance—and already the heat and sensation had started to evaporate, leaving her with an uncomfortable shivery feeling inside. She wrapped her arms around herself in a vain attempt to bring some warmth back to uncomfortably chilled skin.

She hadn't wanted to move apart from him; hadn't wanted to break out of that cocoon that had formed around them. From the moment they had moved, Dario turning away from her, a cold, creeping sense of reality had started to invade the little bubble of delight she had been living in.

'What am I doing?'

She actually muttered the words out loud as she kept her eyes fixed on the back of Dario's dark head, the width of his powerful shoulders.

Was she really planning on heading out of here

with him? With a man she had only met…her eyes slid to a clock above the cloakroom door…less than an hour before.

The main door opened with a heavy swish, someone who had gone outside for a sneaky cigarette coming in and leaving it partially open. Alyse balanced on her toes like an athlete readying for the gun to sound the starting point. She could go now…

But even as she took a step forward she caught the wave of cold and damp that came into the hall from behind the new arrival. His jacket was splashed with water too, warning of a change in weather outside. She would need her coat…and her coat…

Was in Dario's hands, the fine black velvet looking impossibly soft and delicate in the grip of those long, tanned fingers.

She couldn't get her feet to move, freezing where she stood, her eyes locking with his over the heads of the people around them. He knew what she had had on her mind; she could tell it from the faint fast frown that drew those dark brows together, the narrowing of the blue eyes.

'Helena!'

Behind her, just beyond the doorway into the ballroom, Alyse heard an uncomfortably familiar male voice raised in greeting and just the sound of it brought a rush of a whole new set of feelings. In the space of an uneven heartbeat she was brought back to the moment she had arrived at the ball, the desperate plan, only half formed, to make sure that Marcus saw her with someone else so that then perhaps he would take no for an answer.

A swift sidelong glance over her shoulder brought confirmation of the slow creep of unease down her neck. Marcus was here. Suddenly, from wanting him to see her with someone else it had become the last thing she wanted. She wanted to get out of here now and let this evening that had suddenly turned magical in contrast to weeks of tension and strain continue. Pushing herself into action, she turned her feet towards Dario.

'Thank you.'

It sounded as if she had run up a flight of steps rather than across the smooth marble tiling.

'I'm going to need this…' She was already pushing one arm into a sleeve of her coat as she spoke, manoeuvring herself so that she could hitch it up over her shoulder. 'Have you seen the weather outside? It's pouring with rain.'

The shiver she affected was meant to be in response to the conditions outside but it was given an added edge by the worrying sense of unease as she saw the way his gaze went over her head, skimming the entrance hall as if looking for someone.

Automatically, his hands came out to help her pull the other sleeve over her arm, lifting the fall of blonde hair from her shoulders and smoothing it down over the black velvet.

Hurry—hurry! Alyse urged him in the silence of her thoughts. *Please, let's get out of here before Marcus intervenes.*

'We'll have to get a taxi…' she said, pushing her arm under his and curling her hand around the strength of bone and muscle under the fine silk of his jacket. 'Or we'll get soaked.'

She was almost tugging him on his way, urging him towards the door.

'No need,' Dario muttered, nodding towards the uniformed man who held a large black umbrella that he had fetched from a nearby stand above their heads, protecting them from the lashing rain.

'Your car, sir...'

The sleek black vehicle had come to a growling halt at the kerb, the back door opened for Alyse to make her way under the protection of the umbrella. She had only just slid into place on the soft leather seat when the door was slammed after her, and Dario made his way swiftly to the other side. An instant after that, the chauffeur, obviously needing no instructions as to their destination, put the car into motion as he pulled away from the kerb.

Alyse's mood seesawed again, taking her from a need to escape to another, even more unsettling feeling. One that left her breathless and suddenly cold, in spite of the warmth inside the car. Dario's fixed determination had disturbed her so that she could almost believe that she had been kidnapped, taken against her will.

And yet she knew she had been a party to it. More than that, she had been so swamped by the response of her senses that she wasn't thinking straight. She had been burning up with hunger, the sensual need that had uncoiled in the pit of her stomach and radiated out along every nerve. If they could have moved *then*, been instantly transported from the ballroom to wherever they were going, then she wouldn't have had a moment to think, to allow any hint of second thoughts to slide into her mind.

But now, when it seemed that the cold of the evening was seeping into her bones, a slow sneaking sense of apprehension destroyed that wonderful heated knowledge that this was *right*. That it was what she had been looking for all her life. The restrictions she'd had to put up with in order to help care for her ailing mother had limited her chances for the sort of fun and spontaneity her friends enjoyed. Tonight was going to be so very different.

Twisting in her seat, she glanced back the way they'd come, the brilliantly lit doorway to the hotel shielded from the rain by the canopy that flapped furiously in the wind. The weather had driven almost everyone indoors so there was only the doorman on duty. But as she watched a single figure emerged from the hotel doorway and stood, feet planted firmly apart on the red carpet, his whole body turned in their direction, his gaze obviously following the progress of the car as it sped away. The lamplight gleamed on the bright red-gold of his head, making it plain just who he was. He couldn't be anyone else.

Marcus Kavanaugh. The man whose single-minded campaign to bully her into marrying him had blighted her life for the past few weeks. She had done everything she could to make it plain that he meant nothing to her, but it hadn't worked. Of course she'd had to be polite. He was her father's boss's son after all. But politeness hadn't worked. And now that her father had joined in the campaign to see them married, insisting it was the match of the century, she'd felt hounded, trapped, driven into a corner.

It was the memory of how the other man had behaved this morning that made her shudder faintly. She could still hear Marcus's voice telling her that she would regret it if she gave him the runaround any more, and some dark edge to it had made her blood run cold. It was that that had pushed her into the plan she'd had for tonight.

Hastily, Alyse turned back, huddling into her coat.

'Cold?'

Dario's enquiry sounded innocuous but there was an edge to it that brought her eyes up to his in a rush, wary green meeting assessing blue.

'You shivered,' he pointed out.

'Did I?' The inanity of the conversation brought home to her the strangeness of the situation she was in. It was the sort of overly polite small talk you made with a complete stranger when you had just met for the first time.

But that was what Dario was. A stranger. A tall, dark, devastating stranger, and yet a man she had connected with from the start. One whose touch had lit a fire inside her when he'd held her on the dance floor. A man who had driven all thoughts of common sense or self-protection from her head when he had whispered, 'Let's go somewhere else…' in the same moment she had used the exact same words.

Could this be real? She couldn't have this sort of connection in so short a time. And yet this was what she had planned on happening all along. This was supposed to be her get-out-of-jail-free card, wasn't it?

Once more, she made herself look back over her shoulder, seeing the blond man raise his hand to hail a taxi as the car turned a corner and he disappeared from sight. She couldn't hold back a smile at the thought that, no matter what else happened, at this moment Marcus was very definitely out of the picture. The rush of the sense of freedom to her head was like the effect of strong alcohol.

'Feeling better?'

He'd caught the smile—that much was obvious—and wanted an explanation for it. She was never going to tell him the real truth—but then that truth had nothing to do with him. Just as what happened from now on had nothing to do with Marcus. The result was the same, but the one thing she hadn't expected when she'd come up with the whole crazy plan was how much she had *wanted* to do this.

'I could feel even better,' she murmured, sliding over the seat and moving closer to the big, lean body of Dario Olivero. Wanting, needing his arms around her again. 'Yes,' she sighed as the heat from his closeness thawed some of the chill of apprehension inside her. 'Like that.'

He couldn't see her face, Dario reflected as she rested her head against his chest. But the faint purr in her words told him it would still be there on her lips. She felt like a small cat, curled up close, the blonde silk of her hair brushing his chin, the aroma of her perfume swirling around him, making him inhale deeply to draw in more of it. Held as close as she was, she couldn't be unaware of the heat and hardness of his body, the way his heart kicked up at every move she made so that it was almost impossible to keep his breathing steady and controlled. When her head tilted slightly upwards towards his, he knew that she wanted him to kiss her. But not now, not yet.

'We'll soon be there,' he told her, the swift sidelong glance towards the chauffeur meant to imply that they needed to wait until they were alone. And that was definitely true. But there was more to it than that.

He wanted to know what that smile had meant. And why it had appeared on her lips, warming her expression, just after she had looked back through the car window. There had been nothing there to make her smile. Only that one glimpse of Marcus.

And Marcus was nothing to smile about.

Dario's own smile, reflected in the black glass

of the window, was grimly triumphant, the flash of lights as they passed showing up the cold curve of his lips, the determined set of his jaw. Marcus had lost this round—and, with any luck, the rest of the contest.

'Just round this corner.'

And, as he spoke, the car swung round the bend, sending a spray of dark rainwater up over the kerb from a puddle that had gathered as a result of the storm. A short way down the road, they pulled up outside the building where his newly bought apartment took up the whole of the top floor.

'We're here,' Dario urged Alyse, his tone suddenly rough with the knowledge that if he didn't get her out of here and up to that penthouse *fast* then what little was left of the control that had been fraying mercilessly with every sway and pitch of the vehicle that brought her slender warmth even closer to him would snap completely. He would have to have her under him, his hands plundering her soft curves, her silken skin, and to hell with the audience of José the driver or anyone else.

'Time to get inside…'

The image of being inside her that the words flung into his brain was almost his undoing. He grabbed at Alyse's shoulders, wrenching her up from the half lying, half leaning position before he claimed her hands. Folding his around both of hers and pulling her along with him, he exited the car backwards, not even flinching as his broad shoulders met the force of the wind, the slash of the icy rain that was splattering down over his head.

'Come on.'

He pulled his jacket up high to cover her head like an improvised umbrella, protecting that silky hair from the onslaught of the downpour.

'José, I won't need you any more tonight…'

He tossed the command at his driver as he slammed the car door shut behind them, not needing the man's nod of agreement—or the knowing smile that said his employee had already recognised that fact before they'd arrived.

It was like travelling blind, Alyse reflected, her eyes not quite focusing in the glare of the brilliantly lit building after the darkness of the night. She knew that she was crossing a highly polished floor, heard Dario speak some greeting to the man at the desk as they passed, and then they were at the polished steel entry of a lift, the doors sliding open immediately in response to his long bronzed finger pressed on the call button.

So she had to be grateful for the curve of his arm around her. It felt safe and supportive there, the heat and scent of his body enclosing her, and it was as if that warmth was melting away the worries, the apprehension she had felt at first in the car. Now she felt her limbs soften, leaning towards him, resting her head, her weight against the power of his body. The clean scent of his skin surrounded her, blended with some sort of lime cologne, and she gave herself up to the delight of the physical sensations she was experiencing.

'Alyse…'

His tone was soft, slightly roughened at the edges. She lifted her face, her eyes connecting with his, seeing the intense darkness of his pupils, the tiniest edge of blue around their rim. For a moment she was held, mesmerised, unable to look away, and instinctively her lips parted, a faint sigh escaping to blend with his hot breath as his mouth descended towards hers.

His kiss was warm, slow, infinitely seductive. It took her mouth in a wave of languorous delight, lifting her up onto her toes to wrap her arms around his neck, tangle her fingers in the black silk of his hair. The arm that was curled around her shoulder tightened sharply, drawing her closer, bringing her up against the hardness of his body. Lean, strong fingers stroked down the delicate skin of her neck, slipping under the collar of her coat, making her shiver in need. Her heart rate kicked up sharply, sending her blood pulsing through her body, so that she wriggled even closer in burning awareness.

He felt the same, she could tell. There was the undeniable evidence of the hard swell of arousal pressed into the bowl of her pelvis, the faint groan that escaped from between their joined lips before he brought his mouth down harder, stronger, crushing her lips back against her teeth.

'Dario…'

Somehow she choked it out, not wanting to lose the pressure of his mouth on hers. He tasted wonderful, and the moment that his tongue slid over her lips, tracing the seam where they joined, had her sagging against him, losing her breath, losing all sense of where she was.

Would the lift never reach its destination? She wanted to be there—somewhere, as Dario had said, they could be alone together, private, intimate. Yet at the same time she didn't want this moment to end. She wanted to go on and on for ever in this warmth and closeness.

But even as the thought crossed her mind the compartment jolted slightly, came to a halt, throwing her off balance and right into Dario's arms as the doors slid open again.

'We're here.'

Somehow he managed to ease his keys from his pocket and unlock the door while still holding her close, never easing his grip on her arm, her waist.

In spite of the darkness it was obvious that the room was huge, no light illuminating it other than the reflection of the buildings and the streetlamps far below. The faint gleam of the heavy swell of the river was like a silver ribbon, and over to the left the ethereal spider web of a blue circle that looked impossibly delicate to be the London Eye.

She barely had time to adjust to the change in light or look round any more before Dario had tossed his jacket away to the side, heedless of whether it landed on a nearby chair or not, and reached for her again.

'Come here,' he muttered, his voice rough, his accent thickening on the words. 'I've been waiting—wanting to do this ever since the moment I saw you.'

His hands were clamped around her shoulders, rough and bruising, but Alyse neither fully registered it nor truly cared. All that mattered was the passion of that beautifully cruel mouth on her lips, on her skin, the pressure of the hard frame of his chest crushing her breasts. The heat of him surrounded her, flooding her body along with the burn of her own arousal until she was astonished that the pair of them didn't go up in flames.

'I—I—yes…'

It was all she could manage, all she could snatch in, in the moment he allowed her to breathe before his mouth took hers again. His hands closed over her arms as he swung her round, half walking, half carrying her towards the shadowy shape of a huge dark sofa. Her shoes slipped from her feet as he lifted her up, left behind on the soft carpet as his right hand reached round to the back of her neck, finding the zip at the neckline of her dress, swiftly and expertly tugging it down. The release from even the slight constriction of her clothing was like a rush of release to her feelings. Inside the delicate lace of her bra, her breasts stung, pressing against the soft silk, seeming to demand the attention of those strong, rough-palmed hands, and she moaned her encouragement as he stroked his powerful fingers down her body, making her writhe upwards to meet his touch, wanting it stronger, harder. Wanting more.

Then she was lying on her back on the settee, the soft buttery leather cool against the skin that his hands had exposed. And Dario was coming down on top of her, the heavy heat of his skin, the weight of his frame crushing her back into the cushions. One long, finely trousered leg pushed between hers, easing them apart so that she could feel the swollen heat of him pressing against her, crushing into her pelvis, coming so close to the throbbing core of her femininity where the bite of primal need fought against the restriction of their clothing.

'Dario...'

She was reaching for his hands, wanting them on her, wanting to place them where she needed his touch most. She was trying to draw them down to her yearning flesh, but at the same time she wanted to reach for *him*, hungry for the heat of his skin, the taste of him hard upon her mouth.

'I want—I wa...'

But her scrambled words were halted, all train of thought shattered by a sudden violent sound. Someone was at the door, banging hard and slamming a fist against the wood until it seemed that it might actually shatter under its force.

'What?'

Braced hard against the leather settee, Dario froze, his whole body stiffening, his dark head coming up, slightly cocked towards the door, listening intently.

'Who?' Alyse whispered, but he stilled her with a glance, laying one finger across her mouth to silence her. And now, although the scent of his skin was so very close, when all she had to do was to open her mouth and take him in, taste the intensely personal flavour of him as she had wanted just moments before, it was suddenly the last thing she could do. The last thing she dared to do until she knew who had intruded on their seclusion, blasting their way into the heated intimacy they had created and threatening to destroy it totally.

'Olivero!' Another bang at the door clashed with the darkly furious use of Dario's name. 'Open this door, damn you! Open it now!'

A slight gleam in the moonlight showed how Dario's eyes slanted once, briefly, towards where Alyse's head rested against the leather-covered arm of the sofa, then swung back again in the direction of the door.

'Open this door, you bastard! I know you're in there—and Alyse with you too.'

'No!'

The word escaped Alyse in a panic as she recognised the sound, even though distorted through the wood. She knew just who was on the other side of that door, and the fury in his tone reminded her uncomfortably of his threatening warning earlier that day.

'Olivero, you coward, come out and face me…'

'Dario—no!'

Alyse's cry was drowned by another slam of a heavy fist against the wood, and as she reached for him Dario was already levering himself up and off her, that last insult clearly too much for him to take.

Not troubling to rake a hand through his disordered hair or even to smooth down his rumpled clothing, he was striding towards the door, twisting the handle with a violent movement and yanking it open ferociously.

'Well?'

The momentary silence that greeted his appearance, the angry demand of his single word, made Alyse's skin crawl, a cold slimy trail of apprehension sliding down her spine. From where she lay she could see the door, and the man who stood on the other side of it. She had been right, as she knew she'd had to be. The red-gold hair, clashing painfully with a furious scarlet face, the blazing blue eyes were unmistakable. The furious intruder was Marcus Kavanaugh.

But what was he doing here? And how?

He had seen them leave the hotel, had watched them drive off together. She had seen him staring after them when she had looked back through the rain. But how had he known just where to find them? He wouldn't have had time to catch a cab and trail them to Dario's apartment, so how had he known to come straight here and to catch them…?

'Alyse…'

Marcus had turned his attention to her now and, with a small sound of horrified embarrassment, she scrambled up from her place on the settee, forcing herself to her feet. She might have wanted him to get the message—but not like this.

'What the hell are you doing here?'

'I would have thought that was obvious.'

Marcus's spluttering blaze of fury was bad enough, but the edge of laughter in Dario's retort was far worse, setting her teeth on edge and bringing home to her just how dreadful this must all look. She had been sprawled on the settee, her hair tumbling down around her face and shoulders, her legs wide apart, and her clothes…

Cheeks flaming, she tugged her skirt down, struggled to pull her dress up around her shoulders once again, desperate to restore her appearance to a degree of order. Her hands shook so badly that she couldn't reach the zip to pull it up and when she tried to draw Dario's attention to the fact, telegraphing wildly with her eyes and her brows that she needed help, his only response was a blank-eyed stare. Either he didn't understand or…

Her heart quailed inside her, her stomach turning over in sudden nausea. Was it possible that Dario knew only too well what was troubling her but had no intention of making any move to help her? It certainly looked that way. He had barely spared her a glance; instead, all his attention was focused on his raging adversary.

'I— This isn't what you think, Marcus…'

She stumbled over the words, lost them completely when she saw the way that Dario turned, casting a darkly contemptuous look in her direction as if he could barely believe that she had actually said such a stupid thing. Listening to herself as the idiotic comment hung in the air between them, she couldn't believe it either. There was only one possible interpretation of the scene in front of Marcus, and that was the right one. It had also been the one she had wanted him to have, but that had been before this dark fury had erupted around her—and before Dario had seemed to turn away from her.

'And what the hell else would I think it might be?' Marcus spat at her now, making her flinch from the poisonous venom of his tone. 'Unless you're trying to claim that he forced you?'

'I— He… No—I'm not claiming that…'

How could she do any such thing, even to save herself from this hellish embarrassment? She just wished that Dario would say something—anything—to break the tension that stretched tight between the three of them. But after that one demonic touch of humour, the coldly blazing scorn he had turned on her just moments before, he had now frozen where he stood, arms crossed over his broad chest, dark brows drawn together, a silent, watchful observer of the scene in front of him.

'Not that I'd put it past him,' Marcus stunned her by declaring now. 'A man with his reputation.'

'Rep…reputation?' Alyse managed, stunned

to learn that Marcus seemed to know something about Dario—more, in fact, than she did herself. 'What...?'

But Marcus wasn't listening, intent instead on turning the venom he had directed at her previously onto Dario himself.

'Dragged up in the gutter by a mother who was anyone's for the price of—'

It was only the tiniest movement. Just a tensing of Dario's long body, a curl of his fists, a hint of a step forward. But that, when combined with the black thundercloud of his frown, the way his sensual mouth was clamped hard and tight into a thin line, was enough of a warning to have Marcus biting off the last of his insulting sentence and clearly backing down. He obviously didn't think that it was safe to risk baiting Dario any further, however much he might want to.

And the other man's reaction turned Alyse's legs to water at the memory of the way that this had been just what she had planned as part of her original scheme in the first place. It had all seemed so exciting, so brilliant—so *possible* when she had come up with the idea as a way of getting rid of Marcus's unwanted attentions.

Give him the impression that she was involved with another man, that she was seeing someone else—maybe even sleeping with someone else—and then surely he would back off and leave her in peace?

But now, finding herself in exactly the situation she had anticipated, with Marcus at the door, having found her and Dario in a decidedly compromising situation—far more compromising than she had ever planned—things were not at all as she had foreseen. For one thing, Marcus, though looking disgusted and furious, didn't seem to have the intention of turning round and walking away, as he had in her mind when she'd imagined this happening.

And Dario…

She risked a glance at the tall, dark, glowering man to her left, and immediately wished she hadn't. He wasn't actually snarling but he might as well have been and she could practically see his hackles rising in hostile threat to the intruder into his territory. The sparks that seemed to flash between the two men made her feel like some tasty but already wounded prey that was the subject of a face to face confrontation between two powerful and equally ravenous lions.

Giving up on trying to fasten her dress, she folded her arms tightly around her waist, as much to hold herself together as to keep the blue silk from falling into a pool on the carpet at her feet.

'No matter what my reputation,' Dario drawled now, making Alyse start because she was so used to him being silent, 'it seems that Alyse doesn't give a damn about it, *mi caro fratello*.'

My—*what?* Alyse shook her head faintly, unable to believe she had heard right. The stress must be getting to her so that she was imagining things. He couldn't have said…

But, whatever he had said, it had been deliberately provocative. And it had the desired effect, enraging Marcus so that his whole face went white with fury, pulling taut over his bones.

'Marcus…' she tried, desperate to have this appalling stalemate broken, to avoid what she was now starting to fear might actually bring these two to blows. There was something here between these two that was evil. Something she didn't understand but if she could just avoid an actual fight…

'Look, I'm sorry if this has upset you, but really you know I never said…'

He wasn't listening, all his attention focused on Dario's hard, set face. But, even as she watched, Alyse was stunned to see the faint flicker of a smile on the Italian's sensual lips. A smile that was there and gone again in a moment and had nothing warm about it at all.

'I could kill you…'

Marcus's threat, directed at Dario's impassive face, was a low, savage mutter, one that sent a horrified shiver slithering down Alyse's spine. In a panic she stepped forward, her hand coming out as she forgot about holding her dress up and could only think about stopping him.

'Marcus, I tried to tell you that I couldn't see any future for us, so I thought—'

'Thought you'd teach me a lesson?'

'No—I…'

But her voice had no strength, no conviction. Wasn't that really what she had wanted to do? To convince him that she was not for him? That she wasn't at all interested in the proposal he had pushed at her so unexpectedly and had kept pushing for days.

'You thought you'd rub my face in it,' he snarled, the look he turned on her scraping over her body like the burn of acid.

It was only now, when that hateful look paused and lingered deliberately, that Alyse became aware of the betraying damp, darkened patches directly over her breasts where Dario's hot mouth had sought out the sensitive peaks that had strained against her bra. The realisation dried her throat in a moment.

'No...' she tried but, even though her lips moved, no sound managed to come out. And when she glanced uncertainly at Dario, the darkness and focus of his eyes told her that he had something else on his mind other than belief in her declaration.

From a shadowy corner of her thoughts came an uncomfortable memory of the time in the car when she had looked back and seen Marcus staring after them. She'd been careless enough to smile just briefly. And Dario had caught it. Could he think this was what she had wanted?

'Well, you couldn't have made a better job of

it than this, you bitch.' Marcus was continuing his rant. 'You must have known if there was one thing that would guarantee I'd want nothing more to do with you—something that would turn my stomach—it was the sight of you getting down and dirty with my bastard brother.'

CHAPTER THREE

MY BASTARD BROTHER.

This time there could be no doubt about it, though Alyse's thoughts reeled in disbelief at what she heard. She hadn't been sure earlier—*mi caro fratello*—but in plain, straightforward English it couldn't be clearer.

But that just wasn't possible—was it? Marcus was a solid, stolid Englishman with the pale colouring and eyes that marked him out as pure Anglo-Saxon. He had nothing of Dario's stunning golden skin and sleek black hair. Those blue, blue eyes that met hers in a stare of blank confrontation were the only thing that could seem to connect the two. And *bastard* brother…

'Half-brother, to be more accurate,' Dario put in now, though it stuck in his throat to even acknowledge that connection. 'Though definitely the bastard.'

She hadn't known that—or certainly not all

of it, he realised. If the confusion that was written on her pale face was genuine. Somehow she had managed to avoid hearing about the scandal that had exploded in the gossip columns years ago when he had turned up at the Kavanaugh home to carry out his mother's last wishes and claim acknowledgement from his family. But that was impossible, surely. When her father was employed by Marcus and his father, tangled up in everything the younger man did, then even Lady Alyse Gregory must know something of what was going on.

'I…'

That unsettled stare went from his face to Marcus's and back again, no sign of anything but confusion showing in it. So it hadn't been because of who he was that she had chosen him. Obviously any man would have done.

So would she have gone through with it if they hadn't been so rudely interrupted? Or had she calculated this down to the precise second so that they would be caught together at just the last possible moment?

'The last man whose leavings I'd want to touch.' Marcus was really feeling savage now.

Oh, that had hit home. He had caught her on the raw there, and Dario had to admit to a twist of admiration at the way her head came up, her eyes flashed. At last she looked like the woman she was. The product of years of aristocratic heritage, of pure blue-blooded breeding. The woman Henry Kavanaugh dreamed of having as the mother of his grandchildren.

'I'm nobody's leavings! And if you hadn't refused to take no for an answer, then I wouldn't have been forced to…'

The impetus given her by the rush of indignation had obviously ebbed, and she turned a wary, uncertain look on Dario, clearly realising that she had just dug herself even deeper into the hole she found herself in. There was more to that look too. She wasn't asking but summoning him to her aid. She actually expected him to come to her assistance, confirm her story. But if she thought he was going to give her a helping hand, then she had better think again. That 'forced' had hit home, barbs sticking into his skin.

'I wouldn't have had to…'

The careful amendment did nothing to soothe Dario's mood. He was keeping out of this one until she had decided which way she was going to jump.

'You'll regret this.' Marcus's tone was low and savage.

'I already do.'

So now they were getting closer to the truth. That last comment had the ring of conviction in it. Obviously Lady Alyse Gregory would regret her unthinking and indiscreet lapse of control. Particularly as she had now discovered that she had thrown herself into the arms of the Italian bastard that Marcus had revealed him to be.

Clearly his half-brother thought so too. There was actually a smile of triumph in those pale eyes.

'And nothing happened? Then come with me now and we'll forget all about this foolishness.'

Wrong move, brother, Dario thought to himself. Even on his short acquaintance with her, he was pretty damn sure that Alyse would not respond well to that autocratic 'come with me now'. The only way he could have made matters worse would have been by snapping his fingers at her as if he was calling a dog to heel.

And Alyse Gregory was no obedient pet. That

was plain from the way her mouth tightened, and she shook back the mane of golden hair.

'No.'

She had to say it, Alyse acknowledged inwardly. There was no other option. Given a choice in the matter, she would have walked out of here right now and never looked back at either Dario or Marcus. She had no idea just what these two brothers—*brothers!*—were up to but she had no wish to get caught in the middle of whatever personal war they were intent on fighting.

But leaving meant letting Marcus think that he had won. And that was the last thing she wanted. Hadn't she set out on this crazy venture in the first place as a way of making sure that he left her alone? That he stopped plaguing her with expressions of how beneficial it would be for the two of them, blending the aristocratic blood of her line with the wealth and security that he could bring to the table. She had never been able to get him to accept her refusal, and if she left with him now then it would all be to do again.

'No,' she tried again when he looked unconvinced.

'Alyse…'

'The lady said no,' Dario drawled unexpectedly from behind her. 'You lose.'

You lose! If earlier she had felt like some vulnerable prey, now the sensation was much more like some tasty bone being fought over by two bad-tempered dogs.

What did he think she was? Some sort of trophy—just a notch on his bedpost? Not that they had got as far as the bed! Just let them get rid of Marcus and she would make him pay for that.

Dario moved past her, taking hold of the door and moving it to block Marcus's entrance.

'Goodnight, Marcus,' he said pointedly.

'I swear you'll regret this.' It was so different this time. The voice of darkness with threat threaded through every word. 'You'll…'

'Goodnight, Marcus.'

Dario pushed the door even closer to being shut, blocking out the sight of Marcus's enraged face. Alyse found that she was holding her breath, not knowing what she would do if he refused to leave. Would they have to call the police?

She could just imagine what her father's reaction would be if she was involved in some scandal that hit the newspapers, tonight of all nights. He had asked her—begged her—not to rile Kavanaugh, to keep the family name out of the gossip columns. It would just destroy her mother, who had recently retreated into one of her black depressions. That was why she had decided on the plan that was supposed to make Marcus reject the idea of marriage. A plan that now seemed to have had more effect than she could ever have dreamed of.

'Damn you to hell, Olivero!' Marcus flung one more violent outburst at the other man.

But then, to Alyse's relief, he finally turned and marched off down the corridor, swearing as he went.

'At last.'

Dario kicked the door shut behind him, his smile an expression of grim satisfaction as he turned back to Alyse.

'I think we've seen the back of him.'

'Mmm…'

Alyse was preoccupied with finally hitching her dress up so that it sat securely on her shoulders again, struggling to get her hands on the pull of the zip at her waist, to restore her appearance to normality.

'So where were we?'

She hadn't seen him come closer, prowling soft as a hunting cat, so she jumped violently when he touched her, warm and soft on her cheek.

'What?' Her head snapped up, her fumbling grip freezing on the tab of the zip.

His hand was on her hair, long fingers tangling in the fall of blonde, smoothing through the silky strands when she realised just what he meant and tensed up sharply.

'You think we— You can just take up from where you left off?'

'Why not?' He actually sounded genuinely puzzled. 'What's changed?'

'What's... You...'

The words spluttered to a halt inside her head, shock, disbelief and sheer blind fury warring to find the uppermost spot. Fury won. It was the memory of that casually triumphant '*You lose*' that did it.

'You dare to think that nothing's changed?' She flung the words at him, not liking the way that they simply rebounded off his hard, set bone structure.

'Dare?' he echoed dangerously. 'What's to dare about it? We both know why you came here—or we did until dear Marcus interrupted everything. But now he's gone…'

And so had the mood. From the heated sensuality, the primal hunger she had been feeling before, she was now swamped with bitter disappointment that was the result of his cold conviction that they would just take up from where they had been interrupted. He made no concessions to the way that the mood had been shattered by his *brother's* arrival. The way they had fought over her like dogs over a bone.

The struggle to deal with the let-down made her feel as limp as a balloon that had been pricked by a pin, all the air slowly seeping away. She wasn't prepared to investigate the bitter sting that might have been disappointment.

Dario had made her feel wonderful. His touch had aroused her, his kiss had enticed her. But most of all he had made her feel beautiful—and special. She had wanted him so badly and thought that he wanted her too. But that had been before she had become aware of just who he was. Before she had been caught in the middle of the private war that Dario and Marcus were waging between them. She didn't know what had started it, but it was blatantly obvious that they detested each other and that they would do anything at all to score points over one another. She had no intention of being used to make Dario Olivero feel that his half-brother had lost and he had *won*.

'I don't think so.'

She twisted away from him, biting down hard on her lower lip to hold back the small cry of pain as his fingers caught in her hair, tugging painfully at her scalp. Refusing to let him see that it had hurt her, she tossed back the tumbled mane and looked him straight in those blue eyes. How had she never seen how cold they could become? Had her infatuation blinded her so that she hadn't recognised how much they resembled Marcus's eyes? They might be a deeper, richer blue, but the way they froze over when he was angry was exactly the same.

'What the hell's going on?'

She caught Dario's dark frown and made herself face it defiantly.

'Haven't you got it yet?' she challenged, almost defeated by the swift narrowing of those blue eyes, focusing them like lasers on her face. She forced herself to go on before her nerve failed her completely. 'This wasn't anything real. Not at all. It was just a bit of fun.'

'Fun.'

The way the word was snatched in through his clenched teeth was like the hiss of a cobra just before it sprang forward to bite. So much so that Alyse actually took a hasty step backwards, away from attack.

An attack that didn't come. Instead, Dario had frozen into complete stillness before her, his powerful body seeming to be carved from stone.

'Do you usually use people for *fun*?'

'I didn't use…'

Her courage failed her in the burn of his glare. She hadn't used him—at least not in the way he'd meant. But when she'd started out on this plan, with that crazy idea in her head, of playing for attention from someone else, then wasn't that using?

And hadn't that plan been at the forefront of her mind when she had first seen Dario, dark and dangerously devastating, on the opposite side of the room?

'So are you claiming that you just met me—fell head over heels and into my arms?'

Pretty much, Alyse acknowledged to herself. But she wasn't going to admit that. His head was already way too big to let him know the effect he had had on her. Knowing that he believed he was the winner, and Marcus the loser, she had no desire to feed his ego any more.

'As if…' she said scornfully, not caring if that just deepened his conviction that she had been using him from the start.

Any thought of *using* had ceased to be the case from the moment that she had met him face to face. It had flown out of the window, along with her self-control and any sense of self-preservation. She had thought that he felt the same too. But how could this hard-faced, blank-eyed, icy-voiced male standing before her ever have been capable of the sort of passion that she had believed had gripped him just as it had her?

Was it possible that he had known who she was from the start? That even their 'introduction'—that dance!—had been carefully planned, calculated for the best possible effect? Remembering now, she could recall how his eyes had narrowed when she had given her name. He had known who she was—and obviously he knew of Marcus.

'I want to go home.'

As she spoke she was looking round the room, hunting for the clutch bag she had discarded so carelessly in the moment that Dario had taken her into his arms, the shoes she had kicked off as he lifted her from the ground, carrying her towards the settee. Before the ominous bang at the door had smashed into the heated, unthinking mood.

'I want to go home,' she repeated when there was no response. Had he not heard her or was he totally withdrawn behind that cold, set mask that had covered his face?

'OK.'

If she'd thought he might object—that he would have tried to persuade her not to go—then she couldn't have been more mistaken. Instead, he just shrugged and turned away from her.

'Fine.'

A harsh gesture, just the contemptuous flick of

one bronzed hand, pointed her across the room, away from him.

'There's the door.'

That was it. But had she hoped for anything more? Had she wanted him to argue, to try to persuade her otherwise? She had to be all sorts of crazy if that was so.

Padding across the floor in her stockinged feet, she grabbed her bag, picked up her shoes. Just the thought of trying to cram her feet into them again tonight was almost too much to take. She hadn't actually worn them properly since she had got into Dario's car to come here.

Here. She didn't even know where *here* was. She'd been too intent on Dario to notice any landmarks they might have passed.

'But how will I…?'

He didn't let her finish the question, anticipating perfectly just what she was about to say.

'The concierge downstairs will call you a taxi. Charge it to my account.'

And that was it—over—done with. He had switched off from her so completely she might already be out of the room. He hadn't been able to get what he wanted from her; she wasn't in his bed, which was all that he had planned on, so now he couldn't wait to be rid of her.

'Is this how you usually treat your dates?'

The deep blue glance he turned on her was cold enough to freeze right through to her soul, shrivelling everything inside her. A long pause, and then he raised one hand, the index finger extended deliberately.

'One,' he drawled coolly, ticking off the point with his other hand, 'this was no *date.* Merely a chance encounter. And, two—you were never *mine.*'

He didn't add the 'thank God' that was clearly on the tip of his tongue, but he didn't need to. She could read it in the iciness of his eyes, the burn of dismissal that seared her from head to toe.

'Now, would you mind leaving? I have things to do.'

To drive home the point, he flipped open the case of the tablet computer that was lying on a nearby table and tapped the screen, his attention focused firmly on the appliance.

It was as if she was no longer there, and if she had any sense at all left then she'd make sure that that was in fact the case. Without another word, she hurried across the room. He didn't even spare her another glance as she pulled open the door and made her way out of it.

She'd had a narrow escape there, Alyse admitted to herself as the door swung to behind her. She'd seen the flash of something dangerous in Dario's eyes before he had turned away and she was glad to get out of the room unscathed. She could only hope that Marcus wasn't still hanging about somewhere. He'd been furious but, strangely, in this uncomfortable aftermath she didn't feel half as unnerved by his blustering fury as she was by the glacial stare Dario had turned on her.

Dario, *Marcus's half-brother*!

Her mind still reeled under the impact of that revelation. How, at a huge event, in an enormous room crammed with hundreds of people—had she been unfortunate enough to pick on the one person who could put her in a worse situation than the one she had been trying to avoid? What was that saying about being caught between a rock and a hard place? Her legs suddenly unsteady, Alyse almost missed her step on the stairs and had to grab at the bannister for support.

She had got away this time and, with luck, she had convinced Marcus that there was no point at all in coming after her with his unwanted attentions. But was that the end of it? Why was she plagued by such a cold, sneaking suspicion that there was more to come?

That she had simply jumped right out of the frying pan and into the fire.

CHAPTER FOUR

THE RING OF the doorbell was the last thing that Alyse had been expecting.

The last thing she wanted too, if the truth was told. She was waiting for her father to come home because her mother had been asking for him and was getting more anxious with each minute that ticked by. She wasn't expecting—or wanting—any other visitors at the house tonight.

Her first instinct was to ignore the summons. Her father would never use the doorbell because of course he had his own key. Rose and Lucy, her best friends, were away on a skiing holiday, one she should have been sharing with them. But she had decided that her mother needed her more, her illness so bad this time that Alyse had had no option but to take leave from her job at the art gallery to give the twenty-four-hour care the older woman needed.

Marcus, thank heaven, seemed to have got the

message after the encounter in Dario's apartment. He had not appeared at the house for the past couple of days, when before he had been on the doorstep at every opportunity, it seemed. A situation that had been made all the worse by the fact that her mother's depression was worse than it had been for some time.

So at first she sat still, hoping that she couldn't be seen from the street. But the unexpected visitor was clearly not being put off by the lack of response, and if she wasn't careful that persistent ringing at the doorbell would disturb her mother and have her coming downstairs.

Alyse prayed it wasn't Marcus again, coming back for round two. Well, in that case, perhaps he would be put off rather than attracted, she reflected as she caught a glimpse of herself in an ornately framed mirror that hung on the wall as she crossed the hallway. The simple red skirt and cream T-shirt she wore was hardly the look of any man's sexual fantasies. But surely Marcus had got the message by now.

The ringing at the door got louder, more strident, as if someone had pressed their finger on the bell and left it there.

'Oh, all right—I'm coming.'

She pulled open the door then stared in horror at the strong, dark figure standing on the door-step.

'You!'

Dario Olivero might be far more casually dressed than the elegant evening wear of two nights before, but in the worn leather jacket, navy T-shirt and tight blue jeans he was no less impressive than on the night of the ball. If anything, the casual clothes threw the carved beauty of his features into stronger relief, and the faint glow of the spring sun in the garden made his tanned skin look golden against the sleek raven's wing colour of his hair.

'Me.'

For a moment, he hadn't quite recognised her, Dario admitted to himself. When the door to her father's house had first opened, he had thought that she might be some sort of domestic staff. The polish and sophistication of the glamorous society beauty he had seen at the ball was missing, the elegant silk gown replaced by a casual skirt and loose-fitting top, her feet pushed into simple flat pumps that matched the red of her skirt. Her hair hung loose around her shoulders, soft waves that his fingers itched to touch, and, even without a trace of make-up, her skin had a fresh, natural glow that made her look years younger than the twenty-three he knew her to be.

He had spent the past couple of days telling himself to forget the woman who had thought she could use him to anger his hated half-brother. Faced with this other, very different Alyse, he knew without a doubt just why he hadn't succeeded. The woman at the ball had haunted his thoughts, tormented his nights with burning fantasies of the moments she had been underneath him on the settee, her legs splayed to accommodate him, her mouth hot on his. But he had told himself that he wanted nothing more to do with a woman who'd planned only to use him to make his brother burn with jealousy. *This* woman drove all such thoughts from his mind and left him with a knowledge that rocked his sense of sanity. The knowledge that this woman was one he would never be able to forget.

That she was the reason he was here now, instead of forgetting her for good, as he had vowed only two nights before.

But the forty-eight hours that had passed in between had changed so much. Two days before, he would have been satisfied with putting a spoke in his half-brother's plan to use marriage to Alsye to secure his father's favour. Since then he had learned so much more about what was going on. And the delivery of a most unexpected letter, the first and only letter he had ever received from his father, one that had followed him here all the way from Tuscany, had only added to the shifting shadows behind everything that was being played out on the surface.

The depth of his brother's scheming had been no surprise. His father's intervention had been totally unexpected. But now that he had actually met Alyse, he had recognised that she at least was unaware of the darker schemes in which she was being used. She was as much at the mercy of her own father as he had once been at his.

He had vowed never again to let Marcus's cold-blooded scheming succeed if it was in his power to stop it. There was a much older vow too, one that he had made to his mother years before, a promise she had drawn from him on her death-bed. A vow that meant he had to respond to the slightest hint of reconciliation with his biological father, even if it stuck in his throat to do it.

And if that vow gave him more reason to see the beautiful Alyse Gregory—to get her into his life on his terms—then so much the better.

'What are you doing here?' The way that Alyse's heart had lurched against her ribs at the sight of him made the words come out breathless and uneven.

Dario smiled; at least that was what she thought his expression was meant to be. Just a grim twist of his mouth, the sensual lips curling up slightly at the corners.

'And hello to you too. Thank you for the welcome.'

'You're not welcome!'

If she had opened the door to find a waiting panther, sleek, black, dangerous, standing before her, her nerves couldn't have twisted any tighter into painful knots. And she couldn't get her heart rate to settle down into its normal steady beat.

'Fine.'

He was turning away, about to head off down the drive again to where a powerful car waited in the sunshine. It should have made her feel thankful, but instead the knots in her stomach tightened brutally and she was left with an uncomfortable nagging feeling that she had missed something.

After all, he had to have come here for some reason and she didn't trust his apparently easy response to her dismissal.

'Wait!'

At first she thought that he hadn't heard her or that if he had he wasn't going to respond. But then his long strides slowed, he came to a halt, turned a sidelong glance over his shoulder in her direction. And waited.

'Why have you come here?'

'I wanted to return something to you.'

'Return what?'

He turned at last, but slowly, almost lazily.

'Do you want to do this out here?'

'I suppose you'd better come in.'

She pushed the door wide and marched into the hall, leaving him to follow or not as he chose. He prowled after her and it was unnerving how she was aware of every step, every movement even though he was behind her. The whole atmosphere inside the house changed in a moment.

Had he brought the warmth of the garden inside with him? Or was it possible that just the heat of his body could alter the temperature so much? Because suddenly she felt uncomfortable in the long-sleeved shirt that only moments before had seemed perfectly fine for the day. The slam of the door as it closed behind Dario made her start so violently she was sure her feet had actually lifted several inches off the floor.

'OK.' She made herself swing round to face him. 'Just what is it you're returning to me?'

Dario's mouth quirked slightly in disconcerting amusement at her tone.

'A cup of coffee would be nice.'

'There's an Italian coffee bar down the street,' Alyse tossed at him, wanting this over and done with and him on his way.

He didn't take the bait but his eyes went to the partly open kitchen door through which, much to Alyse's fury, it was easy to see the coffee maker she had just filled and switched on before his knock had come at the door. The wonderful aroma of freshly brewed coffee filled the air.

'One coffee!' she conceded irritably.

She pushed open another door, the one that led into the sitting room, wanting him to go that way and so take away some of the pressure she felt. He wasn't even standing *close* to her, for heaven's sake! But Dario Olivero could fill a room simply by being in it, and the warm scent of his skin, the blue gleam of his eyes made her nerves burn in a heated response that she knew must show in the rise of colour to her cheeks.

'One coffee,' she muttered again, not really knowing whether she was trying to drive the point home to him or convince herself.

If it was Dario she was aiming her words at then they had no effect. When she made her way into the kitchen he was right behind her, silent-footed like a hunting tiger.

She opened a cupboard door, snatched two mugs from the shelves, banged them down on the worktop then reached for the glass jug of coffee. It shook in her hand, threatening to spill scalding coffee all over the surface, and it was the last straw for Alyse. Dumping it down on its hotplate, she swung round to face him, her breath snagging in her throat as she realised just how close he had come. She wanted to put out her hands, flatten them against the broad stretch of his chest under the clinging navy cotton and push him away. But, not knowing whether she would react too strongly, risking near violence in her response, or if the temptation to touch those corded muscles, feel the heat of his skin through the soft material might just be too much for her, instead she put her hands behind her, gripping tight to the edge of the worktop in order to stop them going anywhere more dangerous.

'So what is it that you say you want to return to me?' She emphasised that 'say' so that he could be in no doubt at all that she really didn't believe him.

'This.'

He reached into his jacket pocket, then held his hand towards her, palm upwards so that she could see something small and golden, the rich sheen of pearl gleaming against his skin.

'My earring!'

The earring she had worn on the night of the ball and had only realised that she had mislaid somewhere when she had undressed for bed, her still-shaking fingers only finding one piece of jewellery in her left ear lobe.

'I must have left it…'

'In my apartment.'

The quiet confirmation had no trace of triumph in it but, all the same, she felt as if the easy words had scoured a much needed protective layer from her skin. She couldn't meet his eyes, focusing all her attention on the earring in his hand, feeling really rather foolish. She had believed that it was all just a made-up story. She'd even allowed herself to think, just for a moment, that perhaps he hadn't been able to forget her. That he had actually wanted her far more than he had let on. That he might want more than just a heated one-night stand.

Instead, it was something much more ordinary, and he really was returning the piece of jewellery that he must have found after she had left. He would have done the same for anyone at all. It was nothing at all to do with *her*.

'Well…'

He was waiting for her to move, watching her intently, a gleam of something—amusement?—

challenge?—in those blue eyes. His hand was still between them, palm held out, the earring nestling against the bronzed skin, and she knew that he was waiting for her to make a move to take it.

It would mean touching him. It would mean brushing the skin of his palm with her fingers, feeling its warmth, absorbing some trace of him…

When his mouth quirked at the corners again she knew that there was a definite challenge there. She had to move now or face the accusation of cowardice that was clearly hovering just at the tip of his tongue.

'Thank you.'

Swallowing down the twist of nerves, she reached forward, aiming to snatch it up without actually touching him. But the painful awareness of the way he was watching her meant that she mistimed the movement, fumbled clumsily, missed the earring and let it drop back onto his palm.

'Sorry…'

Dario bit down hard on his lower lip, catching back the unexpected laughter that almost escaped him. Alyse had struggled so hard not to let her fingers make contact with his in a vain pretence that she wasn't interested in him at all.

Who was she trying to fool? She had felt the phosphoric flare of response between them from the first moment and it was still there, no matter how hard she was trying to deny it. It was there, in her eyes, the wash of colour over those beautiful cheekbones, in the dryness of the lips she held partly open, breathing rather too fast, unevenly through the narrow space. If he had any doubt—which he did not—then it would all have been driven away by the fast, flurried slick of her tongue over the softness of her bottom lip, leaving behind a sheen of soft moisture on the unpainted skin.

The purely male urge to bend and take her mouth, tasting that essence of her, was almost uncontrollable. But, with a grim struggle, he forced it back down again fast, praying that she wouldn't see the fight he had to control his stinging arousal. If he so much as touched his mouth to hers it would not be enough. One taste, one brief moment of inhaling the special scent that was all her, and he would be lost. He would have to take more. And more. Until he buried himself in her body and was lost for good.

There was too much at stake to rush things now. He wanted this woman until his whole body hurt with need, but that wasn't the only reason why he had come here today. This was no everyday seduction. She was the key to beating his half-brother once and for all; and maybe even to opening the door into his father's world just a tiny crack.

Because, for once, it seemed that Marcus, uncharacteristically, had played his hand close to his chest, and when he had seen Alyse face up to his brother he had known that she was the person to have on his side in this.

'Your earring,' he said pointedly, unable to suppress a smile as she still hesitated, her fingers hovering just above the tiny item of jewellery where it rested on his palm.

But then she clearly gathered herself. Those green eyes flashed upwards, just once, at his face. Part defiance, part challenge of her own that made him want to meet her head-on, take what he wanted right now and not have to bide his time, to watch and plan.

He'd never had to wait for a woman before. But this time, with her, he reckoned she'd be worth it.

So he tilted his hand slightly towards her, angling it, encouraging…

'Ms Gregory.'

'Thank you.'

Her tone might have been stiff and formal but her touch was not. It was fast and awkward, snatching at the pearl in a way that made his skin burn where she touched him. The faint scrape of the pale pink painted nails against his skin made a burn of hungry heat pool low in his body. It was all he could do not to curl his fingers up, closing over hers, to hold her, draw her closer to him.

But not yet. She was already as wary as a wild bird he had enticed to come closer by laying down a trail of breadcrumbs. Move too fast and she would fly away.

'You're welcome,' he told her, smiling inwardly as he saw the way her shoulders relaxed at the careful formality of his tone. 'So—about that coffee? Black, no sugar.'

'Of course…'

Coffee was the last thing he wanted, but he

could enjoy taking the opportunity to watch her as she went about making it, the press of her neat bottom against the red cotton of her skirt, the elegant length of her legs as she stood on tiptoe, reaching up to collect the milk from a shelf in the fridge. His fingers itched to stroke her silky hair and he rammed them hard into the pockets of his jeans to keep them away from temptation.

'Heard anything from Marcus lately?'

The question was almost Alyse's undoing and she had to bang the milk bottle down onto the glass shelf in a pretence that she was responding to his comment that he didn't want it. She'd been glad to turn her back on him, needing to get away from the sensual pull he exerted simply by existing. She'd thought she'd managed to control herself pretty well, welcoming the chance to turn away before she betrayed herself, but now he was threatening her composure in a very different way with the unexpected question.

'No—nothing.'

Concentrating fiercely on pouring coffee into mugs, she was still aware of some inexplicable tension in his lean body, one that had been echoed in the apparently innocuous question.

'But then why would I? He must have got the message on Monday night.'

If his question had been unnerving, then his silence now was even more disturbing. Mug in one hand, she swung round to face him.

'You don't think he got the message?'

It hit hard to think that she might not be free of Marcus as she had hoped. After two months of persistent pressure, she had been so looking forward to getting her life back on track. All she'd needed was for her mother to feel well again. Or so she'd thought.

'Oh, I've no doubt he saw just what you were trying to tell him. But if you think that will be an end to it then you're very much mistaken. It's not the message he wants and I've never known my brother to give up on anything he wants if he's determined it's for him.'

'And he's determined that—what is for him?'

Dario reached forward, took the mug from her precarious hold but made no attempt to drink from it.

'You, of course.'

'What?'

He was joking. He had to be joking; he couldn't

possibly be serious. But his eyes had no amusement glinting in them, and there wasn't even the hint of a smile around that sexy mouth.

No—that was a mistake. Looking directly at his mouth threatened to drive away the ability to think, to follow through the questions that his reply had stirred in her mind. And she had to think; his sombre expression told her that. It also warned that there was more to this than she had ever anticipated. But all she could think of was the feel of that mouth on hers, the taste of it, the hard pressure…and then its heated caress over her skin, down her neck…

'But I—on Monday, I—we—made him think…'

'Don't imagine that that will put Marcus off for good.'

'He can't want *me* that much. Oh, OK, he has been showing me attention for a while—but it's only just lately that he has become more insistent.'

Just before her mother had become ill again this time. Ellen Gregory had had one of her manic moods just after Christmas and she had been high on life, enjoying herself, she'd said, going out to events, to parties where neither Alyse nor her husband had been able to go with her. Then, three weeks ago, she had fallen down into the expected slump, retreating to her bedroom and not talking to anyone. Alyse had seen the change in her father's demeanour then too; he had become quiet and withdrawn as well.

It had been around that time that Marcus had started calling round even more regularly. It was also when her father had asked her to encourage him—or at least not to reject him out of hand. She didn't understand just why Antony Gregory had suddenly become Marcus's advocate but she'd tried. After all, he was the son of her father's boss and she didn't want to cause any trouble between them.

But Marcus had become just too insistent. He'd been dropping hints about the possible repercussions if she turned him down. That was when she had come up with the plan for the night of the ball. She had been sure that if he saw her with someone else—someone she seemed so much keener on than him—then he would get the message and back off. In fact, the only good part of that whole humiliating evening was the thought that at least Marcus would stay away. But now Dario was claiming that his half-brother would not be deterred by anything that had happened.

'No…' She shook her head worriedly, struggling all over again with that feeling of being a bone being fought over by two determined dogs. 'Yes…'

Dario put down his untouched coffee mug on the nearest worktop and reached for her. Still so disorientated by the unexpected news, she let him lead her out into the hall, where he turned her until she was facing the long, ornately framed mirror in which she had glimpsed herself earlier as she'd crossed the hall.

'Look at yourself…'

It was murmured against her hair, the warmth of his breath brushing over the soft skin of her neck. Momentarily, her eyes closed as she fought against the need to lean back into his warmth, to feel the strong support of his body, let the scent of his skin enclose her. But immediately they snapped open again as she recognised the danger of giving in to the temptation.

'Plain, pale and unsophisticated,' she returned

tartly, green eyes clashing with his blue ones in the reflection in the mirror.

His mouth was partly hidden but she felt his laughter in the length of his body rather than seeing his smile.

'And you expect me to believe that? So tell me, Alyse, are you fishing for compliments?'

One bronzed hand stroked the blonde hair back from one side of her face, tucking it behind her left ear, and the feel of his touch made her shiver in needy response. A pulse that throbbed through her body centred between her legs, making her ache in yearning.

'Because I'll feed you flattery every minute of the hour, if that's what you want. Is that how Marcus wooed you, hmm? Was it by praising your beauty, telling you he had fallen head over heels for you?'

Something like that, Alyse acknowledged inwardly. He had told her she was beautiful—told her that he wanted her. But that had been at the very beginning. Just lately he had been pushing for marriage without any care or compliments. He'd insisted she would never find anyone better than him. That it would be to her advantage to accept his proposal.

But the scary thing was that where Marcus's compliments had sounded excessive, insincere, disturbingly so, she wanted to trust Dario—to believe that the words he described as flattery were real.

'Is that what you want? Will that please you?' he asked now, and something in his tone snapped her out of the foolish, hypnotic daydream that she had been lulled into.

'Not when you don't mean it!'

Snatching her head away from his caressing hands, she whirled round to face him so fast that her hair swung out around her head, slapping him in the face and catching on his eyelashes, the hint of late-in-the-day stubble at his jaw, trailing across his mouth.

Slowly he reached up, brushed it away carefully, fingers lingering on the soft strands.

'Just what is happening?' she demanded. 'Why did you really come round here this afternoon?'

She knew she wasn't going to get any answer she wanted when his face remained cold and unyielding, the muscles around his mouth tightening, drawing it into a thin line.

'Ask your father,' he tossed at her, cold and hard.

'What does my father have to do with this? I'm asking you. What is this between you and your brother—half-brother,' she amended hastily when she saw the flare of rejection in his eyes.

'That is none of your business.'

'But you're making it mine—you and Marcus are bringing it to my door, and I don't want it. I don't want to get caught up in your nasty, petty little civil war... What?'

Her nerves skittered, making her heart jolt against her ribs as she saw the way he shook his head, his mouth grim.

'I'm afraid you can't say that. You're already involved—and it isn't just you.'

Cold sensations slithered down her spine at his words. Her throat felt blocked, as if there was something tightening round it, making it impossible to breathe naturally. Sucking in a deep, much-needed gasp of air, she forced words from lips that were suddenly painfully dry.

'You've danced around this for too long,

Dario—and I've had enough! I want you to tell me just what you mean. You claim that you and your brother are involved and who else?'

'All of you,' Dario put in when she struggled to go on. 'You—your father—your mother…'

'My mother?'

Now she was worried. The thought of her mother, shut in her room upstairs, the curtains drawn to block out the sunlight, the bedclothes pulled over her head as she fought the demons of her depression, twisted in the pit of her stomach. She knew that Ellen had been high—higher than usual—for some weeks so that the moment when she came tumbling down must inevitably feel truly low in contrast—but was there something more than that? Something that threatened even more darkness.

'What do you mean? Stop throwing out veiled threats…'

'Not threats, Alyse—at least not from me. Marcus is the one who is threatening you and your family. He is the one who holds your future in his hands—or thinks he does.'

She wanted to scream, to turn her hands into fists and pummel them against his chest—anything to stop him playing with her as a hunting cat toyed with a mouse. But instead she fought to gather her composure.

'Tell me.'

Dario pushed both hands through the thickness of his hair. His eyes searched her face, seeming to be looking for evidence that she really wanted to know the truth. What he saw must have convinced him because he gave a faint nod.

'Your mother has been gambling—at the casino.'

'That's not possible…' Alyse put in. Her mother had been so depressed recently. 'She hasn't been out of the house for days—a couple of weeks.'

Instinctively, her head turned towards the staircase, listening for any sound that might indicate her mother had actually emerged. But all was silent, as it had been all afternoon.

'This was a couple of months back.'

When Ellen had been in a hyper state, full of zest and the conviction that nothing could go wrong with her life. Alyse fought to control a shiver at the dreadful possibilities. In one of her high phases, her mother had no sense of restraint or of danger.

'How much did she lose?'

The amount he named made her head spin, turned her knees to water. And the black cloud that had been hovering on the horizon came rushing closer with a terrible sense of inevitability.

'There's no way we can afford to pay that amount off—not all in one go.' Or even if they were allowed to pay by instalments; it would still be ruinous.

Something in Dario's face told her that this was not all of it. There was more—and obviously worse—to come.

'Go on. Exactly what has Marcus to do with this?'

'He really hasn't told you?' His laughter was a sound of incredulity, the humour grim, as dark as could be, and he shook his head in disbelief as he spoke. 'You surprise me—he has been so much more subtle than I'd ever anticipated. Or perhaps he's learned how to play the clever game—close to his chest after all.'

'He...'

From the back of her mind slid a memory of the day before the ball. Marcus had started to say something… 'Your father wants this every bit as much as I do. More.' And later, her father—her father who had looked so pale and strained recently, but she had put that down to concern about her mother—

'My father…' The strength had gone from her voice, leaving it just a whisper. Her father had encouraged her to see Marcus, to welcome him to the house. Then he had encouraged her none too subtly to consider the younger man's proposal.

But it was worse than she could ever have imagined. Her father had tried to help his wife by taking the money she needed secretly from the company he worked for.

'Embezzlement…' It was a horrible word. A scary word.

Even scarier if you stopped to think just who her father had taken the money from.

'Kavanaughs… Oh, Dad, how could you?'

Alyse knew that the colour had leached from her face. She could feel it seeping away as her heart slowed in horror.

So now she knew just why her father had looked so low, so worn for the past few weeks.

He had tried to save her mother and only got in deeper as a result. Then he hadn't actually pushed her towards marriage with Marcus, but he had made it plain that he would be glad if it was to happen. Of course he would. The Kavanaughs would be unlikely to sue the man who was to be Marcus's father-in-law.

'No wonder he wanted me to agree to marry Marcus.'

But it still didn't explain why Marcus had suddenly become so determined on pushing for *marriage*. Pushing so hard, making her feel so trapped, that in the end she had determined on the crazy plan to get away from his attentions. Not knowing the full truth behind everything, she had taken a wild, thoughtless leap.

I swear you'll regret this. Marcus's words, ominously threatening, came back to haunt her. She had thought she'd got away with avoiding the issue of his proposal, but she had never known the darker elements behind it. The threat that Marcus could now hold over her. It was as if the sun had gone right behind a thick bank of cloud, leaving her shivering in miserable shock.

'You knew all this?'

'I do now.'

He'd known about Marcus's original reasons for wanting to marry Alyse, of course, Dario acknowledged privately. The way that his half-brother had set out to win his father's approval by fulfilling the older man's dream of linking the Kavanaugh family with the Gregorys. An aristocratic daughter-in-law and then, hopefully, later a titled grandson. It would be the final way of achieving a long-held ambition that Henry had failed to achieve for himself.

But not this. He'd known his half-brother was a louse and always had been. But he'd never anticipated finding out about this particularly vicious piece of blackmail. And they called *him* the bastard son!

'But you didn't think to tell me the other night?'

'I didn't know it all then and, for all I knew, you might have been totally happy to marry Marcus. It wasn't until I saw you with him that I realised you weren't that keen.'

'So you decided to have me all to yourself!'

A lazily raised eyebrow quirked in response

to her outburst. 'While you were busy using me to get rid of my half-brother.'

'After you'd used me to make him angry—jealous.'

He wasn't going to deny that. It had been his plan at first. He'd seen an opportunity to thwart Marcus and had taken it. One small taste of pay-back for all the years of viciousness from the man who society called his brother. But now it seemed that Fate had handed him a stronger case for a true revenge—and maybe even a way to make his father notice him at last.

And a way to get this woman into his bed until this sexual hunger that flared like phosphorus between them burned itself out. He would make it worth her while, and it would certainly be to his advantage in every way.

'I reckon we both used each other.'

His casual shrug was bad enough, Alyse thought, but the smile that went with it was ap-palling. Like his carelessness, it was cold, cal-lous, unfeeling. It told her that she had meant nothing to him—except as a weapon to use against his brother.

'Well, I hope you enjoyed yourself!' A heavy

strand of hair fell forward over her face as she flung the words at him, and she reached up a hand to push it back. 'Was it fun? Satisfying?'

'Not as satisfying as I'd hoped…' Dario began but then she saw his mood change abruptly as his eyes followed the movement of her hand and his frown alerted her to the fact that something was wrong. 'Alyse…'

'What…?' Alyse managed as he reached forward fast, caught her hand, turned it towards her. 'Oh…'

The pearl earring, forgotten all this time, slipped from her hand to land on the tiled floor with a small clatter. But Alyse wasn't watching where it fell. She was staring at her hand, at the imprint of the jewellery where the earring had been clenched tightly in her grip. So tightly that it had dug into her palm, breaking the skin and making it bleed.

'Oh!'

'Here—let me…'

He had her hand in his, smoothing her fingers out of the way as he pulled a handkerchief from his pocket, wiped it softly over the torn skin. Then he rolled the cloth into a pad and pressed it down on the small wound, curling her fingers over it to hold it in place. His touch was warm and surprisingly gentle.

She'd hardly lost any blood but still her head swam and she felt faint. His dark head was bent over her hand, the scent of his hair and his skin reaching up like an intoxicating cloud to stir her senses even more. If she just made the tiniest movement then her hand would brush against its softness, making her want to clench her fingers tight around it, hold him closer. Surely, this near to her, he must hear the heavy pounding of her heart, see the throb of her pulse, blue under the skin at her wrist.

'Dario...'

It was just a whisper, thick with the reaction of her senses to his strength, but this time a strength used to help rather than to restrain or to hurt.

'Alyse...' His own response brushed his mouth against the place where her pulse beat, the warm stroke of his lips making her legs weaken, her whole body swaying towards him. It was still there, hot and strong, no matter how hard she might fight against it; she was still lost at the feel of his touch, the caress of his lips. She wanted to reach out and smooth her free hand down his cheek, know the warmth of his skin, the faint roughness of the bristle that shadowed his jaw-line.

She wanted more…

'Alyse…!'

It was her name again but called in a very different voice, in a very different way. High-pitched and sharp and slightly petulant, it came from the higher floor of the house, floating down the stairs to where they stood in the hall.

'Alyse!'

'Mum…'

She turned to head for the stairs, found his hand had closed over hers and she had to pull against it but he wouldn't free her. When she swung back to face him he was looking deep into her face, the smoky darkness of his eyes telling their story of hungry desire, so like the stinging need his kiss had woken inside her. Whatever this was, it had reached out and ensnared them both so that it only needed the tiniest connection to start it all off again.

'I have to go!' It was an angry whisper, even though she knew that her mother's bedroom was too far away for her to be heard. 'My mother needs me. She *needs* me!' she added more forcefully when his dark head moved in stark denial of her reaction.

'Don't go...'

Did he know what it did to her to hear that softly husky voice, the mixture of command and entreaty that threatened to tie her insides into knots as her own need warred with the sense of duty—and despair—that her mother's call had woken in her?

'I have to see what she needs. I *have* to...' she repeated when his grip on her hand had loosened and it was something much more basic and primitive that kept her from moving. 'I have to do something! After all, there's nothing I can do about everything else.'

If she looked for an answer in his face, then there wasn't one there. His eyes were closed off from her, just blue opaque ice, revealing no feeling at all. He'd presented her with the details of Marcus's plan—marry him or see her father go to jail—and now it seemed he was prepared to leave her right in the lion's den.

'I have no defence against Marcus. There's nothing to fight with.'

He blinked just once, drew in a breath that seemed to go right to his soul.

'There is,' he said, his voice rough and husky. 'There's me.'

Alyse's eyes wouldn't focus. She couldn't see what was in his face, didn't know how to interpret it. He couldn't mean…could he? But if he meant what he said, then what else was involved in it? She longed to reach out and meet him halfway, and yet she didn't know what he was offering so the thought of it terrified her in the same seconds that she wanted it so much. Because, whatever he offered, she knew it had to come at a price.

Men like Dario didn't offer help—particularly not help to the extent that would be needed to solve this terrifying dilemma—without wanting something out of it for themselves.

She didn't know how to answer him, and her mind felt as if it was being torn in two. So it was a relief to hear her mother's voice calling to her again, that sharp-toned 'Alyse!' more demanding now, more urgent. Grateful for this one thing that she *had* to focus on, she tore her hand from Dario's, forced her feet into motion, ran up the stairs two at a time until she reached the half landing part way up.

Gasping for breath in a way that had nothing to do with her fitness or the steepness of the stairs, she came to a sudden halt, leaned over the bannister, looked down into the hall and into his face, upturned to watch her. He hadn't moved an inch but was standing exactly where she had left him, obviously waiting for an answer, knowing she would have to give him one.

'Wh-what…?' she stammered, fighting to get the words past the knot in her throat, the uneven beat of her heart. 'How…?'

The curl of his mouth told her that he had been expecting her reaction. She needed him and she had no one else to turn to. And he had only had to wait for her to realise that.

'Tomorrow,' he said quietly, almost casually. 'I'll give you till tomorrow. Come to me then and I'll tell you everything.'

And with another of those half-smiles, cool,

careless and touched with a deep, dark satisfaction, he turned on his heel and strolled out of the door.

CHAPTER FIVE

'YOU CAN'T MEAN IT!'

Alyse's glass froze halfway to her mouth, then was set down again with a distinct crash as it landed on the polished wood of the dining table.

'I don't believe it! You have to be joking.'

'No joke.'

Dario toyed with the base of his own wine-glass, his attention seeming to be elsewhere, though that was something that Alyse knew to be a pretence. He might not be giving her the focused attention she was directing at him but he was fiercely aware of how she was reacting. He knew her gaze was directed straight at him, he just didn't choose to meet it or show any response. He'd made the blunt, emotionless announcement and now he was waiting for her to calm down before he discussed further details.

But how could she calm down when what he had suggested was *this*?

'I said that I would help you and I will—but on my terms.'

And it was those terms that had made her head swim.

'I don't understand—why do we have to get married?'

'You make it sound as if it was a sentence of execution.'

It might almost be the same, Alyse admitted to herself. Except that at least a summary execution would be short, fast and over with.

'It's a lifetime's sentence.'

'Really?'

The look he turned on her now was sceptical and frankly questioning.

'I offered marriage—not commitment and devotion for life.'

Well, that told her, didn't it? If she had been dreaming of rings and flowers and happy ever afters then that fantasy had just been splattered in the dust at her feet. But then she hadn't been dreaming at all, except of a chance of a way out of the terrible situation she now found herself in. The truth was that she was still so stunned at the thought that he had actually said that he would help that she'd had no possible idea just what Dario might be prepared to do.

She'd been an idiot, she realised now. No one was going to offer to help her and her family pay the huge debts that had mounted up without demanding something pretty steep in return.

But this!

'Doesn't marriage usually demand both of those—or at least the intention of both of them?'

'If you believe that then you must have stars in your eyes. Oh, perhaps some idealistic fools set out with the idea of keeping those vows they make, but they very rarely stick to it. At least we'll know where we stand—a marriage of convenience to get us both what we want.'

'Just a marriage of convenience.'

She struggled to match him for calmness and certainty but it was impossible. She might not have been dreaming of rings and flowers and happy ever afters with this man—she'd have been crazy to contemplate it—but deep down she flinched away from the description of marriage that he'd put before her. One day, some day, she had hoped that she would meet someone who would love her as her father loved her mother, above and beyond everyone else. Surely every woman dreamed of having a man feel that way about her?

'One with a planned ending,' Dario continued. 'So there are no mistakes, no illusions. No one can claim they were led into it blindfolded.'

'Of course not.'

The smooth stretch of polished wood between them on the table suddenly seemed like a huge expanse of arid desert. The meal he had served her lay congealing on her plate, impossible to eat.

'I certainly couldn't claim that.'

In fact, when he had first made the suggestion it had been so blunt that she hadn't been able to believe she had heard right. So much so that her initial response had been to demand, 'Is this meant to be a proposal? Because it really doesn't sound like it.'

'You didn't exactly sugar-coat it.'

'I don't usually soft-pedal on my business deals,' Dario retorted.

Well, she knew that. She might only have had a few hours since he had left the house and before she obeyed his summons to come round to his apartment, but she'd put them to good use. She'd spent an age on the internet, finding out all she could about Dario Olivero—and there was a lot to find out. His origins might have been hazy, and it was obvious that he had grown up in circumstances very different from the power and affluence he knew now. In fact, it seemed that he had had no connection with the Kavanaugh family or their wealth until just a year or so before. Which explained why she had never heard of him, even though her family had known Marcus's for years.

But where his beginnings were shadowy and dark, he had soon left that part of his life behind. He had built himself the hugely successful wine business in Tuscany, winning award after award for the full-bodied reds, the subtle whites his vineyards produced. No doubt he had provided wines for the Kavanaughs' hotels and that was how he had come into contact with his half-brother. He had certainly built an empire to match—and outstrip—theirs, which was why he could now offer to take on her mother's debts and remove the threat of arrest and prosecution for her father. He had made a fortune several times over because of exactly what he had just said—that he was known for ruthlessness and determination in all his business dealings as in the rest of his life.

Oh, yes, the ruthlessness extended to his relationships too, apparently. No woman stayed around too long—though there had been plenty of them, all beautiful, wealthy and glamorous. But their regular turnover was proof, if she needed proof, of the fact that he had meant that declaration that he wasn't offering 'commitment and devotion for life'.

But exactly what was he offering—and why?

'I checked everything you said with my father,' she said, playing for time.

'I knew you would.'

'He confirmed everything.'

'I knew he would.'

It had to have been the most uncomfortable and upsetting conversation she had ever had with her father. Antony Gregory had blustered at first, then broken down, and in the end she could see that he had been barely holding on to his self-control and his eyes had been swimming with tears. Alyse had been appalled to see how low he had sunk. Even at this late stage, she had let herself hope it might not be as bad as Dario had revealed. Instead, she had found that it was already so much worse. Her father's embezzlement of funds from the Kavanaugh business had been discovered; Marcus had threatened him with exposure, with arrest… And she could be in no doubt at all that her own behaviour on the night of the ball had made things so much worse.

'Marcus is clearly out for revenge for what he saw as his huge humiliation, and he told Dad that he has just until the end of the week to "sort something out" before the police are informed…'

The memory of her father's face floated before her. But those tears had been for his wife—and himself—not for his daughter or the way he had been pushing her into a marriage that she loathed the thought of. In the past twenty-four hours so much had been turned on its head. With the realisation of just how both her parents had been involved in putting her neck in the noose that now surrounded it, she was forced to look again at the image of marriage they presented.

She could still have no doubt that her father loved his wife. So much that he would risk his own name, his freedom, in order to protect the woman he adored. There were those who would say that Antony Gregory loved not wisely but too well, and Alyse had once felt that way, too. But the revelations of the past days had rocked her world, shattering everything she had once had confidence in. Everything she'd thought she knew—the financial security of her home, her faith in her parents—had been snatched away from her, and she was left knowing she had been lied to, used as a pawn by the people she should have been able to trust the most.

'Which is why you're here.'

Could anything make him show any sort of emotion? All through the meal he had remained sphinx-like, almost unmoving. He had eaten as little as she had, though Alyse couldn't possibly imagine that he was as nervous and apprehensive as she was, but that he must be as sparing in his appetite for food as he was in his movements and the stark elegance of his clothes. An immaculate white linen shirt hugged the powerful lines of his shoulders and exposed the bronzed skin of his throat where it was open at the neck. Black trousers hugged the lean hips and long legs, his narrow waist emphasised by the leather belt with a heavy silver buckle.

Obviously he hadn't had the crisis of confidence that had assailed her as she'd prepared for this evening. After the talk with her father she had had no doubt just how important this meeting was but as she didn't know just what to anticipate, it had been difficult to work out exactly what to wear.

In the end, deciding this was, after all, a business meeting, she had picked out a pale green shift dress that was one of the ones she wore to work, adding metallic flats and pulling her hair back into a high ponytail. It had seemed right at the time—but now…

What the heck did you wear to a businesslike proposal of marriage?

'I appreciate so much that you're offering to help…but…but why do we have to be married?' Her voice trembled so much that it mangled the last word.

'Can you think of anything else that would really put Marcus off? Because, believe me, if we're to deal with this problem properly, it won't just be possible to offer to pay off your father's debts and be done with it.'

'It won't?'

Was there something else behind all this—something he wasn't telling her? But he had said 'we' and she had to hold on to that. She couldn't do this alone and she was relieved and strengthened to think of having Dario's ruthless determination on her side. He, at least, was offering her a way out.

'Why not? Surely an engagement…'

Dario put down his glass and studied her across the width of the table. The candles flickered in a faint draught, throwing different, changing patterns over her pale face, shadowing her eyes. The sky beyond the windows was darker than he had realised, bringing home to him the fact that the evening was closing in around them. She had arrived later than he had anticipated, obviously because she had taken the time to have the much-needed talk with her father. But time was not what they had much of—not if they were going to make sure that Marcus didn't get the upper hand.

'An engagement won't be enough.'

An engagement might deter his half-brother but it would never fulfil the demands their father had made; the conditions he had put into his newly changed will.

Dario's grip tightened on the stem of his glass until the knuckles showed white. It had come as one hell of a shock to realise how ill his father had been over the past months. So much so that he had changed his will—and had actually written to his illegitimate son to let him know about it.

Coming that close to death, Henry Kavanaugh had feared that his long-held dream to have a grandchild, preferably one with a claim to a title, would never be realised. He held no illusions about Marcus and his louche lifestyle, so he had made marriage the condition for a very special bequest in his will. Being a cunning old fox, he had decided to hedge his bets and for the first time to recognise that he had two sons. He would have a grandchild in Kavanaugh House before he died, even if it meant that he had to acknowledge the bastard son he had denied until now.

Looking into Alyse's shocked green eyes across the table, Dario almost smiled, then clamped his mouth tight on the revealing expression. He had never anticipated getting married either. Had always vowed that it was not for him. When he'd come back to England this time, it had just been with the determination to thwart Marcus's plan. Then he would turn and walk away, for good this time. But then that letter had arrived and he had been offered the opportunity to take this one stage further than he had ever dreamed.

If he had known about that will sooner, then he might have had time to plan another approach to this, another way round it. But Marcus, damn his black soul, had made sure that he hadn't found out a thing until the very last minute, by which time his half-brother had already made his play for Alyse. He wasn't going to be wrong-footed again.

'Why won't it do?'

'Because Marcus doesn't want to put your father in jail—though he'll go that route if he has to. What he wants is you.'

'Oh, now you're…'

She was shaking her head violently so that the sleek blonde ponytail swung round, coming dangerously close to the candle flame. Dario leaned forward and moved it out of reach but then he stayed where he was, leaning halfway across the table, his face so much closer to hers.

'If you're going to tell me that I'm joking then I suggest you think again. Do you think that I would even be discussing this here tonight if there was any other alternative?'

Was it just the new shadows on her side of the room or had she lost all colour completely, her eyes suddenly shockingly dark in contrast to the pale green of her dress?

'I—but—oh…'

One hand came up to her mouth, her fingers pressing against her lips to stop the awkward, uncertain flow of syllables. She still wore the pearly pink varnish on her nails and just the memory of those oval nails scraping over the skin of his palm, the longing to know that gentle rasp on other more intimate parts, had him hardening, fast and painful, so that he was grateful for the fact that his lower body was hidden under the protection of the table. Time enough for that later, when everything was settled. He couldn't afford to be distracted, to risk moving too fast and having her turn and run before everything was decided.

He saw the moment that she rallied and welcomed it. He wanted the proud, defiant Alyse he had seen on the night of the ball, when Marcus had thought he could call her to heel and had failed miserably. Trampling fragile, weak women underfoot did nothing for him. He left that sort of thing to Marcus. He might have the upper hand here and now—and he would use it to get what he wanted—but only because it was what Alyse wanted too. She just wasn't quite ready to admit it yet.

'I'm not stupid,' Alyse told him, a new flash of defiance in her eyes as they reflected the flicker of the candle flame. 'I know he fancies me—in fact, I'd go so far as to say he's been obsessed with me for some time. But I've given him no encouragement. Even though my father made it clear—for reasons I understand now—that he would welcome Marcus as a son-in-law. But I made it plain I wasn't interested.'

'Which, knowing Marcus, would only have made him more enthusiastic.'

Dario's mouth twisted cynically at the thought.

'He always wanted what he couldn't have—to deny him was the way to pique his interest.'

'That wasn't why I was doing it!'

'Do you think I don't know that? You were prepared to go to ridiculous extremes to get rid of his unwanted attention.'

Though she'd been quick enough to drop the whole idea once Marcus had interrupted things. He'd let her go that time. He'd never forced an unwilling woman and he didn't intend to start with Alyse Gregory. When she came to him—and she would come to him; there was no room at all for doubt about that—she would be as warm and willing as she had been in the heated, primitive dreams that had plagued his nights since that first meeting, heating his blood so much that he woke, damp with sweat, his heart pounding in arousal and it had taken a long cold shower to restore any sort of balance to his mind and body.

There were better ways of dealing with that burn of carnal arousal—and he reckoned that waiting would mean a more potent satisfaction in the end.

'You really don't know, do you?' he added

when he saw the faint frown that drew her golden brows together, creasing the smooth skin of her forehead. 'You come with a perfect pedigree as far as Marcus—the whole Kavanaugh family—is concerned.'

'Pedigree? You make me sound like some sort of cat.'

'But only of the thoroughbred type.'

The deepening of her frown made Dario smile in response. Did she really still not get it? He liked that in her—that she didn't think of her title as something that anyone might find valuable.

'*Lady* Alyse...'

Understanding flashed over her face but she blinked hard, obviously not quite believing it.

'He thinks that matters?'

'His father does—enough to feel that a marriage to Your Ladyship would enhance the reputation of the family.'

It all made a sort of sense, Alyse supposed. If things like titles mattered so much—which it seemed they did for Marcus. It would explain why he had hounded her for so long. Before, he had just been an irritant, but now that he had this hold over her family…

But Marcus's father and Dario's father were one and the same man.

'Does that do it for you? The whole title thing?'

She saw the way his eyes narrowed sharply and wondered if she'd blundered in where she should have feared to tread. But then he laughed and leaned back in his seat again, reaching for his wineglass.

'Oh, *certamente…*' he drawled, something like real amusement warming his voice. 'Where I was dragged up, in the back streets of Casentino, we were obsessed with becoming lords and ladies—it was all we ever talked about.'

Alyse managed a smile because his comment was clearly meant to be humorous but she couldn't ignore the way it stung to think of him growing up as he had said.

'Your— Marcus's father didn't do anything to help you?'

It was like seeing his face turn to stone as she watched.

'Kavanaugh didn't acknowledge me—or my mother—for years. She was only some Italian peasant he had spent a drunken night with when he was staying with his wine supplier and she was working in the man's house. She tried to tell him she was pregnant but he refused to even see her.'

'What happened to your mother?'

'She died when I was fifteen.' The storm cloud that had settled over his face grew darker with every word. 'I tried to get help from him when she became ill but…'

He flung up his hands in a gesture of dismissal, mouth clamped tight shut over whatever else he might have wanted to say.

'I'm sorry…'

She wanted to know how things had changed after that. Because they had changed somewhere in the past years. Dario was here now, obviously with some connection with his family, even if it wasn't on friendly terms. As she watched, Dario stood up and prowled across the room to the window and then back without looking out.

When he was this close he was so tall and imposing that she had a crick in her neck just looking up at him and the width of his shoulders blocked out the fading light from the window. Although he had said that he would help her, she didn't feel *safe* with him. Only in less danger than she had felt once she had known the truth about Marcus's scheming. The terrible fear that had crept over her when she had heard the full story from her father's lips, seen the pallor of his face, the shadows under his eyes had been almost more than she could bear, and if Dario would help her lift that then she would go with Dario—whatever the risks.

'If you marry me, then, as your husband, it will be my duty to help you and your family. And when your family's debts are paid then Marcus will have to leave you alone…'

'It's not that—' Put like that, it brought home to her all the more reason why she should feel this whole deal was just too good to be true. 'It's— What will you get out of this?'

Something changed in his blue eyes, like a wash of dark water flooding over them, but then, to her astonishment, they cleared again. Dario smiled down into her concerned face and, as he did so, he held out his hand to her, palm upwards, as he had done when he had brought back the pearl earring to her the day before. Dazedly, she put her own hand into his and felt herself being drawn up to her feet to stand close to him.

'Do you really have to ask?' he said, long fingers coming under her jaw, lifting her chin towards him, exposing her mouth to his dark-eyed stare. That stare told her what was coming and she wanted it; she welcomed it so that she didn't know if she was the one who lifted her face even closer or he bent his head to do the same. She only knew that their mouths met perfectly, no hesitation, no awkwardness.

After the heated passion of their first encounter she was unprepared for the gentleness, the way that this kiss seemed to draw out her soul and place it firmly in his hands. Where that had been heat and fire, this was like melting into the sun. She was adrift on a sensual sea, swaying on weakened legs, leaning into him, needing to be closer…closer…pressed up tight against the hard muscled lines of his body. His arms came round her, gathering her even closer, hot, hard palms stroking down her back, burning through the pale linen of her dress. He cupped and held the swell of her buttocks, lifting her so that she came into even closer contact with the heated hardness between his legs. The burn and pressure of it against her pelvis made her pulse throb deep inside, the sting of arousal like an electrical burn at her most feminine core.

'Dario...'

Unable to stop herself, she slithered closer, writhing softly over the point of their intimate contact until she heard him groan aloud in response and their mouths parted enough to let him snatch in a hasty breath.

'Strega...' he muttered, stroking his right hand upwards to where her breasts ached against him, the other broad palm flattening across her bottom to hold her where he wanted her, where that intimate contact was inescapable. 'Witch!'

Well, if she was a witch then he was a sensual enchanter. He had barely kissed her half a dozen times and yet she was already desperate for his touch—for more. Knowing she would die if he didn't...

Her thoughts splintered into incoherence as that wandering hand closed, warm and strong, over the curve of her breast, cupping it through the fine fabric, setting her on fire all over again. She needed this.

'Bella strega,' Dario muttered against her lips once again, his tongue slipping along the seam of her mouth, teasing it open, tasting her. *'La mia bella strega.'*

It was so darkly sensual, so possessive that just for a second it was like a splash of cold water in her face, making her pull back an inch or two until she could meet the darkness of his eyes, seeing them hazed with the same passion that had put a flare of colour along those high, carved cheekbones.

'*Your* beautiful witch!' she managed in a voice that sparked with emotion—but whether with delight or indignation even she couldn't begin to tell.

She only knew that that possessive mutter had sliced into the heat haze that blurred her mind, bringing home to her just what this meant. That it wasn't the start of something wonderful, or just a one-night stand. It was the opening into the marriage that Dario had proposed—for purely business reasons.

'What is it?' Dario lifted his dark head, blue eyes searching into hers as if he wanted to read her mind. 'No second thoughts—no pretence.'

'I'm not…'

'And don't even try to claim this is not what you want because I know when a woman is responding and any fool can see that you want me as much as I want you.'

Lifting the hand that had been tormenting her breast, he trailed the back of it softly down the side of her face, still watching intently, and smiled as he saw her shiver in uncontrollable response.

'My damn brother might have told you that he thought you were beautiful—that he wanted you until you were sick of it. But if I say it, then it will be true. I do think you are beautiful—I do *want* you, Alyse.'

Her name was a groan that pulled on something deep and primitive inside her soul.

'I want you so much that it's eating me up alive not to have you in my bed, not to possess you…'

There was no room for doubt on that point at least. The conviction in his voice, in his eyes, told its own story. He wanted her in a way that no one had ever wanted her in her life before. Being the child of an all-encompassing love like that between her parents meant that she had often felt as if she was on the outside, looking in, as now it seemed she had been, except for what they could get from her. She had never moved out of the house, into her own flat, because her mother needed her help and support. She was her mother's carer, her father's help. He had even tried to persuade her to accept Marcus's proposal because of the way it would rescue the family. But *this* was all for her.

I want you so much that it's eating me up alive...

She felt she could listen to him say that all night. No one had ever said anything like that to her before. Never made her feel so wanted before. The trouble was that she wished she could hear it for the rest of her life and she knew that was not what Dario had in mind. But she could have it for now. She could have that wild excitement, that feeling of being wanted more than any other woman alive that she had tasted so briefly on the night of the ball. She could have that and at the same time she would set her parents free from the fear and the impossible burden of debt that now hung round their necks.

'I want you too,' she acknowledged, too far

gone to be able to lie even if she'd thought of it. She knew she was getting close to saying what he wanted to hear from her, teetering on the edge of giving in to him. But she still didn't know if it was safe.

And yet what other possible option did she have? The alternative was too terrible to consider.

'So you see why I'm doing this. You don't need to ask what I get from this bargain—the answer's obvious. I get you, in my bed, where I've wanted you from the first moment I saw you.'

And between them they rescued her father, saved her mother—and defeated Marcus. It was the only option she had so why not go with it?

What was so very different from the plan she had originally thought of—the path she had originally decided to take? That plan had been to win her freedom. A freedom she now needed more than ever.

Then she had been hunting for a way to win her freedom from Marcus's unwanted attentions. Now she wanted a far more basic liberty—the right to be her own person. She could never truly be that in her family home. She saw now that the near obsessive love her parents had left her no room to really be herself.

She'd planned that she would make it seem that she was attracted to someone else—that there was another man who could take Marcus's place and give her everything that she might have been forced to beg for from Dario's half-brother. Everything and more because she had never wanted Marcus as she hungered for Dario. He had never excited her, never aroused her just by a touch, a look. He had never promised her the open door into a world of wild passion, of sensual hunger and equally powerful sexual satisfaction.

And if her father went to prison, leaving her mother alone, then that was the end of her own dreams of freedom. She could never leave her mother to cope with the dangerous highs, the dreadful depressions that assailed her.

OK, so this wasn't the sort of marriage she had once dreamed of. But hadn't life shown her that that was just a fantasy anyway? Dario had made it plain that he wanted her, and he excited her, opened up new worlds to her. Wasn't that what she wanted for herself? Hadn't she come back to his apartment of her own volition on the night of the ball? Wouldn't she have been prepared to sleep with him—give herself to him without a single qualm? With the only thought in her head being the pleasure that she knew she would get from the encounter—the pleasure they would both give each other?

And if after that one night Dario had said that he wanted to see her again, that he wanted more, wanted the relationship to go on, she would have been up for it—wouldn't she? More than up for it—it would have been what she'd most wanted to hear. And she would have gone along with that happily.

So why was she balking at the word *marriage*? Because of her childhood dreams, the way that she had believed that her parents had the perfect relationship?

Her body knew what it wanted but if she fell into his arms now—into his bed—as she wanted to, what would happen then? When he'd had what he wanted why would he hang around, let alone do anything else to help her? Dario was offering her a way out. Everyone else had lied but he seemed to be totally straight with her.

'How do I know I can trust you? How do I

know you'll keep your word? What is there to ensure that I get anything out of this and not just that you get all you want...?'

'And you don't want me?'

Soft and wicked as a snake's hiss, it left her floundering. But Dario didn't seem to need any answer as he smiled slow and wide.

'Will a contract suit you? A fully legal document—drawn up and signed by both of us? Our own private pre-nup—with the conditions and benefits spelled out clear and precise. What we each get out of this and what we'll have when it's over and done with. When the marriage breaks up and we each go our separate ways.'

But what would he get out of it? Apart from the satisfaction of thwarting his half-brother. Would that be enough? Certainly, it seemed that Dario loathed Marcus enough to make it worth his while to go through this pretence of a marriage.

That and the fact that he would get the other thing he desired—her in his bed, where he had wanted her, he said, from the moment he had first seen her. It made her mouth dry, set her head into a spin. She didn't know whether the wildness inside was the result of fear or the delirium of sexual hunger that Dario somehow seemed to be able to spark off in her just by existing.

Was that enough to satisfy a man like Dario? Was she enough to satisfy him?

'It'll have to be signed, sealed, completely watertight—everything spelled out, every last detail. No loopholes…'

'You can instruct my lawyer yourself,' Dario replied, totally unfazed by her demand. 'And of course you don't have to sign anything until you're completely satisfied.'

He made it sound so fair, so completely reasonable—as if she could have any and everything she wanted. As if this truly was a contract between equals, giving and receiving on both sides. And yet she knew that that was just not the case.

Dario was the one who got what he wanted. She was the one with so much to lose. If she didn't sign then Dario could just walk away, sexually frustrated perhaps, but not truly damaged. She would be left in the nightmare her life had just turned into—with her mother desperately ill—because surely this would plunge her into deeper, darker depths than she had ever sunk to before. And her father would be in prison for crimes he had only committed to protect the woman he loved.

It was just too horrific. It would destroy them both.

She had the opportunity to help them as she had the courage to take it. And at the end of it—whenever that end came—she would have the freedom she most longed for.

She sucked in a deep, strengthening breath, swallowed hard.

'See your lawyer then,' she said and was relieved to hear that her voice sounded strong enough to convince anyone that she was perfectly at ease with her decision. 'Get this contract drawn up, then bring it to me and I'll sign it. And let's get this show on the road.'

Dark triumph flared in Dario's eyes, in his smile.

'Then come here—'

He reached for her again, and just the feel of his hand closing around the bare skin of her arm set all those wild, yearning sensations spiralling in the pit of her stomach.

It was too much like the way it had been on the night of the ball. Too close to that moment when he had crowed over Marcus, telling his half-brother that he had lost while Dario had won. She didn't want it to be like that; didn't want to go back to being the bone tugged between the two snarling, angry dogs. This was something different—something new—and she wanted it to stay that way. She wanted to be more in control than before.

'No…' She managed to put a teasing note into it, even added a smile and a brief, light kiss to the tip of his nose. 'Not until our wedding night.'

'How very old-fashioned of you.' She didn't know how to interpret the intonation he put on that.

'Well, that's me—an old-fashioned kind of girl.'

She turned a slanting, coquettish glance on him in an attempt to dissipate the storm clouds she could see gathering in those sapphire eyes. 'Oh, don't worry—you'll get what you've paid for—but not until the ring is on my finger.'

She'd gone a step—several steps—too far there. Those clouds hadn't evaporated. If anything, they'd grown darker, deeper. Now she waited, breath catching in her throat as he studied her face, considering his answer. Inwardly she tensed, expecting a nuclear explosion. To her relief, it didn't come.

'All right then, *mia strega*—we'll do this the traditional way. Not until our wedding night—*but then...*'

He let the sentence trail off but he didn't need to say it. She could fill in the spaces herself and her mind threatened to blow a fuse under the impact of the wild, sensual images of the night ahead of her.

'I'll see my lawyer tomorrow—get that pre-nup drawn up as soon as possible. Because I don't intend to wait for you, *bellissima*.'

It was only what she'd expected. Alyse felt a blend of excitement and apprehension bubbling up inside her. She couldn't believe that this stunning, devastating man could want her so much that he would go to these lengths to get her. Even to tying himself into a marriage of convenience that was going to cost him a small fortune as a bride price. Deep inside she felt a new kind of thrill, a quiver of rare, stinging excitement at the thought.

But then he dropped her right back down to earth by adding bluntly, 'I want you in my bed before the month is out—or sooner. Marcus won't wait for what he's owed—and neither will I.'

CHAPTER SIX

'YOU LOOK LOVELY!'

'Thank you, Dad.'

Alyse managed to respond to her father's comment with a smile that frayed slightly at the edges. She had to be thankful that her father was smiling too, and he seemed almost ten years younger than he had done two weeks ago. With the huge debt he'd owed completely paid, and the threat of imprisonment now only a bad memory, he looked as if a huge weight had been lifted from his shoulders. No tears now, but Ellen had already been sniffing sentimentally into a handkerchief before she had left for the church. But at least they had been happy tears and there had been a new lightness in her step as she'd headed for the car.

'You are sure—you're happy?' he asked now, his expression grave as he searched her face for the truth. 'It is all very sudden.'

Now he asked! Now he was concerned! The words stung at Alyse's brain and she had to bite down hard on her lower lip to stop herself from letting them escape.

'Sudden but right!' she said as warmly as she could.

She hoped she hid it well, and that her smile was convincing. She had made Dario agree that they would let her parents think that this love affair was real, if sudden and overwhelming. The rush to get married was because of the passionate way they felt about each other—and Dario had determined to show his love for his prospective bride by paying off her family's debts.

But the truth was that none of this felt real to Alyse. It was as if she was functioning on the other side of a huge sheet of plate glass so that she could see her parents, talk to them, hear their responses, but she wasn't really *with* them. She could no longer see them as she had done before. Once she'd realised the truth about the way that they had both been involved in almost forcing her into a marriage to Marcus she didn't want, she had seemed to step back from them, putting a distance between them that right now she couldn't bridge. At the same time, Dario was the one person who felt fully real to her. He was the person she had chosen, the one with whom she had thrown in her lot. Her future lay with him for as long as it lasted.

Already she was moving away from her parents towards a life that was at last her own. Or at least the one she had chosen for now. It might be just a business arrangement, but Dario hadn't realised how important a gift he was giving her in her freedom.

'Yes, it's a lightning romance, Dad, but sometimes that happens. You'd only known Mum for a month but you always told me that…'

'I knew she was the one for me.' Her father nodded his agreement.

'So there you are—lightning strikes and you are left with no choice.' Alyse slid her arm through his, grateful for the strength and support. She had only to get through today and…

The thought of what lay ahead at the end of the day almost ruined her determined attempt to look confident and happy. It was one thing to play the happy fiancée for the past couple of weeks, quite another to know that she and Dario would be alone tonight and for many more nights to come.

Just the thought made her mouth dry painfully.

It was crazy but the closer today had come, the more she had felt her nerves tighten into painful knots of apprehension. At the start of the fourteen days before their wedding was to take place, she'd thought it would be so hard to play the devoted fiancée but in the end it had been ridiculously easy. Dario strolled through the performance with a quick, easy smile here, a lingering touch there. If they stood close together he hooked his arm around her waist, drawing her closer. His fingers often tangled in the fall of her hair and, if her parents were near, he stole sneaky kisses, pretending to be shy or diffident about showing the way he felt in front of her mother and father.

Which was ridiculous. She doubted that Dario Olivero had ever had a diffident day in his whole life. And she had the evidence of his blazing kisses, the sensual touch that seared a protective layer of skin from her body every time it touched her, the heated caresses that aroused her in a heartbeat.

But, strangely, it was those less forceful touches that scorched right through to her soul and made her want him, need him more than ever before. If she could have done so without backing down from her insistence that they wait until their wedding night, she would have grabbed him by both of those tantalising hands and dragged him off upstairs to her bedroom, never caring who was watching. But the one time she had tried it, it had been Dario who had held back. Dario who had eased himself away from her clinging grip, who had shaken his head slowly, almost regretfully, and leaned forward to press a lingering, enticing kiss just beside her right ear.

'Not until our wedding night,' he had whispered softly, the smile on his lips communicating itself to her through the warmth of his breath against her sensitive skin. 'I promised.'

He had enjoyed himself by keeping that promise whilst driving her to distraction as a result. She had almost been driven to beg, but the knowledge that he would enjoy refusing her had kept the words from her tongue when they had almost escaped.

But *tonight*... Tonight he would have the right

to possess her body as fully and as often as he wanted. And it was that 'right' that weakened her blood, made her legs feel like cotton wool beneath her.

'Ready?' her father whispered, pausing at the door into the church to squeeze her hand.

'Ready.' Alyse nodded, though she doubted if that was quite the right word. If someone could be ready and yet totally unready at the same time, then that was how she felt at this moment.

Looking down at her hand where it rested on her father's arm, she couldn't miss the gleam of the brilliant diamond ring Dario had given her.

'I don't need it!' she'd protested when he'd slid it onto her finger just before they had gone together to tell her parents about their marriage. 'It's only for show.'

That had earned her a dark frown and a reproving glare.

'None of this is for show,' he'd growled. 'At least not where Marcus and Henry Kavanaugh are concerned. We might know about the agreement we have, but no one else ever will.

Everyone must think that this is for real. And, to ensure that, we have to do things properly.'

There was 'proper' and then there was this stonking great gem that flashed and sparkled, emblazoning their association in the most blatant way. And it was made all the worse by the fact that somehow he had found out about her love for vintage jewellery and the brilliant diamond could never have been matched in any modern design. This was so much the sort of glorious jewellery she might have chosen for herself—if she could possibly ever have afforded it—that it took her breath away.

'Come on, love,' her father urged, bringing home to her the fact that she had been hesitating too long, not taking a single step forward towards the altar. If she wasn't careful she was going to give away the fact that this was not at all the real love match it was meant to be.

'Let's go.'

Her feet felt unsteady as she walked, the floor seeming to rock beneath her so that she felt disturbingly seasick. She clutched at her father's arm, put all her weight on him as she gathered her breath, trying to force her eyes to focus so that she could see straight.

But seeing straight meant that she could see where Dario stood, tall and proud, shoulders squared, long back perfectly straight, at the end of the aisle. She couldn't see his face, of course, so there was no way to read what he was feeling. Nothing like as nervous as she was, that much was obvious. But did he think that this was worth it—that marrying her was worth all he had paid for her?

Alyse wished that he would turn round. That she could see his stunning face and remind herself…

The thought evaporated in a second as Dario did exactly as she had wished, turning his dark head to glance back over his shoulder. That one second where their gazes met, clashed, shook her world from top to bottom. Of course he was here. He was a businessman and he had organised this business deal so obviously he was going to see it through to the end. He was known for being ruthless, unyielding, never wavering until he had what he wanted. So why that quick, unsmiling, dark-eyed check over his shoulder to watch her approach?

Had he doubted that she would come here today? Not Dario—how could he ever doubt that? She was his investment. His stake in the deal. He would know that she had no alternative but to come here today or see her parents destroyed.

They had reached Dario's side now. Was it her imagination or did he seem taller, bigger, more powerful as he took a step closer? The formal morning coat fitted him to perfection, but with the restraint of it, the elegant crisp white shirt and silvery-grey cravat, he seemed so much more distant, alien to her. She didn't know this man and yet she was signing away her life into marriage with him. Panic fluttered like a trapped butterfly halfway up her throat, so that she needed to gasp in air to relieve the sensation.

She felt her father ease her hand from his arm, pass it into Dario's keeping, but she couldn't look at him, couldn't look anywhere but into those probing blue eyes. His hand closed around hers, warm and strong, but, frighteningly, it felt like imprisonment rather than support.

'Thank you…'

She heard her father's heartfelt words to the man who would soon become his son-in-law. In spite of herself, she couldn't help wondering whether he would have said the same to her at just this moment if she had agreed to marry Marcus. Or was it just Dario who he saw as his rescuer?

Rose, acting as her senior bridesmaid, eased the bouquet of lilies from her nerveless spare hand but Alyse barely noticed them go. She couldn't look anywhere but at Dario, couldn't register anything but the warmth and strength of his body beside her. The scent of his skin and some cool, crisp cologne reached out to enclose her but she couldn't register any of the sensuality that had been her response on so many other occasions. This felt all wrong—so cold, so calculated. So dangerous. And Dario himself stood taut and inflexible, as if he was armouring himself against any feelings the place and the event might create. He was not going to ease up, not going to *give*. He was here to receive his due—

the conqueror who was entitled to his prize and he was going to take it.

'You look beautiful.'

The intonation on the last word was so unexpected that she jumped in reaction and felt his hand tighten around hers just for a moment. She couldn't miss the way that his assessing gaze slid over her hair, left loose under the delicate coronet of flowers in white and gold, took in her face and moved on down to the simple white dress. He almost controlled his reaction but she saw the way his mouth tightened and his eyes narrowed.

'Th-thank you. I—'

She wanted to explain about the dress. She guessed that she knew what he was thinking under that unmoving expression. He was wondering what had happened to the couture gown he had expected her to wear, created by the designer he'd sent to her. It must be obvious, even to a man, that the simple sleeveless sheath that clung to every slender curve was not the creation of the French designer he had chosen.

'I...'

She opened her mouth to speak. But the celebrant had stepped forward and begun to speak and the moment was lost.

She did look beautiful. Dario tried to focus on what the priest was saying but it was impossible to clear his head from the first impressions he had of Alyse as she'd walked down the aisle towards him, taken her place at his side.

He didn't know what he'd been expecting, but it was not this. Oh, he'd known she would be beautiful; she could never be anything but. From the first moment he'd seen her from across the room at the ball, she had knocked him off balance and he'd never been able to think straight since. At least not where she was concerned.

'If any person present knows of any lawful impediment…'

The celebrant's voice tuned in and then out of his hearing like a faulty radio receiver. If anyone did decide to say there was a reason why they should not marry, then he wouldn't hear it. But, all the same, the words were echoing over and over inside his head.

Damn it to hell, didn't he, of all people, know why they shouldn't marry?

Why they shouldn't go through with this travesty of a wedding—this making of vows in a church, before a priest—it went against all he believed a marriage should be.

Oh, not for him. He'd never considered marriage for himself; he just wasn't made for it. But as an institution…as the dream that his mother had longed for all her life and never even come close to, it could mean—should mean—a great deal.

Just for a moment he let it drift through his head to question what might happen if he said that, yes, he knew of a reason why they should not be joined together. Would his mother's ghost rest any happier then?

Because his mother was part of why he was doing this. It might be too late, but perhaps, even now, he could give her her greatest wish, if only posthumously. She had always dreamed of seeing her son in Kavanaugh House, where she'd believed he belonged, inheriting his father's name in that way at least. But he also knew that she had always wanted him to marry for love.

Alyse hadn't asked for love. It had all been about the money and getting bloody Marcus off her back, once and for all. That hadn't been any sort of a lie. Marcus would not have been deterred by anything except a formal marriage contract, signed and sealed and legally unbreakable. As to the other results that this marriage could bring, that was between him and his father.

In that moment as silence descended as the celebrant finished '…or for ever hold your peace…' Alyse shifted slightly beside him, her hand trembling in his.

Immediately he looked down at her, just in the same moment that she lifted her face to look up at him and he saw the faint quiver of her mouth, the huge darkness of her green eyes. Hell, but she was beautiful…

But this whole event was not at all what he'd been expecting. No matter who she was marrying, and even if the ceremony had been arranged in what many might think was indecent haste, the wedding of Lady Alyse Gregory was a society event. One that might have been expected to be celebrated with show and formality. He'd been prepared to pay for that. Instead, it had turned out to be this pared-down, simple event in the village church near where Alyse had grown up.

She had even turned down the offer of a designer to create her dress. And when he had expected no-expense-spared, glamorous style, the simple silk sheath she wore was a major shock and not one he was comfortable with. He didn't like the way it made him feel.

His fingers tightened around the hand in his. It felt ridiculously small, delicate in his hold. The simplicity of her dress, the understated make-up and hair, brought words he'd never wanted into his head. Words like *vulnerable* and *gentle*. Words he'd never connected with any woman before—and wasn't at all sure how he felt about connecting them with this one, here and now, in these circumstances.

'Dario?' The priest was smiling, looking into his face, and it startled him back to the present.

He'd missed his cue. Missed the moment where he'd been asked, 'Do you take this woman…?' and now everyone was watching, waiting for him to give his answer.

Alyse's hand twitched nervously as if she was about to pull away and in hasty response he clamped his fingers tight around hers again, holding her still. He wasn't going to let this fail, not this close to the finishing line.

'I do,' he said, firm and strong, and could almost feel the visible relaxation of the congregation in the church behind him. A quick glance down to the woman beside him saw the way her eyes had widened in shock and concern. Had she really believed that he wouldn't go through with this? But then she only knew the half of it. The half that affected her directly.

'Alyse…'

It was her turn to be asked that question. Her response came quicker, sharper as if she wanted it said; needed it done.

He'd treat her right, he promised the spectre of his mother, who haunted his thoughts. She'd get everything she wanted out of this. After all, what she wanted was easy to provide. Money, first and foremost, and freedom for her parents. Freedom for her from Marcus's damned pursuit of her. And the sexual fulfilment that would come from them being in bed together. The consummation of desire that he'd been hungry for from the first moment he'd seen her.

Just the thought of it made his grip on her hand tighten, the pressure of skin on skin a silent promise to her—and to himself—of what was to come.

'I do...'

They were the words Alyse had been worrying about ever since she'd woken this morning. Just two simple words but they'd spun round and round in her thoughts, threatening to drive her crazy. Two words to change her life. Once she'd said those two words, there was no going back. She would be married to Dario and their prenuptial contract would become legal and binding.

That was what she wanted, wasn't it? If she didn't go through with this then her parents would suffer and she would never know the truth of Dario's lovemaking. The dreams that she had of him during the night, erotic dreams that still clung to her mind like thick, sticky cobwebs, and left her damp with sweat, her bed a mess of tangled sheets, told her how much her body hungered for his. And tonight...

Her mind hazed at the realisation that she was

thinking of hot, passionate sex right here, before the altar, with her hand tight in Dario's.

He hadn't let go of her hand. If anything, he held it tighter, and didn't let go all through the vital questions. Did he think that she might run away? That she might escape him and leave him with her part of the bargain unpaid? He'd already made good on his promises. She knew, because her father had been bubbling over with the news that all those terrible debts had been paid.

So was she the only possible loose end he felt might escape him? Did he think that perhaps she would dodge out of what she owed him and run for her life?

Something disturbingly close to her heart ached at the thought. She couldn't…she wouldn't.

'I do…' she said again, unthinkingly, and heard the ripple of amusement from the pews behind her at her apparent need to emphasise the point.

There was no echoing smile in Dario's dark face, though. His expression was sombre, unrevealing, and his eyes like bottomless dark pools, threatening to drown her in their depths.

Somehow she made it through the rest of the service. The vows were made, the ring was on her finger—another bigger, broader one on his, and they were now pronounced to be man and wife.

'You may kiss the bride…' just about registered in her numbed brain as Dario swept her off her feet in a huge enveloping hug, lifting her to meet his mouth as he crushed his hard lips against hers in a fiercely overwhelming kiss.

The unexpected display of passion knocked all the breath out of her body and had her clinging to him for support, glorying in the feel of his strength surrounding her, the play of powerful muscles under the expensive material of his morning coat, the scent of his skin blending with the tang of some citrus and bergamot cologne. She could do this! Oh, dear heaven, she *wanted* to do this!

The moment seemed to go on for ever but, at long last, Dario released her, taking his mouth from hers and letting her slide slowly back down until her toes were on the floor. Which meant that her ear was just level with his mouth.

'Now let anyone claim that this isn't for real,' he muttered, clearly taking a dark satisfaction in the way that a ripple of applause spread through the church. 'Welcome to my life, Signora Olivero.'

Why didn't he just say 'Welcome to my bed'? Alyse wondered. Because that had been all there was in that kiss. Passion, primal, sexual need—but nothing else. If he had taken her out and branded her as his, he couldn't have made a more blatant statement of possession. He had got what he wanted—and she would be all kinds of a fool if she tried to read anything more into it.

Somehow she managed to make her way back down the aisle, her hand tucked into Dario's arm to support her. She exchanged smiles with her family, her friends, and it was only then that it was brought home to her just how much the congregation was weighted in her favour, with just a few friends who had come from Italy to be with Dario today.

As he walked at her side Dario stood tall and proud and, although he turned his head, nodded to acknowledge the congratulations of everyone, there was a distinct tension about him, one that only she was aware of. If she glanced up at his face, she saw that the smiles that came and went like a flashing neon sign did nothing to reach his eyes while that narrowed blue gaze was flicking around the church, looking left and right as if he was searching for someone.

Whoever it was, he didn't find them. They got to the end of the aisles and then out into the sunshine without there being any moment when he registered anyone special. It was shocking how lonely that made her feel for him. His mother had died, he'd said, and of course the one member of his family that she really knew about—Marcus—was hardly likely to be at the celebration of this particular wedding.

'I'm sorry—' she said, unable to hold back as they snatched a moment alone, waiting for everyone else to come out of the church behind them.

'Sorry?'

The look he turned on her was unfocused and opaque, totally without any emotion.

'My family—they did rather monopolise the church—and you—'

'Why should that matter?' He frowned. 'It is how it is.'

'But you...' she tried again, stumbling to a halt

as he shook his head in rejection of her attempt to reach out to him.

'It's nothing, Alyse. Nothing matters but us. I don't do family.'

At that moment the light wind blew a large white cloud in front of the sun, blocking out its warmth and making Alyse shiver in sudden response. But it was more the effect of Dario's words that had struck home to her rather than the sudden chill. They sounded not just as some explanation for the effect the past had on the present—but also as a cold-blooded decree for the prospect of the future.

CHAPTER SEVEN

'I CAN'T REALLY believe I'm here...'

Alyse shaded her eyes against the burn of the setting sun as she stared out at the beauty of the countryside that surrounded them. The view from the stone terrace of the huge villa was spectacular. Away towards the horizon were some of the vineyards Dario owned.

'Why not?' Dario's tone was sharp.

The truth was that she'd never thought he'd take her to his home. Dario was a man who valued his privacy—the limited amount he'd told her about his life, his past, made that plain. So she had never expected to be whisked away from the reception and hurried onto a private jet for the flight to Tuscany. Now this unexpected insight into the private and personal life of the man she had married left her feeling as if her feet weren't quite on solid ground.

'I never thought we'd have a honeymoon,' she

said hastily, not wanting him to see the truth in her face.

Things were inside out. They should have been doing this—learning about each other—*before* the wedding ceremony. Now here she was realising just how little she knew about the man the world would call her husband. The man whose bed she would share tonight and every night for however long this marriage of convenience would last.

'I said we'd do things properly.'

'So you did.' She hoped that her smile didn't look as forced as it felt. How could he make a statement sound like a reproach? 'And everything was completely—proper.'

It was strange how different that word could sound, the subtle way its meaning varied. Everything about the day had been totally appropriate for a hasty, passionate, romantic wedding. But no one could ever have described the events that had led up to this marriage-business fusion as being 'proper' in the way that usually had the word 'prim' in front of it. How would everyone in the church—her family—have felt if they'd known that basically she had sold herself to Dario for an appalling amount of money? The reasons behind it didn't really change anything. There was an ugly word for what she'd done.

'It was wonderful, all of it.'

She didn't need to force any enthusiasm into her voice as she turned to face him. With the formal wear of the day discarded for something more suited to the warmer temperatures in Tuscany, he was now wearing a loose white shirt, sleeves rolled up to expose the length of his arms, and well-worn faded denim jeans. Once they'd reached the villa he'd even kicked off his shoes and now padded barefoot along the sun-warmed terrace. Against the rosy brickwork of the building behind him, its colour enhanced by the glow of the burning sunset, his monochrome form looked stark and dangerous. But he had been so generous, more than she had ever had the right to ask of him.

'A very special day.' A couple of hasty steps took her close enough to press a spontaneous kiss against his lean cheek, roughened by the long day's growth of dark stubble. 'I know everyone thought so too.'

'I can't say I give a damn about what everyone else thought,' Dario muttered roughly. 'So long as you enjoyed your day.'

'Oh, I did!'

Alyse didn't let herself consider his choice of words. *Your day,* not *our day*—or even just *the day*—as if he had no part in it, other than paying for every damn thing, of course.

'It was lovely—thank you.'

Her lips were still just inches away from his face; she could smell his skin, taste him on her mouth, and her eyes were locked with his sapphire ones that had now turned a deeper, darker blue, Her stomach flipped over, her pulse heating and setting her blood pounding.

'I'm sure I'll find it was worth it.'

It took a stunned second or two for the full meaning of his words to hit home and make her heart clench tight in apprehension but in the same moment she already knew that she didn't care. He might call this the recompense for all he had paid out, the return that he had paid for, but there was more to it than that for Alyse. This was pure sensuality, a deep and darkly primal need that flooded through her as she pressed her mouth to his cheek again, feeling the scrape of bristle, the heat of flesh, the tightness of a strong muscle that jerked underneath her kiss.

'That you're worth it.'

A sudden swift movement and it was not his cheek that she was kissing but the full burning pressure of his mouth on hers. His kiss had no give to it but took and demanded as clearly he believed he was entitled to do.

He *was* entitled. This was what she'd promised him. But from the moment that his mouth collided with hers she knew that she didn't give a damn. This wasn't just about what Dario had bought and paid for. It was what she wanted; what they both wanted and now was the time. The fire they had lit between them might have smouldered slowly for some time, pushed underneath by circumstances, by Alyse's decree that she wanted to wait until their wedding night, but right now it flared into wild flame in the space of a heartbeat, searing hot and hungry through both of them.

'I've waited long enough for this,' Dario muttered harshly against her mouth, tilting her head back with the force of his kiss so that the setting sun burned into her eyes. 'Too damn long.'

'Too damn long,' Alyse echoed on a sigh of acquiescence.

In this moment she had no idea why she had ever imposed that crazy sanction. Why she had ever thought it was important that he should wait—that they both should wait. This was what she'd wanted then; what she wanted now and the intervening two weeks had only made the hunger so much harder to bear.

Flinging her arms up around Dario's neck, she tangled her fingers in the jet-black silk of his hair, feeling the burn of need pulse deep inside her.

'Too damn long,' she repeated with even more emphasis.

She felt the sardonic laughter that shook his powerful frame like a new sensation against her skin, an unexpected caress that crushed the fine linen of her turquoise sundress against breasts that already felt tight and hot, hungry for his touch.

'So why the hell...?'

She pushed the rest of his question back down his throat with the force of her own kiss.

'Because I could,' she told him sassily. 'And because I was a fool.'

'Too damn right you were a fool—and I was a bigger one to agree. But not any more.'

His hands were busy at the back of her dress, tugging at the zip, dragging it down to expose the line of her spine, but at the same time he managed to swing her off her feet and up into his arms. The hand that supported her back slid in between her dress and her skin, smoothing over fine bones, adding heat where she was already burning, hunger where she was already so needy.

'Not any more,' she managed because all she could do was to echo his rough-voiced statement. It was exactly the way she felt.

She had only the most basic knowledge of the villa. They had arrived less than an hour earlier, their bags taken to their room by some unseen member of staff. Then Dario had suggested a glass of wine on the terrace so she had no idea where they were going, but it didn't matter. Dario was in charge and Dario knew exactly where he was going.

With each step they mounted on the way upstairs, he paused, dragging another kiss from her lips, crushing her against the wall to hold her exactly where he wanted her. The plaster of the wall was cool against her skin, a stunning contrast to the raging fire at the points where her body was crushed up against his, and the even fiercer one that burned deep inside, just inches away from the hot caress of his hand.

'This is what it's all been about.'

Dario's tone was thick and rough, each word punctuated by another greedy, snatching kiss, crushing her mouth, taking her soul. One of her sandals slipped from her feet and tumbled down the stairs, followed almost immediately by the other. Alyse heard the sound as a drum roll of inexorable passion. Inescapable and unstoppable. This had been inevitable from the moment they had met and she didn't want to delay another second. She had managed to get her hands between them, ripping open his shirt so wildly that buttons spun off and dropped to the floor. She thrilled by the feel of his hard, warm chest, lightly hazed with crisp, dark hair beneath her fingers. She scraped her nails over the beautiful olive skin, feeling his heart kick in response, his groan of need making her smile against his shoulder.

When Dario kicked open a door at the top of the stairs her heart jumped so wildly that she could hardly breathe. Her blood was pounding in her ears as he carried her across the room, dropped her with little ceremony onto a downy white duvet on top of the bed. Hating the feeling of separation, the breath of cold air that came between them, she moaned a complaint, reaching for him at once.

'Momento...'

He was throwing off his clothes, his shirt already half off after her urgent attentions. It was dropped to the floor, his trousers and black boxer shorts following swiftly. Then he bent over her, taking her mouth again, nipping, sucking, tracing his tongue along the join of her lips, enticing his way inside to taste her more intimately. Alyse was already trying to shrug herself out of her dress, the top half gaping wide to expose the peach silk and lace of her bra, the flushed curves of her breasts.

'Now—now...Dario...'

'No—wait...'

Wait! Her body screamed the hungry reproach but already Dario had turned his head, the heat and weight of his long body holding her imprisoned on the bed as he tugged open a drawer in a nearby bedside cabinet. After a moment's stunned confusion, Alyse realised what was going on.

'No need…'

She reared up to whisper the words in his ear.

'I'm safe…in all ways.'

'Safe?'

He spared her a glance, though it was obvious that he had to fight against his body's needs to do so. Already the heated thrust of his penis was hard against her thighs, but still he held away from her even though she opened her legs beneath him.

'Best to be sure.'

'I am…'

But already he was sheathing himself, his movements firm and competent, turning kisses on her pouting mouth as he set out to distract her, keep her hungry at the same time.

'So am I—now…'

It was rough and raw, deep in his throat as

his teasing mouth moved lower, tongue trailing over her peaking breasts, his teeth closing over the edges of her bra, tugging it down so that his tongue could slide over the delicate skin he had exposed. Then he closed his lips over the pouting nipple, sucking on her through the silk and letting his teeth scrape across the distended flesh, tugging softly.

'Damn you…damn you…' Alyse muttered, cursing him for the delay and yet unable to resist the stinging pleasure of his mouth.

She writhed beneath him, open and hungry, and yearning for the fulfilment his passion promised.

'Come into me, Dario,' she whispered against his ear. 'Take me—make this real…'

She broke off on a high, sighing cry of completion as he moved his big body, slid inside her, pushing deeper and deeper until she felt totally filled, totally given up to him.

'So right…' she sighed. 'So—so right.'

'So right,' Dario agreed, his voice rough and uneven, as he started to move, to press in and out, taking, giving, putting himself totally into her arms as she closed them around him, held his strength tight against her.

Alyse was lost, adrift on the heated waves of passion that swept over her, taking her higher, higher, faster and faster. She felt her muscles bunching, contracting, gathering themselves towards the fulfilment she was reaching for. She was gripping Dario tight, abandoning herself to him, throwing her head back and letting his name escape on a moan of need as he quickened his pace, thrust into her again and again.

'Dario… Oh, Dario!'

She was totally focused, totally lost, abandoning herself to him as the convulsions of delight broke over her, driving her beyond reality into the force of the starburst of pleasure that exploded all around her, forcing the wild, high cry of his name from her lips as she gave herself up to it.

It was a long, heated, sensual night, one that left them sated with each other's bodies, abandoned to exhaustion in the end when they could physically take no more. It was early morning when Alyse finally stirred, stretching and staring around her sleepily, acknowledging the ache of muscles tired by the night's activities, the faint soreness where love bruises marked her skin.

As Dario stirred lazily beside her, rubbing his face into the pillow as he woke, she noticed the aftermath of their passion, the garments discarded here, there and everywhere on the floor where they had tossed them aside in their rush to fulfilment. Stretching out a lazy hand, she reached for her own clothing and surveyed it ruefully.

'You tore my dress.'

She held up the turquoise linen dress or, rather, the remains of it. It was ripped from top to bottom, coming apart at the seams.

The look Dario turned on it was careless, indifferent, but shaded with a rich seam of dark triumph.

'It was in the way.' He lifted those powerful shoulders—shoulders that were now marked with the attentions of her hands, her nails, even her teeth. 'I'll buy you another one.'

Lazy, hazy blue eyes, still filled with the after-effects of the mind-blowing passion that had taken them by storm, mocked her indignation, and his smile was even more slow and indulgent.

'And then I'll rip that one off you too. But I have to admit that I prefer you as you are now…'

His gaze slid over her naked body, caressing the flushed lines of her cheeks, the curve of her shoulders, her breasts above the fine cotton sheet she had pulled over her as she sat up. A moment later an equally caressing hand followed the same route. Smoothing her skin, curving over her breast, cupping its weight in his palm.

'Yes,' he drawled softly, 'this is how I'd like you to stay for the rest of your life.'

'A little impractical.' Alyse's voice was tight with the effort she was making not to respond to his touch.

'Who gives a damn about practical?' Dario's hands were now curved under her breasts, his thumbs toying with the nipples, still pink and tender from his earlier attentions. Alyse shivered as his slightly roughened pads rubbed across the swollen skin, sending burning arrows of need shooting down to pool with moist heat between her legs. 'This marriage is not about practical. It's about this…'

Another sweep of his thumbs, harder this

time, had her throwing back her head and gasping in air.

'Isn't it…?'

This time he rolled her nipples between his fingers, blue eyes very dark as he watched intently, his mouth just curling at the corners as he saw her response.

'Isn't it, *bellissima*?'

Alyse threw caution to the winds. To hell with restraint—and with anything else! Who cared if he thought she was a total pushover where he was concerned? That was the exact truth, wasn't it? So why was she trying to hide it from him? It only delayed the pleasure and the satisfaction she was now longing for all over again. And she didn't want to delay for any reason.

'Yes,' she whispered, low and hungry.

'I can't hear you.'

Deliberately provoked and not giving a damn about it, she let her eyes fly open, stunned to find that he had moved closer and his mouth was almost touching hers. She had only to speak to taste his skin against hers but she wanted more than that.

'Yes, damn you—yes!'

This time she took the initiative, almost throwing herself at him, taking his mouth with hers as she pressed him down onto the bed, flat underneath her.

'Yes...'

She kissed him hard and long, her hands making slow sensual forays along the length of his body, her mouth smiling against his as she felt the way the powerful muscles bunched and jerked under her touch.

'Oh, yes…'

She let her fingers tiptoe over his burning skin, along the hair-roughened length of his thigh to where the neediest part of him strained against her, hard and hungry as before. When she drifted her touch over him she felt him jump beneath her teasing torment, a rush of Italian curses spilling from his lips.

'Now what was that you were saying about pleasure?' she teased, looking down into his face where deep dark eyes glazed with passion, high cheekbones were heavily marked with the burn of need.

Her hands moved again, stroking, tormenting,

squeezing lightly till she felt him buck hard underneath her.

'Was this what you meant?'

'Almost!' His voice was rough and raw, cracking at the edges.

'Almost?'

She barely had the time to get the word out, no chance to wonder what he might mean, when he grabbed her hands in a bruising grip, yanked them away from their tormenting journey. Holding her arms wide, he used his greater strength to twist himself out from underneath her, turning her upside down as he did. When she landed on her back on the bed, he was there, on top of her, crushing her down into the soft mattress before she had time even to breathe, let alone speak.

'Almost,' he grated again. '*Quasi, la mia bella strega*. But this…'

He brought her hands up over her head, held them firmly on the pillow, one of his larger hands holding both her wrists imprisoned tight as he pushed his knee between her thighs, opening her up to him as his lips tormented her aching nipple, suckling and nibbling, drawing into the heat and moistness of his mouth.

'This,' he repeated, coming into her with one hard, forceful thrust, making her toss her head against the pillows in heated delight as she felt the power and strength of him stretching the muscles that were so ready, so hungry for him there.

'*This* is what I meant.'

CHAPTER EIGHT

'TALKING OF DRESSES...'

Some time early in the morning, when the faint rays of dawn were just beginning to creep over the horizon seen from the unshuttered windows, Dario stirred again sleepily, twisting on his side to reach down and snatch up the tangled remnants of the turquoise dress from where it lay on the bed. Flopping back onto the pillows, he held it up, threading it through his bronzed fingers.

'What was wrong with the wedding dress Lynette designed for you?'

He said it casually but, because she had known that this was coming, she felt her stomach muscles tighten, the lazy, satisfied warmth seeping away in an instant.

'The one you wanted me to wear.' To impress Marcus. His father. To show the world that she was his.

'You didn't like it?'

'It was beautiful—but…'

But she had felt as if she had been swept off her feet by a raging tsunami, going under for the third time until she couldn't see, couldn't hear, couldn't breathe. The ground had been swept from beneath her feet, and everything was running away from her. She felt the same all over again now, but for very different reasons.

'But I wanted some say in what I wore. Surely you understand that it's every girl's dream to pick out her own wedding dress.'

'I see,' he said but the look he turned on her said that he saw but he didn't understand why she would have chosen such a plain, simple design when she could have had the services of the couturier he had hired for her. 'But I would have paid…'

'And that's exactly why I didn't want it.' Alyse pulled herself up on the pillows, wishing there were fewer shadows in the room so that she could read his face more easily. 'You have already given us so much; I couldn't take any more from you.'

'It was your wedding day. I would have been happy to give you whatever you asked.'

'And you can't see that it's that *asking* that makes all the difference?'

Dario frowned darkly, trying to make sense out of something that turned everything he'd believed about her on its head and left him feeling as if the ground beneath him had suddenly shifted.

'I wanted you to have whatever you longed for—the wedding of your dreams.'

He'd wanted it to be that way for the wedding at least. When their marriage was never going to be a love match, then he could make it the sort of day she would have wanted. He couldn't do anything about the emotions.

'Or perhaps the real truth is that really you were planning on doing just what *you* wanted.'

The sudden tartness in her soft voice brought his head round sharply. She lay propped up against the pillows, her blonde hair tumbling in wild disorder around a face that had suddenly tightened unexpectedly.

'You weren't really thinking about me.'

'Why the hell would I give a damn what my bride wears—especially when we both know that this isn't a marriage of love but one of convenience—purely a business deal?'

She clamped her lips tight shut then turned and stared out over the horizon, blinking hard in the glow of the rising sun.

'Because you wanted to rub dirt in Marcus's face to show him what he'd lost. And because you wanted your father to see what you were getting.'

There should be a thought in his head in response to that. But the truth was that there wasn't one. Just a blank space on which was etched the disturbing question—was she right? Had he really wanted her to wear something more expensive, to have all the flowers and the bridesmaids' dresses and the decorations imaginable—because that was his way of showing his father and his half-brother?

Well, if he had then it had all come back in his face to bite him. In spite of receiving an invitation, Henry Kavanaugh hadn't even shown up at the wedding. He'd sent a letter of congratulation—well, it was supposed to have been congratulations but it came with a sting in its tail that had been impossible to ignore. He could have his father's recognition at last—but at what a cost! It was a good job that this marriage had at least given Alyse what she had wanted from it—her parents' security—because it sure as hell hadn't given him any such thing.

'I thought all women had their dream weddings planned from the moment they could choose their first dress. That any woman had it all thought out—every last detail—and all they needed was the groom.'

'Any woman, hmm—?'

She turned to face him now, her neat chin coming up, openly defying him, as her green eyes flashed a challenge.

'Any woman?' she echoed cynically. 'So is that how you see me—as just *any* woman? Any woman who would do in your bed.'

'Hell, no!'

Fury pushed him to deny it. Fury at the accusation and a rush of something darkly uncomfortable that he didn't actually want to look right in the face.

'You could never be just any woman. Do you think I would go through all this—that I would sell out my freedom and invest so much money in your family just to win *any* woman?'

He had had to mention the money, Alyse told herself. *Thanks a bunch, Dario!* If there was a way of making her feel low and cheap—correction: low and too *expensive*—then it was that. And he had sold out his freedom, had he? What the blazes did he think that she'd done? Why did he think she was here? Because she had wanted the money?

But of course that was how it would seem to him.

And, face it, Alyse, that was such a big part of it. No—she couldn't allow herself to think that. It hadn't been the money that had been the final weight in the scales as she'd tried to decide what to do. It had been because of Dario himself. Because she had wanted to be with him, under any circumstances.

'Besides, I was caught in a dilemma,' she said hastily, needing to distract him. 'You were offering one thing and my mother wanted me to wear *her* wedding dress.'

'Your mother wore that dress you had on at the wedding?'

He'd seen straight through the story she'd been about to tell.

'Well, no—but in the end I chose not to wear hers.'

'Any particular reason?' he tossed at her with apparent casualness, but she shivered at the thought of just what lay below the careless question.

The truth was she hadn't been able to bear to think of her mother's dress, handed down from one generation to another, as a symbol of her parents' love for each other. Once it had been what she'd dreamed of but now she saw how dangerous that obsessive love, one that left no room for anyone else, could be. It was that love that had got them into this mess after all. She hadn't wanted to wear anything that tied her to her parents for this wedding that, while it might be only about business and money, was also about passion and a way of breaking free from the life she had known.

'I wanted to save that for—for a proper wedding.'

'Proper?' He pounced on the word like a tiger on its prey. 'Define *proper*. Because I'm sure you don't mean it has to be oh, so correct and following every rule of polite etiquette?'

The way he pronounced the last word was so careful, so almost correct but not quite, that it tugged at her heart to think that for the first time his near perfect command of the English language had actually deserted him. It made him sound disturbingly vulnerable—but there was no way she could let herself believe that that was in fact the case.

'One that means something…something more than…'

Oh, dear, she was digging a hole right at her own feet and with every word it just got deeper.

'Something more than…?' Dario echoed ominously.

'Oh, you know what I mean, Dario. This isn't real. It isn't a genuine marriage—it's a business deal—one where you buy and I…'

'You do what? Sell yourself?' Could his voice get any more dangerous?

'Well, we both know there isn't any real feeling on either side—other than a raging burning need to get into each other's pants, of course.'

'Of course,' he echoed, clipped and icy. 'And did you explain this to your mother?'

Alyse flinched away from the ice in his words as it suddenly drained all the warmth from the sun.

'Of course not. Do you think she'd have been able to watch me walk up the aisle as a bought bride? She would have gone into a state of total collapse if she'd known that this union paid for all the ruinous mistakes she and my father had made. I just told her what I've told you—which was that I wanted to choose—and pay for—my own dress.'

This was her marriage, her wedding, her choice.

'Not every daughter wants to wear her mother's dress. Most women want their own special clothes for a special day.'

'Not my mother.' It was a flat, emotionless statement. 'She never had a wedding—never mind a dress.'

He'd touched on this once before but had made it obvious that he didn't welcome her interest in his past. But perhaps now he would let her probe a little further? It would distract him from the dangerous path his thoughts had been on, and besides she really wanted to know.

'Your father never acknowledged her?'

She might have wanted to free herself from the complications and lies her parents had told recently, but at least she had always known she was their daughter, and they had never left her in any doubt of the fact that she had been wanted, even if as a further proof of their love for each other.

'Neither her nor me. She didn't know he was married and he didn't trouble to tell her. She was supposed to have been a one-night stand and then to forget about him as he forgot about her. But then she found that she was pregnant.'

'Did she tell him?'

The way that his hands raked through the tousled blackness of his hair gave away more than he was prepared to reveal in his voice.

'Of course she did—or tried to. She wrote—she even found out his home address and saved up all she could afford to travel to his door. He wouldn't even see her. The door was shut in her face.'

Alyse's nails dug into her palms as she tried to imagine how the poor woman had felt.

'She tried again—when I was born. She took me with her and was so sure that my *father*...' he made the word sound like poison '...couldn't turn away his own son.'

There was a long pause while Dario stared out at the rising sun with narrowed eyes.

'He could. She didn't get over the doorstep and one of the servants was sent to tell her to go away or the police would be called. But she didn't give up. She tried again on my first birthday and again every year after that. She never gave up until she became ill with cancer. That year I went. I had to ask him to help her.'

How could eight simple words be filled with so much bitterness, so much emotion held back and yet clear in the sound of his voice? He had hated going but he had done so for his mother.

'I knew she had loved him in spite of everything and she would die happy if she could just see him. Or if he could do something to help ease her pain.'

'And did he?'

A brusque shake of Dario's dark head gave her the answer she was expecting.

'Not a word, not a sign. Mamma died feeling totally abandoned. But in the end it turned out that my father had never got the message. That he hadn't been in the house when I called. It was only later that I found out why.'

'Marcus?' Alyse questioned and saw again that single sharp nod that signified agreement.

It was as if the sun had suddenly gone behind a deep dark cloud, taking all the warmth from the air. The rivalry and hatred between the two brothers had deep roots and a long time to grow.

'I swore I'd never have anything to do with them ever again.'

'So how did you know about my mother's gambling—my dad's problems?'

Dario's smile was a travesty of any sort of amusement.

'I didn't want anything to do with the Kavanaughs but I have contacts—it's easy to get information if I want it. That was how I learned that Henry had had a stroke and that now Marcus was in charge.'

And he had wanted his revenge on Marcus

for the way the older brother had denied Dario's dying mother the chance of any peace of mind.

'From there it was an easy job to discover that my damned brother was making a play for you—and why. You were just the sort of trophy wife that would be the icing on Kavanaugh's cake and, best of all, you could be manoeuvred into accepting his proposal when it was either that or see your family destroyed.'

'And that was why you came looking for me from the start?'

He didn't trouble to deny it but he didn't show any sort of concern at her accusation. But it damaged something inside her when she knew he'd moved straight onto the attack, to get his revenge on his brother, the way his father had rejected him and his mother.

Her thoughts were reeling back to that first evening she'd met him, on the night of the ball. He'd come straight across the room to her and she'd thought it was because he couldn't help himself—that he'd been so attracted to her. But then there had been that moment when she'd introduced herself and just for a second he had reacted unexpectedly. She had barely noticed it at the time but now she could hear his voice saying her name and something in the intonation of it caught on her nerves.

'You introduced yourself to me—remember. I had my suspicions but then you confirmed them.'

'So is that what I am to you too…' her voice cracked on the question '…a trophy wife?'

Dario twisted in the bed so that he was looking down into her face.

'You're the only wife I'd ever want. I told you, I don't do family.'

Which was like giving her something and snatching it right back with the second breath. Was she still just a pawn in his game to outwit and take retribution on his callous family?

'If it helps,' Dario said slowly, something in the way he looked at her telling her that he had read her thoughts in her face, 'I never expected to want you as much as I did from the moment I saw you.'

'So it wasn't just to get at Marcus—and your father?'

She was ridiculously pleased to know that at least.

'Never just that. There was something there between us like an electrical storm in the moment we met. And you felt it too—don't deny it.'

'I'm not denying it.' Alyse looked deep into his eyes as she spoke, wanting him to know it was true. 'I can't.'

'It was inevitable—it would have happened once we met, no matter who you were, no matter who I was.'

His hand was on her as he spoke, strong fingers moving up her arm, over her shoulders. At first the softness of his touch made her shiver as the nerves beneath her skin began to tingle in instinctive response. Another moment and her pulse had set up a slow, heavy thud that made the blood pound inside her head.

'Inevitable…' she murmured, her eyes half closing as she gave herself up to the pleasure of his caress.

'Totally…' Dario's voice was low, the sound of it like warm smoke coiling around her. His hand was moving down her body, so slowly, so gently, and this time when she shivered it was in a rush of newly awakened need, the tiny moan that escaped her impossible to hold back as she shifted restlessly against the soft white sheets.

'Totally inevitable,' she sighed again as he pulled her underneath him and proceeded to take her senses by storm until she was totally incapable of saying or thinking of anything else but him and the glorious sensual power of his body taking possession of hers.

CHAPTER NINE

'*BUONGIORNO*, SLEEPING BEAUTY...'

Dario dropped a kiss on Alyse's smiling mouth as she yawned and stretched, slowly coming awake.

'Are you ever going to wake up today?'

'Mmm?' she murmured, stirring slightly and then curling up under the covers in the way he had come to love. She looked like a small, delicate kitten twisting herself into a ball and his fingers itched to stroke down the clear line of her spine, watch her arch into the caress, press herself against his palm.

'Are you going to get up?'

'Wake up, maybe...'

She turned a slow, sleepy smile on him, one that twisted his guts into knots of hunger, made his body harden in an instant.

'But I didn't plan on getting up at all today.

In fact, I planned on staying right where I am but…I thought you might want to join me.'

Reaching out, she aimed for his hands, but then brushed against his leg, frowning as her fingers felt the linen of his trousers.

'Oh, but this won't do—won't do at all.'

She pursed her mouth into a moue of sulky provocation.

'You have to take these off—and everything else.'

'Alyse!'

He blended reproach with amusement in order to hide just how much he wanted to do exactly as she said. At least with her eyes still half-closed she couldn't see the hard and hungry evidence of his body that gave away the fact that he was just pretending to object to what she was saying.

'Dario!' She mocked his tone perfectly. 'I don't know why you're objecting—I think we should spend all day in bed. Eat a little—perhaps drink some wine but only in between—when we need refreshment. The rest of the time, I think we should make love again and again and again.'

She writhed sensually as she spoke, adding further discomfort to his hardened state as the movement brought her naked body clear of any covers, the shafts of sunlight slipping through the gauze at the windows highlighting the creamy skin of her breasts, the pert pink tips of her nipples that made his mouth water to remember the way they tasted.

'But we did that yesterday—and the day before…'

'And can you think of any better way of spending our time?'

Her eyes came wide open, gleaming emerald in the sun as she stared at him.

'Or have you tired of me? Is that it?'

'Tired of you?' His laughter was shaken as the way she sat up made her breasts sway softly. 'Hell, woman, do you really think that's possible?'

But the faint frown that drew her brows together bothered him. It looked as if there was something that was troubling her—but what? She had been warm and passionate, giving and hungry for pleasure all through the night, as she had been for so many nights since they had arrived at the villa. He had found her totally insatiable, impossible to resist. In fact there had been that one time, the first morning, that they had both been so turned on that he had forgotten his never-without-a-condom rule. If it hadn't been for the fact that she was on the Pill…

He snatched his mind back from the erotic path it was following and made himself look deep into her questioning eyes.

'How could I be tired of you? Did I seem tired last night…well…' this time his laughter was more natural, rather self-deprecating as he recalled the way they had finally fallen into exhausted sleep, unable to keep awake any longer '…except for once.'

That shadowed look was still there so he put his thoughts back onto the track of distracting her—and going on with the plan he had come in here to suggest.

'I thought we could go out for the day. You should see something of Italy.'

'Go where? What's near here?'

'Well, there's Bologna or Florence—Pisa. Oh, no.' It was a light-hearted groan as he saw the new light of interest in her eyes. 'You want to do the tourist thing? See the Leaning Tower?'

'I can think of another leaning tower I'd rather see…'

The direction of her stare, the wicked curve to her mouth made it plain exactly what she meant.

'But if that's not on offer—then Pisa it has to be. Is that close to the Campo Santo as well?'

'Within walking distance. Why?'

Something of that teasing look had gone from her face.

'I was told there were some frescoes there that are worth seeing. Oh, don't look like that!' she added as she caught the fleeting expression of disbelief that flashed across his face. 'I did study the History of Art at university.'

He'd always assumed that she had taken the unchallenging job because she was comfortable coasting, enjoying her parents' comfortable lifestyle. But he was learning he had been so wrong about so much.

'You did? Then why the hell…?'

'Was I just working as a receptionist?' She supplied the end of the question for him. 'At least I was working in the art world—but my mother was so often ill and she needed someone close to look after her. That's why I still lived at home. But don't worry…' she hurried to say it in order to get rid of the dark clouds that had come rushing over his face '…that's not going to be the way it is any more. For one thing—I'm not going back to the gallery. I gave in my notice as soon as we…as we came to our arrangement. And for another…'

'How long has your mother been ill?'

'She's had the mood swings as long as I can remember.' Alyse's mouth twisted into a grimace of distaste. 'I grew up knowing I had to be careful—not upset her any further.'

Her mother couldn't help the emotional seesaw she lived on, she knew, but, looking back, she could see how her father had indulged his wife, always tiptoeing around her 'delicate sensitivity', always caring for her—or asking their daughter to do so—in a way that made sure she never truly faced up to the repercussions of her actions. Until this final terrible mess that they would never have got out of if it hadn't been for Dario.

'You've done quite enough for her,' Dario put in roughly, and she nodded slowly in agreement.

'It's up to my father now,' Alyse agreed sombrely, knowing once again that amazing sense of freedom that she had woken up with every morning since Dario had made his proposal about their marriage. It was only now, since she had come to Italy with him, that she had got rid of that sense of being used, of being a pawn in her parents' lives rather than free to live for herself. It was weird that even when she was tied by the pre-nup that she had signed she'd felt more liberated and more alive than ever before. 'I can't live my mother's life for her. I can only live my own.'

'So—the frescoes.'

'And all the rest of it—the Leaning Tower—the whole tourist bit.'

Alyse felt her mouth curve into a smile, her mood lightening as she tossed back the covers, pushed herself to her feet. 'Just give me half an hour to get ready…Dario?'

Seeing how his eyes were focused on her naked body, she smiled then wagged a pretend reproving finger at him. 'No! You promised me a day out.'

'A day out…' Dario managed, his throat dry with desire. 'And then we go back to bed.'

*Back to bed...*Alyse thought much later that day, as she tossed and turned in the huge bed, trying to find somewhere comfortable to rest her throbbing head. She doubted that Dario had had *this* in mind when he had planned on getting her back into his bed.

But the headache that had threatened on the journey from the Villa D'Oro had turned into a full-blooded migraine by the time they had seen the frescoes and, knowing what was coming, she could only beg Dario that they head back immediately. They'd just made it before the sickness began and she had been completely out of things for the next twenty-four hours.

She wouldn't have blamed Dario if he had dumped her on his staff and left, but she couldn't have been more mistaken. From the moment they'd arrived back at the villa, he had lifted her off her feet and carried her carefully upstairs to the bedroom. There he had undressed her with gentle hands, so very different from the heated way they had torn at each other's clothes only the night before. He'd laid her down on cool, smooth sheets, brought the medication she needed and, much to her embarrassment, the bowl that had soon become vitally important.

The rest of the time had been something of an unpleasant haze. The one thing she had known was that if she needed him Dario was there, his voice soft in her ears, his hand cool on her head. He wiped her horrible sweaty face with a damp cloth and fed her sips of water when she could manage to keep them down.

At last, after the usual forty-eight hours, she had felt the nightmare receding and, having slept through the second night, she eventually felt well enough to get to her feet. Changing out of her crumpled nightgown and pulling on a white cotton robe, she made her way downstairs to find Dario sitting on the terrace, a mug of coffee in his hands, staring out at the green and gold landscape across the valley where the dawn was just beginning to break, gilding the mellow brickwork of the villa in its light.

'Buongiorno, mio marito...' she said, startling him so that he looked round sharply, obviously dragging himself back from wherever his thoughts had taken him.

'Buongiorno, mia moglie.'

Impossibly, considering the fact that it was his native language, he seemed to be the one struggling with the use of Italian. Or perhaps it was the fact that she had called him 'husband' that he was having a problem with.

'Should you be out of bed?'

He was on his feet, bringing a chair closer, plumping up cushions for her.

'I'm fine, Dario. It's usually all over and done with in a couple of days. It just looks awful while it's happening.'

But she sat down rather hastily anyway. She might be feeling better but she wasn't quite ready for the sight of Dario, shirtless and barefoot, in only a pair of long shorts riding low on his narrow hips.

'But I'd love something to drink—is that lemonade?'

'Naturalmente.'

He poured her a glass of the cool, cloudy liquid, ice chinking against the sides as he passed it to her. Alyse drank with relish, thankful to have something to ease the tightness in her throat. There was something very different about Dario this morning, but she couldn't put her finger on just what.

'Does that happen often?'

'Luckily, no.' Alyse focused her gaze on the rising sun over on the horizon so that she didn't have to meet his eyes as she remembered the way she'd been the previous morning. 'I'm sorry…'

That made his dark eyebrows snap together sharply in a frown. 'Sorry—what for?'

'Well—you didn't exactly sign on for the role of nurse.'

He'd wanted a lover, someone attractive and desirable in his bed. She hadn't felt at all desirable over the past couple of days, and she didn't know where he'd slept but it hadn't been in the same bed as her. She had a vague memory of waking once or twice and he had always been in a chair near to her bed, his long body sprawled uncomfortably, head resting against one hand as he watched her.

'For better, for worse. In sickness and in health,' Dario quoted sardonically.

Those vows belonged to a real marriage. She didn't want to think about the rest of them, the way that it went on to the line 'Till death us do part'. That was a vow that was never going to be met in this marriage. It was shocking how much that hurt.

'How long is this marriage supposed to last for?'

She was horrified by the way the words slipped past her unguarded lips. How could she have spoken her thoughts out loud—and, even worse, without a trace of the uncertainty she really felt about it? Instead, she sounded impatient and demanding and obviously Dario thought so too as his frown darkened ominously.

'You're already tiring of things?'

'N-no.' Alyse gulped down a hasty swallow of lemonade in an attempt to ease the way her throat seemed to have closed up. 'I mean…who could ever tire of living here…?'

Her rather wild gesture took in the sweep of the valley before them, the sparkling blue of the swimming pool off to the right, the long, winding drive down to the road.

'It's heaven but…'

But not her heaven. Not the sort of paradise she should get to love too much because one day it was going to be snatched away from her. In just the way that, at some point in the future, Dario too would leave.

Awkwardly she choked on her drink as she realised just where her thoughts were headed. She had thought of Dario and *love* in the same moment, dreading and regretting the fact that he would be snatched away from her when he tired of this pretend marriage. Probably all too soon. After all, the last couple of days could not have been the fantasy non-stop sexual orgy he had hoped for.

'Why did you bring me here?' she asked, not daring to go too close to the thoughts that were inside her head.

'You know why.'

'You wanted to do things properly.'

Suddenly the refreshingly tart taste of the lemonade had turned to bitter acid. She had known the 'honeymoon' image of their trip to Tuscany had been just that—a pretence to make everything seem real—and she'd been all right with that at the beginning. But things had changed so much in the past three weeks that it was all so totally different now and she was only just beginning to see how that had happened in such a short space of time.

'And I wanted you to see my home.'

My home, not *our* home. *Oh, come on, Alyse! You knew it was that from the start—when you first arrived here. So why should it matter so much more now?*

Because at the start she had felt so very differently. Because in the beginning she had been so grateful to Dario for what he had done, and that wonderful sense of freedom had made her head spin with the joy of it. She had been hugely attracted to him, had wanted him passionately… but she had never felt like this. Never felt that it would break her heart when the time came to leave Villa D'Oro—and him.

Because—somewhere along the road since their fake engagement, their marriage of business deals and sexual need—she had fallen crazily in love with her husband of convenience. The thought was so disturbing, so dangerous that she wanted to think of anything but that.

'Did…did your mother ever live here?' she asked for something to say, needing to distract herself—to distract him from the sudden thickness in her throat, the unexpected rough edge to her voice.

'Not live here, no.'

Dario's voice hitched on the last sentence. He had never been able to help his mother when she was ill. He hadn't earned enough to give her the comfort he had longed to find for her, but at least he could find a way to remember her.

'I bought the villa in my mother's memory. She had always loved it when she was alive, and once confided that her dream would be to make a home in such a place.'

'It's a magical place.'

Dario could only nod, privately acknowledging that the Villa D'Oro had worked some sort of magic on him since he'd arrived here this time. He'd been living the past weeks in a self-indulgent, indolent haze, content to spend his days showing Alyse the beauties of Tuscany, and at night rediscovering the beauties of her body. They had indulged themselves in other ways too, eating good food and drinking the best wines his vineyards produced. It had been a long, lazy, hedonistic existence—the sort of holiday that he never took—and no one would ever believe he could have been so idle for so long. He'd never wanted to before.

I wanted you to see my home, he'd said and now he realised he'd never said that to anyone ever before. Not to any other woman. In fact he'd never brought a woman here.

And yet he'd stayed here for several weeks now, off duty in a way he'd never been before. A couple of days in the Villa D'Oro and he was usually itching to get back to work. But not this time. Something had changed this time. Alyse had changed things.

'I wish my mother could have seen this place, just once. Seen her dream.'

But that was another thing that Alyse had changed. He knew that in his mother's mind, her dream would have included him with a wife—a real wife. He couldn't stay and pretend that he had a marriage. It felt wrong when the union was just an illusion, even if he was acknowledging his mother's other dream—that of seeing him united with his father.

'And I wish she could see you now,' Alyse put in softly. Just the sound of her voice tugged on something sharply inside him, making him stare into the sun so intently that he almost felt it would sear the sight from his eyes. Or any shadow of his so-called family from his mind. But it would take more than that to erase those unwelcome thoughts. The ones he had thought he wanted and now could only feel as a weight on his shoulders, a dark shadow that lay over even a day as beautiful as this one.

'I invited my father to the wedding,' he said suddenly, seeing Alyse's start of surprise at the abrupt change of subject. 'He didn't turn up.'

That hadn't been unexpected, Alyse knew, though she couldn't forget the way he'd been looking around as they'd walked down the aisle—looking for someone. In spite of his cynically nonchalant approach, had he actually hoped that his father might turn up when his rejected illegitimate son had married that 'trophy wife' Marcus had failed to win?

I don't do family. It was no wonder that Dario had tossed out that cold-blooded declaration. He had never had a family to learn how to exist with.

'He's a fool,' she said earnestly. 'An idiot not to want to connect with a son that any other man would be proud of.'

'You think?' He shot her a sideways, darkly sceptical glance, one that had shadows in it that were nothing to do with the effects of the sun on the horizon.

'But of course—you've dragged yourself up by your bootstraps from very difficult beginnings. You've made a fortune for yourself, unlike Marcus, who had all the privileges and education from the start.'

'I thought that way once,' Dario stated flatly. 'All the money I made—each thousand then eventually each million—I let myself believe that this time he had to notice me. When I matched him euro for euro—when I outstripped him…'

His bark of laughter was so bleak, so raw, so totally without any touch of humour that it made Alyse wince back into her chair, blinking hard to force away the burn of tears at the back of her eyes.

'You'd have thought I'd have got used to the silence by now.'

'Like I said, your father's a fool. You're the son who proved himself—not just the son who inherited everything.'

That made Dario twist in his seat so that he

was looking directly at her, his dark head blotting out the sun. He could see her perfectly, but his face was just a black silhouette against the rising glow.

'And what about the son who had to blackmail a wife into his bed?'

She hated the way he asked that. Hated the black thread of cynicism that ran through the words.

'You didn't do that! You didn't *blackmail* me. I was willing—so willing.'

When he lifted one black brow in mocking question she was up and out of her chair in a moment.

Moving across the terrace, she bent down and kissed him on the mouth, long and slow. The white robe and the neck of her nightgown gaped as she did so and she saw from the way his eyes darkened that he was clearly well aware of it.

'I was willing…' she repeated, sliding onto his lap, feeling the pressure of his erection, hot under the cotton of his shorts, against her body as she straddled him. 'I still am.'

'Alyse…' His hands came up to hold her, burying themselves in the fall of her hair as she increased the pressure of her lips against his partly open mouth.

'Let me show you how willing I am.'

With her hands between them, she tugged down the zip of his shorts, freeing him so that his powerful shaft came up against the moistness of her where she sat above him. It took only a moment or two's adjustment, taking him firmly in her hand to position him just right before she sank down onto him, hearing his groan of dark satisfaction as she took him into her.

'Does this look like blackmail to you?' she muttered thickly as the hunger took hold of her. 'Does it?'

But Dario was beyond speech and he could only shake his dark head in response to the question as Alyse began to move, sliding up and down with deliberate pressure. He held still for a few intense moments until he gave a moan of surrender, reached out and dragged her closer, pulling her head down to his, crushing her mouth with his as he abandoned himself to her.

CHAPTER TEN

DARIO READ THE email message over again, cursing under his breath as he did so.

How the hell had time got away from him so badly? It never had before.

The meeting he'd been sent a reminder about had been planned months ago. Before he'd married his convenient wife. Hell—before he'd even met Alyse. It had been the reason he was originally in London when he'd found out about Marcus's nasty little underhand scheme to blackmail Alyse into marriage.

But that had been before the night of the ball. The night he now thought of as the night of Alyse. The night that had knocked him completely off balance. And he had never been able to think quite straight since.

An example of that was the fact that he had actually forgotten this meeting. He never forgot anything. Certainly not something like this.

Cursing again, he slammed down an answer—'I'll be there'—and stabbed his finger on 'send'.

Perhaps this reminder was important in other ways too. It had prompted him to realise just what was happening—and to see what needed to be done to stop the rot. This meeting was important—he couldn't get out of it—but what really mattered was the business with his father. That had to be dealt with and sooner rather than later. Something burned in his guts at just the thought of it, but he knew there was no getting away from it.

'You should pack your bags after breakfast.'

The command came at Alyse over the table. Breakfast was usually her favourite time of day, with the sun not yet too hot, both of them still slightly sleepy and something of the intensity of the closeness of the night still lingering around them like scented smoke. But today was different; that much was obvious from the moment she'd woken to find that Dario was no longer in the bed beside her. He had already been up and dressed and it was as if the unexpectedly formal rich blue shirt and black trousers were like a coat of armour, closing him off from their normal regular routine.

'Oh?' She paused with a spoonful of yoghurt halfway to her mouth. 'Why?'

'We're going back to England.'

Dario's focus was on his tablet computer, a faint frown drawing his brows together as he read through opened emails. He'd never done that before either, and it made her shift uncomfortably in her seat.

'Just like that?'

She didn't trouble to iron the unease from her voice and at least it earned her a pause in his focus, the blue eyes flicking up sharply to fix on her face.

'I have business to attend to.'

Which was perfectly reasonable, so why did it make her feel so troubled? She had known that their idyll at the Villa D'Oro couldn't last for ever; in fact she'd been waiting for Dario to decree that their 'honeymoon' was over. So why did her stomach feel as if a thousand butterflies were battering their wings frantically against the sides, looking for escape? The yoghurt didn't taste right either, she thought, hastily putting the spoon back in the bowl and reaching for a glass of water. The truth was that she wasn't at all hungry this morning. She'd felt that way for a couple of days but, mixed in with the upset of Dario's announcement, it felt worse today.

'OK, then, I'll get on to it.'

'Do that. The car will be here at ten.'

So soon? He had woken up this morning and decreed that it was time to get back to work and that was it. No explanations—just a snap of the fingers and she had to obey. The tiny bit of yoghurt she had eaten seemed to curdle in her stomach, all pleasure in her food ruined.

The sight of the smoothly made, fresh-sheeted bed that greeted her as she went into their bedroom seemed to symbolise all that had just happened downstairs, making her sigh in despondency. When she had woken the covers had been in the wild tangle they had created last night. Several pillows had been on the floor, the one that Dario had used in the night and that still smelled of his hair and skin tucked underneath her cheek, where she had tugged it when he'd eased himself out of the bed. Now all that wonderfully sensual jumble had been smoothed away. The bed looked pristine and immaculate, as if nothing so wild as uninhibited lovemaking had ever darkened its sheets.

Lovemaking…

Alyse tugged open a drawer and started pulling out a bundle of her underwear. Why call it *love*making when the truth was that to Dario it was simply sex that he had paid for? As in that damned pre-nup she had signed.

But… Alyse's head came up sharply as she tried to remember just what else had been in that contract. She couldn't properly recall…and the sudden movement had made her head swim so badly that she had to sit down rather rapidly on the bed rather than fall to the floor.

She didn't want to get on with the packing, she admitted to herself. She wanted to stay because here at least she was in Dario's home. Here, they had the illusion of a marriage. If they went back to London then things would change. Dario would no longer be the man he was in the sunlit warmth of Tuscany. He would focus on his work and she would be installed in that huge apartment, a kept woman. And the worst thing of all was that she would have to try to convince everyone that she was blissfully happy—deeply in love with Dario and he with her.

Well, the first would be easy enough—but, even if Dario played his part well, she'd know he just didn't mean it.

She didn't want this to end and she was afraid that returning to London would do just that—end it. It seemed inevitable that, once this 'honeymoon' was over, reality would set in. Reality and the prospect of facing up to what she had really done in marrying Dario—and, even worse, giving her heart to him.

He'd provided the pre-nup because she had demanded it, and he had kept his word on the way he had helped her parents out of the monstrous hole they had dug themselves into. But he hadn't explained any further details, made it clear just why he thought this marriage was worth it to him. Other than thwarting the half-brother he detested. She'd thought that he might set a period to the length of their marriage and had been frankly surprised that he hadn't done any such thing.

I offered marriage—not commitment and devotion for life.

His words came back to haunt her. This wasn't a real marriage, so inevitably it must end at some point—but when? How long would Dario want to keep her with him, in his bed, in his life? Until he tired of her. But how would she know when he did? And how would she cope when he discarded her?

While they'd been here at the Villa D'Oro, she'd been able to enjoy his company, share his bed, had been the focus of his attention and, loving him as she did, she had revelled in it. But what would she do when he told her it was over? How would she handle seeing him with someone else? She felt nausea rise in her throat at the thought.

'Enough!' she told herself sharply. She'd been told to pack, and Dario would certainly scent a rat if he came in and found her sitting on her bed, staring at the floor. He'd want to know what was up, and she couldn't possibly tell him. Pushing back the queasiness that still bothered her, she got to her feet and turned towards the wardrobe. The prospect of flying while she felt like this only added to her discomfort.

The flight to England, short though it was,

turned into a journey from hell. From the moment they took off until Dario's jet landed in London it was a battle to keep the sickness she was feeling from showing. To make matters worse, she now had to deal with a growing suspicion that there could be a disturbing, shocking explanation behind the way she was feeling. One that seemed to drain all the strength from her body and kept her silent and still until they reached his apartment at last.

'I'm going to have to go out again… Sorry, but it can't be helped.'

That 'sorry' would sound more convincing if he wasn't already halfway to the door, but Alyse was actually relieved to see him go.

Using the excuse of needing painkillers—praying Dario would take her withdrawal as being caused by the arrival of her period—a period she had now worked out was in fact well overdue—she had managed a diversion into a chemist's and had snatched up a vital testing kit, pushing it to the bottom of her bag, where she now felt as if it was close to burning a hole in the leather.

'No problem. I understand.' Her reply was vague, offhand, her attention elsewhere.

The door had barely slammed shut behind him before she turned and headed for the bathroom, pulling the pregnancy testing kit out of its packaging with shaking hands. She had to know.

I don't do family.

Oh, heaven, why did she have to remember that line, and the absolute conviction with which it was spoken, right now?

She knew Dario didn't 'do family' and who could blame him after the way his father and his horrible half-brother had behaved? How could a man who had grown up unwanted by his father, disowned and ignored, and then pushed away as the result of Marcus's scheming, ever want to 'do family'? The ghastly old man hadn't even bothered to come to the wedding, after Dario had made the effort to ask.

What was the time she was supposed to wait for this thing to develop? Three minutes?

How was she supposed to stand still and watch it for three minutes…? It was an eternity—dragging out unbearably.

Clutching the white stick in her hand, Alyse

paced round the bathroom and then, when that was not enough, into the living room. Desperate to distract herself from the waiting, the ticking by of seconds that seemed to last for ever, she tried opening cupboards, pulling out drawers. It was an aimless exercise, simply filling in time, but…

'Oh…'

Shock blurred her eyes, and she let the test stick drop from her hand into the last drawer she'd opened, then hastily snatched it up again, her eyes fixed not on it but the papers it had landed on.

'No…'

The headed notepaper was an immediate giveaway, the Kavanaugh name emblazoned across the top. *Henry* Kavanaugh's name. The letters danced before her eyes as she grabbed at the papers, crumpling them in a shaking hand.

Why had Dario's father written to the son he had discarded and abandoned, and then scorned when Dario had tried to make contact, to break down the barriers between them? There were actually two letters, but right now she couldn't get past the first one because when she focused on it the date it had been written struck her like a blow to her chest, taking away every trace of breath.

This letter had been written before their wedding. Before Dario had paid off her father's debts. Before even he had come to her to suggest their business deal marriage, with her as the convenient bride. But how convenient she had never even begun to guess. She had thought that Dario had offered the marriage as a way of helping her parents because he had wanted her so much. Because she had been enough for him. Now she was slapped in the face by the fact that there had been something he had wanted so much more—something she could never give him but that he could use her to get for himself.

She'd thought that with Dario she had found herself, and her freedom at last, but she had been used, deceived, betrayed from start to finish. And this was the cruellest deceit of all. The worst lie.

The last lie, she vowed silently as the letter slipped from her weakened grasp, falling back into the drawer in the same moment that Alyse remembered the test stick that she still held in her hand. The three minutes were well and truly up.

'Oh, no.'

Her head spun wildly, sickeningly, as she looked down at the window where the result was displayed only too clearly and with no room for mistake.

Pregnant.

Pregnant.

'Oh, no, oh, no…no, no!'

'Oh, no—*what*?'

She hadn't heard the footsteps or the door open behind her but there was no mistaking just who had come into the room. She didn't even need to turn round to see. There was no mistaking Dario's presence, Dario's voice.

'I couldn't leave—I knew something was up. So what is it? Just what the hell is going on here?'

CHAPTER ELEVEN

'I'M PREGNANT.'

Alyse couldn't think of any other way to answer him. And really, why hedge about it, or try to sugar-coat things? There was no easy way to say it. She might have wished for a little time to catch her breath, to get used to the idea herself, but now that Dario was here there was no point in trying to do anything but tell him the truth. And the reality was that she wanted the truth to be told. From now on, nothing but the truth.

'I'm pregnant…' she said again in a very different tone, an irrepressible, overwhelming note of awe creeping into the words.

The only response was total silence from behind her but she didn't dare to turn round to see what sort of expression went along with that total stillness. She just wished he would speak—

say something, anything so that she could know what she was dealing with, understand a little of what he was thinking.

She heard Dario draw in a rough, ragged breath and let it out again. He was still giving nothing away.

'You're sure?' he said at last and that had her spinning on her heel, whirling round to face him whether she was ready or not.

'Of course I'm sure! I can read.'

She waved the white stick wildly in the air then pushed it towards him so that he could see it for himself.

'Pregnant. That's what that word says. *Pregnant*. With child. Expecting. I'm having your baby, Dario…and if you say "How?" then I'll…'

'I'm not going to.' Dario's tone was flat, emotionless. 'I'm only too well aware of just *how* you became pregnant. But when—the night before you had the migraine?'

'Or after it…the time on the terrace.' It was ridiculous to blush at the memory but she still felt the fiery colour rush into her cheeks. 'I was so sick that I hadn't taken my pill for a couple of days.'

When she'd seduced him out there in the sunlight without a thought for the possible consequences. Consequences that had now become all too real.

It was the last thing he'd considered when he'd realised something was up, Dario acknowledged to himself. He was all sorts of a fool because it should have been one of the first thoughts that had come to mind, but the truth was that he hadn't even considered it. They had used contraception every time but two. And, in spite of those two slip-ups, he had known that she was on the Pill.

He'd damned well forgotten how sick she had been. No tablet could have stayed in her stomach after the onslaught of those two days. So there was little doubt exactly when this had happened—or even where.

The only question was what they did about it.

For the moment his mind wouldn't move on to answering that question. All he could think of was the fact that Alyse was pregnant with his child. His eyes went to the flat plane of her stomach, the curve of her hips in the tight denim jeans she had worn to travel in. There was no sign, no swell of a baby bump. But how could there be? It was still so early…

How could something so totally invisible have such an impact that it left him feeling as if someone had punched him on the jaw, stunning his brain?

He was going to be a father.

'That was very special…'

He could see that he'd stunned her in turn. The lush pink mouth that had opened to say something else now stayed slightly open, bemused and silent. Did she really not think he'd spoken the truth? How could she doubt it when his body had hardened and ached from just the memory?

'But I know…' She was struggling to speak firmly, making him frown. 'I know you don't…'

I don't do family. Oh, he'd been so sure when he'd said that, burning up with conviction. And he still wouldn't cross the road to any member of his living family. His so-called father had made sure of that. But a family he'd never met. *Dio mio*, a family he'd made—they'd made between them? He'd never thought it would ever be a possibility, had made damn sure that it was never likely to be, and so he hadn't prepared himself for how he would react if it happened.

I don't do family.

He was going to be a *father*.

But, having spent so much of his life trying to prove himself to the father he had never had, what the hell did he know about being a parent? Wasn't that something you learned by example? By watching the way your father behaved…

Hell, no! His thoughts shuddered away from the idea of ever being anything like the man who had merely been his mother's sperm donor. Because there was no way that Henry Kavanaugh merited being termed anything else.

He had nothing to compare it with. Nothing that told him what this sort of a family would be.

Where the devil was this going? He might have been the one who was most unsure about this, but Alyse sure as hell looked every bit as uncomfortable as he felt.

'I…'

He opened his mouth to answer her but he had hesitated a moment too long and already she was rushing in to fill the silence.

'But don't worry. I won't ask anything from you.'

If she'd thought to appease him, ease his anger, Alyse recognised, she couldn't have been more wrong. The burn of his glare told her that, and the world tilted around her so that she had to grab at a chair for support.

'You won't need to ask,' he declared, clipped and cold. 'I know my duty. I gave you an allowance once we were married—though I see no sign of the way you've spent it.'

Ice-blue eyes swept over her worn jeans and loose red shirt, and the thought that he considered all he'd done for her as his *duty* was more than she could bear. Would that be his attitude to this baby too? That he would consider his part in its life as his *duty*?

'Why would I need anything from you? There's nothing I can spend the money on. I mean—you gave me all those clothes, even after the wedding, more jewellery than I could possibly wear.

I lived in a palace in Tuscany—and now here in a penthouse…'

Her hands waved wildly, indicating the huge room, the wide expanse of London beyond the huge plate glass windows. The frown that was his response made her legs turn to water. Had she blundered in, declaring that she considered this place her home? Was that never to be? Was this how it ended?

He'd never put a time limit on their convenient marriage, but had it really come quite this soon? But of course the news she'd hit him with went against everything he wanted from life. And, as that appalling letter in the drawer had revealed, what he wanted in life was far from *her*. Instead, she had only been a means to an end to get what he really wanted from his father—recognition and revenge.

'I had more food than I can eat—'

The bitterness of her recent discovery put more venom into her words than they merited and she watched as Dario's black brows drew together in a dark frown. Was he beginning to guess that there was something else behind all this? She wasn't going to let him off.

'What else could I need?'

What else, other than a man who really wanted to be married to her? Who *loved*...?

No! Her mind danced away from that thought. She couldn't let it in, didn't dare to let it sneak through any crack in her defensive armour and take root in her mind, in her heart.

'We had a contract.'

'We did.'

But a contract was all they had. She was the fool who'd allowed herself to consider the possibility that there might be more.

'And I meant to keep to it, but a child... A child is not in the contract,' Alyse managed, getting control over her voice only by making it sound as stiff as her lips and spine.

'To hell with the contract! Unless...'

He suddenly broke off, fixed his burning gaze on her face until she squirmed under the force of it. She pushed her chin upwards to meet that blazing blue glare, trying to hide the way her stomach was quailing inside, tying itself into agonising knots.

'You weren't planning to abort...?'

'Oh, no—no!'

He sounded furious, appalled. No wonder, when the letter she had seen made it clear that a child was an essential part of the other contract—the one he had with his devil of a father.

'But a child was definitely not part of the plan—there was nothing about it in the pre-nup.'

Because neither of them had thought that would happen. She had thought that she was protected. He had thought that she was—and they had taken that one crazy risk…

Or had they?

Dear God, but was this worse than she had thought? Had Dario deliberately 'forgotten' about contraception so that they would end up in just this situation? Her mind already felt bruised from what she had learned. Only now, slowly and unwillingly, was she beginning to face up to all that must lie behind it.

She knew that she couldn't live with it. It would tear her heart in half to leave, but it would shatter it beyond repair to stay, knowing why he had wanted her, why he had married her.

'You don't have to stay married to me—to "do the right thing"—just because I'm pregnant,' she managed through lips tight with the cold despair that gripped her. 'I can manage on my own…'

'And just how will you manage? You left your job to come to me. I will provide for the child, of course…'

Of course… He would want to be seen to be doing his duty by the baby.

'And you have your allowance.'

'Are you saying I'll still be entitled to an allowance even as your ex-wife?'

'Ex-wife?'

He made it into a sound of pure disbelief, his dark head going back as if she'd slapped him.

'This marriage isn't over. We are not separating. I will not let you go!'

It was the most brutal of ironies, Alyse acknowledged miserably, that just a few short hours ago—less—those might have been the words she most wanted to hear from him. That she would have thought she was dreaming if he had told her he wanted their marriage to continue—that he had no intention of separating from her. But now she knew exactly why he was saying that, and that knowledge turned her hope of a dream into the darkest, most bitter nightmare.

'Of course not.' She laced her response with pure acid, watched as he actually dared to frown at her tone. 'That just wouldn't do, would it? You'd never satisfy your father that way.'

'What the hell has my father…?'

'He won't pay out on an *ex*-wife and child, will he? Not when he wants a respectable marriage, a legitimate grandbaby. You have to give him everything he asks for, you know, otherwise you'll never be able to move into Kavanaugh House—the *family home*.'

He was catching on now. The mention of Kavanaugh House had done it. She saw those blue eyes look behind her, go to where the drawer she had pulled out still hung open, the letter from Henry Kavanaugh clearly seen inside it.

'The letter.'

Alyse had once been told how close the emotions of love and hate were to each other. She'd never fully believed it, but now she thought she really understood. Dario stood before her, tall, dark, stunning; the man she had fallen in love with. But he was also the man who had betrayed her. He had lied to her, used her to get what he wanted every bit as deliberately as her parents had. She hated that. She hated him for doing that to her.

'Yes, the letter. The letter your father sent you before you ever asked me to marry you. Do you remember what it says—or do I have to remind you?'

'Hell, no…'

Dario needed no reminder about what that letter said. How could he when it had burned into his mind ever since he had first read it. It was the letter that had started all this. That had made him see there was a way that he could do more than thwart Marcus in his half-brother's campaign to take Alyse as his wife and so fulfil the old man's deepest wish. Getting the family estate, and Kavanaugh House as his reward.

It was that letter that had sent him to the Gregorys' home on the day that he had discovered the financial mess Alyse's father was in. The mess that Marcus had been determined to take advantage of and force Alyse to be his bride, even though she had made it plain that that was the last thing she wanted.

The letter that had held out a tempting suggestion of a possible reconciliation, or at least an acknowledgement of who he was and the fact that Henry Kavanaugh was his father. He would even be given the family home if he, rather than his half-brother, was the one to give the old man the fulfilment of his dream. Something that his mother had dreamed of right up until the day she'd died.

'My fa—Kavanaugh wrote to tell me that he'd changed his will. He offered me an acknowledgement of the fact that I was his son.'

'And a nice big, juicy carrot in the shape of Kavanaugh House.'

'That wasn't what I wanted.'

'No?' Alyse's scepticism cut like a knife, all the more because he couldn't deny it. He had to admit that the thought of beating Marcus that way, of inheriting what his half-brother most wanted, had seemed at the time to present itself as the most perfect form of revenge.

At the time.

'How can it not be what you wanted?' Alyse

challenged. 'When your mother tried everything she could to get your father to acknowledge you, year after year? When you say yourself that you worked so hard—made your fortune with the hope that he would recognise you as his son, or at least know that you existed. Well, didn't you?'

'Yes.'

He was not going to deny it. That had been how he had thought, what he had wanted. It all seemed so long ago now.

'I wanted that.' Or thought he'd wanted it. He'd lived so long with the emptiness inside him that he'd thought he'd finally found a way to fill it.

'And do you want this child?' Lightly, she touched her body, fingertips resting on where the baby—*his baby*—must lie, tiny as yet, and already turning his life inside out, changing things so totally. 'Do you?'

'Damn you to hell, yes!'

He might not know how to be a father, but there was one thing he knew for sure and that was that this baby—his child—would never feel unwanted as he had done. He would always be there for it, and he would never, ever turn away from it. He would be the best damned father he knew how to be.

'Because it will give you everything you ever wanted?'

'Yes.'

Too late, he realised that his response could be interpreted so very differently from the way he'd meant it. She wouldn't believe it if he tried to tell her what he really meant. And who would blame her?

Silently, Dario cursed the way that Alyse had discovered his father's letter before he had had time to resolve the problem. He'd been on his way out to talk to Henry just now. To tell him that he wanted no part of his scheming and manipulating. He wanted to put all that behind him so that he could move on. Move on into the sort of world that offered a future instead of tying him to the past.

'No,' Alyse said now, her fine-boned face set into a cold, determined expression, her green eyes hooded, hiding every emotion from him. Her hand still rested on her belly, but it seemed to Dario that this time the gesture had changed from one that was a gentle indication to a sign of protection, defending her child against the world.

Against him? It was like a knife going through him.

'No. Now you claim this child—*now* you "do family."' Her voice rang with defiance, with rejection. 'Well, there's something you need to know. I will never, ever let my baby be used as a bargaining tool, as your father did with you. As he wants to do with it now. Oh, don't look so horrified, Dario. I'm not going to deny you access, if that's what you want.'

'If I— Can you doubt it?'

'Oh, yes, I can.' Alyse's eyes blazed green fire into his, openly challenging him to stop her, to contradict her. 'You don't do family, remember.'

'I was a fool when I said that,' Dario put in sharply but either she didn't hear him or she deliberately ignored his interjection, going on with her declaration as if she had determined to get it all out and no one was to stop her or divert her from what she had to say.

'But I'll do it for you. You can see your child—have access to your child whenever you want. But you can't have me.'

Dario's shoulders had just begun to relax, some of the tension leaving his body, when she hit him with that last comment, slapping him in the face with it so that his thoughts reeled.

You can't have me.

The words sounded like the slamming of a door. A sound he knew only too well. It was like going back all those years, to when he was fifteen. When he had stood on the doorstep of Kavanaugh House, pleading—begging—for his father's acknowledgement, for Henry's help for his dying mother. And the door had shut in his face.

…even as your ex-wife. The words she'd flung at him echoed round in his head. He'd thought she was testing him, seeing how much he was committed to caring for this child. He'd never actually thought that she was already seeing herself as his ex—and their marriage as being over.

'You can't have me,' Alyse repeated. 'I want more than this. More than the "allowance" you give me.'

'If you want more, you can have it. How much…?'

She didn't hesitate, not for a second, and he

knew what she was going to say before she'd even opened her mouth. He thought that he'd seen the face of rejection before, but never, ever like this.

'I don't want an income—I don't want maintenance. I don't want anything from you. All that money you paid off for my mother and father.'

'I could afford it—and it was worth it…'

And it would have bought him what he wanted—his father's recognition. But was that worth everything he had paid for it?

It *was* worth it. Alyse wrapped her arms around her body to stop herself from falling apart. He had spoken of their marriage in the past. It seemed he had already put it behind him. Something she had struggled with and so far found totally impossible.

'I want to do this…'

'But I don't want it! In fact, what I really wish I could do is to pay you some of it back. You gave me—us so much when you paid off the gambling debts, got Marcus off our backs…'

'It was in the agreement.'

'But I can't just take everything. I doubt I'll

ever be able to repay you what you gave us—I'll always be in your debt.'

'And did you not think that you have already paid off your *debt* already?'

Dario's mouth twisted around the word *debt* as if he was tasting poison.

'Don't you think that what you've already done to fulfil our contract will count as repayment against whatever "bill" you think you owe me?'

No, she couldn't answer that one honestly. Not when he stood so tall and dark between her and the window, a black oppressive silhouette looming over her.

'Why would I think that?' she hedged.

'Well, if you're reckoning up—if you really want to balance the money paid out against the benefits received, then—'

'Then our marriage, short as it is—*was*—has to reduce my debt just a bit?'

She gagged on the words, unable to believe he actually thought that way. That he would balance their days—their nights—together against the money she had cost him in some appalling reckoning of gains and loss. But, of course, he hadn't got what he'd wanted, had he? His father, cold, calculating, scheming, was not likely to pay out in any way when Dario hadn't come up with everything he demanded.

Like father, like son?

'Does it? So tell me, Dario, what do you think I might have paid off—how much has my bill been reduced, do you think?'

He didn't answer her, but then she didn't expect him to. His scowl might have stopped a lesser woman in her tracks, but the truth was that Alyse couldn't have halted if she'd tried. The deadly combination of pain and anger had made her tongue run away with her, no chance of reining it in or holding it back.

'So let me see—we've been married…what…? Four months? Making lo—having sex, what? Ten times a week? More? Even at that estimate, that's over one hundred and fifty times. So how much have I earned? How much per night?'

'I don't think like that.'

'Well, perhaps now it's time that you did. Because I need to know. How much have I paid off my debts to you, hmm? Surely you can give me some idea?' The pain was too much, burning like acid through her heart. 'I mean, what do you normally pay your whores?'

If she had tossed something foul right in his face then his head couldn't have gone any further back and, before his eyelids dropped over his eyes, she saw that they had lost all colour, his pupils just black slits.

'For your information, I don't associate with whores—no matter how much or little they cost me. Every woman I've ever been with has known how valued she was, great or small, and all—*all*—were happy with the way things were. But you…'

Astonishingly, he seemed to have lost control of his breathing. Something choked him to a halt, making him shake his head savagely, pull in a raw, ragged breath before he could go on.

'You come way too expensive. You cost far too much.'

You cost far too much.

Alyse felt sure that he must hear the sound of her hopes shattering and falling into pieces all around her. It was only now that she acknowledged her wild, foolish, naive dreams. Dreams that she had barely really recognised. It was only now that, just for a minute, she allowed herself to acknowledge that she had actually imagined that he might have said he didn't want to let her go.

But she'd forgotten the real truth about their marriage. Forgotten that to Dario it was purely a business deal and that that was all he wanted from her. Her place at his side, her body in his bed. Her name on the certificates that would make his father fulfil his promises. No commitment, no feelings except for sexual passion, no emotions creeping in to spoil the conditions that had been part of the contract.

She had dodged the real issue—that Dario didn't love her. And not loving her obviously meant that he wasn't prepared to put up with this change in their circumstances. He'd made that plain in that flat, cold statement.

You come way too expensive.

He'd warned her, hadn't he? Told her straight. So why should it hurt so much, tear at her like this to realise that he'd meant it? Because when had Dario ever said anything that he didn't truly mean?

'You're so right. You couldn't afford me now—and it would never be worth it, not for me. I want more than a man who marries me for what I can bring him…'

'I *wanted* you!'

Was that fury or accusation in his voice? Either way, it was too little too late.

'I want more than that too. I've spent my life being used by other people and I can't let it happen any more. My parents used me to get them out of the mess they were in—either through marriage to Marcus, or then to you. Your father used you, played you like a pro… Marcus would have used me if he could—to get his father's approval, the damned family home—and you…you…'

She choked up, tears thickening in her throat, blocking her from speaking. And if there was anything that could have stopped her from going on, if there had been any sort of chance for them, then if Dario had spoken now it might actually have had some effect.

But instead he stood there, dark and silent, blue eyes clouded and opaque, no trace of any emotion on his face. He had no comeback to offer her. There was no chance of any denial, any protest—fool that she was to even hope for it. He was taking everything she was throwing at him and putting up no defence. Probably because he thought he didn't need to defend himself—or because he knew that there was no way he could even try to deny what was the real truth behind his actions.

'Well, it stops here,' she managed, no longer needing to fight to keep her voice calm and cold. That happened all on its own as she acknowledged the way that Dario had not argued against the truth. 'It stops now and it's never going to happen again.'

Had he turned to ice? she wondered in the frozen silence that greeted the end of her outburst, the final words falling in a desperate cry into the emptiness around them. Had the coldness of his life, his thoughts—his heart—finally reached out and enclosed him so that he couldn't move or say a word? But then what could he say? He'd made no move to deny her accusations, offered no expression of feeling—of any sort of feeling—but instead had just stood there, still and mute, and never tried to interrupt or say anything.

And now that she had fallen silent he still wasn't going to speak. Or move. Or act in any way.

It stops now and it's never going to happen again. Her own words came back to haunt her, sounding like the final full stop, the death knell to everything. He wasn't going to even try to protest, to change anything.

It stops now…

'Yes.'

Just one word, low and flat—Dario's only response. Nothing more.

He'd barely spoken when there was a tap at the door that still stood open from the moment that Dario had walked in, finding her with the pregnancy test in her hand…and those appalling letters in the drawer.

'Excuse me…'

José, the chauffeur, who had been sitting in the car for Dario to come back and give him instructions to drive him somewhere. But he'd obviously decided that, having waited so long, he might as well make use of his time by bringing up the cases they had brought back from Tuscany. He deposited them on the floor now, hers and Dario's standing side by side.

'Shall I put these in…?'

'No.'

It was Alyse who spoke, rushing in while Dario still stood as if he had never said that single word.

'No, José—will you please take my case back down to the car and then—' She glanced at Dario, feeling now that her own face must be as set and stiff as his. She could feel her jaw muscles aching with the battle for control, her eyes not focusing quite right.

'I assume you'll let José drive me?'

'Where are you going?'

Could he sound any less interested? The question had no intonation in it whatsoever. No trace of any sort of feeling.

'I don't know yet. But I'll let you know.'

That brought a tiny touch of reaction, his eyes narrowing sharply as he frowned a question.

'I promised you that you'd have access to our child,' she told him. 'I'll keep that promise.'

It was as much as she could manage. She couldn't take any more. So, determined not to break down, to risk turning back in case the sight of him standing there took all the strength from her and tempted her to turn back, she spun round on her heel and marched from the room, leaving José to follow with her bag.

If she so much as hesitated, if she turned round just once, Dario told himself, then perhaps he might find some words—might find something to say to make her change her mind. But what words would do that? What could he say except that one single syllable—that 'Yes' that had been all he could offer before?

Because what else was there to say? He couldn't refute her accusations of wanting her because he believed she would give him what he hungered for. They were all true. In the beginning, at least. But the fact that things had changed did nothing to reduce the way they had been there in his thoughts, driving him on, driving him to her.

He couldn't contradict her declaration that this stopped now—and it never happened again. It was what he wanted. It was how it should be. No more lies. Never again.

So *yes* was the only possible answer. Unless he could find something to put in its place. Because he had to find something or the future was going to be impossible to face.

But it was only as the silence of the empty apartment settled down around him and the rooms seemed to echo with the hollowness of space that he realised just what had gone and how much he had lost.

CHAPTER TWELVE

'WHAT ARE YOU doing here?'

Alyse couldn't quite accept that she had actually opened the door to Dario. She didn't even know that he remembered she had a friend called Rose, let alone knew where Rose's flat might be. When she had walked out on him, this had been the only place she could think of to go to, to hide out there, trying to work out just how to rebuild her life and face a future that had suddenly turned into an arid desert. The last thing she had expected was that Dario would track her down and come to her here.

'How did you know where to find me?'

'I thought about trying your parents' house first. But then, of course, I realised you'd not go back there again—' he almost laughed at her response, the expression of rejection that must show in her eyes '—no matter how desperate you were.'

Dario's voice was low and husky and he looked rough, his jaw darkened by a day's growth of beard, shadows like bruises under his eyes. She'd thought that she looked washed out, several nights without sleep showing on her face when she'd looked in the mirror this morning, but quite frankly Dario looked worse.

'So I asked José where he'd taken you.'

Thinking only of getting away, fighting nausea, almost all of her energy focused on keeping the tears, ever at the back of her eyes, from slipping to her cheeks, she'd asked the chauffeur to drive her to Rose's office. Obviously, Dario had followed the trail from there.

'I told Rose not to let on…'

'I know—but I managed to persuade her.' Even the half-voltage rough-edged smile he turned on reminded her of just how persuasive Dario could be when he wanted. 'I told her I had something important for you.'

'You did? I didn't leave anything behind.'

'No, this is something I want to give you.'

He lifted one hand, showing her the large document file he held in it.

'No…'

Alyse had to admit it, her heart had lifted just a tiny bit, felt a weak little twist of hope when she had seen him, but now it dropped right down into the pit of her stomach, making her feel horribly nauseous as she took two instinctive steps backwards, her eyes fixed on that file. She could only imagine the one thing that had brought him here like this—that duty he felt towards his child, and to her as the mother of that baby. And she couldn't bear that that was all.

'Can I come in?' His diffidence surprised her but she could hardly leave him standing in the hallway so she beckoned him in, only to find that he was holding out the file as he came towards her.

'I don't want it!'

Alyse found she was shaking her head more violently now, her hair flying around her face as she did so.

'You've done enough, more than enough, already.'

A wave of his hand dismissed it as only a hugely wealthy man could dismiss such a huge amount.

'Didn't you listen?' she managed, holding her

body stiff and straight so that he couldn't see the way she was quaking inside, not knowing if she could handle this. 'Whatever it is, I don't want it.'

It had torn her apart to leave him, to see him, she believed, for the last time. Now he had come after her, come back into her life and even if it was just for the shortest possible time she knew that parting would have to be done again. She had barely got through it the first time. She didn't know how she would do it again.

'I can't cost you anything more.'

'Oh, but you can. You have to.'

It wasn't anger that had affected him so badly, Alyse realised with a sense of shock. There wasn't fury in his eyes but something else, something that looked disturbingly like pain. But what had put that there?

'I can't…' she began again then broke off in consternation as he pulled a document from the file, held it out to her. 'What?'

Dario said nothing but continued to hold the papers out to her. Slowly, she reached out, took them, forced her eyes to focus, read partway, then, unable to believe what she had seen, went back and read again.

'What?' she repeated, unable to get her head round this, unable to think any further. 'Dario—this is…?'

'The deeds to the Villa D'Oro,' Dario supplied when she couldn't. 'The legal transfer of the property from me to you.'

So now she understood just why he had said she cost too much. He was actually handing over his home—the home he had bought in his mother's memory—the home that held the only connection he had to his family—to her. She could only begin to guess at what that had cost him, in all senses of the word.

'You can't…'

'I can and I have. What do I need with a house that big? I would only rattle around in it. But you—and the child—you'll need a family home.'

Alyse had thought that her head was spinning in shock already but it was when he said the words 'family home', the dark intonation he put on them, that something exploded in her mind, sending her reeling away across the room, needing to put a hand out to the wall to support her.

'Kavanaugh House…' It was a strangled gasp. Could he part with the villa because he already had the Kavanaugh family home tied up legally safe and sound? 'Your father…'

Dario had known this was coming but he still hated to hear those words on her lips, to know that his father's malign influence still reached this far.

'No,' he said, putting every ounce of conviction into the single word. 'Damn it to hell, Alyse—*no.* He has not had any part in this for a long time. Not since the day I married you.'

She needed more than that, he could see. And he was happy to give it to her.

'I'll admit that when I heard how Henry wanted you as his daughter-in-law, that he would delight in the connection to your family so much that he wanted to reward Marcus—give him a huge part of his inheritance early—I was determined to wreck those plans. And then when Henry…' he would never honour that man with the name of *father* ever again '…when he sent me that letter—offering me his recognition, the acknowledgement of my being his son, if I was the one who married you…'

He pulled out another document, one that Alyse recognised this time. The letters from Henry Kavanaugh telling Dario how he would be rewarded if he presented the old man with first a daughter-in-law with a title and then a grandchild.

'I was tempted, I admit—' Dario shook his dark head as if in disgust at his own weakness. 'But after our wedding I no longer wanted any of that. Or anything to do with him.'

There was still doubt in her eyes; she was still not convinced. But he had to try. His father was dead to him—the only thing worth fighting for was this.

He held out his hand towards her, gesturing towards the letters.

'Give them to me.'

She seemed frozen to the spot so he reached out and took them from her nerveless hands. With several brisk, sharp movements, he tore the paper in two and then in two again, ripping it over and over until it was in tiny irreparable pieces that he tossed to the floor so that they lay like confetti around her feet.

'But I don't understand.' She looked as dazed as if they had been something cold and shocking that had hit her in the face.

How could she understand when he didn't fully comprehend what was happening himself? He only knew that when she had taken herself and the baby—his baby, his family—away from this relationship that something had shattered deep inside. He had hated the way she had talked about needing to repay him, the way she had equated every night in his bed with something that was part of what she owed him, something that could be equated with money—the cost for every time they had been together.

What do you normally pay your whores?

The terrible words swung round and round in his head, threatening to destroy him in a way that was far, far worse than the rejection his father had ever turned on him, the way that Marcus had made sure that the door was slammed shut in his face. He had been able to survive those wounds and live on. The way he had felt since that day when she had walked out had left him fearing that this injury might just be fatal.

'Dario…that letter would have given you everything you wanted. Your father— No?' She broke off on the question as he shook his head violently, stamping the shreds of the letter under his foot as he did so.

'No—damn it to hell, no!'

Black fury was raging inside at his father, and at the way that man could still reach out and touch his life, make Alyse feel this way, make the woman he…

It was as if a huge sheet of glass had suddenly descended, cutting him off from reality, silencing the rest of the world and enclosing him so there was only Alyse and himself in existence.

Only himself and the woman he loved.

'No.'

It was all that he could manage. The only thing he could say. The only thing she had to believe.

'He gives me nothing. Nothing at all.'

'But he does…'

Alyse couldn't find a way to get a grip on what was happening. The letters that Dario had just destroyed completely had told him that, after all these years of rejection and loneliness, he could be recognised as Henry Kavanaugh's son.

'He'll acknowledge you…'

So was he prepared to give that up? Give up the dream he'd held for his mother's sake? And why?

'He'd accept me only because of what I bring him—not because of who I am.'

And she could understand that, couldn't she?

A shocking realisation hit home and had her shaking in despair, unable to accept what he'd done.

'How can you give me Villa D'Oro—your family home—unless…'

'You think I'd only part with the villa because I now have possession of the Kavanaughs'…'

Dario's voice failed him and he could only toss his dark head in rejection of even the thought.

'You couldn't be more wrong. I have to give you Villa D'Oro because I can't live there. Not without you. If you're not there it's not a home—and most definitely not a family home. Without you, it's just an address, a place with no soul, no heart. You are the heart of that place. You turned it from a house into a home, and without you it will always be empty.'

Something in her face gave him the nerve to move forward, reach out a hand to her. But only to reach it out. He didn't yet take her fingers in his, knowing there was still more that had to be said.

'As for Kavanaugh, I want nothing from him. I need nothing he can give me. Whatever he offers, the cost is just not worth it. I'm not a Kavanaugh. I'm an Olivero. My mother's name—and the name I hope my child will bear too.'

Unbelievably, it seemed that Dario's emotions were running away with him. For the first time Alyse actually saw him lose control, struggle with composure, fight for the ability to go on.

'And this man dares to want you—*you*!—only as the mother of his grandchild, the inheritance of a title. You are so much more than that. Worth an infinity more than that. And our child will never, ever be known only for what he or she brings to the status of our family.'

'Our family?'

It caught on her tongue, choking her. It threatened to stop her breathing because of what it said. It said so much more than she could ever have imagined or dreamed. And had he really included her in there too—in his *family*?

'We don't have a family,' she managed through a mouth that was painfully dry so that her tongue seemed stiff as a piece of wood. 'All we have is a business arrangement, one where you paid for what you wanted…'

She couldn't go on, despair crushing her lungs so that she couldn't catch any breath.

'What I wanted?' Dario echoed the words as if they were poisonous. 'Damn you, no.'

She couldn't understand the reason for the rawness in his tone, the harshness of his voice.

'You paid for me in your bed—you…'

The words were snatched from her as her head spun in disbelief as he pulled out another document. This one she recognised when he thrust it at her wildly. She didn't need to read it. It was the pre-nuptial agreement she had signed before their marriage. Was it really only four months? Sixteen short weeks? It felt like a lifetime ago.

'I know you never read it fully. So read it now, damn you—read it properly.'

It was almost impossible to follow his command as the words danced and squirmed before her eyes. She could barely take it in but she knew that she had to. Every expression on his face told her that—the burn of those blue eyes, the patches of white where the skin was drawn tight and hard around his mouth and eyes, etched against the side of his nose.

So she read it once. Then read it over again because she couldn't believe what she was reading. She hadn't signed this—had she?

But there at the bottom of the page was her signature, along with the black scrawl that was Dario's name. Making it legal and binding—to him.

Because, apart from the formality of the wedding, the only things that really mattered in this document were the things it locked *Dario* into doing.

She had believed that Dario had demanded that she marry him to share his bed—to become his lover—and that those were the conditions that he had written into the pre-nuptial agreement he'd had drawn up. That basically he had bought her, body and soul, for the price of the rescue package for her parents. A hugely expensive rescue package for which he'd been justified in demanding a very high price.

But not the price she'd thought he'd insisted on.

'You—you only wanted to *marry* me.' Her voice was filled with the shock of realisation. 'You didn't...'

The contract tied her only to marrying him, changing her name to his. He hadn't put down in writing that it was to be 'a proper marriage', one that meant she was to share his bed, share her body with him. She had thought, had believed, that he would make it a condition of his bailout package for her parents that she had to sleep with him, but that was not the case.

'I married you because I wanted you. Yes, I wanted to see my father and my damned half-brother defeated in their foul little plan. I wanted to make sure that Marcus didn't get his filthy hands on you. But no, I didn't want to buy you like some very expensive prostitute. I wanted you in my bed—but you had to come there of your own choice. After that, I wanted a willing woman in my bed. I've never forced a woman in my life and I certainly didn't intend to start with my wife, even if you only married me because I bought you. Because I paid off all your family's debts.'

'No...' She struggled to put any strength into the word but, looking into his face, seeing the dark intensity etched there, told her that she had to go on, had to make this so very clear. She couldn't bear to have him thinking anything else. 'I married you because I wanted you too. You were the one who insisted on marriage... You did!'

She almost laughed as she caught the touch of shamefaced acknowledgement in his expression. But the laughter shrivelled as she thought of the significance of what that expression meant.

'Yes, I thought that the only way I would win my father's recognition was by marrying you—but that delusion was shattered on the day of our wedding, when he didn't even trouble to attend or even acknowledge my invitation. It was all what he wanted, how he wanted it—and nothing more.'

I don't do family. In her head Alyse could hear those words as he had spoken them outside the church. The terrible, bitter disillusionment that had sounded in them then.

And, even as she thought it, she heard him echo the words from her own thoughts.

'I don't…do family.'

'I know…'

It was a sigh of resignation and acceptance. But then that sigh was caught up, cut off between one breath and another as she paused to think, to register that he hadn't said exactly what she'd believed. Not quite.

'What? What did you say?'

For a couple of uneasy seconds she thought that he wasn't going to respond to her challenge. But then a slight brusque inclination of his head dismissed whatever second thoughts he was having.

'I don't know how to do family,' he said, low and tight. 'But, with you, I found I wanted to try.'

She couldn't believe it. She had to have heard wrong. There was no way he could have said…

But looking into those blue eyes that she loved so much she could see the shadows that clouded them. She could hear the rawness in his voice that threatened to pull his words apart, unravelling them totally.

'When…?' It was barely a whisper.

'The first night at the villa, and ever after that.' His eyes held hers, burning into her, willing her, begging her to believe. 'I could have told you then. I should have told you—but I knew then I would never want to let you go,' Dario said and there was no doubting the depth of conviction in his tone, the shadowed certainty in his face. 'I just didn't know what to call it.'

'And—and now?' Her voice was just a thin thread of sound but she knew the moment he caught it, saw the stunning change in his face. It was as if someone had lit him up from within, but at the same time he didn't dare quite reveal all that was inside him.

'And now I'm admitting that it's love. I'm in love with you. I love you so much that I hate the way you'd even think I'd only pay to have you in my bed. I need you in my life—I love you so much that I want you to be with me for ever. Want you as my love, my wife, the mother of my child.'

'But you—' she began then broke off as he moved forward, taking her hands, holding them tight against his chest.

'Don't say it—' he begged and she knew the words hung unspoken between them. 'Don't remind me of how stupid I was. How ignorant and unable to recognise… I didn't know what a family was. I only knew that it had to be more than what my father and my mother made of a blood family. That there had to be more than the blood ties that bound me—unwillingly—to Henry and to Marcus.'

'They're no family to you!' Alyse interjected sharply, unable to bear the thought of the way his so-called family had treated him.

'I know—and I didn't want them to be either. I wanted the sort of family that you had. The sort of family where your father cares enough to risk jail to save your mother from breaking down completely. And where you were prepared to sign away a part of your life to help them both. Dear God, but I wanted that.'

'Really?'

'Really.' It was firm and strong, totally sure. 'I'd always vaguely understood that the appeal of a family—a real family—the reason for it being was a very special closeness, a need of each other and caring for each other. You can't order it, you can't buy it, no matter how much you pay—it has to grow and become real. It started to grow the first time we made love. And it was there between us that day on the terrace.'

'It was there before that,' Alyse said softly. 'It was there when you cared for me—when you nursed me through the migraine—for better, for worse.'

Dario's smile was wry, softly reminiscent.

'That led to today—to the baby. And now…'

His hand slid down over her belly, curved protectively over the spot where his baby nestled, tiny as yet, but growing into a real child, a person, a member of their family.

'Now, our child will be loved for who it is, not because of anything it brings to our marriage except itself. Just as I love you for who you are and I always will. I don't know how to be a father but I'll be the best damn *papà* I can be.'

Suddenly his voice dropped, fell from the declaration he'd made into a raw and aching whisper.

'I still don't know how to do family. I just know I want to try. With you.'

I just know I want to try. With you. What

braver, greater declaration could there be? How could she ask for anything more?

'And I want to try too,' she said, her voice deep with conviction. 'With you as the man I love. The father of my child.'

Alyse leaned forward, offered him her mouth, and knew the soaring sense of true happiness, true fulfilment as he took it in the longest, most loving kiss she had ever experienced. She moved into his arms, feeling safe and secure there and knowing she would never, ever want to leave them.

'Let me tell you something,' she whispered, the softness of her love and her happiness in her smile. 'I don't really know how to do this sort of family either. Not one where I'm the mother and you—my love, my husband, my future—are the father. But I do know one thing. We'll learn together. We'll make a real family. And that's all that anyone could ever ask for.'

* * * * *

Six

Avoid greediness—neither take unsporting shots nor kill in excessive numbers

Seven

Avoid selfishness—let your fellows have the sport which is rightly theirs

Eight

Never shoot at a quarry you have not fully identified

Nine

Respect and conserve the natural scene

Ten

Regard shooting as a means to an end and not an end in itself

The Complete Shot

John Marchington

Adam & Charles Black   London

First published 1981
by A & C Black
(Publishers) Ltd,
35 Bedford Row,
London WC1R 4JH

ISBN 0-7136-2145-1

Marchington, John

The complete shot.
I. Title
799.2'13 GV1153

ISBN 0-7136-2145-1

Filmset by August Filmsetting,
Reddish, Stockport.
Printed by
Butler & Tanner Ltd
Frome and London

Contents

Illustrations

All photographs are by the author, with the exception of that shown on the jacket and numbers 4, 5, 11, 15 and 16, which were taken by his wife, Janet. Some of these photographs have appeared in the *Shooting Times and Country Magazine* and *The Field*, and the author is grateful to the Editors for their permission to reproduce them herein.

To my sons – James, Nigel and William –
the best of shooting companions.

Preface

Beginners to the sport of shooting have been well catered for, over the years, by a succession of instructional books, but little has been published for the experienced shot. This absence may reflect a belief by publishers that once a shooting man progresses beyond the novice stage he has little desire to learn more of, or delve deeper into his sport. My own experience is to the contrary, for the articles I have contributed to *The Field* over the last fifteen years bring forth a steady stream of 'Letters to the Editor', or correspondence to my home. Some writers agree with my views, others disagree (usually with pleasant courtesy), and some seek to expand a line of thought. What, however, is now relevant, is that all are experienced shooting men anxious to debate all aspects.

Hence this book. It is not, in fact, directed at a particular section of the shooting community but will, I trust, be of interest to all. The complete novice will glean much from it, and, hopefully, even the most experienced will have their thoughts and attitudes stimulated. It should also be of use to the man of expertise in one department who is about to try his hand elsewhere – for example, the traditional driven pheasant shot, shortly to stand in a grouse butt for the first time.

I have assumed a reasonable level of basic knowledge in all readers, and you will not have to skip pages on how a cartridge works, and like material. I have also assumed, and this is more controversial, that most shooting men are not deeply interested in technicalities. We all wish to understand choke, patterns, striking energies and similar aspects of ballistics and, in particular, the best compromises for our most practised form of shooting, but, for most of us, this is a means to an end only. I have not dwelt over-long on such details.

In spite of all I have done and written I am not an overall expert in the field of shooting and nor is anyone else. It is far too diverse and complicated a subject. Some men will be excellent marksmen, others indifferent shots but authoritative on gun-making. Experts exist on training dogs, pigeon shooting and walking-up snipe. Here and there you will find masters at downing driven grouse, or lesser subjects such as ferreting. But nowhere exists the man who can justifiably claim to be an all-round expert. What I can claim is that I have personally done all the things of which I write, and done them with enthusiasm and an enquiring mind.

I hope you will find the outcome both interesting and helpful.

A contrast of settings – walking-up partridges in September and cock shooting in January.

Chapter 1
The changing scene

I have written this book on the assumption that the readers will be perceptive and intelligent participants in the sport of shooting, and interested in all its aspects, whether of practical application or merely adding to their overall knowledge. Full enjoyment of any experience, be it drinking a good wine, admiring a picture, or watching an excellent dog at work, calls for a knowledge of the background and I can do no better than start by tracing the history of the sport and the attitudes of the sportsmen.

If we widen our definition of sporting shooting to include bows and arrows we can go back to the Magdalenian period of approximately 30,000 B.C., although it is doubtful if the sporting aspect was much in evidence. As tribes united, controlled larger territories and gradually evolved into civilisations, so game came to be hunted for sport as well as simply food, but the evidence of sporting activity is thin. We know, for example, that the wealthy Ancient Egyptians would use a form of throwing stick against wildfowl, but the first evidence I can trace of shooting for sport in this country occurs in *The Master of Game*. Henry IV discovered his Master of Game, Edward, Second Duke of York, was plotting against him and had him locked up in Pevensey Castle from 1406 to 1413. During his imprisonment he translated a Continental book, *Livre de la Chasse*, into English, and altered it to conform to English practices. Appearing as *The Master of Game*, it contains an interesting reference to shooting running hares with both longbows and crossbows.

Our interest, however, lies with the history of sport with firearms; that is to say missiles propelled by gunpowder or later, more sophisticated propellants. The first suggestion of firearms in this country appeared about 1310, that is a century before *The Master of Game*, but the next chapter covers technical developments in guns and, beyond observing that the sequence of progression was, in simple terms, matchlock, wheel-lock, and flintlock, we will consider the progress of the sport rather than the weaponry.

Although only a week before I wrote this a noble Lord had an article published in a sporting magazine in which he claimed sporting shooting, 'as we know it', only began in the eighteenth century, I beg to differ. Much hangs upon the words, 'as we know it', but, as I see it, any act of firing at game with a gun for sporting purposes must fall within our definition. In 1548 Sir E. Bedingfield wrote to the Earl of Bath expressing concern over the future of hawking as a result of 'such persons as dayly do shoote in hand-gonnes or beat at the fowles in ryvers and pyttes, so as ther is no fowle that do remayne in the countrye'. Of course, much of this would be shooting for the pot, but there has never been a clear division between shooting for sport and shooting for food.

There is clear evidence of wildfowl shooting in the sixteenth century, but 1621 saw the publication of one of the most important books for the shooting historian, Gervase Markham's, *Hunger's Prevention: or, The Whole Arte of Fowling by Water and Land.* In this Markham gives an invaluable catalogue of the various devices for taking all manner of game and, while the relative lack of priority given to the gun shows it is only one of the normal methods at the time, it is clear that shooting is firmly established, not just for 'Hunger's Prevention', but as a sport. Regrettably space prevents quoting at length from this fascinating book, but the introduction to the gun cannot be omitted:

> The next Engine to these is the Gun or Fowling Piece, which is a generall Engine and may serve for any Fowle great or little whatsoever, for it hath no respect at which it striketh, being within the leuell: And of the Fowling Piece you shall vnderstand that to be the best which is of the longest barrell, as fiue foote and a halfe, or sixe foote, and the boare indifferent, as some what vnder Harquebush, for these should the best charges, & carry the furthest leuell, which is a principal thing to be regarded.

Markham's detailed instructions on stalking fowl, either by natural cover or using a stalking horse, his advice on aiming and dog training, and many other aspects, combine to make it clear that by 1621 shooting was well understood and practised.

Perhaps his Lordship, with whom I have gently disagreed, may have had in mind the practice of shooting at flying or running quarries, feeling that the sport, 'as we know it', did not encompass stationary targets. If this is so his claim for an eighteenth century origin may well rest on a poem by A. B. Markland, published in 1727, and called, *Pteryplegia: or, the Art of Shooting Flying.*

The general tenor of the verse suggested that 'shooting flying' was a recent development and the temptation to accept this is enhanced by the poet's obvious practical experience of the sport.

Further support for the eighteenth century comes from that meticulous writer, H. C. Folkard in, *The Wild-Fowler*, (1859), who quotes Whitaker's *Richmondshire.* In fact I have no difficulty in producing evidence for a seventeenth century introduction to shooting flying. Quite obviously it was not a practice which developed almost overnight. As guns improved both in weight, balance and the means of ignition, so would different men, at different times and places, attempt shots at moving targets. The question is when the practice became common. Consider these additional facts. In 1644, Alongo Martinez de Espinar, a Spaniard, dealt with shooting flying partridges in a book on general shooting. Spain is not England, but sporting practices travelled quickly and we have irrefutable evidence that shooting flying reached England by 1686, for in that year Richard Blome's *The Gentleman's Recreation*, contained the passage:

> It is now the mode to shoot flying as being by Experience found the best and surest Way: for when your Game is on the wing, it is more exposed to danger: for if but one shot hits any Part of the Wings so expanded, it will occasion its Fall, altho' not to kill it: so that your Spaniel will soon be its Victor, and, if well disciplined to the Sport, will bring it to you.

Given this vital passage we can date the commencement of sporting shooting 'as we know it', with surprising accuracy. Markham, a most diligent author, obviously knew nothing of it in 1621, yet by 1686 it was, 'now the mode'; a phrase suggesting the practice was well established. Taking a middle date between the two gives about 1650, so, until, if ever, contrary evidence appears, I place the beginning of shooting flying in the mid-seventeenth century.

The literature of shooting is very sparse until an extensive three volume work in 1801–1802 by the Reverend Daniel, but his useful contribution was almost immediately overshadowed by Colonel Peter Hawker's *Instructions to Young Sportsmen* (1814). However much we may criticise Hawker for the single-minded ruthlessness with which he pursued game, he is owed a great debt for his invaluable book. In this he tore aside the obscurity surrounding the sport and provided for later generations a mass of details of guns, gun-makers, powder, shot, quarries, tactics, dogs, and every other conceivable aspect of the sport.

Up to a few weeks before I wrote this passage it had generally been assumed that *Instructions* was Hawker's sole book on the sport. It was known he had written of his Army experiences and also a small book on playing the pianoforte, but no bibliography listed any further work, nor had any of the specialist booksellers I deal with heard of any. By pure chance, at the beginning of 1980 I was corresponding with an elderly, and very authoritative, collector of rare shooting books who mentioned he had heard a rumour of an unknown book by Hawker in America. Springing to the scent I was able to trace this great rarity to the possession of Mr F. P. Williamson in Maryland, and it required but little research to confirm the author was *the* Peter Hawker. Titled *The Sportsman's Pocket Companion*, it was published in

1801, when Hawker was only 15, and, obviously, many shooting men would wish to own and read a copy. Happily, at the moment of writing, I have been able to arrange for the Game Conservancy to publish a limited edition later this year, thereby making the book available to interested purchasers and enabling the Conservancy to earn some funds.

The nineteenth century was, for the well-to-do sportsman, a wonderful period; indeed, in writing *The History of Wildfowling*, I refer to it as the Golden Age. The wide gulf between the rich and poor ensured that the former had little competition from the latter in the shooting field, (or anywhere else for that matter), and the law imposed harsh penalties for poaching. (Little more than a century ago a man convicted of night poaching for a third time faced deportation for seven years.) Men of means had both the money and the time to follow their sport and many did with near fanatical enthusiasm. Some, such as Folkard, the Scottish lawyer, combined their shooting with industrious careers but others, of whom Sir Ralph Payne-Gallwey, Bart., was an example, allowed shooting to occupy most of their time and energy. Low taxes and great estates generated enormous wealth, but the story of the excesses of the pheasant shoots of the closing years of the century is told later.

On the technical side the outstanding advance began with the detonating cap which was soon adapted to the pin fire cartridge. Very quickly the gun trade, then in its prime, invented the centre fire cartridge, and so permitted the evolution of the breech loader, which had been an understood but impractical improvement until then.

Although the nineteenth century was a period of massive technical advance, it also saw less obvious, but equally important progress in the minds of men. At the start of the century there was little regard for the quarry, as witness Hawker and others advocating long range shooting with large shot in the hope of wounding, but in the closing years a more humane trend appeared, particularly from Abel Chapman, a man of wide interests and vision.

The changes in the sport during the twentieth century have had little to do with either the development of guns and ammunition, or variations in the forms of shooting, and, for all practical purposes, a nineteenth century sportsman would have no difficulty in taking part in a present day shoot. Instead the very substantial changes have been social and environmental. The century of the common man, as sociologists enjoy labelling it, has so improved the leisure, wealth and travelling ability of most people that shooting is now the sport of a far wider cross-section than was previously the case. Coupled with this growth, and partly as a consequence of it, has come the tremendous pressures on the countryside which have absorbed substantial acreages of land, drained many wet lands, industrialised some coastal areas, and created extensive pollution problems. All is not black, for we tend to view the problems from a biased angle and ignore the good aspects. Development and technological progress has been responsible for a great improvement in living standards and one cannot enjoy the benefits that flow from motorways, sewage works, power stations, hospitals, schools, factories, and all the other 'land eaters', and then grumble about the disadvantages.

The shooting man of a century ago could have been described in a few lines, for the great majority would have come from the same social drawer, but a description of his equivalent in the latter half of the twentieth century is far more difficult. One of the attractive features of the sport is the lack of class boundaries, and, as a Labour Government found when contemplating restrictions against field sports, the roar of indignation came from men of all levels. The background of the individual may determine what he shoots at, but it has nothing to do with whether he shoots. To this extent the sport plays a minor, but useful part in helping national harmony, for people who are often at loggerheads come together in common interests and causes. A visit to the Game Fair will demonstrate this adequately.

While the principles of driven shooting have changed very little in the last hundred years, the structure of the sport has. The arrival of the railways made it practical for sportsmen to travel widely and, for the wealthy, opened the era of the shooting house parties. However, travel was still sufficiently awkward to prohibit a visit of less than two or three days and the estate had to be large enough to provide extensive shooting. The twentieth century was not long advanced before two major influences, the motor car and war, changed the pattern. The social upheavals of the 1914–1918 war, and particularly, heavily increased taxation, saw the break-up of most of the large estates, and reduced the size of most shoots. Concurrently, wealth was being redistributed, with the upper strata of the manufacturing and commercial worlds benefiting and, in many cases, looking to shooting for relaxation. The outcome was a rapid expansion in syndicates and this swing from private to syndicate shooting has continued in the driven game sector throughout the century. (Forty per cent of the members of the Game Conservancy now belong to syndicates.)

The changing attitudes and pressures of this century have combined to produce a shooting man very different from his contemporary of the last century. The experienced shot who embodies the best outlook and philosophy of our time is by no means necessarily an excellent marksman. He is probably competent, but quite untroubled by his inability to achieve a very high percentage of kills to cartridges. And compared with the nineteenth century sportsman he is less concerned with what he kills and more interested in his surroundings. His work is probably more demanding, both in time and pressure, and hours spent in the countryside are consequently sharper and sweeter. As an experienced shot he will have a good understanding of all forms of the sport and, being naturally observant, will miss no detail of the day. He will know his natural history, have a passing knowledge of agriculture and be an ambassador of the sport whenever he encounters hostility from town dwellers. And, not least, he would never countenance shooting without a dog. In a nutshell, the essence of a complete shot is not just his ability, but this attitude to the sport, the quarries and the environment.

Inevitably, in assessing the sport, the thinking and sensitive man has to look squarely at the ethics of killing for sport. The average, uninformed member of the public is instinctively hostile and, while we may not welcome this criticism, we should at least appreciate and understand it. We grow accustomed to killing creatures, but few town dwellers have killed anything larger than a fly, and the concept is repugnant to them. Guns, to the public, are associated with violence, crime and war. To take these brutal weapons and use them to slaughter beautiful and gentle birds and animals is beyond comprehension – we, the sportsmen, must be depraved. I cannot feel too incensed by the behaviour of young 'anti's' who set out to disrupt sport, for I can see their point of view. They are young, idealistic, often from the universities and polytechnics, and therefore lively and positive people, and they see what to them is a social wrong within their power to protest against, if not right. Of course, they should have more regard for the freedom of the individual and more respect for the laws of trespass, but, when one looks at the savage, mindless, violence to be found in modern society, such protests are minor.

But, moving away from a consideration of the views of the uninformed, what do you think of the ethics of shooting? Obviously you favour the sport or you would not be reading this book. And so must I or I would not be writing it. But this is not to say I am without reservations. Let me lay my conscience bare, the better that you may examine your own.

The arguments to be advanced in favour of shooting are quite strong and, in the process of advancing them, it is possible to delude oneself over the deeper issues. Our first line of fortifications, as it were, is the charge that no-one can attack our sport if they are, themselves, flesh eaters. How can a person who ate bacon for breakfast, trout for lunch and lamb for supper criticise me for shooting a pheasant? Well, the reply will go, I have to eat to live, but I did not kill the creatures – you did. Someone, we respond, has to kill the creatures we eat – no-one criticises slaughterhouse workers so why sportsmen? Because, comes the response, overwhelming the front line trenches, they do it for a living and you do it for fun.

And so we do. When we strip away the euphemisms of 'pricking' instead of wounding, and 'bagging' instead of killing, we kill for pleasure. Of course, our sport produces a useful crop of food, but few of us would bother to shoot if all we gained from it was meat in the freezer. Moving to another defence, it is a very forceful argument that shooting alone preserves the considerable acreages of coverts, cover and rough corners which are invaluable sanctuaries for wildlife in a shrinking countryside. But we cannot honestly claim we shoot for this purpose – it is a beneficial spin-off and not a principal cause. Nor can we claim we shoot for the pleasure of being in the countryside and the healthy exercise it brings, for this could be achieved by hiking or bird-watching.

Granted that the benefits that shooting brings, in many ways and to many people, are substantial, we are being less than true to ourselves if we do not face the issue that shooting involves killing for pleasure.

Consider me. I love children, dogs and animals generally. I feel deeply for people in distress, ill-health or poverty. Show me an injured creature and, assisted by my family, I will nurse it back to health. More than once I have taken physical risks to save sheep trapped on mountain ledges, and when I lose an old loved dog, am inconsolable. I am far from being a hard man. And yet I kill things.

And further, to complicate the complicated, I love the things I kill. A woodcock's eyes; the liquid note of the curlew; the magical world of the grouse; a rabbit's bounding energy; the sheen of a cock pheasant's rump – these, and all the other wonderful aspects of our quarries, I love. Yet I kill them. And so, my reader, do you and likewise tens of thousands of other basically good and kind men.

It is fair to argue that the distress we cause them is nothing like so great as our critics believe; in fact, there is not, in the context of their world, any distress at all. They are protected from the grey thread of certain death that runs through the rope of each human life, for wild things cannot foresee death. Nor can they reason, and the snipe flushed by a sportsman's spaniel is no more frightened than when disturbed from the same spot, only hours earlier, by the shepherd's dog. Neither do the pheasants, flushed by the beaters, fear death or injury as they plane towards the guns. They may, after a few shoots, anticipate noise, but no more. It is the pattern of life for wild things to be wary, suspicious and easily alarmed. In this context our efforts in seeking, flushing and firing at them do not cause unnatural alarm or distress and need not trouble us. Nor does killing the bird cleanly cause it pain or distress and it is a fair claim that shot game dies more easily than most humans. The defence is even stronger if we consider the alternative ways in which the creature would have died had we not shot it – most of them more protracted and painful. Provided, of course, we kill cleanly . . .

The last paragraph has the merit of factual accuracy and has done much to remove the charge that shooting is cruel. It has, however, once again led us from the central issue, that we kill for pleasure. We can defend the circumstances in which we kill wild creatures – what we cannot defend is the fact that we want to do it.

The thought has cast troubled ripples across the smooth enjoyment of my shooting for many years past, and doubtless it will do so all my life. The explanation, of course, is very simple, albeit often advanced as a startling discovery by sociologists, for man has hunted since the very beginning and such a deep-rooted instinct cannot be cast off in the relatively brief spell of time in which we have moved from hunting our meat to farming it. When all the myriads of words written on the rights or wrongs of field sports blur into a confused mass I see myself and a spaniel working an unkempt hedge-row along a Norfolk field. It is frosty and still. Somewhere, close by, a rabbit lies tensed as a spring, but quite motionless. The spaniel knows it is near and so do I – the dog moves in brief, bounding rushes, then stands stock still, head cocked, listening and peering. I am totally alert and involved, balancing and watching for the slightest movement. Tomorrow I will wear a grey suit and tie and work indoors with paper and complex affairs but, now, I am man the hunter – ageless. My forefathers for thousands of years have felt, as I feel now, the absolute concentration and thrill of the hunt.

This same, sharp, skin chilling tingle of excitement and apprehension comes to me in many places – on the high hills when we cast for a covey of grouse we know lies close, or huddled in the marsh grasses and watching the black dots of approaching wildfowl. It is a harsh sport, but it is also the true pattern of life and death, without the veneer of civilisation under which we shelter.

All sensitive sportsmen will share my reservations about the act of killing, but we all face the same great anomaly – that without the hunt and the kill the whole essence of the sport would disappear. We can only resolve our individual consciences and hope future generations will not judge us too harshly.

Chapter 2
The gun

That men are attracted by guns is beyond dispute; what is less clear is why. Probably it has much to do with the feeling of power guns engender, for it is the nature of men to wish to control and dominate and guns are great equalisers – big strong men and little weak men are all the same size once armed. This, however, is the appeal of a gun at its crudest level and there are more subtle attractions attached to sporting guns. These stem from the instinctive desire of humanity to own and enjoy those material things necessary to survive in comfort and safety. Such instincts explain why immediately a man and woman unite they want to buy a home – not rent, where their security is tenuous, but buy their own personal castle. It also explains why twentieth century man has persisted in burning solid fuels in his home even when an adequate, cleaner and more convenient system of central heating has been installed. Locking the door of one's own private cave and sitting by the warmth and security of an open fire stirs instincts formed over tens of thousands of years. And so with a gun – here is a hunting weapon, an ingenious twentieth century implement certainly, but in the eyes of instinct just the latest in a long line of tools necessary to secure food. Shelter, warmth and hunting tools – the basic essentials of existence and, although we have almost lost sight of these fundamentals under our complex veneer of civilisation, nothing has changed.

And so a gun has a special place in the heart of its owner, which cannot be equalled by a set of golf clubs, or a tennis racket. Perhaps a fishing rod with which one has shared triumph and tragedy over many years may approach this, but no other instrument of pleasure can really equal a much loved gun. Of course, feelings will vary – the formal driven game man who carries his gun, or pair, in a sling for most of the day cannot feel for his weapon as does the all-round shot. In practice most readers of this book will have several guns, but there is likely to be one favourite. For me it is the number two of my pair, designated my general gun and used on all occasions other than driven game. My hands have worn the chequering almost smooth, my thumb and finger have polished the safety catch and triggers, and, in spite of much care, the stock bears some scars. I have carried that gun many hundreds of miles through sun, snow, gale and frost. With it I have sheltered under peat hags on Scottish hill tops in August rain and sat out long cold hours in Cambridgeshire pigeon hides. It has shot mallard at dusk by the Hampshire Itchen, blackgame on the Yorkshire fells, woodcock on the Sussex Downs, snipe in the Hebrides, rabbits ferreted from Surrey hedgerows and partridges on Norfolk stubbles. It was my gun when my favourite spaniel was a puppy and went where she went throughout her life. I expect that when I am a very old man, poking about in a thick hedgerow with an elderly spaniel, it will still be the gun on my arm. If it were stolen tomorrow the cheque from the insurance company would be only a very partial compensation.

There is ample evidence throughout the literature of the sport to show that shooting men of all periods had affection for their favourite gun, and certainly the earlier guns lent themselves to loving to a greater extent than ours. One has to be knowledgeable and look closely to pick out the differences between the highly developed and near-identical guns of today, whereas a century ago, when external hammers were still much in evidence, guns could be seen to be individuals at the merest glance.

In considering the origin of the gun one must first look at the origin of gunpowder, and the various authorities suggest it was known in India and China long before it first appeared in Europe. In 275 A.D. Julius Africanus wrote of 'shooting powder', and a form of gunpowder was used at the siege of Constantinople in 668 B.C. and the siege of Mecca in 690. In 846, Marcus Graecus, in *Liber ignium*, gave a recipe for gunpowder of six parts saltpetre and two parts each of charcoal and sulphur. This is very close to the modern formula. The Saracens used gunpowder in 904, the King of Hungary in 1073, the Greeks in 1098 and the Arabs in 1147. There was artillery at Toulose in 1218 and Roger Bacon died in 1292 leaving a written description of gunpowder. Gunpowder was first introduced to this country in the fourteenth century but was not manufactured here until the latter half of the sixteenth. The first written evidence of firearms in England came in 1338 with an indenture listing the various cannons included in the equipment of the King's ship and in 1373 Chaucer wrote in his *House of Fame*, 'Swift as a pillot out of a gonne.' The 'gonne' of this period was crude in the extreme; a tube to take the powder and projectile, set into a wooden holder or stock which was rested on the shoulder. Ignition was achieved by placing a loose match to the touch-hole.

This basic lay-out lasted for a long time and progress centred mainly on improved methods of ignition. First came the matchlock, a simple pivoted lever, with a slow match secured in one end. Pulling the opposite end, the trigger, lowered the match onto the flash-pan and touch-hole. By the beginning of the sixteenth century the Germans were developing the wheel-lock which, like its successor the flintlock, produced sparks by the clash of flint and steel. The steel wheel was powered by a spring and, when released

An excellent example of an early 18th century flintlock. Made by William Turvey of Oxford in 1720, this fowling piece is six feet, two inches long.

by the trigger, a serrated edge revolved rapidly against a flint. For a hundred years the wheel-lock reigned unchallenged but, early in the seventeenth century, the Spanish produced the first of the flintlocks. These are so well known that the briefest description should suffice. The flint is screwed into the jaws of the cock and, when the trigger is pulled, a spring propels this forward to knock the cover plate of the flash-pan forward, thereby exposing the priming powder. The hammer is not the falling cock but the vertical steel face of the cover plate, which receives the blow from the falling flint and, at the same instant, plays its part in producing the sparks. Here was an ignition system so ingenious and reliable that it was to last for some two centuries until, early in the nineteenth century, a Scottish clergyman, the Reverend Alexander John Forsyth, LL.D., invented the percussion system of ignition. This depended on the fact that certain fulminate explosives could be ignited by percussion rather than fire and, at first, the fulminate was contained in paper or thin metal and placed in the flash-pan to be struck by the falling cock. During the nineteenth century the English gun trade was very active and such men as Egg, Wilkinson, Lancaster, Lang and

Westley-Richards quickly produced advances, culminating in the copper cap upon a nipple, with a flash-hole leading into the breech. By the 1850s the muzzle-loading percussion gun was both highly functional and elegant and many fine examples exist to this day. They were not, however, convenient, for the standard equipment included a ramrod, shot pouch or belt, powder flask, caps, cap-charger, paper for wadding, spare nipples and a nipple-key. One last great advance remained – the invention of a practical breech-loader. I write 'practical', because various breech-loaders had appeared at various times from the beginning of the sixteenth century, but none had performed satisfactorily. It was the invention of the percussion ignited cartridge, by a Frenchman in 1840, and its development into the pin-fire cartridge seven years later, which opened the way for practical breech-loaders.

England was rich in gun making talent, fuelled by the willingness of wealthy customers prepared to pay for the best, and new ideas abounded. In this highly competitive market the better ideas quickly triumphed over the less sound and progress was rapid. By 1862 a Mr Dow was showing a centre-pin fire cartridge at the Internation Exhibition, but history suggests he was better at invention than patenting his ideas. In the event Eley Bros stepped into the picture and the firm has remained prominent ever since. The centre-fire cartridge created the opportunity to position the lock-work within the body of the gun and the first hammerless guns appeared within a few years. Again, improvement followed improvement in rapid succession until the design of the side-by-side, hammerless ejector was so refined that gun-makers of the twentieth century have made no improvements of significance. One fact will illustrate this – the Anson and Deeley action, which exists in millions of shotguns the world over and is still in production, was patented in 1875.

This history is, of course, of the very briefest, but limited space forbids a closer look. There is much, much more of interest and I recommend W. W. Greener's classic, *The Gun and Its Development*. Although first published in 1881 it is not scarce for it ran to nine editions and there are modern reprints.

All of which leads us to the present day, and to the point at which many books on shooting lay down a specification of the right gun to use, what it should weigh, how it should be choked, and so forth. Such instruction is all very well for the novice but for experienced shooting men, such as my present readers, there is no more a standard gun suitable for all than there is a standard wife. And taking the analogy a little further, you should use the gun, and marry the girl, with which you are happiest and hang convention. I have no right, nor has anyone else, to lay down firm rules on the 'right' gun, and suggest that he who deviates is in error. However, some consideration of various aspects of this complex question should interest the majority and, possibly, stimulate some doubt among those readers who acquired an unsuitable gun years ago and have accepted it ever since.

Firstly, heresy though it may be, I do not think the average, sporting, shooting man is greatly interested in ballistics. Men who shoot only clay pigeons are, and so are all riflemen and those who are scientifically inclined, but there is that about the temperament of most country-loving sportsmen which leaves them cold to figures, graphs and diagrams. This is not to say that we are totally indifferent to the subject, but discussion at a shoot lunch is more likely to centre on dogs than plating percentages. I will not, therefore, load this chapter with technical data on breech pressures, points of choke, and the like, but try to concentrate on commonsense views on difficult questions.

All questions and problems relating to sporting shotguns should be considered against the background of two vital facts – firstly, they are short range weapons, and no combination of boring, shot or load can lengthen the range by more than a few yards. Secondly, their whole function is one of constant compromise. For any given size of target at a specific range there is an ideal barrel boring and size and weight of shot. Anything different is imperfect and as, for all practical purposes, no two shots are ever identical, the great majority of shots are made with less than perfect combinations of boring and load. The problem for the individual is to evaluate which combination of boring and load is going to be most nearly right, on the maximum number of occasions, for the type of shooting he enjoys more frequently.

Given this requirement it is at once obvious that there can never be a universal specification for the most suitable gun.

Little time need be lost in deciding on the best bore size, for this has evolved over the years from the application of our first fact – that guns are short range weapons. As little can be done to improve the range it is pointless to carry a heavier gun than is necessary and after many generations of trial and error, the twelve bore is the most frequent choice. There is a case, to be examined soon, for something heavier for wildfowling. In the opposite direction, something smaller is sensible for ladies and youngsters to meet the twofold need of reducing both weight and recoil. It is easier to solve the problem for a lady than a youngster for the former's size is usually constant, whereas the latter grows steadily larger and heavier. Some fathers advocate actually starting a boy on a twelve and letting him 'grow into it', but this is a mistake. Granted recoil can be solved by giving him two inch cartridges which will give less of a kick than the standard cartridge, in the lighter, twenty bore; however, the weight problem will both tire him if the gun has to be carried any distance, and more important, implant a bad style of shooting. Watch any youngster mount a gun which is too heavy for his strength and he will lean backwards, to counteract the weight, rather than balance on the front foot. Excessive weight also makes it harder for a young shot to swing correctly and leads to 'poking'. The question of selecting the right gun for a youngster demands more consideration than it often receives and I go into greater depth in Chapter 13.

A twenty bore makes a grand gun for a lady, offering a combination of adequate killing power with a worthwhile reduction in weight over a twelve. Personally I have little time for a sixteen bore, for one loses relatively little in weight yet is faced with the difficulty of replenishing cartridges when in out-of-the-way places.

And so back to twelves. At regular intervals somebody fuels the flames of the automatic and pump gun dispute and the correspondence columns blaze with heated and contrary views. The outsider would deduce a wide gulf of opinion between equal protagonists on this issue but, if this was so, automatics and pumps would be encountered frequently in the field. In fact, they are rare because the majority belong either to clay shooters or novices. Some are, of course, used for normal sporting shooting, but not by the more informed sportsmen. It is worth assessing the reasons briefly. On a purely practical basis automatics and pumps are very functional and, because their design permits high volume mass production, relatively cheap. (This automatically means they appeal to the less discriminating market.) In appearance and balance they are inferior to the better class of side by side or over and under. The complicated loading system renders them more liable to malfunction and, possibly the major shortcoming, the difficulty of viewing the breech makes them less safe. These drawbacks might be tolerated if the principal advantage of being able to fire from three to five shots in rapid succession gave a substantial benefit. In fact, such a facility is entirely contrary to all principles of sportsmanship and so automatics and pumps stand condemned. There will, no doubt, be a sprinkling of readers who will wax indignant over my lofty dismissal of these weapons, but they fight a lost cause as my view reflects that of the great majority.

The conservative approval of the conventional side by side sometimes, mistakenly, leads to vague, undefined, criticism of over and unders, but there cannot be a logical objection to this design. Whether or not two tubes are positioned horizontally or vertically affects only the sighting plane and has no bearing on ethics, balance, safety or appearance. In fact, shooting men of the future, unless they are wealthy, may have to use over and unders, for they are easier, and therefore cheaper, to manufacture than side by sides. No doubt the gun trade will eventually tell us that a single sighting plane improves marksmanship.

Although it is a simple matter to justify the use of a side by side twelve bore it is harder to complete the specification in detail. Guns for wildfowling have their special needs, but individual preference still gives wide scope for argument even on guns intended for ordinary game and rough shooting. Weight is an example. The rough shooter, who fires relatively few cartridges in a day, will willingly accept greater recoil in exchange for carrying less weight. (I am rather assuming all readers will know that the greater the weight of the gun the less the recoil for a given cartridge.) The driven game shot, conversely, carries his gun but little, yet fires many cartridges. At first thought he will be pleased to settle for an extra half pound or so of weight and avoid a stiff shoulder. But it is not so simple – consider another aspect. I submit that the standard load game cartridge is not just adequate but too heavy for the range at which most driven game is shot. Additionally, there are many circumstances in driven game shooting when the *speed* of aiming and firing is paramount – examples are partridges bursting over a hedge or pheasants flitting over a narrow ride. Combine these two factors and there emerges a good case for using a very light gun, with a light load cartridge, adequate for the job, to keep the recoil within acceptable bounds. Some readers may feel the advantage of a light gun is more than lost when standing at a drive known to produce high birds and facing the alternatives of being either undergunned or using a heavier cartridge producing an unpleasant recoil. Which view is right will depend on several personal factors, including such wide variations as personal physique and how often one shoots pigeons over their roosts, and I have no wish to follow each thread of reasoning to its weary conclusion – my concern is to show how every man can have his individual needs and preferences.

Choke is another technical consideration on which men, waiting impatiently in barn or lodge for the rain to stop, can argue endlessly and all are right for none can be proved wrong. Here, again, I am not going to complicate our thinking by producing diagrams or circles with a profusion of dots in them. Most readers will know the vital ballistic principle that pattern fails long before penetration, or, in other words, the power of a pellet to penetrate the quarry continues after it, and its fellows, have deviated so far from the original line of sight, and one another, that a hit by a sufficient number to achieve a kill is remote. For the purpose of considering choke all we need to bear in mind is that narrowing the end of a barrel confines the shot into a smaller diameter throughout its entire flight and, by maintaining the pattern for longer, increases the range – precise figures on what degree of choke will produce what alteration to the percentage of pellets in a certain sized circle at various ranges will merely cloud our minds in considering the basic principle.

Immediately we come once more to the impossibility of producing precise answers from circumstances of infinite variations. The targets of a game shooter are far more constant, in range and size, than those of a rough shooter and so he, at least, should be able to lay down firm requirements for choke. Only hours before I wrote these words I was shooting driven pheasants on the Sussex Downs. On the last drive before lunch I stood in a very small clearing in an oak wood, looking at a 'window' to the sky of some fifteen yards diameter. Being mid-November the leaf was on and the pheasants could not be spotted in advance. Choke was unwanted and a blunderbuss preferred. The first drive after lunch a woodcock flitted through the wood at twenty yards again calling for maximum speed. On the second drive the birds were flushed from a covert on a hilltop over the Guns set in a deep valley. The birds were not, as some guests, broken men surrounded by empty cases and not a bird to show, have claimed, out of range, but a fully choked left barrel was almost essential. So, within a couple of hours, my ideal boring for the shot of the moment varied from cylinder to full choke, and this at driven game. For the rough shooter the position is even more complex. I can walk through a bog in the Hebrides and have a snipe spring at three yards and a mallard at forty-five. An hour later, on the high ground, I can flush a covey of young grouse under my feet and wish for cylinder boring in both barrels and, minutes later, put up an old cock grouse at maximum range and need full choke.

There is no need to labour the point – no matter what form of shooting one follows each individual shot calls for a varying degree of choke and, this being impossible, the problem is to decide on the best compromise. Once again I am deliberately avoiding statistics – precisely how many pellets are placed into a thirty inch circle at forty yards from a load of $1\frac{1}{16}$th oz. of no. 6 shot fired from a half choke barrel is not relevant. The quality of the decision will benefit by one's ignoring such complexities and remembering instead that the ability to kill the quarry at the longer ranges is only purchased by having a narrow shot spread at the shorter range which, obviously, increases the chances of missing closer targets. Conversely, results with nearer quarries can be improved by opening the choke but reducing the range.

Fortunately we are spared the agony of having to make a single decision over choke by the ability of a double-barrel gun to carry alternative borings and most experienced shots will have developed the instinct to select the barrel to suit the shot. As a general rule the rough shooter will want the greatest contrast between his barrel borings and the man who only shoots driven game the least. As another general rule the most common mistake is to have too much choke rather than too little. In the last century, when the effectiveness of choke boring was established, the shooting fraternity rushed to adopt it as the answer to their long felt need of increased range. Various books of the period record how many sportsmen discovered a fall-off in their marksmanship and the gun trade, having been well paid to produce guns with heavy choke, were then well paid to take it out again.

In theory the best borings for a rough shooter's gun are cylinder or improved cylinder in the right barrel and full choke in the left. In practice, and because of the views in the preceding paragraph, I have my own left barrel on my 'general' gun, bored three-quarter choke. A rough shooter knows that, in a full season, he is sure to encounter a wide variety of shots but some driven game men have a lesser variety than others and can standardise their borings accordingly. For example, the man who shoots driven partridges in September and October and then changes to relatively low pheasants for the rest of the season might well elect for improved cylinder in both barrels. However, for the man expecting greater variety, and certainly my own preference, a good combination is improved cylinder and half choke. Granted half choke will not be best for those really high birds but, for the reasons advanced earlier, taking the season through, a more open boring is best.

And now, just to demonstrate there are no inviolable rules, here is a contrary argument, to wit that for humane reasons all barrels should be not less than half choke. If we accept, as we must, that the duty of every sportsman is to avoid wounding the quarry whenever possible, then the reasoning has strength. Most shots are taken at relatively close ranges. With a tight choke the quarry is either missed cleanly or decisively killed (the fact that it is badly smashed is irrelevant) and the risk of long range wounding reduced.

Before leaving choke I would stress that choke and pattern are entirely different. Choke determines how densely the pellets are packed at a given range but it does not ensure an even distribution of pattern. Obviously a regular pattern is essential, for if you strip even such a relatively large quarry as a pheasant of its feathers and then disregard those parts where a hit will not have serious effect, at least in the short term, there is not a great deal left. Any 'holes' in the pattern will mean a miss or, much worse, pricking and for smaller quarries this risk is magnified. Now when we consider good pattern distribution we move into a grey area, for how many shooting men have actually plated their gun to judge its performance? Few, I suspect. And how many guns, nowadays, are actually carefully plated and regulated to achieve first-class patterning before being released from the factory? Obviously the better class of guns are, but in the highly competitive lower end of the market such a time consuming measure would be economically impossible.

I have already stressed how unscientific smooth bore shooting is and a further examination of pattern will underline this statement. When a gun is plated we see only the path along which each pellet travelled before impact, but there is no indication of timing. In practice, as a charge of shot travels through the air the distance between the first and the last pellet is known as 'stringing'. This can amount to several feet and, assuming the quarry is moving rapidly, this delay will mean a different striking pattern to that achieved on a stationary plate. The effect can be illustrated by imagining a shot fired at a rotating flat disc, the rotation representing the movement of the quarry. On a stationary disc the first and last pellet in the string might have struck within an inch of each other but on a rotating dish the time delay can create a considerable gap. Further consideration of this will show that the occasional lucky shot, when we kill the quarry with just one pellet in the head or heart, does not always come from a 'flier' on the edge of the pattern. It could have been a pellet well in the general pattern which arrived early or late, with the unfortunate creature avoiding the main charge.

Finally, before leaving patterns, we must remember that the pattern achieved by a particular boring varies according to the variety of cartridge used. If you are anxious to ensure a certain performance from your barrels then have them bored and plated with your normal make and load of cartridge.

For some pages past I have demonstrated the impossibility of having an ideal gun to answer our widely differing needs throughout a season, and the logical solution is to own two guns of differing specifications. Given sufficient money this is an attractive solution but it ignores one vital fact – *none of the various technical considerations I have listed even begin to compare with the importance of pointing the gun in the right direction*. Shortly I will discuss shot sizes and, here again, we can dwell on the pros and cons of different sizes but, as with chokes, pattern, weights, barrel arrangement – any technicality you care to name – marksmanship is everything and the rest almost nowhere. (One of the best shots I ever knew used his grandfather's gun with the choke almost shot out and whatever cartridges he could get hold of.) Now marksmanship, as we will discuss later, is an art and not a science and no artist can keep changing his tools. Unless two guns match, the theoretical technical advantages of changing from one to another for different forms of shooting are outweighed by one's reduced performance. This is, in practical terms, difficult to achieve, for few men can afford a pair of matched guns and those who can are hardly likely to take such an asset rough shooting. A compromise is possible, for an absolutely exact match is not vital – provided the fit is the same and the balance reasonably similar they will do. (Even this compromise clashes with the earlier dictum that the rough shooter's gun should be lighter than the driven game man's.)

There is certainly a strong case for the man who possesses a 'pedigree' gun, which will almost certainly be bored for driven game, obtaining a cheaper but similar gun for rough shooting and having this bored differently.

When I first began to think seriously about the technicalities of shooting I spent much time considering cartridges, and weighing the merits of different loads of powder and shot. I suffered from a young man's common fallacy that the more pellets I sent up the barrel the greater the chance of a kill. This gradually dispersed under the pressures of many a sore shoulder, the realisation that aim was paramount, and, most important, the assurance of a much respected gunsmith that constantly firing heavy loads was harmful to the gun. Thus encouraged I settled for a $1\frac{1}{16}$th oz. load and concentrated my worries on which shot size was best. Little thought was needed to show that there is no simple answer. Returning to my bog, with the close snipe and the distant mallard, many experienced shooting men would select number 7 or 8 and 3 or 4 respectively. This choice stems from the theory that at close ranges even very small shot penetrates and pattern density is more important and that at long ranges heavy shot is required for penetration. However, if you ask an advocate of this theory to justify it in precise ballistic terms he is rarely armed with relevant data. Nor can he often dispute a counter-argument that large size shot at close ranges kills equally well but leaves the quarry less badly smashed (fewer pellets). To which can be added the claim that, as pattern fails before penetration, long range shots need more smaller pellets rather than fewer large ones.

In practice there is little point in deciding on the best shot sizes for short, medium and long ranges when one has no idea at what range the next shot will be taken. Granted there are some specific occasions when one can forecast the immediate future with fair certainty – the driven pheasant man taking his stand at a drive famous for high pheasants knows it will be long range work, and the early September partridge shooter walking up roots knows they will rise close but these are the exceptions. For the great majority of the time one has no idea of the likely range of the next shot and attempting to vary the shot size for the expected task rarely gives any practical help. What it does do, greatly to the shooter's disadvantage, is to distract the mind from the all-important task of seizing the opportunity with single-minded concentration. Up comes the gun and part of the brain is troubled by matching the range to the shot size in the breech. However, I will concede there is a case for standardising on a larger size shot in the left, that is more heavily choked, barrel. I followed this for some years but it involves stocking with and carrying two shot sizes, and loading one barrel from one pocket and one from another. The system caused minor problems and irritations and I doubt I bagged any more through it.

There is no more an ideal shot size than there is an ideal choke and the best solution is to settle on one size, indeed one cartridge, and fire that and nothing else. As time passes one gains absolute confidence and confidence does far more to kill quarries than varying shot sizes. Which conclusive statement leaves only the question of which shot size to adopt as standard.

It is sensible to begin the enquiry by considering the objective. Our wish is not just to bag what we shoot at but to kill it cleanly – selecting heavy shot because a lucky pellet might break a wing or otherwise disable the quarry at long range is totally unacceptable to any proper sportsman.

How best then to kill cleanly with shotgun pellets? Pellets kill for either of two reasons, but usually through a combination of both. The first is shock, which occurs when the quarry is struck by a number of pellets none of which would necessarily be serious individually but which, in total, depress the animal's vital forces so severely as to cause death. The second cause of death is a pellet or pellets striking a vital organ, or organs, so severely that they cease to function. The former is the more humane as death is virtually instantaneous, whereas with damage death can be prolonged. Obviously the more pellets that strike the quarry the better both for the greater shock and the improved chance of one or more hitting a vital organ. Equally obviously there is no point in increasing the number of pellets by decreasing the pellet size to the point where they lack sufficient penetrative and shocking power.

From these facts we can derive a specification for the best shot size, namely that it must be sufficiently large to have adequate striking power at the maximum range at which we are likely to shoot. Anything larger than this optimum size will give extra striking power, which is not important, and decrease the number of hits, which is. (This statement underlines the risk of wounding by using large shot at extreme ranges.) To reach a decision we must first decide on maximum range, and this has to be a realistic maximum and not the occasional barrel stretcher at a distant crow. If I state that forty-five yards should be maximum range for normal shooting, many readers will think this too low, but most shooters over-estimate distance and the sixty yard kill turns out to be fifty and the fifty, forty-five. Forty-five yards, *accurately measured*, is a long way. Of course animals are killed at much longer ranges than this, but many more are wounded. It is not a question of whether we can kill at more than forty-five yards but whether we should try.

Let us, then, take forty-five yards as the maximum range. To enquire further, with accuracy, calls for facts which are not all available. Ballistically there is a pleatitude but, ideally, we need to know the striking energy necessary for a pellet to penetrate, for example, the skin of a rabbit or the breast feathering of a mallard, and still retain sufficient force to damage an organ. Eley's *Shooters' Diary*, gives what it calls a 'rough guide to the maximum requirements for a clean kill', and says small birds need two pellets of 0.5 ft lb, striking energy; medium birds three of 0.85 ft lb, and large birds four of 1.5 ft lb. I wrote to Eley to ask details of the research on which this data was based, but was told it had been repeated for many years and the source was lost in the past. Sir Ralph Payne-Gallwey carried out experiments, in the last century, by strapping newly-killed pheasants to the underside of kites, flying them at various heights, and firing at the carcases. However, for reasons too involved to detail here, I am reluctant to accept his conclusions. In the absence of anything better we must work on the Eley proposals.

At once all manner of questions arise; for example, is a cock pheasant a medium or large size bird? (It is certainly large to a partridge but small to a capercaillie.) If large, then at forty-five yards it needs striking with pellets whose energy at that distance has not fallen below 1.5 ft lb. If medium then 0.85 ft lb will do. Turning to the established facts we know that, from a standard game cartridge, and at forty-five yards, number 5 shot strikes with an energy of 1.61 ft lb, number 6, 1.20 ft lb, and number 7, 0.86 ft lb.

So, if we class a cock pheasant as a medium bird, then number 7 shot will do at maximum sensible range, but if a large bird, number 6 is slightly too small. The view I have taken over the years is that a pheasant is larger than average so number 7, at the longer ranges, is on the light side, but that number 6 is adequate. There is a case for number 5 but, as we concluded earlier that the more adequate, hits the better, then number 6 must win. Of course, not all shooting is done at pheasants but most of the quarries are sufficiently close to the pheasant, in size, weight, and protective covering, for it to be a realistic norm. Obviously for either lesser ranges or smaller quarries, smaller shot would be better, but we must arm in the expectation of meeting the larger quarries at the longer ranges.

The conclusion that number 6 is the best all-round shot size, will not come as a surprise to those readers who have used it for years, but I hope the logic by which I justify the advice will remove any lingering doubts that might arise after listening to someone advocating four's or eight's. However, I most certainly do not recommend number 6 for geese, where a heavier punch is essential. Quite how heavy I would not like to say, for I have not shot enough geese to feel able to pronounce with authority. Applying the reasoning we have just concluded I think the favoured B.B. is too heavy and it would be better to use number 1 shot and improve pattern density. This, however, must depend upon strict discipline over range which, in the wide open spaces of a marsh, and too often with a touch of goose fever, is not always evident. Although heavier shot is often recommended for hares, I disagree. They frequently present a going-away target and are easily wounded rather than killed cleanly. At the ranges at which it is reasonable to shoot them number 6 is adequate.

To a very large degree all I have written up to now is a justification of the norm in gun sizes, weights, chokes, and shots and the essential message has been that details matter far less than shooting straight. Now we move into an area both less precise in opinion and definition and fascinating in scope – the matter of the best weaponry for wildfowlers. A century ago the twelve bore was regarded by wildfowlers as a cripple-stopper for punt-gunners and all the authorities recommended large bores firing heavy charges. The largest shoulder gun was the four bore, and a double-barrel version would weigh a little over twenty pounds. A double eight bore was around fourteen pounds and a ten bore eleven to twelve pounds. Gradually, as the century grew to a close, a combination of increased technical knowledge and common sense turned opinion away from the heavier guns and the occasional author, Abel Chapman and Henry Sharp being front runners, began to recommend twelve bores for wildfowling. This trend continued into the twentieth century and by the thirties the major contest was between ten and twelve bores. Since then the availability in this country of heavy load cartridges for magnum twelve bores has meant the decline of the ten bore. Not only is the ten unable to fire a heavier charge than the magnum twelve, but it weighs more and ammunition is not easily obtained.

So for the wildfowler the practical choice lies between a medium weight, standard twelve bore and a magnum. Now I am aware that, not many pages back, I argued that the advantages of always using one familiar gun, or its twin, outweighed technical considerations, but there are exceptional circumstances in wildfowling. For a start the conditions are usually cold and the gunner will wear considerably more clothing than usual. This will not just warrant but actually require a shorter stock; possibly by as much as a quarter of an inch. Next the postures in which the wildfowler shoots will be totally different to those familiar on land. Occasionally he will be lying down; frequently kneeling; rarely standing and almost never able to move his feet. With these problems his shooting style will be so cramped that if technical changes in his weapon bring positive benefits then a gun which differs from his norm may be justified.

Some differences are not changes which would affect marksmanship. For example, it is better for a wildfowling gun to be a non-ejector. The simpler mechanism is less likely to be affected by mud and water and the ability to reload quickly is hardly ever required. More fundamentally, it is unwise to bring a gun of high value below the sea wall. The abrasive qualities of the mud will dull and scratch the stock and the salt will stain and rust the metal. A less valuable gun can be found without necessarily altering weight or balance, but another recommended feature, a pistol, or half-pistol grip, becomes significant. This feature is reputed to increase the holding ability of the right hand when wet, muddy or cold. It may, but personally I have never experienced any difficulty in holding the gun when, at last, wildfowl come into range.

These points, whilst fun for the enthusiast to conjure with, are really only detail. The crux of the matter is whether to use a standard twelve bore of familiar weight and balance, for reasons of marksmanship, or move to a magnum twelve bore for reasons of range. The answer is not simple, for if it was the wildfowling community would not, after a couple of centuries of debate, still be undecided. As we have seen from the almost universal adoption of the standard twelve bore the shooting community is capable of polarising on the most suitable gun and there must be more complicated factors at work below the high water-mark. There are, and the principal consideration is that far more targets occur for the wildfowler at extreme range than for the inland shooter. The land based shooter might enquire why all wildfowlers are not armed with magnums, but the ability to shoot further, effectively, exacts a price. To run through the ballistical considerations for a wildfowler's gun would be a lengthy task and bore non-wildfowlers. But on shot sizes, the relatively heavy feathering of wildfowl and generally, the longer ranges require an increase in shot size to number 4 or 5. Now the heaviest charge one can reasonably fire from a standard gun is $1\frac{1}{8}$ oz. and this weight of number 4 shot, through a full choke barrel, should kill at fifty yards. To fire a heavier charge, regularly and without damaging the gun, means changing to a magnum, but increasing the charge by $\frac{1}{8}$ oz. only adds two yards to the effective range. At $1\frac{1}{2}$ oz. the range rises to 57 yards, and with $1\frac{5}{8}$ oz. the heaviest magnum twelve bore cartridge made in this country, 59 yards. In other words an extra $\frac{1}{2}$ oz. of shot has added less than ten yards to the range and for this modest improvement one has to move from a familiar gun and hump extra weight. Even worse than carrying the heavier gun is the problem of swinging it with speed onto a close teal, or similar fast quarry, speeding past at dusk.

Convincing though this condemnation may be the counter-argument is strong. Nine yards may not be far but it does increase the range by nearly twenty per cent and, in the context of wildfowling, this modest extension is often critical. And even when the extra weight of shot is not necessary for range it delivers a heavier than normal blow against a very tough quarry. Also for geese a magnum is almost essential and it is obviously better to use a familiar wildfowling gun, rather than a strange weapon.

Personally, my mind is unresolved. I have an excellent twelve bore magnum, by Lincoln Jefferies, with a prominent foresight and raised rib for shooting in poor light, pistol grip, wildfowl engraved on the action, and three quarter choke in both barrels. It delights every wildfowler who handles it and has served me very well. But it *is* heavy and sometimes its weight causes me to miss chances. Conversely, I kill many duck with a standard twelve bore, but sometimes yearn for the extra range of the magnum. Hopefully wildfowlers will never reach a conclusion, for arguing the merits of magnum *v* standard twelve bores is all part of the fun.

It is not through oversight that I have failed to deal with the question of balance in guns. I cover it in the next chapter, on marksmanship, for whilst balance is achieved technically the result is important in determining how well the owner shoots.

As I wrote at the start of this chapter, I am concerned not with repeating technical data but looking at the practical aspects of guns. One question, which I find bothers sportsmen a great deal more than points of choke or shot loads, is the startling increase in the cost of guns. To give one simple example, a plain, middle quality English boxlock, by Webley and Scott, could be purchased twenty years ago for under £100. Today a boxlock by W. & C. Scott, the successors to Webley and Scott, costs over £2000. Even allowing for inflation this represents a staggering increase and, applying the only practical test, a man would have to work about three times longer to buy one now than twenty years ago.

It is interesting to look very briefly at recent history. At the turn of the century the English gun trade was extensive and active with some two hundred firms producing guns of all classes. Good workmen abounded, craftsmanship was high and wages low. Although the First World War brought great social changes, none of these led to fundamental changes in the structure of the gun trade and, apart from a flow of Belgium guns at the bottom of the market, English sportsmen shot with English guns. (My Norfolk uncle still shoots with a double-barrel, side by side, Belgium twelve bore he bought, new, for £5.) It is hardly necessary to detail the changes that began after the 1939–45 war. Rapidly increasing wages, coupled with decreasing hours, soon had their effect on such a labour intensive product as a gun. B.S.A., one of the most famous names in medium quality guns, ceased production. Greener's, fathered by W. W. Greener, the author of several classic books on guns, was absorbed by Webley and Scott. Slowly the ability of this country to build the middle and lower ranges of sporting guns was eroded, even though demand rose. Ironically it was the increased wages and leisure time enjoyed by so many which also created an enlarged market.

The Belgians were delighted and prospered until the fifties, when rising costs hit them and the French took over. Their's was only a brief victory for the Spanish were gaining strength and the French were soon pushed aside.

Perhaps the best illustration of the sad decline of the English trade is seen in the battle of the giants – Webley and Scott for England and A.Y.A. for Spain. The Webley 700 model had been produced virtually unchanged for many years. It offered a well made, side by side, boxlock ejector, guaranteed to give excellent service and probably outlast its owner. A quarter of a century ago there was no serious foreign competitor in its price range, and Webley's directors could have been forgiven for thinking the 700 would go on selling far into the future. This complacent scene was shattered by the arrival of the A.Y.A. no. 2, also a side by side, modelled on the design of the classical best English guns. The workmanship was, of course, inferior to our best, but it offered a sidelock ejector, with chopper lump barrels and other technical features superior to the Webley. Worse, it was offered for a few pounds less than the 700 and this price differential was maintained for some years – as the Webley rose so did the A.Y.A., but always remaining a little less. In the beginning British buyers were wary; stories of badly tempered metal and other shortcomings circulated. But the years passed, the A.Y.A. gave good service and gradually buyers made their choice on merit and not rumour. The relative sales figures are not at my command but certainly A.Y.A.'s sales went up and as they did the financial benefits of volume production helped to keep the sale price down. Soon the gap between the two guns widened, which, of course, created a vicious circle – as the 700's price increased so sales went down, which pushed the price up. By 1979 the Webley 700 was £1150 and the A.Y.A. no. 2 almost half. The end was inevitable, and the last of the English middle range manufacturers stopped producing shotguns. From two hundred gunmakers at the start of the century, the numbers had shrunk to ten, all concentrating on the top end of the market.

It was a sad tale of the decline and death of an industry, but no sooner had the corpse been buried when a new birth was recorded. In February, 1980, just days before writing this, I was invited to London to the press announcement of the formation of a new company to manufacture middle-grade guns. Harris and Sheldon, the parent company of Webley and Scott, had taken the bold decision to rehouse the leading craftsmen, and the machinery, of the old company in fresh premises and fund a new firm with £250,000. To emphasise the long traditions and background of the new venture they had resurrected the name of W. and C. Scott, Ltd, originally formed in 1834, and manufacturers of some excellent sporting guns before eventually combining with Webley's to form Webley and Scott. The declared policy of the new company is to manufacture traditional boxlocks to a very high standard, rather than sidelocks of lesser quality and, not surprisingly, the examples shown of the two new models bear a close family resemblance to the old Webley 701. This, the top end of the Webley range, was an excellent gun and, sold in the white and finished elsewhere, carried some grand names in its day. Whether W. and C. Scott, Ltd, succeeds in securing a place in a highly competitive market remains to be seen, but everyone with the interests of English gunmakers at heart will wish it well.

All of which has a bearing on a fascinating question of relevance to the sportsman wanting to buy a new gun. Does the difference in quality between a best Spanish and a best English gun justify the great price differential? To be specific, if I could purchase today, which I cannot for there is a long waiting list, a Holland and Holland 'Royal', it would cost me over £10,000. A no. 1 quality A.Y.A. has the same basic specification and looks very similar, yet costs not quite £2000. Is the difference really worth some £8000 or is one paying for a name plus the cost of maintaining expensive London premises?

To help one arrive at a conclusion I talked to a director of one of the leading London makers and to another from A.S.I., the importers of A.Y.A. guns into this country. Both were very helpful, very fair and both were in agreement to a surprising degree.

The position can be most constructively examined by accepting that a best English gun is, to all intents and purposes, perfect, and then considering how far short the A.Y.A. falls. A good analogy can be made with Rolls

Royce and standard motor-cars. Before the war the Rolls Royce was, virtually, perfect and the mass-production car a very long way short. In recent years there have been great advances in technology, design and materials and mass-produced cars have improved dramatically in all respects. But the Rolls, being virtually perfect at the start, has had much less opportunity to improve. The gap has been greatly reduced, and so it is with the guns we are considering.

How much reduced? Very much to my surprise, a man closely involved in English gun manufacture, and concerned to support their case, told me that a best Spanish gun was ninety to ninety-five per cent as good as a top English gun. Perhaps this is exaggerated, but certainly even the strongest advocates of English guns conceded that the differences were not startling and, by no stretch of imagination were the qualities in proportion to price.

Where then do the differences occur, do they effect the performance of the guns and are English guns worth five times more? Beginning by dispelling a popular illusion, there is no saving made by using cheaper metal. (Such a practice would be pointless, for the difference, per gun, between the very best gunmaking steel and medium quality material is only a few pounds.) However, the walnut blanks for the stock are another matter, for a really good blank can easily cost £400 and two top quality blanks to make a matched pair may be as much as £1500. But the gap in raw material prices does not end here for A.Y.A. use far larger quantities and therefore enjoy the benefits of bulk buying.

This leads to a critical factor – volume production. Every business operation has various fixed overheads – premises, insurance, advertising, office staff, etc., etc. and every businessman knows the list is endless, and the cost of these overheads has to be built into the selling price of the product. The more you make the smaller proportion of the selling price represents external expenses and the more is value for money in materials and workmanship. Inevitably a considerable proportion of a best English gun must represent low volume production and expensive overheads. (Expensive London premises must be well furnished, well maintained and staffed by a good calibre of employee.) Low production also prevents a manufacturer equipping his works with the most modern automatically controlled machinery; a statement which may surprise those readers who believed best English guns were entirely hand made. In fact, all gunmakers would prefer to shape both timber and metal to outside tolerances by automatic machine work, whenever possible, then hand finish, for the process by which surplus material is removed does nothing to alter the quality of the hand finishing. Of course, a London maker can send his work out for machining but the contractor will want an adequate profit and the overhead cost of transport, setting up the machinery for short runs, and other factors, will be high on such a low volume.

A.Y.A., on the other hand, claim to have some of the most advanced gunmaking machinery in the world. As an example, five stocks at a time are produced from the blanks on a profile cutting machine. Of course some will argue that no machine can emulate the work of a man but this is far too sweeping. There are some functions, engraving is an example, at which men excel but there are others where it makes not a jot of difference. A truly flat surface is no flatter whether cut by a machine in two minutes or filed by a man in an hour. This point questions the validity of the claim that a best English gun takes x hundred hours to make. No doubt it does, but is this essential craftsmanship or the lack of advanced machinery?

The barrels provide a good illustration of the relatively minor, but not insignificant, differences between the two classes. Both are produced from excellent steel and both are chopper lump forged. Both, I am sure, will be very well bored on good machinery, but it is unlikely they will be entirely concentric. In practice, the thickness of the walls of each tube will not be similar at any given point – they will not be perfect tubes. These minute variations will not effect either performance or safety, but on an English gun the small amounts of surplus metal will be removed, partly to achieve perfection and partly to make the top and bottom ribs fit better. Both here and abroad the finished guns will be plated, but whereas in Spain this is a check to ensure reasonable patterns, here careful regulating takes place.

Engraving is another example of where the money goes. My English informant claims an English engraver may spend as much as twice as long as his Spanish counterpart, and this was not denied by my Spanish advocate. However, an English gun will probably be engraved with a special design selected by the purchaser, whereas the Spanish will have a standard rose and scroll which, because the engraver knows it by heart, can be done far more quickly. The former will give the owner more pleasure, but it is questionable whether it makes the gun much more valuable.

To say there are many other factors would minimise the position – the truth is that every action concerned with building a gun can be done perfectly or rather less so, but there is no point in giving more specific instances for I have demonstrated principles and must now try to sum up.

Firstly, and remembering our comparison lies between a top A.Y.A. and a best English gun, any differences have no bearing on performance, at least in mechanical terms. England claims its guns will last longer – Spain denies this. Properly looked after both should see their owners out. Balance is a very contentious aspect for it owes so much to personal preference. It can, of course, be altered, but for reasons to appear in the next chapter, it is better for balance to be built in from the start rather than achieved by adding or subtracting weight later. On this point English guns must score, but some will rank the benefit very small. Certainly in terms of general appearance and technical performance the gap between the two is small and nowhere near the great price differential. Equally, for the man who merely seeks a well built, quality gun which will be both reliable and a pleasure to use, the A.Y.A. will serve him well. Whether he buys this or an English gun will make no difference to the quantity of game he bags.

Why, then, buy a best English gun? Because it is perfect. Because the best materials have been worked on, regardless of time and expense, to produce a gun as near perfect as man can make it. The difference between it and its Spanish competitor is small but it is there and best English guns are for perfectionists who want the very best and do not mind paying for it. Much of the enormous difference of £8000 is not immediately obvious, but has to be sought by close inspection. It is not so much one or two outstanding features, but that every visible or hidden part, large or small, will stand up to the closest scrutiny. Some of the value can be seen and touched, some lies in the special individual character acquired by guns which have seen little of machines and much of craftsmen. And some of the extra cost cannot be found in the gun at all, but has gone to fund the calibre of men and organisation necessary if a firm is to have the quality of premises and staff required to sell top guns to top people.

There are many people in this world who are willing to pay a high price for perfection, aware that the ultimate in craftsmanship can only be obtained by disregarding production costs. For this reason it is not really fair to compare the A.Y.A. with a top English gun for one is not comparing like with like. The one is built as a high quality shot gun, to be used for sporting purposes. The other is on a higher plane and can justify its existence, both as a supreme example of the gunmaker's art and an investment, even if never fired. Whether or not we individually own a top English gun, we should, nonetheless, be pleased that it is a field in which this country still leads the world.

Chapter 3
Marksmanship

When Gervase Markham wrote *Hunger's Prevention* in 1621, marksmanship was one of the less testing problems, for the method of ignition was so cumbersome and slow that the accepted practice was to stalk the quarries and shoot them when stationary. The sportsman, he wrote, must seek concealment in hedge, bank, tree or any shadow, and when,

> he is gotten within his Leuell and hathe the Winde fit and certaine, then hee shall make choyce of his marke, which (As before I said) would in no wise be a single Fowle, hauing more within your leuell, but rather the longest and largest Ranche or File of Fowle you can finde, for since one shoote is as much as you can get at one time and in one place, it is meete you put it to as greate vse and profit as you can possibly, which done you may instantly and speedily discharge.

In the first chapter I concluded that the practice of 'shooting flying' was established about the middle of the seventeenth century and, with this transition from stationary to moving targets, the sportsman began his unceasing quest for improved marksmanship. Our sporting forefathers were well aware of the importance of allowing the correct lead, as witness some apt lines from *Pteryplegia: or, the Art of Shooting Flying*, written by A. B. Markland in 1727. Advising against excessive lead, he wrote:

> For, too much space allow'd, the shot will fly
> All innocent, and pass too nimbly by.

And on too little lead:

> Too little space, the Partridge, swift as Wind,
> Will dart athwart, and bilk her death behind.

Although aware of the principle of lead the earlier writers lacked any scientific means of measurement and all underestimated. Even Hawker, in the early nineteenth century, thought a foot or two would suffice. It is not, however, necessary to be a mine of ballistical details to shoot well and there is no doubting the nineteenth century contained some very fine shots. Just how fine and how many is another matter and, in my view, the *average* shot of this century is probably just as good as the average of the nineteenth.

It is, of course, impossible to prove this, but logic supports the case. In virtually all spheres of physical activity performances have improved and if our standard of marksmanship has not improved there is no reason to think it has gone back. Additionally, technical changes have favoured the twentieth century sportsman.

Opponents of my view can quote substantial evidence of nineteenth century marksmanship. Consider Hawker on 14th September, 1812: 'With the exception of some random shots out of reach, and three snap shots at rabbits in high grass, the above first-barrel shot at the hare is the first miss I have made this season, making sixty shots in succession without missing, besides some birds killed and lost in the standing corn, etc.' And on 1st September, seven years later, he killed 45 partridges and a hare with 50 shots.

Such extracts prove nothing. Hawker would not have quoted them had they not been exceptional and he was an exceptional man. What we would dearly like to know is the kills to cartridges percentages of his butcher, baker and candlestick maker. 'Granted', will reply the proponents of the nineteenth century marksmen, 'but what about those outstanding shots who graced the formal pheasant shoots of the last half of the century – where are their twentieth century equals?' In reply I will defy all the lore of the history of shooting by questioning whether this select band were, in all the circumstances, outstanding shots. To qualify as 'outstanding' a man has, in my view, to be outstanding at all forms of the sport – not merely one form *in which he has quite exceptional practice.* Consider the facts. The social structure of nineteenth century England gave the wealthy or privileged sportsman prolific driven shooting throughout the season, and not on a spasmodic basis but six days a week. The large estates vied with one another to produce record bags and each individual Gun frequently enjoyed more shooting in a day than most modern sportsmen have in a season. A few statistics of personal bags will suffice. On 8th September 1876 the Maharajah Duleep Singh shot 780 partridges at Elvedon. In 1893, in Hungary, Lord de Grey shot 240 partridges *in one drive.* Lord Walsingham, shooting in Bluberhouses, Yorkshire, on 30th August 1888 killed 1070 grouse, and, again in one drive. Sir Fred. Milbank, at Wemmergill killed 190. Perhaps the shortest, but most telling statistic is that in the lifetime of the 2nd Marquess of Ripon, from 1867 to 1923, he shot 556,813 head.

Now it is possible, but very unlikely, that fate contrived to have born to some of the wealthiest houses of Britain the most gifted shots of the century. I prefer to see it differently – that men of good natural ability at sport were presented with a unique opportunity to enjoy unlimited practice at one form of shooting. It is no wonder they became highly proficient and many readers, presented with driven game in profusion for some years, would become equally skilful.

But enough of the past: we must think not of what others did but of what we should do. I will start with a theory which should offer comfort. Bodies being infinitely variable in their construction it follows that identical performance at physical things is impossible. Running is a good example, and the different combinations of heart, lungs, muscles and other components, allow outwardly similar men to perform to very different levels. Shooting is also physical but involves more complex machinery. The eyes have to note movement, speed and direction. Nerves have to pass information through the body and muscles have to react. That strange factor 'timing', must play its instinctive part in fractions of a second. These and other functions must operate in every shot fired and, returning to our analogy of runners, there is a limit to what our individual bodies can achieve. A runner can train until his body is at its highest peak in development and fitness but beyond this he cannot go. Equally every shooting man has a personal level which, by constant effort and practice, he can reach but cannot better. Depending upon the time available, and application, a man will come close to, or fall well short of his personal peak, but the message I am anxious to spell out is the futility of feeling frustrated and disappointed at failing to reach that which was never within one's grasp.

Put simply – everyone has a natural ability as a shot and it is impossible to improve beyond this. If you have shot for years, thought about your performance carefully, had experienced coaching and generally done all you can to reach your personal optimum, then there is no point in tarnishing your pleasure by fretting over your marksmanship.

(As an aside, it is worth remembering that when you shoot badly the only person who really cares is you. The other Guns are well content, for it makes their performance look better, and the host is probably reflecting that if he had a few more guests like you he could add another day at the end of the season!)

The next reassurance is to beware of the fallacy of believing there is a 'right' way to shoot. It is certainly true that most of the best shots follow certain basic principles, but many equally good shots have their personal idiosyncrasies. A couple of months ago I watched a most awkward shot win a highly competitive clay shoot. His stance was ungainly, his head sunk down and twisted and his elbows held too high. Any experienced shot would have dismissed him as a novice – except that he never missed a bird all day.

Over the years many fine shots, and fine coaches, which is not necessarily one and the same, have written at length on marksmanship. Their sincere purpose has been to advise others on how to hit what they aim at and to this end they have given very detailed instructions on every aspect. With very few exceptions indeed the details have been of how the writer shoots, and, because people vary so much in physical construction and temperament, such general advice cannot be correct for all people in all respects. The man who, by nature, is slow and careful simply cannot throw up his gun and fire in an instant, anymore than the tall, willowy and light man, who is greatly affected by recoil, can place his feet fairly close together and shoot from a strictly vertical position. This is not to dispute the essential principles of good shooting technique, but rather to stress that there is no need to follow in slavish detail the words of the masters. Sometimes a deviation from the norm stems from an original bad practice which has not been wholly eradicated, but again it may have crept in to suit a special peculiarity of the individual – perhaps without his realising either its existence or purpose. If a well proven coach picks on some idiosyncrasy of yours and explains precisely why it is bad, then it must go. But unless a good, convincing reason is offered have no part in an operation intended merely to tidy up your style.

A surprisingly large number of shooting men have never considered the various actions of body and gun involved in marksmanship and, while this knowledge is not essential for success, it does help in analysing failure. Whichever particular style of shooting you favour it makes no difference to the performance of the gun and the ballistical problems involved – the variations are simply individual methods for solving them. As a start let us look at what has to be done to hit a moving target.

The considerations can be based upon a bird flying at right angles to the sportsman at a range of 35 yards and at a speed of 40 m.p.h. It is unlikely that any readers will have misunderstood the advice of some writers to ignore lead and shoot at the target, but to dispel any possible illusions let it be clearly stated that it is absolutely essential to give lead, that is to say to shoot in front of a moving target. This lead is necessary to allow for the distance the target will move in the time elapsing between making the decision to fire and the arrival of the shot. However, this interval falls into two important areas, which can be distinguished as discharge time and flight time. Discharge time begins when the brain, content with the visual situation reported by the eyes, issues the order to fire. Time then runs while the instruction is passed to the finger; the trigger is pulled; the lock operates and the hammer falls on the cap; the cap explodes and ignites the powder; the powder burns, the gases produced generate great pressure, and the wad and shot burst open the crimping and travel up the barrel. At the moment the shot charge emerges from the barrel this complex sequence is over and the discharge time ends. The critical factor to remember about discharge time is that the shot-charge remains in the barrel – in other words, until the end of the sequence the aim of the gun can be varied.

With the flight time, however, the charge has passed beyond human control – rightly or wrongly the commitment has been made. The only factor which will vary the flight time is distance and if we know the speed of the shot it is a simple matter to calculate the time it will take to travel a given distance. Once the flight time is known it is equally easy to assess the distance the quarry will travel in this time and tables giving forward allowances make popular reading for off-form shots. Considering our 35 yard bird, crossing at 40 m.p.h., shows a lead of six feet eight inches is necessary to compensate for *flight time only*.

Now no matter how vehemently some readers may swear that they never give a lead of anything remotely as much as two yards, at any range, I remain quite unmoved. This statistic is not a matter of opinion but hard scientific fact and while some sportsmen may be convinced they lead by much less they simply cannot do so and still hit the target.

So far we have dealt with interesting facts but nothing more. What we now consider is vital, as it is the explanation for the classical advice of keeping the swing going and not 'poking'. (Many missed shots are due to the Gun cramping his swing, and many reasons, of which cold, tiredness, excessive clothing and lack of confidence are but a few, can cause this.) Whilst the flight time varies with distance, the variations, being mechanical only, are constant. Discharge time, however, is made up of both mechanical and human delays and there are differences of timing, not only between individuals but between the performances of the same individual at different times. With a man with a discharge time of 0.25 second the bird will have travelled nearly 15 feet before the shot leaves the barrel. To this must be added the flight time, giving a distance of an extra six to seven feet – in other words, without swinging, the gun would have to be aimed some seven yards ahead of the target; an impractical requirement. Even worse, if the man was just a tenth of a second slower than usual the bird would have travelled a further six feet, causing a clean miss.

All these complications are eliminated, however, by the vital fact that the shot charge does not leave the barrel until discharge time has ended. Provided that the gun is kept swinging with the bird until *the shot has left the barrel*, the length of the discharge time is unimportant for it is automatically eliminated. Put another way – with a swinging gun the only lead necessary is that required to cope with flight time. It is when we start to poke, that is slow or halt the swing before the charge has cleared the barrels, that the effects of discharge time are felt, and then we can miss by ridiculous margins.

There remains one further factor, but I think the practical effect is insignificant and I mention it just for interest. If you jumped off a roundabout travelling at 60 m.p.h. you would not only fall towards the ground but continue travelling at 60 m.p.h. Imagine yourself as the centre pivot of the roundabout and the gun barrel as a spoke radiating outwards. When the gun is being both swung and fired does not the sideways movement of the barrel impart a sideways movement to the shot charge? As I say, I think the practical effect is negligible but some mathematically minded reader might try the calculation.

By killing the last bird in the covey the Gun can allow the natural swing of the barrels to catch up with his next target.

The problem of marksmanship has therefore resolved itself into a very simple matter – provided the swing is maintained, the gun, at the moment of firing, must be aimed sufficiently in front of the target to compensate for flight time. It is just a question of how, and many hundreds of thousands of words have been published, and avidly read, setting out the answer. As all authors on the subject of marksmanship are concerned with one simple act, lasting only a second or so, it is hardly surprising that most are repetitive and anyone wanting to study the views of the experts can confine himself to Churchill's *Game Shooting*, Stanbury and Carlisle's *Shotgun Marksmanship*, and Ruffer's *The Art of Good Shooting*. If, as we are often told, there is a right and a wrong way to shoot then the experts would all agree, so, some years ago, I compared Churchill and Stanbury. To my delight they were at variance on many points. Stanbury recommended the left hand to be so positioned that the left arm is almost straight. Churchill was more concerned with balance, suggesting the left hand should be so placed that the gun felt evenly balanced between the two hands. Having selected the left hand position, Churchill was content for the barrels just to lie in the palm, but Stanbury stated categorically that no weight should be taken by the palm. He required the first finger to lie under the barrels, pointing at the target, and for the bulk of the weight to be taken by the remaining three fingers and thumb. Stanbury warned against allowing the thumb to be above the level of the barrel in case it distracted the eye, but Churchill actually recommended this as a means of cutting out disturbance of aim from left eye vision.

Down below, both were content for the feet to be fairly close, a gap of eight inches or so, and not parallel but pointing slightly outwards. Here harmony ended, with Churchill standing much squarer to the target. A line taken through the heels of Stanbury would point at the target, but with Churchill would be at almost ninety degrees to it. Balance was another area of major difference, with Stanbury emphatic that the weight must be on the left foot for every type of shot, with the right heel clear of the ground. Churchill recommended balancing the weight evenly on both feet, transferring the bulk of the weight to the left foot when swinging to the left and vice versa to the right.

There are other differences between Churchill and Stanbury; between both of them and John Ruffer; and indeed, between all the experts. The pleasure I expressed at the start of this comparison was because the wide range of differences proves it is unnecessary to copy the authors in slavish detail. In many of their recommendations they are, as I said earlier, merely describing how they personally shoot rather than setting out essential rules to success. This is not to say, however, that there is no message to learn from these unquestioned experts – there is, and it is critical. The essence of good marksmanship is gun mounting – done properly you are ninety per cent of the way to a kill. Done badly, a miss is probable.

The vital part played by gun mounting in marksmanship will not come as a surprise to experienced shooting men, for we know that when we mount the gun smoothly and deliberately, and pull the trigger as the butt beds into the shoulder, a clean kill follows. The novice cannot understand this, for if it is essential to mount the gun properly then why not, he reasons, mount it as soon as a target appears in sight and then concentrate on aiming. Nor is this unsound thinking, for in the old days, before the invention of percussion ignition, all men shot this way. They had to, for the delay and uncertainty of ignition made it impractical to bed the butt an instant before firing. Many still do use this method, and often with much greater success than the experts' views would suggest, for it has the merit of simplicity – mount the gun fully, swing the barrels with the target, keeping the lead experience suggests is necessary, squeeze the trigger and keep on swinging. It is not the right way to use a shotgun, being laboured and an unsuitable style for shots that must be taken rapidly. No-one shooting in this fashion will ever become an outstanding shot, but it is wrong to condemn it utterly for there are some men who through age, physical problems of eyesight or other handicap, or just a slow, deliberate character, cannot adopt the recommended technique. Moreover it has the advantage that when off-form the results are not so disastrous as with the more advanced styles!

If a committee of competent men, renowned for being both clever and practical but totally inexperienced in shooting, were formed to advise on marksmanship, they would almost certainly recommend mounting the gun fully, well before the shot was made. All logic cries out for this approach, but you and I know that it does not work as well as the 'instantaneous' method of firing as the butt beds. Why? The answer is a combination of fluidity of movement and time. It is one thing to write at leisure of the various processes of making a shot: to detail all the different aspects of balance and swinging from the hips; picking up the target early, considering safety factors, easing off the safety catch, and so on. Out there, with feet ensnared in sugar beet, mud or heather, sun in your eyes or rain on your glasses, no warning at all and a split second before the target is out of sight – then there is no time to act deliberately and we go back several pages to that critical question of lead. We *must* give the right lead and we must give it instinctively – attempting to calculate the lead and apply it laboriously does not give the consistency of results obtained by letting the eyes, brain and body take over. Churchill was forceful on the subject: 'dismiss all ideas of

To avoid being dazzled the Gun is allowing the pheasant to fly out of the low sun before commencing the shot.

calculated allowance – train the eye and hand to take charge of these matters and learn their job without brain inteference.' (How the eye would pass its message to the hand without brain interference is a detail we will not pursue.) Ruffer, a couple of decades later, echoed the theme, 'When the gun comes into the shoulder and cheek, pull the trigger for better or for worse! You will hit the bird.'

To achieve the right mental approach to shooting it is essential not to think of aiming in the sense of firing a rifle. Although this is the obvious comparison a far better example is catching a cricket ball or striking a tennis ball with a racket. The essence of the problem is instinctively timing a moving object – feeding information on direction and speed to the computer of the brain and getting back instructions to muscles and limbs. The analogy can be taken a stage further for as the quality of a tennis stroke is determined by the preliminary action of a good backswing so is a shot conditioned by the preliminary of good gun mounting.

How best, then, to mount a gun? There is no disagreement between good shots of the need to lock the muzzles onto the target and keep them there throughout the whole process. There is less accord over where the butt should be until raised into the shoulder. Stanbury says, 'the stock is lying along the low forearm, with the butt by your elbow.' Ruffer recommends, '. . . about the level of your chest.' All this proves is that one man likes the stock higher than the other. The only point to watch is that the higher the butt has to be raised to the shoulder the more the muzzles are likely to dip.

So, the target appears, the muzzles are locked on, the body pivots and, with a sweet fluidity of timing, the butt rises smoothly but firmly to the shoulder, beds home as the trigger is pulled and the swing continues. So simple, so straightforward and so difficult to perform really well. If I had to make two vital rules they would be to keep the muzzles on the target and to economise on movement. I have two good friends who both play golf, one badly the other well. The first winds up his swing to an exaggerated degree; the second keeps it short and simple. Logically the less the gun moves in the process of mounting the better. Personally I move the gun almost into the fully mounted position as I 'track' the target with the barrels and the degree of movement in the final act of bedding the butt is small. I do not, however, say this is correct, merely that it suits me. A man will not play his best cricket, tennis, golf, or shoot to his highest potential if he is left uncoached, nor must he be made to conform to a strict, universal pattern. The basics must be right and then individuality can be given reign.

Although Churchill and Ruffer declare boldly that one could forget forward allowance and let the automatic overthrow of the gun look after this, my own experience is to the contrary. Certainly at close targets this applies, but for the average shot I need to apply conscious lead. Here again I would be cautious about urging a personal opinion except that most writers put the same view in one way or another. Stanbury says, 'you must give some forward allowance at long range and you must do it consciously.' A recent synopsis of the top shooting coaches in the country reported Paul Bentley as teaching, 'coming from behind and through the target', Rex Gage an 'accelerating swing', Clarrie Wilson, 'mount on the target and pull out in front', Brian Stevens, 'to it and through it', and Michael Rose, my own shooting doctor, 'behind the target, pulling out in front as far as required.'

On balance I think the man who can genuinely forget about lead is the exception; the majority of us need to apply conscious lead. Where I do accept the Churchill/Ruffer doctrine is as regards the undesirability and impossibility of attempting to calculate and apply lead in X or Y feet. Here we come back to the technique of coming through the target, bedding the butt and firing, all at the same instant. There is something in this combination of actions which makes it easier for brain and muscle to give the overthrow necessary for the correct lead than the more laborious technique of mounting first and then swinging through. 'Overthrow' is a good word to describe this method of applying lead. In fact on a close, fast target I find I throw the gun with such vigour the barrels literally follow through like the head of a tennis racket.

I do not pretend the views I have propounded have set out anything new on the subject of marksmanship, nor do I believe there is anything new to be said. What I have tried to do is to strip away the unnecessary detail, the pursuit of which will only detract from the purpose, and leave the vital main principles. Correct mounting is vital for it automatically ensures the other essentials of giving lead and maintaining the swing.

Occasionally one sees shots, more frequently at clay pigeon shoots, who adopt exaggerated, even grotesque, positions. Bodies are crouched, heads thrust forward, fanciful movements are made with the gun and other posturings performed. Sometimes these are affected, sometimes they have developed unbeknown to the individual. Always they are ugly. Any physical act performed really well carries an aesthetic beauty – it is neat and clean with economy of movement. Merely to watch brings pleasure for the whole act combines simplicity with effectiveness and functional honesty. So it is with shooting. A good shot does not merely hit the target – he does so with grace and makes it look easy.

And, of course, when one is shooting well it is easy. On my good days, and no doubt yours as well, I waste no time over theories or self-doubt. The targets appear, I expect to kill them cleanly and I do. And one of the main reasons why I do is because I expect to. Confidence plays a very great part in marksmanship because the confident Gun hurls his barrels through the target with gay abandon, thereby maintaining his swing. Conversely the man filled with self-doubt is ill at ease, restrained and stiff. This leads to poking, missing, a further loss of confidence and so the vicious circle tightens. (It is interesting to note the difference in attitude between good and bad shots when they perform badly. Bad shots simply miss, but good shots have reasons ranging from defective trigger pulls, low sun, a dog playing up, being late to bed and having a touch of liver.) As few shooting men fire a gun through the summer months the start of every season sees some severe cases of lost confidence needing a wash and brush up. A visit to a shooting school is usually an adequate cure, and is particularly worthwhile if the first day out is to be a major shoot rather than a potter. For many men lack of confidence stems not from worrying about whether they will fail to hit the target, but rather that they will be seen to fail by other men. As evidence, consider a rough shooting excursion on your own with a dog or two. Do you lack confidence over your marksmanship? Almost certainly the thought never crosses your mind and you shoot all the better for it. As further proof, most men shoot better on familiar ground, among familiar faces, rather than among strangers. I am not naturally shy but, at a strange shoot, I much prefer to make my first shots out of the limelight.

This leads to the thought that no cricketer would go into bat, or tennis player begin a match, without some preliminary practice. It is taken for granted that the body needs some preliminary strokes to warm up before it can perform to its best standard. But we cramp ourselves into a landrover, walk stiffly to a peg, stand still getting cold, and then expect to swing and shoot fluently. How pleasant it would be to find a host who started the day by projecting some easily paced clay pigeons from his attic window to allow his Guns to bolster their confidence!

One reassuring thought I can offer the indifferent performer is that the pressure is greater on those with high reputations. Such men are watched by all and any fall from their normal level is noted and remarked. In an effort to put matters into perspective, I once observed, in an article, that the shot you were about to make at the approaching high pheasant was only being watched by eight other Guns, three wives, a picker-up and the chap who drives the game cart. Yet, a few hundred miles away, a man was about to attempt to putt a golf ball into a small hole and was being watched by nine million on television. (Although the logic of the argument is inescapable, I have a suspicion I would rather fail before nine million strangers than a few close friends.)

There is no formula for confidence other than the solid foundation we build over the years. If you know that, year in year out, you shoot reasonably well, then it becomes easier to accept the occasional off day philosophically and this, in turn, wards off the tenseness which can be disastrous. One interesting aspect, although it may be personal, is that there is no logic to performance. I have gone out feeling fit, keen and confident and shot badly and, on other days, suffered from colds, been oppressed by business problems, dull-witted from a late night, or a variety of other drawbacks, and shot to my best standard.

My anxiety to ignore the minor details of marksmanship in order to place emphasis on gun mounting does not mean they are of no consequence. The importance of gun fitting is an aspect on which opinions vary from the man who says, or more usually writes, that a correctly fitting gun is essential, to the man who writes, or more usually says, that the importance of gun fitting is grossly exaggerated. In fact the argument is not over whether it is best to have a gun which fits the individual, but the degree to which this aim should be pursued. Many argue, somewhat convincingly, that Americans hardly ever have their guns fitted yet some of them shoot extremely well. So they do, but logic suggests they do so in spite of fitting faults and have adapted themselves to the gun rather than vice versa. The result of a good shot contorting himself to his gun can be studied at most clay shoots. I wrote earlier that a good shot makes it look easy and one of the reasons is the absence of unnecessary movement. With a well fitting gun, as the butt settles into the shoulder, not the arm, the stock is touching the cheek and the right eye, (or left as may be), is looking directly along the rib *without the head having moved a fraction from its normal position.* To achieve this, cast-off, bend and length of stock will be correct and the grip will be the right diameter for the user's hand. Additionally the triggers will be nicely positioned for the forefinger and the trigger guard will be clear of the second finger. Now if any, or all, of these points fall short of the ideal the owner will compensate but the important point is that the action of gun mounting – that so vital gun mounting – is now further complicated by having to remember to duck the head a little or move it to right or left. In a nutshell, the better a gun fits the easier it is to mount it correctly.

Beware, however, of changing the fit of a gun with which you shoot well. Indeed, beware of changing a gun at all. Many years ago I had an elderly Army and Navy with 28 inch barrels. Lured by the very logical arguments in favour of shorter barrels I changed to a new 26 inch gun. My shooting went to pieces and recovered only when the 26 inch was exchanged for a 28 inch. Later, with the benefit of experience, I concluded the trouble was not two inches off the barrels but a psychological loss of confidence. Not long ago I decided to retire my driven game gun in favour of another of superior specification. My friendly experts recommended slight variations to cast-off and bend, but particularly stressed the need to have the new stock a quarter of an inch longer than the old. Yes, they conceded, I could shoot reasonably well with it but it was too short. So I did as I was told and the results were awful. At this moment the new gun is locked away in the safe awaiting an investigation when the season is over. It may be the longer stock, or balance, or some other factor as yet unconsidered. Whatever it is the fact is underlined that, for no obvious reason, one gun suits a man and another, apparently similar, does not. However great the appeal of something new there is danger in leaving a well tried and proven gun.

Balance is another aspect on which men are not in general agreement and, for reasons to be explained, some men may find a well balanced gun is not necessarily the best for their marksmanship. Balance is not some magic quality which can only be instilled into a gun by craftsmen of skill bordering on artistry. It is a physical feature which can be incorporated in a gun by careful design and controlled manufacture. The fact that all guns are not well balanced is partly because opinions vary between individuals as to what good balance is, and partly because achieving a specific balance calls for greater expenditure than is possible in the cheaper guns. So far as opinions are concerned it is common to see several men inspect a gun and individually declare they like or do not like the balance. Given such personal views, and as there is no such thing as 'correct' balance, the manufacturers of mass-produced guns can hardly be blamed for compromising. Costs affect balance in several ways. Taking extreme ends, and beginning with the barrels, it is cheaper to manufacture safe barrels, which will pass proof, by leaving the barrel walls thick. This leaves weight in the wrong place for good balance, but removing it is expensive. At the other end, the stock, the density of the wood varies. In a top grade gun the adjustments for balance are made individually, but in lesser guns all stocks are bored with a standard hole and weight added.

The balance of a gun is not determined solely by resting the action on a finger and moving it to and fro, finally announcing it is rather heavy in the barrels, or vice versa. This is merely the point of static balance, which is to say the point about which the gun balances when stationary. But guns, in use, are never stationary. We have to move them and, when taking snap shots, move them fast. It is not just the static balance but the moment of inertia which, together, determine the balance. Consider the gun as a pole, of the same length but weighing half a pound. Now attach a three pound weight to one end and a similar weight to the other, thus giving a total weight roughly equal to a twelve bore. Hold it with both hands, a few inches apart, in the middle. Now try to point it, quickly and accurately, in various directions and at various angles. It will be difficult and clumsy because the weight is at the ends and a considerable force is required to move it and, once pointed and aimed, stop it. Positioning the weights at the ends, far away from the hands which exert the power, has created a high moment of inertia. Now reposition the two weights in the middle, between the two hands, and the ease with which the pole can be moved and pointed is transformed. It now has a low moment of inertia. The moment of inertia, low or high, is least when measured about the point of static balance so it is important that this falls halfway between the two hands. In this way the point around which we are trying to turn the gun is also the point around which it naturally wishes to turn. (This may explain individual preferences in balance. The position of the right hand is fixed, but we all have personal preferences for the left, some of them extreme. As the ideal point of static balance is midway between the two hands variations in balance will suit different people.)

So, the well balanced gun will have as much weight as possible concentrated between the hands and the point of static balance midway between them, which usually means no more than four and a half inches forward of the front trigger. This explains why the 25 inch and 26 inch barrelled guns are such fast handlers for not only has the metal come off the extreme end of the barrels, where its moment of inertia is highest, but a similar reduction in weight is possible from the end of the stock. Beware, however, of the caution I uttered earlier. Light, well-balanced guns are not only easier to start moving but easier to stop. One of the advantages of the heavy old-fashioned, wildfowling pieces was that it was well nigh impossible to stop the swing quickly and, 'poking' was not a problem. For men given to this sin there is much to be said for a barrel-heavy gun.

Moving from the balance of guns to that of Guns raises once more the controversy between the experts. Stanbury, the advocate of always keeping the weight on the left foot, argued that the act of transferring the weight to the right foot, when swinging to the right, can easily result in the gun being canted over sideways, especially on a high shot. Personally, I am strongly in favour of keeping the weight on the front foot. I find so doing makes for a smoother and faster pivot of the body to left or right and helps in absorbing recoil. However, many, possibly the majority, distribute the weight equally over both feet and what matters is not how the body is balanced but that it *is* balanced. When we watch one of our companions shoot our eyes are normally fixed on the target. Try, instead, watching the man and observe how the good shots are always neatly balanced and the less good are not. Balance is an aspect coming under the heading of preparation, of which more in later chapters.

Balance and footwork are inter-related, if only because a change of foot position can disturb the balance and it is rarely that a shot can be taken without an adjustment to the position of one's feet. An integral part of the shot is assessing the course of the target, deciding just where the shot will be fired and positioning the feet so they are correct for this angle. It is the need to change the feet positions quickly and accurately which makes it desirable to have them relatively close. And it is because close feet give a narrower and therefore less stable base to resist recoil that I prefer to keep my weight on the front foot.

Some writers advocate actually pushing the barrels away from the body with the left hand to absorb recoil. To avoid the stock leaving the shoulder one is required to pull rather harder with the right than one pushes with the left. In fact one writer suggested an infallible way of always firing as the butt bedded into the shoulder was to allow the right hand to slip slightly along the grip and thereby pull the trigger. For me this is all too complicated – there is enough to do without playing at pushing and pulling with alternate hands. If the recoil bothers you – and it may as the years pass – the solution is a lighter cartridge.

Most of the readers of this book will be settled into their own particular style of shooting and unless you have good reason to think you have a bad fault I would urge you to hesitate before trying to change. Once well grooved a man can go on shooting to his normal standard very satisfactorily but any attempt to leave the groove can disrupt the performance and not necessarily bring long-term benefits.

One misleading fallacy on shooting driven pheasants stems from the oft-repeated advice that one should 'hit them under the chin'. Further confirmation that this is both right and possible is sometimes heard from those who have watched an outstanding shot in action and report, 'you could see the heads snap back'. In practice it is impossible to hit pheasants in the head consistently without also peppering the body and wings. Just to hit the head would necessitate firing the bulk of the charge in front of the bird and catching the head with the fringe of the pattern – a chancy business which would produce many clean misses. Centring the head in the pattern would mean, on the normal assumption of a 30 inch effective spread at the working range, a dense pellet pattern for a 15 inch radius, and 15 inches would include the body and wings. What the advice is intended to convey is the need to shoot at the front of the pheasant, that is the head, rather than be misled by the long tail into aiming at the middle when a slight error would mean a miss behind or pricking the bird. 'How then', query the doubters, 'do you explain the frequency with which some good shots snap back the heads?'. With ease – the body is too heavy to be displaced, the legs are merely thrust against the body and the wings only react when a bone is broken. The head, however, is both light and well extended and just one pellet will cause it to snap back spectacularly. (In passing, I have several times stood on the same level as pheasants in flight and watched the effect as they were shot by Guns in a valley below. The force of the charge actually lifts the bird vertically, although not to a degree which can be observed from underneath.)

At the end of these observations on marksmanship I will draw attention to the considerable extent to which what I call the 'effectiveness factor' varies between men out of proportion to their relative skills as marksmen. We all know the fairly modest shot who somehow makes a much larger contribution to the bag than might be expected and his counterpart who shoots very well but at the end of the drive has surprisingly little to carry. The explanation lies in the ability of the one, and the failure of the other, to make the most of their chances. The one has always worked out in advance the likely flight path of birds as the drive progresses. His hands are never cold and rarely wet. He does not trip over stones, clods, turnips or other obstacles, having removed them earlier. Many other small details have received his attention, including putting cartridges in the gun and looking unwaveringly at the likely arrival point of the targets. In short he loses no chances through neglecting detail. The other does. All this I will deal with later, but the essential point is that the ability to break clays at a shooting school, on a warm day in August and knowing when and where they are coming from, does not guarantee the same competence when a walking Gun in a freezing wind with January cocks breaking in all directions.

To conclude, it is as well to get the question of marksmanship into perspective – being a good shot is very satisfying but it does not automatically make one a better sportsman. The stronger contender for this honour is the Gun who, at the conclusion of the last drive, walks his dog half a mile to look for someone else's lost pheasant.

Chapter 4
Deeper shades of safety

I will not offend you by running through the oft repeated rules of gun safety for, as an experienced Gun, you will know them by heart. In fact the rules can be condensed into one – never point a gun, loaded or unloaded, at anything you do not wish to kill. If everyone observed this simple requirement there would be no shooting accidents. Regrettably they do not, which is why I deem it necessary to include this chapter. Very few other authors agree with me for, on checking my library before starting to write, I find that with few exceptions they divide into those writing for novices, who invariably deal with elementary safety, and those writing for the more advanced sportsmen who mention it very briefly or not at all.

The rules of gun safety are merely sheer commonsense. Anybody who is not actually stupid, which distinction still appears to leave a significant minority wandering around with guns, can learn the principles of gun safety in minutes. It is not, as we are sometimes led to believe, necessary to experience years of training, starting as a bright-eyed boy under the care of the keeper. (Partly this is because safety is so simple, but also because many keepers are far from safe themselves. The suggestion that I can take young Tom shooting without reservation because he has 'Been taught by the keeper', does nothing to calm my fears!)

No – it is not learning the rules of safety but self discipline which is the problem, and the wide variations in human character and temperament don't help here. One particular menace is keenness – not the ordinary keenness of youth to smite a small ball with a bat or a larger one with a boot, but the burning enthusiasm that grips a youngster when he spies his chance of a first pheasant, grouse, or even humble rabbit. At such a critical moment in a young man's life safety will not rank high and we experienced shots should keep a close watch and halt a potentially dangerous situation before it develops.

Unfortunately we cannot halt our contemporaries so easily for, irrespective of how many years they have been shooting, there are some who are inherently unsafe. The reasons vary, but in some cases it is difficult to judge whether carelessness is due to stupidity or absent-mindedness. Certainly when a man who has shot for several decades stands at his peg with his gun in the crook of his arm, pointing directly at his neighbour, it must be one or the other. Such cases have, however, the advantage that they can be seen to be unsafe and action can be taken – or rather it should be; a point to be touched on shortly. The more dangerous man is the experienced shot who is normally safe but given to lapses, for here one has no advance warning. In these cases accidents do not occur through slow and deliberate breaches of the code, like climbing a fence with a loaded gun, but split-second infringements. A partridge shot at head-height with a stop on the other side of the hedge; the classic dipping woodcock in a wood; the behind shot at ground game on a flint covered field with a picker-up too close. The Gun was well aware that such shots should not be taken but on the spur of the moment, he took the chance and pulled the trigger. Why? There can be many reasons – he may have been shooting badly and be desperately anxious to recover form; or had a row with his wife and not care much for humanity at the moment; or have business worries and be tending to drink overmuch; or any one of a hundred reasons. Perhaps one of the most important is temperament, for some men are gamblers and showmen by nature and are more easily tempted to take chances; this may be why some of our Continental visitors, particularly from the Mediterranean area, have a bad reputation.

The problems of safety concern many shooting people, as witness the fact that when I contribute an article to *The Field* on the subject the correspondence pages quickly blossom with a crop of letters. Many add to the debate but some suggest, albeit politely, that if I confined my shooting companions to those who had been properly brought up the problem would not exist. It is, I fear, not only an impractical answer but an illusion. It is impractical because few, very few, people are in a position to choose their shooting companions. Syndicate managers have many problems and cannot always be as selective over the Guns as they would wish. Additionally, shooting men who, like me, do not have their own ground, are only too grateful for invitations – we are in no position to desire to give our approval to the other guests. It is an illusion because unsafe shots can be found at all levels, even among those 'properly brought up', and there is ample evidence for this statement to be found in the literature of the sport. The popular conception of safety discipline in the higher social levels would have us think otherwise, and tales abound of how Lord X or General Y sent some unfortunate Gun home for an infringement. No doubt they did but the gulf between the sinner and the sentencer was large. Furthermore there were unlikely to be repercussions and probably Lord X disliked the fellow anyway and General Y thought he had designs on his daughter. What would be far more indicative of the proper and universal application of safety discipline would be to find accounts of Mr Smith sending home Lord X and Mr Brown dispatching General Y. There are none. Mr Smith and Mr Brown do not. They fume silently, complain to their wives and put up with it. There are many accounts of beaters, keepers, and even other Guns being shot but, provided the culprit was important enough, no retaliatory action. Try it yourself. Complain to your host that the Gun on your right, who happens to be his father-in-law, has just swung through the line. Or that the Gun on your left, the bank manager who has just agreed an overdraft of £150,000 to your host, is firing forward and low when the beaters are close.

This point made, however, it is true that safety practices are best where the background of the individual and more important his parents, involved a variety of disciplines and responsibilities. It is no coincidence that the nearest I have come to being shot was on a large formal shoot when, on an end of season cock day it was decided the beaters should also shoot; and a hare drive in Cambridgeshire attended by all the estate workers.

What then can, and should, we experienced shooting men do about safety? Two things – the first being positive and the second negative or defensive. We should, in the first instance, take the initiative far more frequently in complaining about unsafe gun handling. We have all had the experience of seeing a fellow Gun perform some unsafe action and yet how often do we go to him and remonstrate? Very rarely. He has not harmed anyone and, hopefully, he will not do it again. To tackle him will cause ill-feeling, embarrassment and probably cast a cloud on your day, his and perhaps the rest of the Guns. He will probably deny the offence, get cross and your host will not thank you. How much easier it is to say nothing. I am better now than I was, probably because as I grow older I am more willing to do what I believe to be right even at the expense of personal popularity. Also, I have learnt how to register my protest without creating offence. No doubt, I suggest, he has 'lost sight of my position because he was facing the sun', or some similar route of honourable escape can be offered. It is always readily taken, but the point has been made and is rarely missed.

It may be embarrassing to act, but I believe experienced Guns are under a double moral obligation to do so, doubly so because they owe it to the good name of the sport to do all they can to avoid accidents and to the man, or woman, who might be shot in the future if they do not.

Finally comes the difficult point of whether, if a man is behaving dangerously, you should complain to him or your host – always provided he is not the host! On the one hand the host is, in the final reckoning, responsible for all that goes on and, on the other, one wishes to shield him from embarrassment. (Merely drawing his attention to the bad behaviour might be construed as an implied criticism for placing you and his other guests in jeopardy.) My own view is that if the man is endangering you alone then it is both right and best to speak to him direct. However, if the threat is to others then, while I would not rule out the right of direct approach, perhaps the better course is to speak to the host. (Some readers may feel any complaint in these circumstances should come from the endangered parties and a mere observer should remain silent. I disagree – my whole point is that experienced Guns should take the initiative over safety.)

This is the positive side of gun safety; I wrote also of a negative or defensive side. This consists of a slightly novel approach in that almost all advice on safety is concerned with telling the reader how not to shoot others – I will offer some thoughts, on how to avoid others shooting you. Reduced to simple terms the Guns with whom one shoots can be divided into those you know and those you do not. In an ideal world the Guns you know, and shoot with regularly, would all be safe, but it is a lucky man who has complete confidence over the safety of all his sporting companions. Still talking of ideal situations, one should just not shoot with suspect companions, but shooting is not so easily found as to make this practical. (I admire a Hampshire friend who was invited to a shoot to find not just one but several of the Guns regularly firing too low and close. Many men would have endured it for just one day, but he found his host, spelt out the facts firmly yet politely, and left. In so doing he not only removed himself from danger but, hopefully, caused the culprits to think.)

Of course, it is much easier to escape from dangerous sportsmen of one day's duration than regular companions. However, whatever the circumstances I am in no doubt that the problem *must* be tackled rather than endured. Surprisingly the minor sinner is often more dangerous than the man guilty of major crimes. The latter strikes such fear into one and all that there is little problem in gathering overall support for either a dire warning or his complete removal. It is the man who only infringes slightly who is endured until the one fateful day. I can only repeat and emphasise that, from long personal experience, I know most shooting men will grumble among themselves about careless safety discipline but will rarely protest unless the behaviour is blatant – it is a formula for disaster.

Asking a culprit to cease from his particular sin is one safety step: there also exists the effective measure of keeping a wary eye on both those Guns you know to be suspect and those you do not know but have reservations over. One example, to be covered in detail shortly, is the matter of Guns mixing with closed guns on their arms. Even when I know my man I dislike this, but with suspects I keep well clear of the barrels. Many other opportunities arise for acts of safety initiative. When shooting driven game with a doubtful man to one side or other and with a hedge or other cover between us, I always walk over before the drive begins on the pretext of checking that he is in his final position as I 'want to be quite sure where he is.' I then tell him precisely where I am! Not infrequently a slight adjustment in position will place a thick tree in between and bring peace of mind. There is no point in listing a variety of possible precautions, for the general point is made. However, whatever else you forget when you have a suspect Gun beside you, if ground game or a low bird crosses between you, ignore the game and watch him. If he appears to be swinging through turn your back and crouch at once.

There will, perhaps, be some readers who will be incredulous that such advice is necessary, believing that I exaggerate. If so they live in a favoured world, for it is rare to meet a shooting man without a tale or tales of accidents caused by carelessness, stupidity, or both.

I started this aspect of safety by dividing one's companions into those known and those unknown and I recently wrote a light-hearted piece for *The Field* on playing detective with newly-met Guns to decide whether they were experienced old hands, likely to be safe, or relative novices and therefore suspect. Much can be told about a man by the way he assembles his gun and generally handles it, but experienced Guns can be ham-handed and novices adept, so further clues must be sought. Dress is a useful area. A new outfit from head to toe may mean a burglary or fire but more probably means the worst. Conversely a well-worn outfit of the right type is a good pointer but not conclusive – you may find yourself looking down the barrels of a salmon fisherman just taking up shooting. Two aspects of dress which nearly always bespeak the novice are the absence of any form of hat, and wearing the cartridge belt buckled outside the jacket. Conversely the one factor which invariably denotes experience is possession of a dog obviously well under control. In the article I suggested identifying a novice could be treated as a minor and useful sport, and finished, 'Although an experienced shooting detective would regard it as equivalent to shooting a low hen in October, it is permissible to engage the suspect in conversation. Such direct questions as, 'Do you shoot here often?', are rank bad sportsmanship, but 'Is that a one ounce load you are using?', or 'Did you go north in August?', are, in fishing terms, a legitimate fly for the water. Some replies, for example, 'Could you possibly sell me some cartridges – I got through nearly 200 yesterday', will categorise the speaker at once, but treat with caution the man who suggests his marksmanship is poor. He may be an excellent shot taking out a form of social insurance policy against an off day.

I feel less frivolous about my next point, which is the question of whether guns should be carried broken or closed between drives at formal shoots. For years I have laboured mightily with my pen to make the shooting world conscious of the stupidity of standing together chatting with closed guns. Consider the facts. At the majority of driven shoots some, often the majority, of the Guns will gather together coffee-housing between drives with closed guns on their arms. Inevitably the barrels point at the feet and legs of their companions. To my mind this is a gross infringement of the rule never to point a gun, loaded or not, at anything you do not wish to kill. Yet no-one moves quickly to one side or seems the least concerned. What particularly surprises me is that the participants are intelligent men and usually from the social stratum who have been taught their safety code well. And so, from time to time, I touch on the practice in my articles, stressing how dangerous and unnecessary it is. Years ago I thought it a simple matter to stamp out this anomaly – now I know better. Each article is followed by a little flurry of 'Letters to the Editor', evenly divided between those in agreement and those explaining that participants at formal shoots have all been properly brought up and would never have a gun loaded between drives. Few things drive me to near-fury, but this idiocy does. Not *all* Guns at formal driven shoots have been 'properly brought up'; in fact nowadays many have not. And some who have been are careless, forgetful, stupid or moving rapidly into their dotage. Several times over the years I have had suspicions, watched carefully, and seen a man discover his gun to be loaded after a tête-à-tête.

One of the objections from those who dismiss my views as unnecessary fussiness is the increased risk of damaging a gun kept broken. Certainly if the ground is slippery or the owner not very steady on his feet the gun is at greater risk – so are those standing near if the gun is closed and accidentally loaded.

It is so glaringly obvious that a closed gun should never be pointed at anybody that I cannot accept there is any valid reason for waiving this rule in any circumstances. The suggestion that participants in formal shoots are above human failing is laughable and does not bear serious consideration. I have given up hope of seeing it implemented but I believe it should be a standard rule of formal shoots that guns must always be carried broken or in a sleeve. Granted a gun in a sleeve can be loaded, but the risk of an accident is reduced in two ways. Firstly the act of putting the gun in the sleeve prompts the owner to check it is unloaded. Secondly, once in the sleeve it is carried on the shoulder and the barrels point skywards.

A final example will underline the confused thinking on the subject in the world of formal shooting. One of the standard objections to the use of automatics or repeating guns at formal shoots is the difficulty of seeing, instantly, whether they are unloaded or not. The same problem applies to a *closed* side by side.

It is interesting to contemplate whether driven shooting is more dangerous than the other forms. At first thought it is, as a considerable number of Guns, guns and other people are all involved in close proximity. Statistics would also probably bear this out, for I suspect more shooting accidents occur at formal shoots than elsewhere. In fact, a scientific study might produce a different answer. To draw an analogy, more people are killed in motor cars than riding motor cycles, but this merely reflects the greater numbers travelling by car rather than the degree of danger. If we were to take the number of accidents per million cartridges fired, I suspect driven game shooting would be found safer than other forms. However, even this may not be the correct test. Perhaps the question should be based not on the

Excellent safety drill, with one gun sleeved and the other being passed both broken and unloaded.

comparative numbers of shots fired but hours spent with a loaded gun.

Probably the form of shooting most likely to cause an injury, as distinct from serious injury, was the old practice of woodland shooting for rabbits where a line of beaters drove towards a line of stationary Guns. This near-extinct activity apart, the prize for danger is disputed between driven partridge and driven grouse. Which is the worst is hardly very important, but considering their claims will help to underline the risks. The essential danger factor common to both is the low flight path of the quarries and explains why accidents in these forms of shooting, where injuries occur to the face and upper body, are more serious than with ground game where the legs suffer. Partridges are more dangerous than grouse in so far as visibility is concerned, for their natural habitat usually contains an abundance of hedges and it is harder to see one's various companions than on an open moor. Of course, if the rules are followed, this limitation of sight will not be at all dangerous, for a Gun will not fire below a safe angle in a direction in which he cannot see clearly for a distance well beyond the range of the shot.

But, then, if the rules were followed there would not be any accidents at all.

Personally, I think driven grouse shooting more dangerous than driven partridge, and by quite a wide margin. The very hedges which limit visibility have the virtue of compelling the partridges to rise, but on the moors grouse can pick their height and often come through at the most dangerous levels. There are other aspects in which grouse are worse than partridge. Natural partridge country may not be flat but, more often than not, your neighbouring Gun is roughly on your level. You are unlikely to shoot him if you fire at 45 degrees to the ground you stand on but, on a grouse moor, this is entirely feasible. Apart from the problems of having to memorise contours at every drive, grouse are also harder to pick out against the moorland background and travel faster. One has little enough time to fire as a covey of partridges bursts over a hedge but with grouse the margin is often smaller. They are also, for most of us, a more exciting quarry. Add this combination of facts together and my reasons for voting driven grouse the most dangerous quarry become clear. This is hardly a revolutionary conclusion, for the accidents occurring whilst shooting driven grouse provide sad confirmation. However, a moment's deeper thought will show driven grouse provide an opportunity to follow my earlier recommendation to survive by anticipating trouble. Most of us do the majority of our formal pheasant and partridge shooting in familiar company – in the main our fellow Guns are safe, for those who were not were drummed out at an early age. With grouse the position is different for relatively few shooting men live in grouse country and even those well placed geographically are not always well placed financially. As a result driven grouse shooting is, for most of us, a rare treat enjoyed on only a few days each year. Also, because it is unique to this country, it attracts many foreigners and the numerous jokes of wild shooting by our overseas friends are not without solid foundations. The irresponsibility of foreign Guns is by no means universal, for some countries have a tradition of producing safe sportsmen. There is no point in detailing those nationalities who constitute a risk, but some of them find their way to our moors, and we can find ourselves indulging in the most dangerous form of the sport, among Guns who are mostly strangers and some of whom can be very unsafe. In this situation the wise man will keep a very sharp look-out.

The dangers of driven grouse are well illustrated by a story which, I can assure you, is absolutely true. Several years ago I went to shoot on a moor owned and run by a man with considerable experience of the sport – my lips are firmly sealed as to where and with whom. After breakfast he assembled his Guns and lectured us firmly on the dangers of swinging through the line. My wife accompanied me with a camera and, on the second drive, my host occupied the adjoining butt. In due course a covey passed through, she pressed the shutter and, when I processed the film, we had a crystal clear photograph of our host's gun pointing directly at us. Given this from an experienced Britisher (I will not distinguish between English and Scots) what hope has one from a hot-blooded Mediterranean sportsman shooting grouse for the first time!

As I wrote earlier a safe shot is made not by his knowledge of a few simple rules but the self-discipline with which he applies them, year in and year out. Because the application of this self-discipline takes place in a split second it must be based on an instinctive desire to shoot safely for the right reason; that is for fear of harming others, and not the wrong reason, which is fear of public criticism. Consequently the extent to which outsiders can control the safe behaviour of others is limited. A further complication is that even though a man may have every desire to shoot safely, his actual performance can fall short of others whose motivation is no greater. In part this is because the best of safe shots have safety always in mind and automatically reassess their position, in safety terms, as the day progresses. Ideally the brain should contain a safety map on which all people, dogs, farm stock, and anything else liable to injury, is located, with safe and unsafe angles of shot etched in, the whole being constantly readjusted. At the opposite extreme is the man who thinks about safety only as he raises his gun. The opportunity to calculate safety angles is at its highest at a driven game shoot, for there is ample time for a thorough assessment. Although I was critical earlier of gun handling between drives at formal shoots, safety standards *whilst actually shooting* are usually good. There is, however, one strange infringement which occurs regularly and is never remarked upon. Most Guns adopt a waiting posture with the gun either over their arm or in a 'ready' position in which it points ahead, either horizontally or a few degrees up or down. Eventually the beating line draws near, and on many woodland drives the men eventually emerge less than fifty yards from the Guns and sometimes considerably nearer. As birds flush in the final stages the Guns raise loaded guns and, in the process, swing through the beaters. I can see no difference, in terms of danger, in swinging vertically through the beating line or horizontally through the Guns. To be safe the gun should be held vertically as the beaters draw within range and the Gun should turn rearwards to reload.

Although the major safety discipline must come from the individual, shoot organisers, be they land-owners, syndicate captains or men letting Guns commercially, can and must play a part in safety. Pre-planning is important, as two examples will illustrate. I once ran a grouse moor syndicate and, when the lease commenced, found one butt dangerously positioned some fifteen yards ahead of the rest of the line. The keeper agreed it was dangerously sited, but explained the ground in the correct position was too boggy. It took just an hour of throwing in rocks to create a firm base and move a butt which for half a century had exposed many sportsmen to risk. Again, with friends I took over a shoot where the standard practice, on one of the drives, was to position a stop in a thick hedge. Here he was hidden, vulnerable, and not particularly effective. With the farmer's consent we cut out a short section, replaced it with wire and had our stop clearly visible, safer and completely effective.

There are many similar ways in which risks can be reduced; some constant to all shoots and others applicable only to local conditions. One favourite on grouse moors is to erect small sticks on the butt walls to warn the Gun when he swings too near to his neighbours. Some sportsmen regard this practice as unnecessary and irritating. I welcome it, for it does no harm and may do good.

A shoot organiser who is both firm and forthright on safety makes an important contribution, for he corrects any slackness as soon as it appears and keeps everyone's standards high. Certainly a shoot organiser is failing in his responsibilities if he fails to deal with any unsafe behaviour which he either sees or has reported. In one sense his presence makes this embarrassing task easier for he can act as a spokesman for others rather than making a personal complaint. Nor is a passionate scene necessary for most offenders are very contrite and a few well chosen words suffice.

One potentially dangerous area for syndicates is the question of substitute Guns. A man who has paid a large subscription feels, with justice, that if he is not free on a shooting day he is entitled to send a substitute. He should, of course, only select a replacement Gun he knows to be safe but this requirement is not always observed. It is sensible for a syndicate to emphasise this obligation at the start of each season and anyone who fails should be told so in unequivocal terms.

Most of the views I have expressed so far have been concerned with behaviour at formal shoots, not because standards can be relaxed elsewhere but rather that the sheer numbers of participants make the application of safety rules harder. Wildfowling is, perhaps, the safest form of shooting, for fowlers are usually static, rarely have anyone near and normally fire at high quarries. Rough shooting on high ground is also comparatively safe, for the absence of woodland and hedges gives a clear view. Granted it is easy to fall on rough ground but an experienced Gun will keep his barrels skyward. Rough shooting on low ground, and particularly in enclosed fields and woodland, is considerably more dangerous. The risk rises in proportion to the numbers involved, which is one reason why I believe the best number for rough shooting is two. Beyond this safety demands strict discipline and working to a firm plan which is not altered without all the participants being informed. A major problem for rough shooters is the behaviour of the various quarries, for many fly or run at levels less than perfect in terms of safety. Nor does the relative paucity of opportunities encourage a rough shooter to dwell over-long on the trigger.

The only practical way to conclude this chapter is to repeat the obvious – that the rules are simple and accidents occur entirely through lack of self-discipline. I imagine that all readers who are in sympathy with the theme of this book will agree with the high priority I have placed on safety.

Chapter 5
Fieldcraft and behaviour

My motive in heading this chapter 'Fieldcraft and behaviour' is to draw a clear distinction between those actions taken to improve the chances of bagging the quarry and those done for the good of others – both people and wildlife.

Contrary to popular belief, fieldcraft is not a quality found only in country dwellers, while those shooting men who live in towns spend their sporting hours blundering around, snapping large twigs, walking on skylines and generally committing all the errors against which Boy Scouts and trainee infantrymen are warned. Like the rules of safety, the fundamentals of fieldcraft are simple and can be absorbed quickly by any sensible person. It is their application which counts and, as an example, I know a managing director of a large manufacturing company, whose daily life is spent in board-rooms and chauffeur driven cars, who has a rare ability to camouflage his face with mud, merge into the marsh grasses, and take more than his share of wildfowl. Conversely, I know countrymen who talk too loudly and commit other sins.

Fieldcraft begins with an attitude of mind and while the different aspects can be taught and learnt, it comes more readily to some than others.

Defining fieldcraft is not, at least at first thought, too difficult. Describing it as the art of moving inconspicuously in the countryside is a good start, but falls short of a full description. A better one, for shooting men, is that fieldcraft is taking all the measures necessary to secure the quarry. These few words neatly encompass all the measures, such as dress, movement and tactics, which experienced sportsmen know to be necessary. However, I would like to enlarge the scope of fieldcraft beyond the mere functional purpose of bagging the quarry and treat it as a more wholesome combination of both ability and attitude in which observation and enjoyment of the countryside play a vital part.

I cannot, I appreciate, minimise the major involvement of the hunting instinct, for a large part of the pleasure of shooting comes from allowing the old instincts free reign and pitting one's wits and senses against wild things. Full enjoyment, however, comes from savouring all the beautiful and wonderful aspects of the outdoors and, at least in this area, the town dweller is often more perceptive and appreciative than the country man. The country dweller is often there by chance and not because he wants to be – witness the many youngsters who move to the towns when age allows – but the townee is in the country through choice.

Fieldcraft is therefore not a relatively narrow part of shooting but encompasses most of our actions; in fact, I submit the definition that fieldcraft consists of *achieving one's purpose outdoors with the minimum of noise, disturbance and discomfort, but with maximum observation and enjoyment.*

The beauty of this definition lies in the first four words, 'achieving one's purpose outdoors', for in adopting it, every shooting man can apply it to his own preferred philosophy. For some the day will be a failure unless the bag has been at least up to expectations; for others the pleasure of an unhurried day in the countryside will take first priority. I am certainly not going to pontificate on which attitude is right and which wrong. Indeed, it would be an impertinence for me to do so, for what right have I to tell others what they should enjoy or avoid. All that matters is that men, and the occasional lady, should not just shoot, but enjoy all the aspects of the sport and its surroundings. However, to a large extent I suspect these thoughts are preaching to the converted, for it is the more sensitive and thinking people who buy books and these philosophies will already have occurred to my readers. We must move onto more practical issues.

It is a fallacy to think fieldcraft does not apply to formal driven game shooters. Granted the opportunities are limited but good fieldcraft will enable an experienced Gun to shoot more and do so in greater comfort. Take one simple example. Guns are sometimes transported on a trailer with straw bales as seats. A good fieldsman will select a position with his back to the wind and far enough back to avoid the mud hurled up by the tractor wheels. Taken in isolation this is a trivial action, but multiplied through each day, week and season, this rural commonsense adds up to a substantial whole.

Naturally the scope for exercising fieldcraft is much greater in the non-formal aspects of the sport, whether walking a bog for snipe or flighting pigeons in to roost. Everyone is aware of the two fundamental rules of never showing oneself more than is necessary, or making any avoidable noise. Fortunately for the quarries it is not only novices who break these rules for many experienced Guns are guilty. 'Experienced' is, of course, a relative word. It means that someone has performed or observed an action many times before but there is no guarantee they have learnt from this repetition.

Having written earlier that men should be free to choose their own way of shooting, my own preference is to hunt with zest and efficiency for this, doubtless, was the way men went about it when life depended upon success. Granted mine does not, but it gives me pleasure to do a job as well as

To remain warm, alert and effective in conditions such as these, it is essential to be adequately clothed.

possible. Noise is easily avoided for, with knowledgeable companions, speech is rarely necessary and shouting never. Concealing movement is far harder, but walking in wood or shadow rather than open field or full light is a great help. Most men follow these principles, but fewer avoid unnecessary movement, by which I mean standing entirely still when there is no actual need to move. Watch people at rest – few keep really still, and it is the little movements of hand, head or body which cause the unseen pigeon or duck to swerve away just before it crosses in range. It is a good rule to walk reasonably quickly when you need to move but to stand still and concealed when movement is unnecessary.

My definition recommended the avoidance of discomfort and some stern characters may frown on such weakness. Personally I find life imposes as many unavoidable discomforts, problems and worries on me as I need to better my character and I cheerfully avoid any I can. In fact, there is a perfect alibi to strive for comfort in the words 'achieving one's purpose outdoors', for discomfort mitigates against efficiency. Obvious examples are legion, so let me offer an unusual one. Rough shooters frequently travel considerable distances and by the end may be carrying a heavy bag of game. This is uncomfortable, which diminishes pleasure, and an encumberance, which reduces marksmanship. To my mind measures taken to reduce this are not decadence but commonsense. A simple solution is to plan a route which passes by the car at the halfway mark. If this is impractical, a cache may be made close to a road or track where a collection can be made later, but take care to conceal the bag from vermin, flies and thieves. Against the first and last straightforward concealment will suffice, but note a landmark in case, several hours later and in the gathering gloom, you feel rather foolish. In the early season flies are a major problem, but on moorland one answer is to bury the game in sphagnum moss and roof it over with the same material. On low ground lay the game in an indentation, or a rabbit hole, and cover with grass which acts as a barrier if laid sufficiently thickly.

There is an old Norfolk saying that only fools and paupers are cold. Occasionally, very occasionally, we may be caught out by unexpected weather changes but otherwise we have only ourselves to blame for being cold or wet. The most common failing is not to think ahead adequately, for wearing the right amount of clothing is very much a matter of balancing the anticipated temperature with the degree of movement. In general we tend to dress for the temperature ignoring whether we will be static or mobile, forgetting that even a mild winter day is cold if one stands still for hours. Another fault is wrapping the chest with vest, shirt, two pullovers and an outer jacket, while protecting the legs with just thin pants and a pair of trousers. Long, thick pants are essential to avoid heat loss in cold weather.

The essence of keeping warm is not just to wrap clothing around the body but for clothing to hold warm air, which explains the popularity of string vests. The merits of wool against some of the latest man-made clothes are argued, but, while I have no knowledge of the relative values, whatever material is used it must be thick – there is no point in half measures with clothes when decoying, wildfowling or sitting on a shooting stick in an English winter. Personally, I find a thin undervest, topped with a thick main vest, an excellent combination. Some measures are, however, permanent for the day and in the early season it is best to gain the warmth from top garments which can be removed as the day warms.

When you consider how important it is to maintain the layer of warm air next to the body it is surprising how little attention is paid to the neck. Every time the gun is raised the arms perform a pumping action, driving out warm air around the collar. A silk scarf is a great help in avoiding this loss, as also are wristlets or tight fitting cuffs. Obviously the hands and feet are the first to feel cold and warrant special care. In recent years the insulated mini-slippers have become popular for absorbing perspiration and keeping the feet warm. They certainly perform their function well, but are bulky. Using them means wearing oversize boots, which make for clumsiness and are tiring for walking any distance. On balance I think thick wool socks are still the best compromise. Most shooting men find gloves interfere with marksmanship and it is noticeable how rarely one sees them worn by the best shots. However, gloves are better than hands so cold that they can hardly function. Personally I use mittens which are little less effective than gloves, and do not interfere with sensitivity. On really cold days a hand warmer in the pocket is a great help – provided you can keep it alight, which I rarely can.

Properly dressed one should never feel uncomfortably cold, but two factors can break down the defences. One is wind, about which we can do little except take shelter whenever possible. The other is wet, about which we can do a great deal. Rain makes a day colder even if you repel it. If you fail and your trunk becomes wet, a cold, miserable future looms. Common sense suggests a completely waterproof jacket, although some people seem content with the showerproof varieties. The range nowadays is wide, although in the end it comes down to Barbour's versus the rest. My own preference is for Barbour's, for they 'breathe' better than those varieties based on a plastic or rubber membrane and also stand up to hard wear longer. Their drawbacks are a tendency to stiffen when wet or cold and the need to dress them with the proprietary wax if they are to remain waterproof. No doubt someone will produce a garment to better Barbour's eventually but, having survived all competitors since the last century, the odds are on them.

No matter how good the jacket it will be ineffective if rain runs down the neck. Ideal head covering sheds water as the roof of a house, directing it well clear of the neck. To this end the cap, much favoured by game shooters, is an absolute failure and I cannot understand its popularity. The fore and aft, of Scottish origin, where they know all about rain, is far superior. Whatever the design, a hat made of wool will repel rain far longer than man-made fibres or even a man-made/wool mix. Never buy a jacket without a detachable hood, for in really severe conditions a hood is a godsend. With a good waterproof hood, tied firmly under the chin, and your back to the weather, you will finish up warm and dry when your companions are the reverse. I always keep a pair of waterproof trousers handy in suspect weather. The need for stout material is greater with trousers than jackets for lightweight trousers are soon destroyed by bramble and wire.

Most youngsters, when they begin to shoot or fish, are guilty of acquiring a wide range of supplementary equipment of little real, practical use. How many of us did not purchase a large, heavy sheath knife ideal for gralloching deer, killing redskins, and other unnecessary tasks, but incapable of extracting a thorn from a finger, neatly slitting a rabbit's stomach, or tightening a screw on a gun action. Most shooting men develop beyond this stage and discard the unnecessary, but fishermen never do. Even with maturity, however, I find myself tempted by devices and am always willing to stagger off flighting pigeons under a load of lofting poles, for example. In an effort to protect my body from the enthusiasms of the brain I have evolved my 'simplicity rule', and I commend it to others inclined to over-load and over-complicate. It is this – the proper equipment for a shooting man is gun, cartridges, dog, whistle and knife – anything else has to be justified.

There are, as I wrote earlier, many different aspects of fieldcraft but I will not pursue the matter further. My fundamental purpose is not to produce a list but, rather, to stress how fieldcraft begins with an attitude of mind. However, before concluding, there is one matter of importance, to wit the dispatch of wounded game. It is, I trust, unnecessary to stress that all wounded game should be recovered and dispatched as quickly as possible. I abhor the sight of men killing pheasants by holding the head and twirling the body round, for too often it fails to break the neck. Nor am I happy with the practice, often used by pickers-up, of rapping the bird on the back of the head with a stick, for this is not infallible. Nothing beats holding the body in one hand and breaking the neck by twisting firmly and quickly. For the same reasons it is better to kill rabbits and hares by breaking their necks rather than using the flat of the hand behind the ears. Snipe are neatly killed by pressing in the skull with the thumbnail.

I like men who treat dead game with respect; who see them as attractive creatures and not meat. No doubt a dead pheasant or woodcock cares not whether it is tossed onto an untidy pile without a second glance or laid in a neat row, and I must admit it is not a vital matter. But, a few minutes earlier, these were fine, living creatures. We claim, as men, the right to kill them, but we should at least accord them respect.

These sentiments neatly lead us onto the second aspect of this chapter – behaviour; that is to say the way we treat both the quarries and our fellow men. As the quarries cannot speak for themselves they deserve priority. Attitudes have changed enormously in the last hundred years for it is rare to find, in books of the nineteenth century, any humane observations. 'Browning' was normal and it is common to read advice on taking long range shots in the hope of disabling a bird. An occasional writer expressed concern for the quarries, but it was not until nearly the end of the nineteenth century that the great sportsman/naturalist, Abel Chapman, really expounded the rules of fair play for the game. In general, we can now claim our standards of behaviour towards the quarries are high, but a few inconsistencies exist. Perhaps the weakest aspect is that of long range shooting for, unquestionably, the longer the range the greater the prospect of wounding. On this basis we should criticise men attempting long range shots but our reaction when they succeed is to offer congratulations. Again, wildfowlers are often attacked for long range shooting, particularly at high geese. How can we equate this with reports that the XYZ estate offers some of the highest pheasants in the country and few men can bring them down consistently. What about the birds shot at by the less consistent performers? If there is an area in which the sport still has room to improve it is by tightening up our attitudes on long range shots.

From time to time the question is raised of the desirability of some form of compulsory test to be taken before allowing a sportsman to shoot live game. The great majority of the shooting world, and particularly those involved in formulating attitudes and policies, are opposed to this further infringement on individual liberty, but I must declare an opposite view. Naturally I favour the need for maximum freedom, but all issues must be balanced and the welfare of the quarries must weigh heaviest. It is, to my mind, wrong for a novice to buy a gun and then learn to shoot at wild creatures. Let him first achieve a reasonable standard of marksmanship at clays; learn to recognise legitimate from protected species; how not to shoot his fellows; then turn him loose – not before.

Having taken on ourselves the right to kill we should exercise it with responsibility, as, indeed, we already do in most cases. Shooting can do with men who not only ignore low pheasants, but stop halfway through the afternoon because, 'We've shot enough for the day'. And walk up a covey of grouse, shoot one or two, watch the remainder settle just over a nearby hillock and walk away. Shooting can do without men who keep walking up the same snipe until, at last, they kill it; or feed their pond heavily and kill the neighbourhood's ducks as often as possible. Restraint and moderation are the keywords.

When considering fieldcraft we had the driven game shot in mind less frequently than his fellows for his need to practise fieldcraft, and his opportunities, were less. In considering behaviour of men to men the roles are reversed for the rough shooter and wildfowler have few, if any, companions while the game shot is surrounded, (some would say plagued), by them. This is not to say that there is less scope for bad behaviour among rough shooters; in fact, there is rather more for participants in formal shoots are firmly regulated by numbers and pegs whereas the flexibility of rough shooting allows the greedy shot ample scope. At no time is this more evident than when a man who knows the ground is shooting with one who does not, for it is simple for the former to direct the latter into the best positions when there is unlikely to be any game and then take his turn in the pound seat in the prolific places. Sad, but we have all been victims. (None of us culprits, of course.)

As more people are involved, and the procedures more complicated, the opportunities for behaving wrongly, either deliberately or innocently, are greater on formal driven shoots. Those readers who are thoroughly experienced in driven shooting will learn little or nothing from what follows, but those who are just taking up this aspect of the sport should find it useful.

As a start it is wrong to expect that all the Guns will share your attitude towards the sport. Tom may be an outright killer, gaining pleasure in exact proportion to the numbers he kills each day. Frank may be a marksmanship man, waxing happy or waning sad as his ratio of kills to cartridges rises or falls. William, perhaps, is a drinker and much more interested in his brandy flask and lingering over port at lunch. Geoffrey is an excellent fellow, but old, and irritates everyone by the time he takes to move from vehicle to peg and vice versa. James is noisy, Charles has a hard-mouthed dog, Harry poaches others birds – the list of shortcomings will encompass the entire shoot. So be it – a shoot is a cross-section of humanity, albeit a rather narrow cross-section. If you cannot tolerate what you see as faults in others then the sport for you is wildfowling.

Lack of punctuality is an all too common sin, causing inconvenience to Guns, beaters and all the other participants. Nor are such excuses as fog, icy roads, and the like often valid, for a prudent man listens to forecasts and adjusts his starting time. The same failing causes problems during the day, for the sum total of hold-ups caused by a dawdling Gun is often substantial. The simple and effective remedy is a polite warning and then starting the day, or the drive, without the offender.

Another sin, more often committed by the old-hand than the newcomer is bringing a partially trained young dog, to give it both experience and training. Granted the final polish on a dog has to be applied under field conditions, but it is a matter of degree. There often occur slack periods when there is time to spare which can usefully be applied to a simple retrieve or working a patch of cover. Additionally nothing but good comes from having a well-disciplined young dog sitting by one's side and watching the shooting.

A relaxed and organised Gun, able to concentrate whilst waiting for driven partridges in Angus.

But a display of shouting or whistling at an inadequately trained dog is not acceptable. While this is generally recognised, what is not so often remembered is that this applies whether the dog is young and as yet untrained or old and past all hope of disciplining.

The careful Gun will ensure he is aware of precisely what may and may not be shot. Some shoots will wish to spare partridges, others hen pheasants after a certain date. Further north it may be a hen caper or the only pair of blackgame on the shoot. If you are not given a list of 'protected' species, when arriving at a new shoot, it is wise to ask.

So far I have considered the problems of a Gun in strange surroundings, but some men who behave impeccably in foreign parts are less good at home. One area is the treatment of visitors, who arrive in the complicated world of a new shoot badly in need of help. The host is often too busy for more than a brief welcome and there is a duty, not always performed, of the regulars to make the stranger one of the family. Usually much helpful advice is possible – whether his car is vulnerable to the evening rush of cattle through the yard; how many cartridges to take; the need to change footwear at lunch; does he know Guns number from the left here, and so on.

It should be, but often is not, a standard routine for a visitor to be introduced to every Gun before moving off. Even when this is done there are shoots where the Guns appear to feel the handshake has terminated their social obligations and there is no need to speak to the lonely stranger for the rest of the day.

Almost all shooting men are aware of the basic country rules, such as shutting gates, not leaving litter and taking care not to start a fire. However, these obligations lie more heavily on a shoot than a private individual, in view of the weight of numbers. Consider, for example, plastic cartridge cases – does the farmer really not mind if you finish the season leaving several thousand of them littering his fields or should you make arrangements to have at least the larger piles cleared. Farm crops, as distinct from cover crops, are another problem area. Doubtless permission has been given for the beaters to drive the kale, but should some of the youngsters be discouraged from whacking the crop enthusiastically with their sticks. And, on the positive side, if a Gun found a chunk of old metal in the plough, would he toss it in the hedge or leave it there to damage the combine next July? These are small things, but they are the seeds from which good or bad relationships between the shoot and the farm grow. And the keeper – do all the members of the shoot know not only his wife's name, but how many children they have? Beaters too respond well to consideration or indifference. Changing a drive to save them a wet struggle through soaking cover; arranging hot soup on a cold day; and a word of thanks at the finish; these make the difference between hired hands and a loyal team. And an end of season beaters' supper costs the Guns relatively little but is much appreciated.

Returning to individuals, syndicate Guns should show proper regard for the efforts of the organiser. Such paragons usually do the job without reward and the Guns should do all they can to ease their burden. When, for example, a request arrives for the subscription pay it by return rather than oblige the man to chase you. And if he calls for volunteers to help build a pen, or needs three dozen oil drums as feeders, then do something and at once. If he makes modest mistakes say nothing and at the end of the season write a hearty letter of thanks. Better still organise a shoot dinner at which he and his wife are guests of honour. He deserves no less.

Further individual performances deserving approval include carrying cartridge bags for elderly Guns and not bemoaning one's luck when drawing a bad number and spending a morning watching the birds fly over all the other Guns.

Tipping is an area containing greater scope for error than appears obvious at first thought. I still recall, with sadness, tipping the wrong man and, as I could hardly ask for my money back, it was subsequently necessary to give the right man rather more.

It is pleasant to watch a sensitive man tip a keeper, for the nature of the relationship requires the job to be done delicately. The moment of receiving the traditional brace provides the opportunity, but quite how much to give is sometimes a problem. It seems little time since a tip of £1 per hundred birds bagged was a safe formula which had endured for years. Now inflation has made this amount derisory and any figure I suggest now will be wrong in twelve months. If a stranger, seek guidance first from a regular Gun or guest, for the question could slightly embarrass the organiser. Certainly it is no longer realistic to increase the tip for every hundred birds for it would be inadequate, in these days of smaller bags, to give the same tip for bags of, say, 110 and 190. A sensible scale is a set figure up to 100, then increasing by a small amount every 20 birds. (For the shooting historians of the future this now means, in early 1980, £5 for the first 100 and £1 per additional 20 birds.)

The suggestion is sometimes mooted that tips should be based on one's personal day and not the overall bag; in other words the man who drew a poor number and shot 8 out of a 250 bag would tip low and the fortunate Gun who had a lucky day, high. The argument for this practice is that, theoretically, the tips would average out, the keeper would receive as much in total, and the Guns would donate according to their individual pleasure. Personally, I feel this leaves the keeper too much at risk to human nature, for while the disappointed would tip down it is less certain the satisfied would tip up.

Syndicates should ensure their keeper does not suffer for, obviously, they do not tip after every shoot. When the keeper receives his bonus, Christmas box, or whatever else it is called, the amount should roughly equal the total he might reasonably have received in tips in a private shoot.

It is unlikely that I have told readers anything they did not already know about behaviour in the shooting field for it is, after all, merely common-sense and normal human decency. However, enough bad examples are seen every year to draw attention to the gulf between knowing what to do and actually doing it. Hopefully the preceding paragraphs will lead to a few stabs of remorse and vows to reform.

Not very long ago I attempted to set out the ten most important rules for shooting men and to place them in order of priority. These ten commandments duly appeared in *The Field*, and I think they justify repeating here:

1. Be at all times safe.
2. Strive to achieve clean kills – avoid long range shooting.
3. Retrieve and dispatch wounded game immediately.
4. Place the well-being of your dog before your own.
5. Study to be quiet.
6. Avoid greediness – neither take unsporting shots nor kill in excessive numbers.

7. Avoid selfishness – let your fellows have the sport which is rightly theirs.
8. Never shoot at a quarry you have not fully identified.
9. Respect and conserve the natural scene.
10. Regard shooting as a means to an end and not an end in itself.

Chapter 6
Finding shooting

The most important requirement for consistently successful and enjoyable shooting is not the possession of a top quality gun or the ability to shoot well with whatever gun you have. Nor is it physical fitness, good companions or a well trained dog. It is not even, as most readers will have concluded by now, the tenancy of a good shoot, for all tenancies end one day. It is money. At frequent intervals I read the well worn cliché that money does not guarantee happiness. Granted, but it is a rattling good start towards it. In different spheres of life it secures a better home, greater leisure time, improved education and health facilities, and, in general, a better quality of life. If this is not a major step towards happiness then I am confounded. In shooting terms it overcomes the major problem of finding shooting, for this country offers some of the finest, and most varied, shooting in the world and, at a price, much of it is available.

Naturally this rationing by cheque book favours the better-off, but while there are sound socialist objections to this it is, in practice, a good thing for the countryside and its wildlife. It would be quite impossible for nature to withstand the pressure if shooting was free to all comers. A practical example of this occurred very recently with a change of regime in Portugal when some of the finest partridge shooting in the world was reduced to barrenness in two years. If unrestricted shooting means no shooting then there must be restrictions. The alternative to money is State control and if this is designed to keep out the wealthy how are the fortunate few to be selected from the proletariat? By letting them pay a high fee? Unthinkable, for it is back to wealth. By ballot? Perhaps, but who is then to pay for all the keepering, etc – the rest of the community who are not enjoying any sport at all? Or should the State allow shooting to those who have served it well? Heaven forbid, for here lies the road to political coercion, bribery and underhand pressures. No, much as the working man may complain about sporting rights going to the highest bidder, it is actually an excellent system. A great deal of money, which would otherwise have to come from the community, is poured into rents, keepers, game-farms, beaters, cartridge and clothing manufacturers, and other associated activities. This, in turn, finds its way back into a wide range of pockets, most of them entirely disassociated with shooting. For example, the anti-capitalist will ask what benefit accrues to the less well-off by the landowner receiving a generous rent? The landowner, feeling better off with the rent in his pocket, is more likely to change his car or lay down a tennis court, thereby sparking off a chain of work which, in turn, encourages others to use their, now increased, money.

As a final shot; consider what happens in those Continental countries where the State holds the sporting rights. Does the ordinary man in the street enjoy even occasional shooting at pheasants or partridges? Certainly not; it is let to visiting sportsmen, who pay good money of course, and the locals finish up in the beating line.

Far from attacking men sufficiently well-off to put money into shooting, those less fortunate should acknowledge the extent to which other people's money pays for the maintenance, and even improvement of habitat which nurtures all varieties of game and rears the birds which provide the nucleus of our overall game stocks.

So, money is the major key to shooting. This is not, however, to say that all is lost without it. Giving advice in this chapter is complicated by the fact that the problems of individual readers, in finding shooting, will vary. These will range from the young man with a wife, a baby, a mortgage, a disintegrating motor car and no money to spare, to a retired business man with few heavy commitments, plenty of cash, and bothered only by making a choice between several syndicate vacancies. I can but start with the impecunious and work on, inviting readers to skip those paragraphs of no personal interest.

For those who cannot pay the answers are wildfowling, which we will touch on shortly, and pigeons. (In the right areas, invitations to hare shoots are often obtainable. These will be grasped eagerly by those without shooting but dropped as soon as their circumstances improve.) Pigeon shooting provides excellent sport and pigeons at their best give shots as testing and excitement as great as any but the cream of driven shooting. It also, and this is the nub of the matter, provides a very useful service to farmers, for the damage done to crops at certain times involves substantial financial loss. A man, or men, decoying on these occasions will offer complete protection to a field, and even when pigeon damage is of no importance shooting will reduce the extent to which pigeons 'work' the area and so help when crops become vulnerable again. As a result a keen sportsman, willing to turn up whenever the farmer calls for help, can gain free pigeon shooting over a wide area provided, and this is critical, he is trusted. Farmers are torn between wanting protection from pigeons and a natural reluctance to let a stranger on their ground with a gun. The initial approach is, therefore, all important. Obviously if you have a mutual contact, who will vouch for your reliability, then ask for his help. If not a personal visit gives the farmer a better chance to assess you than writing, and hopefully, consent is more likely. Do, however, pick your moment. Do not visit a man in early August who is desperately trying to harvest his cereals before the weather breaks and has no current pigeon problems. Do call in December when pigeons are eating his kale faster than his cattle. Do not at the first visit ask for pigeon shooting in perpetuity. Seek permission to decoy, (do not use the provocative word 'shoot'), on one occasion, saying when you will arrive, where you want to site the hide and when you will finish. After you have shot, clear up your cartridge cases, and any other rubbish, report on results to the farmer and ask if you can return. Never come without warning the farmer beforehand and make it plain you are always happy to be summoned. Provided you conduct yourself properly you will soon be very welcome and from this may spring other opportunities to shoot. Further, once you have achieved a good reputation on one farm entry on to others is far easier.

The next rung up the ladder is renting a small rough shoot. Times have changed, and for the worse, since 1938 when Julian Tennyson could devote a whole chapter of *Rough Shooting* to listing the desirable aspects of a good rough shoot, without which one would not take it. Now the competition for rough shooting is so intense in most areas that it is unrealistic to be selective – either you take it or the next man will. There are still a few remote areas where finding rough shooting is relatively easy, but these are so few and so distant, they can be ignored.

It is almost impossible to find a rough shoot by looking for advertisements. Few appear, and those that do are either at very high rents or suffer some grave drawback. You may, if you are very lucky, learn of it by chance but, failing this, you have to go and find it. The formula is precisely the same as that required to catch salmon – unremitting effort. Take a map of the area which interests you, call at the nearest farm, introduce yourself, and explain you wish to rent some rough shooting. In the process drive up slowly, shut all gates behind you, stroke cats, pat dogs, speak civilly to the farm hand mucking out a stall, (who is probably the farm owner), and never decline to discuss the weather. You will get nowhere and nor, to your follow-up enquiry, will he know of anyone else who might have ground. Do not lose heart either now or hours later when the sixteenth call has yielded nothing. Keep on visiting, crossing farms off your map, and moving on to the next. In the end you will succeed.

By that time the question of what constitutes good ground for a rough shoot will seem academic, but it is important in assessing how much rent you should pay. In practice the answers are so obvious they hardly need spelling out. Perfection is an area of small fields, bounded by thick hedges with good bottoms and occasional small, warm woods, well shaped for working out by one or two rough shooters. A mixed farm growing cereals and roots with such additions as kale, to shelter pheasants, and rape, sprouts and clover leys, to attract pigeons, will do nicely. And, of course, one wants some extensive water meadows. In other words the sort of small farms I remember from my early Norfolk days, and where the farmers were often only too pleased to supplement their income by letting the shooting. Now the water meadows are drained, the small fields combined into a few large ones by bulldozing out the hedges, and many of the boundaries delineated by barbed wire. Even so all is not lost for all but a few modern farms have rough corners which can be made attractive to game.

It is pointless for me to suggest a scale of rents, for the values will be rendered useless by inflation. The owner will normally quote a rent, which will be as high as he feels able to pitch it, and you must say yes or no. Even if you feel it high it may be wise to take it for a year and assess your view at the end of a season. Men looking for rough shooting are not in a strong negotiating position.

Climbing the financial ladder further we reach the solution of taking a Gun in a syndicate. The advice which follows should be of help both to readers considering taking a syndicate Gun for the first time and for those thinking of changing.

Do not be too mean when considering how much you are willing to pay. Providing driven game shooting calls for certain unavoidable expenses, of which a keeper and rearing are but a start, and sport will be strictly in accordance with the amount of the subscription. Further, in order to attend a shoot one has various fixed expenses and, equally important, a day is given up. Unlike other forms of shooting the success of a day's driven game shooting depends on there being a reasonable flow of game and it is a pity to be bored when the payment of a rather higher subscription would transform the day.

The ideal arrangement is to be introduced to a vacancy in a syndicate by a friend who is an existing member when, hopefully, all the good and bad points will be accurately revealed. And, rest assured, there will be good and bad, for the perfect syndicate never existed. Failing this you must find your own vacancy and tread warily in the process, for there are some bad bargains to be had. The drawbacks vary from bad companions, to poor management producing poor results, and a few outright rogues making money from sporting innocents.

It is much easier to find vacancies in syndicates than rough shooting and, generally at the end of each season a crop of vacancies are advertised in the sporting press. Vacancies are also available through the various sporting agencies. While most of these are, doubtless, genuine, you must approach with caution, for the best syndicates almost always have a waiting list. What, in fact, is a potential syndicate member looking for? In a nutshell, good sport, good management, value for money and good companions – simple enough to write but, when we consider all the complexities of running a syndicate, so very hard to attain.

No good syndicate will find it difficult to fill a vacancy, so beware any enthusiastic attempt to 'hard sell' its advantages. The converse is true, that the manager of a good syndicate will not tolerate too deep an interrogation, but you are entitled to establish some vital facts. One, to which the answer will be readily forthcoming if it is favourable, is the financial basis of the shoot. The ideal is where the entire cost of the syndicate is shared equally between all participants, for then no man is gaining personally and a major source of squabbling is removed. Almost as satisfactory is the arrangement where one or more men put in value by way of rent free ground, poults supplied, or something similar, and the rest contribute money. Next is the syndicate where the organiser has a free Gun for his efforts and the rest share the cost. It is difficult to criticise this for, unquestionably, the organiser has a heavy work load. However, it is an arrangement that can lead to dispute and I prefer to see the work split among the Guns, even though one man has charge.

The least satisfactory arrangement exists where the organiser runs the shoot for personal gain. Fortunately this is rare but, where it exists, there is usually tension and such a syndicate is best avoided. There are other permutations including, and more frequently in recent years, private shoots which take in a few paying Guns to assist with costs. How well the system works depends entirely on the man in charge.

Very few men contemplating a syndicate Gun will be novices to shooting and will therefore learn much about the syndicate by an inspection of the ground. This will, normally, be carried out in the company of the organiser, and as he is nearly as important as the ground, a dual assessment will be possible. Every existing syndicate member will agree that the pleasure of the day is greatly dependent on the general atmosphere of the shoot and this, in turn, depends largely on the organiser. You will not need me to spell out the qualities needed to make a success in this department.

Shortly I will list the desirable features of the ground. You should certainly expect to be shown at least a substantial portion and this should include a sufficient area of permanent coverts, without which it simply is not a shoot. Look beyond more physical features to wider aspects. Is there a noisy motorway close by, or are you in line with the main runway of an airport? And if the owner, farmer or farm manager is met, does he pass with a curt nod or show enthusiasm over discussing shoot details? Ask about the shoot's lease to the ground, for no matter how good it may be there is little point in joining for the last season. Enquire, discreetly, how the present vacancy has come about. Death, or a move from the area will do nicely but an evasive answer should prompt suspicion. Continuing this theme further discover, if possible, what the turnover of Guns has been. A good syndicate will certainly not lose more than one member every year or so – anything higher is not promising. It is reasonable to ask if the organiser would object to your speaking to the out-going member. Obviously your purpose is to seek a reference for the shoot, but no organiser who is confident of his position will object. Indeed, the same theme will run through the discussion – the better the shoot the more openly and readily will your questions be answered.

There must, of course, be a game book and you must inspect it. A history of increasing bags bodes well; a steady fall needs a very good explanation. In general terms the level of the subscription will be in line with the size of the bag – it must be for there are no economic short cuts to producing quantities of pheasants. Now at this point some routine cries will be arising on the theme that the size of the bag is no indication of quality. Of course not but, in assessing a new shoot, numbers, unless utterly falsified, are factual and positive, while the quality of the birds will come from a verbal description, easily distorted. In fact even quality can often be assessed from the game book. If the majority of the season's bag is obtained by the end of November then little can be expected. If, however, no serious shooting has taken place before mid-November and the bags are still good in January, then good birds may be inferred. Your inspection of the ground will also show whether it is favourable for quality and, finally, a direct question to the organiser on what measures are taken to achieve good birds will produce either an informed summary or a blank stare.

As I have observed previously, the effects of inflation make it impractical for me to give advice on reasonable subscription levels, and even in an inflation-free world this would be difficult as costs vary so greatly throughout the country. For example some fortunate areas favour game and the normal production of wild birds allows artificial rearing to be treated simply as a back-up insurance. Elsewhere practically every bird shot will have been reared during the last summer. Some shoots will have ample permanent cover; others will have the expense of cover crops each year. Fortunate syndicates will have a good keeper's cottage within the lease at little extra rent, while others will not and have to make expensive alternative arrangements. The list of variations, and the resulting effect on subscriptions, is endless. One solution is the Game Conservancy. All readers should belong to this invaluable organisation, and a chat with one of the permanent field staff at Fordingbridge will produce sound guidance.

There are other pointers to a good syndicate, one of which is an annual shoot dinner. The desire to prolong the companionship beyond the season's end suggests good relationships. Another is the shoot's attitude to the presence of ladies on shooting days. It is, I admit, a personal view, but I find shoots which encourage the ladies are invariably relaxed and happy.

So far I have written of what the Gun can expect from the shoot, but, obviously, there is an equal obligation due from the Gun to the shoot. This I covered in chapter five.

Many readers will already have basic shooting in one form or another, and merely require some additional days, preferably in a form giving variety to their norm. One solution is to join with friends and take a day or so's driven shooting from one of the many shoots which now ease the cost of their sport by letting a few days to outsiders. In general one can expect such a shoot to be well run and to receive reasonable value for money, not least because the approximate bag will be forecast in advance. For sportsmen who normally shoot on a modest scale such an initiative will produce an exceptional day; probably the high spot of the season. However, for those who regularly shoot driven pheasants there is not much new and exciting to be found in shooting someone else's driven pheasants and much greater interest can be found, for no more money, by journeying further afield for grouse and associated quarries. Granted this will mean, for the majority, a lengthy journey, but it is a small price to pay for the exhilaration of shooting on high ground.

In recent years there has been a substantial increase in the demand for formal driven shooting in Scotland and the north of England from overseas visitors. This demand has reflected both increasing wealth in some areas of the world and the relative cheapness of visiting Britain brought about by a weak pound. Estate owners and tenants have frequently welcomed this potential income, but have had greater expertise in producing the sport than finding and organising the visitors. This has led to the growth of sporting agencies and a very substantial amount of overseas money flows into this country each season from this source. There is also a useful spin-off for we more humble indigenous sportsmen, for once the foreigners have paid the high rents for the earlier, prolific days, good value can be had from, if not the crumbs, at least the unbuttered bread. By October the demand for driven grouse shooting has dropped substantially, and yet in a good year many moors will still have large stocks and the quality of the birds will be far better than in August. As Patrick Chalmers wrote:

Oh, different, different was it once,
   One, 'walked' in August's prime,
Convenient coveys which a dunce
   Could deal with every time;
Are they the self-same birds, indeed,
   That, this late afternoon,
Come, like the levin and will need
   A MAN to 'ca' them down'?

Nor need the sport be confined to grouse for the fringe land of the moor will offer partridges, blackgame and pheasants in different surroundings to those in which we are accustomed to finding them. Inevitably such visits have a certain element of risk for, unless you organise a party, you will be shooting among strangers who may, or may not, be both good companions

Sporting agencies provide an excellent variety of shooting days. Here Paddy Fetherstone-Godley, proprietor of the Avon and Airlie Shootings, works his dog on an Angus moor.

and safe shots. The most important factor is the organiser who, whilst he is quite properly running the business to make a profit, should control events in a relaxed but firm way. My personal experience in recent years has been on the Avon and Airlie grounds in Angus and I have had some superb sport, in beautiful surroundings, which, before the growth of the sporting agencies, would not have been available. It is pleasant to record that I have heard very few men complain of having received poor value at any northern shoot. However, there must be some bad ones and you will be well advised to seek a personal recommendation from a previous visitor before committing yourself.

Sporting agencies do not confine themselves to driven shooting, but as this attracts the highest charges they naturally concentrate on this form of the sport. The opportunities for rough shooting are far fewer and results will be less certain, not least because they will depend, in part, on the skill and tenacity of the visitor.

Other forms of shooting are available for the sportsman prepared to travel, from guides on the Wash who advertise their services for wildfowling, to a West country hotel offering driven snipe shooting. The deeper the enquiries you make beforehand the less your chance of disappointment.

So far I have written of 'journeying to shoot', where shooting has been the sole purpose for travelling. On a less intense scale is the general holiday where some form of casual shooting is available. Usually the ground is fairly barren, for if not the sport would be more highly exploited, but, approached in the right spirit, one can have great fun from such holidays. The opportunities for all these forms of shooting are regularly advertised in the sporting magazines.

Almost exactly a century ago, in 1881, 'Wildfowler' wrote *Public Shooting Quarters*, and for 2s. 6d. you had a 'Descriptive list of localities where wildfowl and other shooting can be obtained'. 'Wildfowler' was Lewis Clements, one-time contributor to *The Field* under that pen-name and later founder of the present day *Shooting Times*. His book demonstrates with painful clarity how much we have lost in the ability to journey to some out-of-the-way coastal area and enjoy unrestricted and carefree wildfowling. The pressures of a larger population with more leisure, more money and ample transport, have forced the local wildfowling clubs to obtain leases of the foreshore wherever possible and there are now few areas where a visitor is free to shoot without first obtaining a permit. The wise procedure is to obtain from WAGBI the address of the local club secretary and enquire the position well in advance. Most clubs are very willing to grant permits to responsible visitors although, as all experienced wildfowlers will know, having a permit and bagging wildfowl are two very different things.

Finally we come to the ultimate way of acquiring shooting – leasing your own ground. At the modest level of renting a few hundred, or even scores, of acres for a rough shoot this is perfection. It is also very difficult and, as I wrote earlier, if the chance occurs do not vacillate – inspect it at once and, all being well, take it. The greater problems occur for the man contemplating the expensive lease of a large area of ground suitable for forming a syndicate. At the start one is faced with a fundamental question of tactics – if you lease the ground in your own name the financial and legal obligations bear entirely on you. But, as the man in possession, you have complete control and can lay down the basis of the syndicate and select the members. Democracies are only desirable for those who would otherwise be oppressed. There is much to be said for dictatorships when you are the dictator, and having control of the ground will allow you to run things the way you believe is best. Furthermore, provided you are scrupulously fair, most syndicates benefit from a strong leader rather than endless discussions between equals. The decision you make must, in the end, be yours alone and will take into account numerous factors, including your financial position; the prospects of obtaining syndicate members in the locality and whether the rent is such that the ground could be relet if you had to give up before the termination of your lease.

Irrespective of who rents it, the first problem is to find the ground. At first thought one would expect the best ground to be snapped up by locals before it entered the open market, but this is by no means so. Some owners prefer to let to strangers rather than locals who will be at the least acquaintances, and possibly friends, when it could be embarrassing to insist on full performance of the tenant's legal obligations if a dispute arose. Others simply want to squeeze the maximum rent from the market and prefer to have tough bargaining with a stranger. Some owners will advertise or instruct an agent to act for them. Others will lie low and these can be lured from cover by inserting a 'Shoot wanted' advertisement. In wording this, remember owners want reliable tenants who are going to build up the shoot and behave responsibly. If you propose employing a full-time keeper, or your members include doctors, lawyers and other solid citizens, then say so. Such an advertisement should be inserted from the beginning of January, or earlier, and allowed to run for some weeks.

Be positive about your search. Write to all the major estate agents in the area giving your needs. Other useful leads will be the local Regional Group of the Game Conservancy and the secretary of the local branch of the N.F.U., both of whom may know of land likely to enter the market. Watch out for auctions of estates and farms and write to the successful bidder, or the auctioneer, afterwards, enquiring if the shooting is to be let.

Provided you are not restricting your search to a very small area it should not prove too difficult to track down possible ground, but before beginning a detailed assessment, think first of general policy. Consider what you are trying to achieve in terms of the annual bag. Is the ground the right size, and if not can you adjust your plans? Is it really within reasonable travelling distance, not just for shooting days, but the frequent close season visits necessary to supervise a keeper? Are there any fundamental problems such as plans to build a motorway alongside the main covert, a new town alongside one boundary or put a major overhead power-line scheme through the centre? Even the worst threats do not necessarily make the shoot unacceptable, provided the rent is adjusted accordingly. In fact, for syndicates where money is tight drawbacks can actually produce ground which would otherwise be unobtainable.

In the world of property a house in very good condition is not necessarily an excellent buy, nor a dilapidated property a bad one – provided the prices are properly fixed, both represent equally good value. In the same way the inequalities between shoots can be largely ironed out if the rent is varied properly, for this will find its way through into the total annual costings. For example, the rent of really good ground will be such that less money is available for rearing. Ground lacking in adequate permanent cover should command a lower rent to allow the tenants to plant annual cover crops. Many factors should influence the rent, even to such extremes as the availability or otherwise of local beaters, but the prospective tenant is rarely able to bargain so closely. There is, however, much more to be considered before arriving at the matter of rent.

Two factors are paramount and must be investigated by personally walking all the ground, not just a sample area. They are cover and the type of farming carried on. Ample, permanent cover is so important that ground so-blessed is already halfway to being a good shoot. Of course, it is desirable it should be in manageable blocks and situated in the best positions to provide high birds, but we cannot demand perfection. Woods vary, and we seek mixed woodland with wind defeating thick hedges around the perimeter, ample, warm ground cover, and 'windows' in the overhead canopy to encourage bottom growth within the wood.

Outside the woods we would like to see relatively small fields, well hedged, and with a good mix of crops, including a preference for cereals, sugar beet and kale. We do not want large fields, many of them down to grass, and bounded by barbed wire.

At this point, let me stress the need for expert advice. Few men would purchase a house without having it inspected by a surveyor who, as a professional, will know what to look for and how much importance to attach to what he finds. In the case of sporting rights the sensible course is to ask the Game Conservancy to survey the ground. Their report will give advice, not just on the ground as it is, but what needs doing in the future.

If you are to maintain reasonable bags throughout the season, it is essential to have enough coverts to provide a sufficient number of drives. The arithmetic is somewhat daunting. Assume you plan to shoot on ten days in the months of November, December and January, and that there will be eight drives in a day. This means eighty drives in the season. Assume, also, that each covert needs resting for three weeks between drives which means it can be driven a maximum of four times each season. The answer calls for no less than twenty coverts, each capable of holding an adequate population of birds. I am not suggesting a shoot with fewer coverts is inadequate, but one starts with problems.

You will be fortunate if your potential landlord also farms the land, for he will wish to co-operate with the shoot. An antagonistic farmer is a major drawback, and it is important to try to assess the situation, preferably by chatting with the farmer if different to the landlord.

Find out why the land is in the market. There should be a good reason why the last tenant did not wish to renew his lease and if one is not forthcoming then probe deeper. You are fully entitled to ask if you may telephone the last tenant to seek his assessment of the ground and a landlord with nothing to hide should not object to this. Equally, the last tenant should have kept bag records and the landlord should produce these automatically. If the numbers have been declining you should be doubly anxious to speak to the outgoing tenant, no matter how convincing the owner's explanations. The cause may well have been the tenant's financial problems reducing the numbers reared or the incredibly bad marksmanship of the Guns. It may also have been the commencement of timber operations in the main covert or major poaching forays from the new town. Ask the man who suffered and not the man who stands to gain by reassuring you.

Other, more minor, considerations arise. If you plan to shoot on weekdays, will enough beaters be available? Can cover crops be planted if you desire, and if so, on what basis of charging? Is the owner aware that you expect the coverts to lie quiet through the season, or does he expect to have men decoying pigeons in an adjoining field? The more thoroughly all the various questions are discussed beforehand, the less the chance of dispute once the lease is operating.

When, at last, the various factors are clearly understood, the question of rent can be settled. Here again the advice of the Game Conservancy will be invaluable for their permanent staff are in regular touch with shoots throughout the country and will know market rents. In general, the initiative of suggesting a rent will come from the owner, and he will be an unusual man if he has not pitched it on the high side. If you are unaccustomed to property negotiations, it will probably pay you to instruct a knowledgeable agent to act on your behalf, for he may well save his fee several times over. Consider, in the negotiations, what you have to offer the owner and make sure you play these cards to their full value. For example, the shoot may be badly run down with almost no stock, no rearing equipment, coverts in bad order and a keeper's cottage in need of renovating. You will face heavy expenditure to correct these shortcomings and it is reasonable to expect a reduced rent for the first few years. Whatever figure the owner suggests, ask what he bases it on. There is little science in valuing shoots, or for that matter, residential property – it is all a question of market value and this is not established with a pocket calculator but observing what similar properties have achieved in the open market in recent months. If the owner can give actual examples, for comparable land, then he has a strong case. If, however, he is guessing then your guess is as good as his. Even if good comparables exist, this is not always binding for, in the ultimate, it all depends on how keen the tenant is to rent and the owner to let.

Assuming that, in the end, you agree a rent it is *absolutely vital* to have the agreement evidenced in a lease drawn up by solicitors. Without this precaution you have little security of tenure and every difference of opinion can erupt into a volcano of argument. Insist on a decent term – five years is a minimum, seven years is better and ten not too many. It is foolish to spend time and money improving a shoot only to have to hand it over to a new tenant just when the results are coming through. Of course, with high inflation a landlord is entitled to look for a higher rent part way through a long-term lease. However, it is better to write in a specific increase to commence at the revision date, for without this it might be necessary to call in an arbitrator.

If possible have a clause included in the lease which gives you the right to assign. You can then, if circumstances make it difficult for you to continue, pass the lease on rather than be forced to pay rent for sport you are not enjoying. Take care over obligations imposed on you in respect of the keeper's cottage. For example, if you accept a full repairing obligation and it is in bad condition at the start, you will be faced with expensive repairs. Include, if at all possible, a clause giving you the right to break if more than a certain percentage of the permanent cover is removed. Without this the owner could cut down the woods upon which the sport depends and still leave you liable to pay the full rent for years to come.

Obviously the more assiduously you and your solicitor seek to spell out your rights the more enthusiastically will the other side list your obligations. In so far as they remove ambiguity, these are welcome, but beware legal requirements involving heavy expenditure. Some owners may wish to compel you to rear, for example, a certain number of pheasants each year. This, on the face of it, is reasonable, but it could be embarrassing and is better avoided if possible.

If you and the owner strike up an immediate friendship there is a temptation to dispense with a formal agreement. Avoid it. Written evidence of detailed agreements are hardly ever referred to until a dispute arises. It is then that their existence can save long and expensive litigation. It is a sobering thought that if more people took care to evidence their affairs properly fewer lawyers would be able to afford to shoot!

Chapter 7
Rough shooting – low ground

The literature of shooting contains various definitions of rough shooting, most of which differ. Personally, I see it in simple terms – all which is not formal driven game shooting is rough, and this includes such variations as decoying pigeons, ferreting and walking up a bog for snipe.

Much as I enjoy shooting driven game, if I had to settle for one form of the sport only it would be rough, always provided I could stipulate that the countryside would be beautiful and the quarries not too sparse. Even the greatest advocate of rough shooting must grow weary of walking flat, featureless fields of, say, north Sussex for a grey squirrel, a rabbit and a snap at a passing pigeon (missed). I have no interest in the interminable argument as to whether rough or driven is the better form of the sport. They are two entirely different concepts, one being a very positive activity and the other far more relaxed, and there is no point in comparing them. Along with many other sportsmen I enjoy both, just as I can enjoy both watching Wimbledon tennis and playing myself. Many of today's driven game shots began as rough shooters and have progressed there by a combination of increasing years and increasing income. It is interesting to reflect that most have the opportunity to partake in rough shooting if they wish but few do. The converse does not apply, for however much rough shooters may criticise the sport of their more affluent friends, few, if any, would decline an invitation to a day's driven shooting.

This point made, however, I suggest that the more enthusiastic a man is about rough shooting the truer a sportsman he is. Rough embodies all the great attractions of the sport, giving ample scope for pitting one's wits, stamina, experience and marksmanship against quarry, weather and ground conditions. Not least, dogs play a major part. This is not a theme I will pursue, for experienced shooting men will have their own positive views and my supporters will need no encouragement.

There are, doubtless, some shooting men who were so unfortunate as to begin their sporting careers at driven pheasant, subsequently progress to include driven grouse and have not moved outside this limited world. The great majority, however, began with low ground rough shooting, which poses a problem for me in writing this book. In covering any other aspect I can be reasonably sure that some, at least, of my readers will come green to the subject, but what can one tell experienced men about low ground rough shooting? In general terms probably not much, but few men have experience in all forms and I will soon move on to specialised aspects of rough shooting.

Considering the general aspects, a major problem is actually finding somewhere to shoot anywhere near heavily populated areas which, logically, is where the majority of readers will live. We suffer from a vicious spiral in which competition for sporting rights pushes up the rent to the point where several men have to share the ground. This produces such shooting pressure that it becomes necessary to rear in order to provide sufficient sport for all and, the overheads of rearing and releasing having been met, it becomes logical to put down more birds. In this way what began as a rough shoot can escalate into a mini-driven shoot with the members taking it in turn to beat and shoot. I am not critical of this; indeed, it is an excellent compromise between the two forms of shooting which I cover in detail in chapter ten, but it is not pure rough shooting.

If you should be searching for rough shooting do not despise small areas, for the productiveness of a rough shoot is frequently out of proportion to its size. For years a friend has allowed my boys and I to shoot some thirty acres of woodland and rough meadows. We never return without several rabbits, pigeons, pheasants and the occasional woodcock or hare. Small areas also escape the attentions of those with ambitions to build larger shoots.

Part of the fun of rough is the planning needed to make the most of the opportunities and this requires careful thinking on how to work the ground. The best principle is to follow a route which will firstly drive the game further into your ground, rather than over the boundary, and secondly into cover where you can expect to get within range. Although I write 'drive', it is not usually a deliberate attempt to drive the quarries, but rather a two-pronged effort whereby if the first attempt to get in range fails the quarry will not be lost, but manoeuvred into a better position. Obviously quiet progress is essential, but some noise is unavoidable, not least the occasional shot. Nor should we overlook how frequently game flees from our sight for, as we are high and prominent and game low and inconspicuous, much sees us and shrinks away unseen. For this reason it is often sensible to begin with a route around the perimeter, for even if it is unproductive it will frequently move game towards the centre.

The plan of action will rarely be constant but will vary with the weather, crop conditions, unavoidable disturbance on your ground, such as agricultural operations, shooting and other activities outside your boundaries, and numerous other factors, not the least being the number of companions if any. For true rough shooting one participant will do, two is adequate and three the most effective. More is a crowd. Three allows a man either side of a hedge or narrow wood and one heading; an ideal arrangement. It is surprising how very large areas of cover can be shot effectively by very few if only the job is done sensibly and thoroughly. Consider a large wood which, in theory, at least, will require fifteen or more beaters. A preliminary reconnaissance may show it narrows to a point containing a thick layer of ground cover. Two men, or even one, commencing by walking along the outside of the opposite edge, and then entering and working slowly to and fro, can eventually drive most of the game in the wood into the holding cover in the point. This is, of course, an ideal situation, and few woods will be so convenient, but most will have a patchwork of good and poor ground cover. Pre-planning, particularly if helped by some cover clearing out of season, will allow the same tactics. The rule is to be slow and thorough.

As an example, last Christmas I went to Norfolk and eventually confronted twenty-five acres of unbroken sugar beet with only two spaniels, three boys and two fellow Guns. The keeper said we would never move the pheasants from the beet. Nor would we had we walked straight down the rows, but I called for a tougher discipline. Slowly but steadily we criss-crossed the field, at right-angles to the rows, and moving several yards sideways for every one forward. Some pheasants we flushed and shot but the great majority either flew low or ran into a little wood at the head of the beet, from whence we finally drove them.

One point to watch carefully in walking game into a flushing area is that there is no emergency exit, by which I mean a ditch or hedge offering an escape route. Ideally such places should be guarded by a companion, but a good alternative is a handkerchief or some other object unfamiliar to the quarry. Given a long, rectangular wood and three or four Guns, time can be saved by working line abreast until a hundred yards or so from the end, when the line can halt while one or two Guns go forward to stop the end. Once positioned progress can resume, but with increasing thoroughness as the end is reached. The sign of a good rough shooter is the care with which he works out the last yard or so.

Making the best of a rough shooting day calls for two of the main qualities of fieldcraft – observation and initiative. As an extreme example I return to the Norfolk visit, mentioned a few lines earlier. On the day my sons and I were to rough shoot for pheasants we woke to a gale and rain. Some sportsmen, lacking in flexibility, would have plodded through the day. I went wildfowling off Brancaster and my third son hid in the lee of a wood and shot forty-six pigeons. It is very much a case of changing plans to take advantage of circumstances. I recall various occasions whilst rough shooting, when we have noticed a pigeon flight line develop. Pre-conceived plans have been abandoned and we have flighted pigeons very successfully until, in the way of pigeons, the flight has petered out.

A rough shooting purist may argue that artificial stocking is contrary to the spirit of the sport. Perhaps it is, but the drawback of leaving the stocking to nature is that the outcome is a natural balance. This is ecologically satisfactory but produces too many predators and not enough sport. Ideally one manages the shoot by keeping down predators and improving habitat, thereby allowing game to multiply. Regrettably what is desirable frequently clashes with reality, which involves earning a living, raising children, house and garden maintenance and a host of other time consuming obligations. As a result if one is to see reasonable sport it is often necessary to put down some pheasants, and I would urge you to consider partridges as well. Granted releasing birds properly is labour intensive, but the bulk of the work can be concentrated into a couple of months, unlike gamekeeping on the old principles, which is never-ending.

Establishing a number of feeder points, with hoppers, which only need replenishing every week or so, can transform the numbers of game on the ground. However, it does raise the ethical question of how far one should carry this policy if birds are released on neighbouring shoots. At one extreme a rough shoot may have a central feed point or two, which only hold birds which have strayed so far from home that their return is unlikely. The other extreme is typified by an example I have seen practised for many years. A friend's main covert, unfortunately, actually touches his boundary at one point. The neighbouring farmer who, need I state, never rears, always plants a narrow strip of kale, running from the wood edge to a large, well-maintained, feed point. Regularly throughout the season two or three Guns appear, enter the kale at the wood edge to cut off any retreat, and work out the kale. It is as close to robbery as one can go without actually committing a crime.

Quite how far one goes to attract birds reared by others is a matter for individual conscience, but any guilt disappears the moment a rough shooter puts down a reasonable stock on his own ground.

Turning to shooting tactics, it is logical to start with partridges. Rough shooters know better than most whether stocks are sufficient to allow shooting and, in any event, they are unlikely to do much harm for wild partridges rapidly learn to become even wilder. The feeding pattern of partridges is the stubbles early in the day, sheltering in root crops at mid-day and then back to the stubbles to feed before the day ends. Or at least it was in the days before the corn was cut and the field ploughed almost without a break. And even when the plough is spared much of the stubble is burnt off. Lucky the rough shooter whose ground includes water meadows or similar permanent cover.

Given, however, that you have partridges the policy should be to work the coveys from the most open ground into the thickest cover, and always commencing from the boundary side. (Old time partridge keepers used the unpleasant term 'fleshing ground' for whichever cover they proposed to drive the birds to for the final act.) Normally the holding cover will be roots and these are best worked at right angles to the rows as this makes it harder for birds to run. Where possible work against the wind, partly to help with scent for the dogs, and partly to prevent noise carrying. Noise, or rather the lack of it, is vital to successfully walking-up partridges. Even in thick cover many birds will lift out of range unless you are absolutely quiet. It is a mistake to allow dogs to work unless they are very well-trained, for the noise involved in attempting to control them will be fatal. Thoroughly done, it is not difficult to walk-up partridges from roots and it is usually better to keep the dogs to heel and ensure closer shots. Retrieving shot birds in roots is often difficult, even when clean killed, for there are few landmarks in a sea of waving green leaves. Nor are companions much help with partridges for they have usually concentrated on their own chances. If a quick retrieve is not possible, mark the spot with a handkerchief and finish the cover, for blundering around for ten minutes is a sure way of seeing coveys flush out of range. Always be particularly alert at the edges and work them well for birds often run forward and squat where the cover ends.

Any rough shoot is enhanced by wet, low ground, for man rarely cultivates it, cover thrives and wildlife abounds. At the least one can expect the normal varieties of game and, given a pond or sufficient wet patches, the bonus of duck. Do not overlook the potential of a stream, however small, for given the right contours some modest damming will form a pond. Some areas attract duck automatically, while others need feeding. One infallible arrangement is where drainage from a cow shed can be led into the low area or pond. Failing this, regular feeding will work, but flight ponds should be operated with discretion. Duck are beautiful creatures, and there is neither need nor justification for a large slaughter.

Not all low ground shooting is done in cultivated English counties and we sometimes find ourselves in extensive bogs and water meadows with snipe as the major quarry. I must confess that although snipe offer such sporting targets I do not pursue them with zest. In the hand they are too small, fragile and attractive, and I cannot easily look into those beautiful, dark eyes. Such was not always my view and many an hour I spent plodding through the bogs of the Hebrides. There is no lack of advice on how to shoot snipe, varying between those who would have you knock them down before they begin to zig and those requiring you to wait until the final zag. In fact, there is no 'right' way, for as I pointed out in chapter four, a man's style of shooting varies with his temperament. A deliberate shot cannot 'snap', any more than a fast shot will wait and retain his rhythm. Nor do snipe behave to a pattern for some never stop twisting and others never start. Take them as they come and shoot when it suits you.

Opinions vary as to the best direction to walk-up snipe in relation to the wind. In theory walking downwind requires them to rise at you, before turning away with the wind. However, they do this so quickly that little real advantage is gained and one suffers the much greater disadvantage that the wind carries the unavoidable sound as you splash about, snapping reeds and plodging through mud. As snipe are very sensitive to noise, walking into the wind usually allows a closer approach. It also forces the birds to fly into the wind, and if this is fairly strong, slows them.

I would remind you of my belief, that if a snipe is fired at it is unsporting to mark it down and pursue it again.

Few species give more sport to the rough shooter than pigeons and this enjoyment is enhanced by the knowledge that shooting winter pigeons actually increases numbers rather than the reverse. To justify fully this apparently ridiculous statement would take too much space so I must ask you to accept a simplified version of a lengthy scientific investigation carried out in the Cambridge area and of particular interest to me as I shot some of the pigeons involved. Although pigeons breed in most months of the year, most of the young to be reared successfully, seventy per cent to be precise, leave their nests in August and September. By October the pigeon population has roughly doubled to what it was in the spring and by mid-winter the birds have to spend ninety-five per cent of the daylight hours feeding merely to stay alive. The great explosion in the pigeon population of the last few decades derives from changing agricultural practices which have made more food available, but the October population merely reflects the breeding conditions of the summer and the available food in the countryside is quite inadequate to see the numbers through the winter and early spring. It is the classic situation of nature over-producing in order that some may survive. The Cambridge study area showed a July population of 63 pigeons per hundred acres. This rose to 154 in September but by February had dropped to 70, mainly through starvation rather than shooting. The logic now emerges. If the ground can only sustain 70 in February it makes no difference if the autumn population is shot or not, for the surplus over and above the capacity of the natural food supply will die anyway. Now consider an individual pigeon alive in September. Left alone it will eat and live until February when, let us assume, it is one of the surplus to die. In this five month period it has eaten a considerable quantity of food which has not enabled it to survive but is now denied to other pigeons. But if shot in September most of this food supply would still be available. In other words, and offered only as a sweeping and general statement, if, of the 153 birds on the hundred acres in September, 53 were shot quickly the food they did not consume might allow the remaining 100 to survive the winter, whereas leaving the whole 153 to guzzle away unharmed might so deplete the larder that by spring the population might be down to the original 70.

Wet, low ground on a rough shoot immediately widens the opportunities and the range of quarries.

In practice, just as changing farming techniques brought the population up so new methods have caused a fall back in the last decade. Much as rough shooters sympathise with their farming friends, we do not wish to lose the pigeon and, it is comforting to think that, if the theory outlined is correct, we can not only shoot autumn pigeons but improve the population in doing so. A very rare case of having one's cake and eating it.

Much nonsense has been written and spoken over the years of the ability of pigeons to resist shot. Probably the myth began with nineteenth century gunmakers, ever alert to the prospect of making guns for some specialised purpose. Like so many tales of little substance, once launched it has survived unchallenged, as witness Tennyson in *Rough Shooting*: 'Another thing to the pigeon's advantage is its toughness – very often a pigeon, literally filled with shot, will carry on quite normally for more than a quarter of a mile, and then crumple up all at once'. The pigeon owes its reputation not to its toughness but its loose feathering. Ducks, pheasants, and other firmly feathered birds can receive pellets without shedding feathers. Pigeons will shed several if grazed by even a single pellet in the right place. Couple this with the willingness of shooting men to take long range shots at pigeons and you have the familiar sight of a pigeon at forty-five yards shedding a few feathers from a stray pellet while the marksman, never doubting it was in the centre of the pattern, remembers the amazing resistance of pigeons. Hit a pigeon with several pellets at a sensible range and it will die just as instantly as any other quarry.

Most shooting men have shot pigeons at one time or another and quickly assimilated the first principle, namely, it is useless to go to the pigeons – to achieve large bags matters must be so arranged that they come to you. I have already mentioned flight line shooting, which is usually opportunism, and this leaves decoying and roost shooting.

Do not be too impressed by tales of experts who can go out and shoot a hundred whenever they want. In the right combinations of weather, crops and pigeon movement large bags can be achieved with reasonable consistency, but there is no certainty to the game. I once went out with a leading expert who set off with confidence and we returned, hours later, defeated. Of course, one failure proves nothing, but over a period of ten years or so I shot pigeons with enthusiasm and, although I went about matters very seriously, success usually required an element of luck. Part of my procedure involved recording the weather conditions whenever I decoyed to see what part, if any, they played in the results. Some answers were obvious – for example, that pigeons would feed happily on heavy clay plough when it was dry but left when it rained and their feet started to ball up. Other aspects of behaviour I never solved, but one important fact stood head and shoulders above the rest – pigeons fly much more frequently in windy weather. Now obviously this is of prime importance for the pigeon decoyer, for the more pigeons that pass the more will be shot. This habit of flying more in rougher weather is illogical behaviour, for, particularly in winter, one would expect pigeons to conserve energy and not waste it by flying more than necessary. (Their relative immobility on still days proves that excessive flying is not essential.) This wish to fly on windy days is not confined to pigeons, but can be seen in numerous species, of which the most obvious are rooks, gulls and coastal wildfowl. However, whatever the reason those seeking good decoying should have as a major priority a windy day.

It is not the major priority, which is an attractive food crop. I often encounter disappointed pigeon shooters who have been summoned by friendly farmers with the news that 'the field is blue with them'. A few shots and the sportsman spends the day wondering why they do not come back. Why should they? Having been driven to a fresh larder there is no reason for the pigeons to waste time and energy returning to the original. In general terms no day's decoying on which there are a good number of food sources available will be very productive unless you operate under a flight line, and even this fails once the flight dries up. Real success only comes with certainty when circumstances have reduced the food sources to a very few and the pigeons must feed from these or starve. Clover leys or rape are examples of foods very popular with pigeons but, except in rare cases, if they can feed on one field of rape then the area offers the choice of a hundred. Real perfection is a day in late winter, when all the kale has been eaten off, and three inches of snow covers everything except just one field of sprouts.

Naturally the experienced shot will decoy where the pigeons are, rather than where he thinks they ought to be. Quite why they are so perverse is rarely obvious but there will be a reason. Sometimes a hardly discernable contour will divert a cold breeze over their heads; the soil may be less sticky; or a drill has failed and a profusion of grain lies on the surface. What the reason is will be interesting, but more important is the existence of a reason. Sometimes the preference of the birds for an area or a flight line is obvious; on other occasions it takes a thorough reconnaisance to spot it. One lesson I learnt was the need to hasten slowly and, no matter how sure I was of the best spot, to spend a short time checking the whole area on arrival. As with wildfowling, the man on the spot enjoys a great advantage over the travelling Gun. He can observe the changing behaviour of the pigeons and, when all the circumstances are right, shoot. But the man who arranges to shoot a week or so in advance has little chance of striking good conditions or exploiting them to the full if he does.

Space does not allow a detailed examination of the complexities of all aspects of decoying, but some basic principles deserve listing. There is much more to building a hide than siting it in the right place for it has to provide both adequate cover and comfort. The ideal hide is so placed that the sun, if any, is at your back, blinding pigeons looking towards you. The wind will blow at right angles to your direction of view, giving crossing shots. It will be roofed in some way, shielding you from the view of both overhead pigeons and rain. The 'window' will be at such a height that you can look and shoot through it sitting, for standing still hour after hour is more tiring than walking. Personally, my preference is to use a high shooting stick so I can rise to shoot. In winter hides formed in hedges or on the edge of a wood usually need supplementing with a camouflage net or strings of ivy. They lack, however, the major advantage of a well built bale hide of being almost draught-proof. In so far as it is possible to be cosy anywhere outdoors in February and March, a thick bale hide with a flask of soup is.

The best decoys are unquestionably dead pigeons injected liberally with formaldehyde and allowed to dry out for several months. For the dedicated pigeon shot the trouble involved in both their preparation and conveying them without snapping off heads or ruffling feathers is worthwhile, but for occasional decoying artificials are more convenient. The basic rule is the more decoys the greater their pulling power and all shot birds should be added to the flock at once. Some may be speared through the head with a sharpened twig, pushed up the neck, and the opposite end thrust in the ground, but the majority need placing in the feeding posture. It is sufficient to lay the pigeons chest down and push the beaks into the ground to hold the heads upright. When there are a good number of dead birds set out bring in the artificials in case the contrast alarms. Do not follow slavishly the advice to set up decoys heading into the wind. By all means make this the trend, but except in strong winds, you will not see a wild flock so precisely disciplined.

Care in setting out the decoys will frequently determine not just whether wild birds come in but where. If you have a good supply arrange the decoys in the shape of a boomerang with the thick centre pointing towards the wind. When forming the 'wings', narrow the width and increase the distance between decoys as you work towards the extremities. Most incoming birds will aim to land in the open area behind the greatest concentration, that is to the lee of the densely populated centre of the formation.

I advised earlier setting the hide to give a crossing wind to the field of view. A wind blowing into your face would have birds coming from behind, unobserved, and a wind from behind would mean pigeons landing towards the hide and spotting every movement. Do not set the decoys immediately in front of the hide or the birds will make awkward shots as they wheel and drop in the last few yards of flight. Aim to have the birds crossing the hide on an even course, and heading for the centre of the decoys which should be some fifteen to twenty yards distant and ten yards or so to one side. On plough set the decoys up prominently on clods of earth and on stubble a circle should, if possible, be roto-scythed, so the decoys are clearer.

Having baited the trap, retire to the hide and remember two important rules. Firstly, once you spot a pigeon approaching never lose sight of it. The temptation is to sink below the hide edge and wait for it to appear in range, but it is a bad practice. When it does appear it is often from an unexpected angle and the shot is rushed. Alternatively pigeons are often suspicious of the decoys and fly past slowly, at a distance. Watched throughout you can decide between shooting it then or giving it a chance to circle and come in again (which it rarely will). Unwatched a long but reasonable opportunity may be gone before you realise it exists.

Rule two is to keep movement to a minimum once a bird appears and, with careful preliminary organisation, there is little need to move. Your eyes peer over the screen; the barrels have been resting in the ready position throughout. As the pigeon approaches the butt eases imperceptibly into the shoulder and the gun fires. He who stands up, fumbles for a gun leaning in the corner, pokes it through the aperture and peers out to obtain a better view will rarely shoot an unsuspecting pigeon. With a good pigeon shooter the only birds ever to have been aware of danger will be those that fall to the second barrel.

Sport is rarely steady when decoying, and the dullest spell usually begins towards the end of the morning. By then the pigeons have eaten their fill and are resting. As the day wears on they 'come on' again and will go to roost with full crops. Usually the best sport of the day is had just after dawn, when every pigeon in the area comes hungry from its roost, but not all men show the same enthusiasm for rising early for pigeons as they do for wildfowl. All too frequently the active periods are brief and, when pigeons are moving, waste no time and concentrate on the job. Contrary to some opinions my experience is that pigeons rarely show concern about seeing one of their number in an unnatural position, even lying on its back. Therefore unless birds are obviously shying away it is better to stay in the hide during busy spells and leave the tidying up until things quieten. One is often faced with the problem of whether to shoot a single bird in range and, in so doing, frighten off a large flock heading in your direction which might provide a right and left. Numerous disappointments encourage me to follow the bird in the hand principle unless I know I am on a strong flight line. When decoys are drawing well, birds will pitch among them if allowed, and permitting some to land and then killing a bird in the air improves the chances of a second barrel kill. Even during a dull spell never leave the hide immediately after firing, for the noise of the shot may put up pigeons in the general area.

Pigeons must never be allowed to settle and begin feeding elsewhere on the field you are decoying, as they will probably prove more attractive to subsequent arrivals than your decoys. Put them off with a shot, but stay hidden for they sometimes appear uncertain as to the source of the noise and may circle to you. Pigeon shooters are frequently performing a useful service to the farmer and, time permitting, he or a helper can be persuaded to drive round once or twice in the day and flush birds from other fields. Another variation of this tactic is the use of crow-scarer ropes, which smoulder slowly and ignite a cracker every fifteen minutes. Carefully sited they will stop birds settling on nearby fields and scare them in your direction.

One problem is how long to persevere in one spot if nothing stirs. It is foolish to display tenacity when pigeons which were feeding on your clover ley yesterday have, in their remarkable way, just discovered a newly drilled field half a mile away and are now eating corn. Equally, moving takes time and may put you out of operation when pigeon movement begins. The wisest course is to leave everything intact and carry out a quick reconnaissance. However, if you are getting little sport but can see a clear flight line or birds dropping in elsewhere, waste no time and move at once.

You may recall that in the chapter on fieldcraft I argued the virtues of minimum equipment. Obviously pigeon shooting calls for fairly extensive accessories but the less you have the faster you can change position and, in general, I think this is more valuable. Lofting poles, for example, sometimes help, but they are a burden. Unless I am very sure of the prospects I prefer to restrict my equipment to a dozen decoys and a length of camouflage netting. However, while I rarely carry more than a hundred cartridges to the hide, it is essential to have a reserve supply nearby or, one day, all will go well and you will be caught out. Carry the net in a sack, which will also take the bag later. Finally, remember to dress heavily for you will be exposed and stationary for a long time.

Roost flighting pigeons in ideal conditions has a good claim to be one of the most exciting and enjoyable forms of shooting. 'Ideal' means a stormy night, preferably with a near gale causing the canopy of branches overhead to heave like an angry sea, and most of the pigeons in the area determined to roost in your wood. Life then becomes a confused blur of noise and movement with the roar of the wind punctuated by the gun and a never-ending stream of grey shapes offering every variety of shot. It is enormous fun.

We have to take our chance with the weather but selection of the wood can be more calculated. Obviously the fewer woods and the more pigeons there are in an area the greater the numbers roosting in any one wood. Cambridgeshire is an excellent example, for the cropping pattern provides good food and maintains a large pigeon population, while the area covered by woodland is small. Conversely, Surrey has too much grass, too little corn, rape, clover leys, sprouts and other pigeon delicacies and far, far too much woodland.

The best bags are made when the shooting men of a suitable area all man their woods on the same evening and the pigeons are kept moving. Ideally the Saturdays following the end of the pheasant season are best, for the woods have been left quiet at dusk for many months. Success is largely determined by location – all the little wrinkles of advice pale into insignifi-

Roost flighting pigeons, with the spaniel tucked under cover.

cance beside being in the right spot on the right day and, as pigeon shooting is not marketed like pheasant or grouse, the secret of successful roost shooting is getting to know the right man.

Given this valuable contact what follows should help to improve results. Unless the wind is very light pigeons will reach their roost point by approaching from downwind. Some parts of a wood appeal to them while others, apparently equally attractive, do not. Surprisingly, they often head for the highest, most exposed part of the wood, although if allowed to land and left undisturbed they then drop to lower positions. Get to the wood at least one and a half hours before dusk, even more if the decoying is quiet, for there is nearly always some movement over a roosting wood. Do not select a position with a 'window' to the sky where branches will not obstruct your vision. Pigeons coming into roost are looking for danger and, in this situation, will usually spot you and jink as you fire. The ideal spot has a complete cover of thin branches as near the roof of the wood as possible. This makes it difficult for birds to spot you, but will only deflect a very few pellets. In the beginning most shooters find branches very distracting, but once one learns to ignore them they present no problem, provided they are reasonably distant.

If a good position is chosen a hide is not necessary. Provided the Gun keeps quite still everything favours him, for the bird is moving and looking through a maze of branches while the Gun is motionless with a clear view of the pigeon silhouetted against the sky. Spaniels with large areas of white, and yellow labradors need placing under cover, but this is all.

It is essential to keep a good look-out for if you spot the bird in good time the game is half won. As with decoying, the art is to shoot the pigeon before it ever suspects your presence, and this means minimum movement. Those readers who have never flighted pigeons before will still have read the advice not to shoot at the high ones, as they will probably circle and come in. Even if you let several by which never reappear, continue to leave them, for firing may frighten others approaching but not yet in view. Never allow birds to settle elsewhere in the wood for they will draw like a magnet. Be flexible – your priority is to keep under the flight line and if it moves then move with it. It may be a shift in the wind or late arrivals from a more distant feeding area but, whatever the reason, stay alert for a change in the line.

If the birds are coming slowly it is sensible to pick-up as you shoot, for this reduces the work to be done in the deep dusk. However, when there is a steady flow of pigeons concentrate on shooting. The difference in kills to cartridges between standing quite still and concentrating on incoming pigeons and looking over one's shoulder whilst picking-up is dramatic. Nor is it sensible to let a dog or a helper retrieve while you shoot as this breaks the rule of absolute stillness.

Two questions have arisen whilst roost shooting which I have never solved. How do cock pheasants, which by late January would normally run like a stag at the sight of a human never mind a shot, know they are in no danger and flutter up to roost within easy range while I fire shot after shot? And, why do pigeons rarely come into their normal roosts in large numbers on still, frosty evenings?

If there is a large pigeon population near you and good roosting woods it is well worth attempting to organise roost flighting evenings during February. Some keepers may not object to continuing into March, but after a few weekends the pigeons become wary, (and, hopefully, fewer), and enthusiasm fades. It is better to do the job well for a few Saturdays and stop.

By today's standards I would have been ranked a deprived and underprivileged child. In retrospect most of the things I lacked were, in the long run, beneficial to my subsequent appreciation of life but, in one respect, fate treated me harshly. I refer to myxomatosis. Granted by the time it struck, in 1954, I was no longer a child but it was still a sore blow for I was a very impecunious young man and rabbits were central to my sport.

The background of the rabbit is interesting. A few years ago I wrote *Pugs and Drummers*, dealing with ferrets and rabbits, and I sought the origin of the rabbit in this country. Modern literature all stated the rabbit was introduced to this country by the Normans, but few authors offered positive evidence. In fact, the belief relies on negative evidence, for there is no mention of rabbits in this country before the thirteenth century and the presumption has been that no mention meant no rabbits. I found this unsatisfactory and, in my book, advance the case for a much earlier introduction. Very briefly I contend it is unlikely that the Romans, who regularly shipped live rabbits from Spain to Rome, spent four hundred years here without introducing them. (Ferreting was a favourite sport of Roman soldiers.) And, moving even further back in time, it is even possible rabbits were well established before the Romans arrived. Rabbits' bones found in Berkshire have been carbon-dated at about 7500 B.C. What is now the English Channel was dry land until about 5000 B.C. and in the period prior to the breach both the vegetation and the climate would have enabled rabbits to survive. Many different species walked or flew across this area to re-colonise England when the last Ice Age retreated – why not the rabbit? This is a gross over-simplification of a very complex problem, but let no-one tell you that, beyond all doubt, the Normans introduced the rabbit.

Far from being a simple, uncomplicated animal the rabbit is actually immensely interesting, not least for its remarkable ability to survive robustly when men, predators and disease combine against it. Those who have passed lightly over the rabbit so far are recommended to look closer.

I suspect even the most lordly game shooters have more of a taste for rabbit shooting than they will readily own to, but the great majority of dogs make no effort to hide their preference. When I come down from the hills after walking up grouse we often pass through patches of bracken with rabbit populations. No matter how tired the spaniels may be after a long day, a whiff of rabbit revitalises them, and great sport is had as the rabbits bolt from one patch to the next.

For most rough shooters rabbits are taken as they come, and no special effort is made to come to terms with them. Where rabbits are fairly sparse this is realistic, but given a good population and ample cover they can be driven successfully. In fact, rabbit driving was an accepted and highly productive form of sport for many years with bags of many hundreds in a day being common on some estates. The Guns would line a ride while the beaters drove the rabbits forward, an exercise which could obviously be extremely dangerous. We tend to think of rabbits as quarries which our dogs flush from thick cover but these are only the ones which have chosen to hide. Rabbits will run from noise just as readily, and just as far in advance, as any pheasant and when an area is to be driven the standing Guns must take up their positions before the walking Guns or beaters line out. Choose the positions carefully, so that the standing Guns have clear and safe arcs of

The Gun has sensibly selected a high vantage point to cover all escape angles of bolting rabbits.

fire on both sides. Obviously walking Guns only fire at rabbits going back and standing Guns do not fire forward. Late winter is the best time when frost has burnt off most of the undergrowth.

Normally most of the rabbit population will be underground and maximum results require these to come up and join in the sport. One method, ferrets, we will cover in a moment, and the other is known graphically as stinking-out. Put simply the technique is to go round the burrows in advance and insert a substance of such foul odour that the rabbits prefer life on the surface. At the simplest level this is done the day before shooting by pushing paper balls soaked in paraffin down the holes. In older days, when labour was cheap, the process often began up to six days in advance and various complicated recipes were used. One of the more sophisticated involved mixing soft soap, black sulphur, tar, spirit of tar, paraffin and train oil and boiling the brew slowly.

Two good rules for rabbit shooting are never to shoot at a rabbit closely followed by a dog and never to take a companion who is not known to be impeccably safe. Rabbit shooting is less dangerous than grouse shooting, but not much.

The problem with offering advice on ferreting is that those who own ferrets will not need it and those who do not own them will not require it. However, for the benefit of those just starting, or even borrowing ferrets for a day, some basic principles may help.

Experts argue on whether to feed ferrets or not on the day they work. I believe in feeding them for they are less likely to kill and lay-up. This problem has now been greatly eased by the invention of the 'Bleeper', a miniature, low frequency radio transmitter, fastened around the ferret's neck, the signals from which are picked up by a receiver held by the ferreter. With this he can locate and dig out the ferret far more rapidly than by the old methods.

Do not ferret among boulders, or under buildings or tree roots, for if the ferret lays-up you will not dig it out. Some people muzzle their ferrets to prevent them killing; others, with whom I agree, say a muzzled ferret which encounters a rat will be badly wounded. Avoid wasting time by ferreting burrows which show no sign of occupants (lack of droppings, no fresh tracks, dead leaves and cobwebs in the entrance). Do not expect a single ferret to bolt rabbits from a large burrow where the occupants know every road and by-way, nor be surprised at a lay-up if you put two ferrets into a small burrow. Quietness is vital, for a rabbit alarmed by sounds above, and reluctant to bolt from the ferret, is more likely to be caught. Avoid, therefore, treading on the burrow and make all preparations some distance away. Enter the ferret at the lowest hole in the hope it will drive rabbits up not down.

There then begins the waiting phase, which may last from a few seconds to an eternity. There is a good case for using a lightly loaded cartridge, for most ferreted rabbits are shot at close range. One ounce is adequate, but I have used the Eley two inch with good effect. Where you choose to stand is important. A rabbit not hard-pressed by a ferret will often sit in a hole entrance before bolting, so even if you do not conceal yourself at least avoid being prominent. Standing against a tree helps. As usual, remaining motionless is as important as being hidden. Never shoot a rabbit in the hole-mouth or you may kill the ferret (which will sometimes be firmly attached to the rear of the rabbit.) If you wound a rabbit always use the second barrel at once, for if it drags itself back into the burrow, a lay-up is certain.

Hopefully the ferret will duly reappear and the extent to which it has been handled and tamed generally will determine whether it will come easily from the hole or back down from you. Awkward customers will attach themselves to a proffered rabbit carcase and can be hauled out. If fortune is not with you and the ferret lays-up there are a variety of measures available before actually digging. Space, however, precludes details and I can but refer you to *Pugs and Drummers*.

Woodcock are not as difficult as we are often told they are. The main reason why that shrewd firm of drink suppliers is not deluged with demands for bottles is that woodcock are solitary birds and one rarely sees two in reasonable proximity at the same time. Apart from the obvious need for care necessary with any low flying bird, I can offer no special advice on how to shoot them, apart from observing that the rapid shot does better with them than the slow, deliberate man. Much as I enjoy the shot, I do not like looking a woodcock in the eye afterwards.

Chapter 8
Rough shooting – high ground

For me this is the cream of the sport. I am exhilarated by wildfowling, excited by driven pheasant and absorbed by rough shooting but, given a choice, I will walk the hills in August and September for grouse. And I do have the choice for a little luck and much effort has secured the lease of a large slice of very wild moors in the Hebrides. Here I can walk all day through seas of purple heather, under blue skies, with the Atlantic sparkling to the west and see neither man, nor trace of his existence. Sport, in terms of shots fired, is sparse, but I love those lonely, savage hills. Time has no significance other than simply bringing night and day, year in year out, and, as I shelter from a passing shower under a rock overhang I may be the first human to stand there since time began.

Next to wildfowling it must be the most testing form of shooting, calling for miles of walking over rough and varying ground. Sometimes, when the clouds drop and the rain slants in from the sea there is no pleasure – just a strong desire to get off the moor and into a hot bath. But the good days belong to those high spots of life that stay in memory. For a brief spell my mind is clear of all the problems of modern living – telephones, constant papers demanding action, taxes, educating children, appointments piling upon appointments. Instead there lies the endless sweep of purple heather, limited only by the inverted, vast blue bowl of the sky, and dotted with sparkling lochans. These are the days to climb to the high ground, which offers the dual attractions of a cooling breeze and a twenty mile view across the Minch to the Outer Hebrides. It is hunting in its most pure and exciting form – a man with a dog and a gun, searching for an elusive quarry in wild surroundings.

Hill walking for grouse is not a sport for the lazy or unfit; indeed it never has been, as witness this extract from *The Oakleigh Shooting Code*, in 1836:

When the guns are expected to be numerous, it is decided to be on the ground as soon as it is light enough to commence operations in a fair way. Birds may be killed above the horizon long before sunrise; but the sportsman's rule is never to fire until the morning is so far advanced that he can plainly distinguish them in their flight against the dark hill-side. They arrange to breakfast at three, (calculating the time by their watches, and not by the house-clock, which may have a way

A visit to high ground offers the low ground Gun a wealth of new sights, scenes and quarries.

of going peculiar to itself), and to be on the ground before four; as the greatest number of birds are killed between four and six, and when there are many competing for a prize it is folly to throw away a chance.

Only just over half a century later things had changed out of all recognition, and Lloyd-Price could write in *Practical Pheasant Rearing and Grouse Driving*, 1888:

That the present craze for large bags of grouse, killed from behind butts or artificial shelter, has revolutionised our ideas of sport as compared with those held by our ancestors, there can be no manner of doubt. The ease with which guns, shooters, loaders, and all the paraphernalia can be carted without any trouble to the ground, and the *otium cum dignitate* with which a man can ride a pony up to his allotted castle, dismount, arrange his cigars, whisky flask, cartridges, guns, and other *impedimenta* with the certainty that he will not be dispossessed from a comfortable seat on his driving stick for some hours, if at all, during the day, has, it is useless to deny, an extraordinary attraction for the present customers of Messrs. Purdey and Atkins.

Not only the 'present customers', but all succeeding generations have experienced the 'extraordinary attraction', but even this palls unless there are sufficient grouse to give reasonable sport. Some ground, more usually in the west, never has had and never will have an adequate stock and this provides opportunities for walking-up. Shooting men are rarely half-hearted about high ground rough shooting – they rapidly polarise into loving or hating it but, as a general rule, men who enjoy rough shooting on low ground are equally enthusiastic on the hills.

Hill walking for grouse and salmon fishing share one common characteristic – a major factor in success is tenacity. Somewhere up in the endless miles of hills, are a few grouse: avine needles in a heather haystack, and the main problem is to find them. The advice that follows will be of little help unless it is applied assiduously. It is not, of course, necessary to make the contest quite so hard. There exist excellent country hotels where you will be driven into the hills by landrover and shepherded around all day by a pleasant keeper. He will know where the grouse, which will be relatively numerous, will lie, and when you have shot some will carry them for you. It will be enjoyable and do wonders for your health. It will not, however, be half as satisfying as solving the problems on your own.

Let us assume you are newly arrived in some area of the Highlands or Islands with permission to rough shoot, but little idea where to start or how. Furthermore while you have your dog it knows no more of high ground rough shooting than you. On this class of ground there is unlikely to be a keeper and reliable advice may be hard to come by. Highlanders are pleasant people; a welcome characteristic, but it leads them to tell others what they think they want to be told whether accurate or not. Additionally even the country people sometimes display an amazing ignorance of natural history. Ask, by all means, but treat the answers with reserve.

Before arrival obtain an Ordnance Survey map of the area. Study it in advance and note those areas where gentle sided valleys run at right angles to the prevailing wind. Eliminate exposed high ground and steeply sloping valley sides. In practice, it is impossible to appraise ground from a map, but with limited time it is sense to start with the more promising. However, no ground can be dismissed without a close inspection.

Next drive along every road and track passing through the ground and, with binoculars, assess the surroundings. Basically you are looking for heather – include in your itinerary those areas with large purple expanses and exclude the green and rock covered. At anything below 2000 feet height is not important. Now take the map and plan a route. It is possible to search for grouse by finding a good area and criss-crossing it thoroughly. It is also very boring. A large part of the pleasure comes from walking the hills, absorbing the magnificent scenery and enjoying the unique sights, such as coming across a golden eagle on a hare carcase, or a great northern diver on an isolated loch. Little of this is achieved by an intensive search of one hillside. Instead plan a walk that combines likely ground already observed with what the map suggests is scenic promise. Greater variety is possible if you can arrange to be dropped at one point and picked up at another, but this holds pit-falls for the inexperienced. Never arrange a meeting at a specific point, for this commits you to covering a certain distance in a certain time and may prove difficult or impossible. The safer plan is to walk parallel to a road, to which you can strike off when time is nearly up. Your pick-up can then expect to find you anywhere along a given stretch.

This flexible arrangement is necessary as it is impossible to be positive on time. The ground may be barren and covered quickly, or productive and there may be frequent detours to cover promising areas. Work on the assumption that you will progress in the general direction you plan (which is very different from the distance you will actually walk) at the rate of one mile per hour. This may sound ridiculously slow, but, in practice, it is realistic.

Hill walking, whether shooting or not, is potentially dangerous. The careless man can easily become lost and even the careful walker can incapacitate himself on the rough ground. By the time it was realised you were in trouble, and a rescue team mounted, it would be dark. The chance of your being found before dawn would be slim and, even in August, the nights can be very cold on the hills. While the prospect of your being marooned is not high, it is only commonsense to take all sensible precautions. I do, and I know my hills as my own garden.

For the newcomer to the hills it is important to take a companion. If he is experienced so much the better, but even if not, at least one can go for help if the other is injured. However, in this event the injured man must be left as warm as possible. At all costs get him out of the wind, even if he has to be dragged some distance. Find a sheltered spot under a rock, or a peat hag or even in a depression. Retain only the minimum of personal clothing and dress him in the rest. Then pack him in a thick layer of heather. Finally, and most important, put up a marker – a handkerchief on a gun, or anything to guide rescuers. Remember you may not be physically capable of returning. Take a long look at the surrounding landmarks and memorise every detail. In particular, pick up some recognisable landmark at the earliest possible point. Telling a rescue party that the victim lies sixty yards west of where the burn forks is far better than 'roughly in the middle of the big valley'.

If you have no companion leave a written note of your proposed route and do not try anything ambitious.

The right clothing is vital both to comfort and, possibly, survival. Most readers will be shooting on holiday expeditions, which means the warmer period from mid-August to the end of September. At this time the problem is frequently not cold, but heat, for the moors can be insufferably hot on still days, when the sun beats down and puffs of heather dust fly at every step. (I still relish the sight of three jolly policemen on a shooting holiday in the Hebrides. I met them last August on a day that promised to grow very warm. They were setting off in wellington boots, waterproof over-trousers, Barbours and hats. I queried whether they would not be rather chilly in the hills, but they felt not.) A good rule is that if you do not feel slightly cold before you start walking, you will soon feel too hot.

Good leather boots are virtually essential. If new, wear them for gardening for a couple of months beforehand. Even if well worn in always take a few plasters and cover sore patches on the feet before they develop into blisters. Have boots large enough to wear one thin and one thick pair of socks. Dubbin them liberally each evening. It does not matter greatly whether they are waterproof or not – water will soon come over the top and, anyway, it cools the feet. I have covered hundreds of miles in old tennis shoes with holes cut in the toes to let water out.

Personally, I abhor walking in trousers and, except on the coldest days, wear shorts. There is a rare freedom in striding across a sphagnum moss based moor in boots and shorts with the sun and breeze on one's legs. A good compromise in marginal weather is breeks of the variety sold by Cambrian Fly Fishers. If the temperature rises one's stockings can be dropped to the ankles and the bottom of the breeks opened. On the good days the thinnest of shirts suffices, but it would be foolish not to plan for trouble. Always take a good jumper and I personally add one of the 'space blankets', a large sheet of plastic coated with heat-retaining metal foil with which to wrap oneself, or a companion, if incapacitated. Equally, or perhaps more important is a pocket compass. With it you need never be lost, even if, as often happens, mist or cloud falls quickly. The lack of it could kill you. Several chapters earlier I wrote of my 'simplicity rule', but I think the above items, and several to follow, are justified, not least because they are very light and small. *Always* take insect repellent – its absence could, quite literally, ruin your day. If unprotected, strong men flee before midges. I find space for half a dozen mini-flares, which would indicate my whereabouts in the dark. Then come two luxuries, or no doubt one at least would be for most men, to wit, a camera. For me it is an essential. The other is a pair of lightweight miniature binoculars. Sometimes they are very useful, for example, in studying a distant hill and deciding whether the heather warrants a visit. More often they are used to watch wildlife at a distance, pick out the road in the valley bottom or observe whether the pick-up car has spotted me.

Of course, on overcast days a waterproof coat is necessary but a problem arises on warm days when showers threaten or the forecast suggests rain later. One can, of course, take a normal waterproof coat, but this is heavy and cumbersome. The solution is one of the lightweight, hooded cagouls, favoured by mountaineers. Rolled tightly it takes up little space and will keep out heavy rain. On these doubtful days it is not worth worrying about wet legs. Few outdoor experiences are more miserable than labouring through thick heather, in the rain, with one's legs festooned with both trousers and outer waterproof trousers. Better by far to wear a waterproof jacket above, shorts below and let the legs get wet. Mine have never leaked yet.

Do listen to the weather forecasts which, contrary to popular belief, are usually very good. There is no fun in getting caught on high ground, several hours from salvation, in heavy rain. Go fishing instead.

Some readers will note I have said nothing of food or drink. A fact of life which soon imprints itself when rough shooting on high ground is that everything you require has to be carried. The burns are full of perfectly good water – why carry drink? If you cannot do without food for several hours then by all means take some – but, in or out of your stomach, it will weigh heavy and distracts from the marvellous appetite you would otherwise have for dinner.

How to carry the various items, plus anything you shoot, is a matter of import. A conventional game bag is a clumsy contrivance for walking any distance over rough ground, not least because the weight of the bag itself is not insignificant. A rucksack distributes the weight better, but is an unusual encumbrance when shooting. Personally I carry the ancillary items in a small canvas bag, hanging on loops, from my cartridge belt, and this arrangement leaves my trunk and shoulders entirely free. Grouse and other quarry can then be tied on the belt, although young birds need tying by the feet as well as the neck. Unless this precaution is taken the constant jolting of the rough going is likely to pull the head off and one feels sad after walking twelve miles for one grouse to discover it fell off some distance back.

After all this detail the question of gun and cartridges seems almost a minor detail as, in fact, it is. Take your normal gun and normal cartridges – they will be fully adequate. How many cartridges is less clear, but a belt full plus a few spares in a pocket will suffice for ninety-nine per cent of hill days – at least unless you get among snipe and are injudicious.

At last you may set forth into the hills, but not without one final caution. The weather can change very dramatically in the hills, but the wide horizon allows one ample warning. Keep a wary eye to the windward and if storms threaten start descending to the lower ground in good time. A characteristic of hill weather, particularly in the west, is days of alternating sun and showers; exciting to experience, but uncomfortable if caught in an exposed spot. By watching both the weather and the ground ahead it is not difficult to reach shelter before each shower arrives even though, at first sight, no shelter exists. There are few hills and moors which do not offer some form of cover in the shape of rocks, peat hags or even the overhang of a river bank. At the worst one can don the cagoul, pull up the hood and crouch with one's back to the weather – it is well worth stopping for a short time to shelter rather than continuing and getting wet.

Set a steady, but fairly slow pace. It is better to keep going steadily than hammer away for twenty minutes and rest for ten. While high ground rough shooting is not intended to be a test of stamina, there is no denying it is hard work, and unless participants are already in good shape some preparation is advisable in advance. This is not to suggest intensive training; rather walking where one would otherwise have driven to toughen up the legs and feet. When my wife and I have a social engagement within a five mile radius, and time permits, I always set off in advance on foot. This provides the dual bonus of not only improving stamina but sharpening the appetite.

The problem, you will recall, is to find quarries in this vast expanse of moorland. I will concentrate on grouse for they will provide the majority of the sport and searching for them will also uncover any alternatives. The movements of grouse, and men for that matter, are principally determined by food, shelter and sex. Sex can be disregarded, for, at the time we shoot, breeding is over and we are chasing the resultant coveys plus the occasional solitary bird or unsuccessful pair. The principal food of grouse is heather, which also provides excellent shelter. Therefore, while it is not accurate to state that grouse will never be found away from heather, this is rare and your search must be concentrated in the heather. And not just any heather. Grouse have strong preferences and, deviating a little, the art of building a good grouse moor is to so 'form' the heather, by burning, that heather of the right age and areas predominates. In the manner of ground we are considering, such optimum conditions will not exist. It may, or may not, be burnt, but where it is the job will be done inadequately and excessively large tracts will go at one time. The art is to find and search those areas of suitable heather and, in this way, the sheer scale of the problem is greatly reduced. Take away those sections which are either heatherless, or covered with unsuitable heather, and that which is left becomes manageable. What, then, is suitable heather. The answer is usually given in years of age, which is totally uninformative to anyone not familiar with *calluna vulgaris*. In practical terms it must be young enough to be nutritious and tender but old enough to have the height to provide cover. To some extent these two requirements are incompatible and the ideal is a mix of young, short heather for feeding, close to longer, older heather for cover. Nor do grouse like a flat, unbroken bed of even, perfect heather, for this makes movement difficult. The preference is for a patchwork of small clumps of varying heather interspersed with short grasses which will not obstruct movement.

This combination of heather is ideal, but the requirement of shelter also calls for protection by contours as well as heather growth. Wind does not trouble grouse unduly, partly because they are used to conditions on the hills but also because wind at floor level, among the heather clumps, is much less severe than at our head height. Even so grouse prefer the easiest conditions and will select an area which is sheltered rather than exposed. Each covey has its own territory and, although this may extend over a considerable acreage, it will initially have been chosen for the shelter it offers. In practice, on a moor it is not so much shelter as being less exposed than other spots and it is important to bear in mind the prevailing wind, for, obviously, areas in the lee start first favourites. This is not to say that ground on the windward side of a hill will not hold grouse, for heather quality is placed before shelter. Nor from a grouse's angle is ground on the windward exposed if it is well broken. Lie on the face of a moor and see how much cover comes from even minor ups and downs. The worst ground for shelter is flat, open stretches – the best, that which is well broken *on a small scale*. Small hillocks and miniature valleys, preferably at right angles to the normal wind, and covered with clumps of mixed heather, are ideal.

Therefore, as you progress, watch for such ground and unhesitatingly change direction to explore any you see. You will develop an eye for good ground and much wasted time and effort will be avoided.

Ideally the route planned will be into the wind to assist your dog to work. We know, of course, of highly trained pointers and setters, but grouse being but a brief, albeit colourful interlude in our shooting lives, you will be working your faithful labrador or spaniel. Avoid allowing it to overwork, for a dog will cover more miles on a moor than is normal on low ground; the weather may be hot and, like you, it may not be fit at the start of the season. When crossing obviously poor ground it is sensible to bring it to heel for a

The fringes of high ground lochs offer the chance of grouse, duck and snipe.

rest. Doubtless you will be able to detect the proximity of game by the dog's behaviour. Keep, also, a watch underfoot for feathers or droppings. (You will be forced to look down every step or so anyway.) Once you suspect the presence of grouse abandon your straight route and work the area carefully, keeping the dog within easy range. (Oh how easy to give the advice – how hard to apply it!) If the scent is faint merely zig-zag through the heather, but once the dog suggests the grouse are fairly near pause and take stock.

Contrary to much that is written, even August grouse are not always easy. Some are, but you have walked too far to take chances and must plan for maximum effectiveness. However innocent the youngsters in a covey, their parents are not, and where they fly will be determined by two factors. If the wind is strong they will almost certainly go with it, for that way lies maximum speed and the fastest escape. If the wind is mild the covey will follow whichever route will take them from your view in the shortest time and if this can be accomplished by flying over a hillock only yards away they can be gone in an instant. So, like a general of old preparing for a cavalry charge, review the ground. Approach from downwind, as this stops them flying with it. They will not, however, fly into the wind, but will slip out sideways and you must stand where you will have them in view. Sometimes the contours of the ground make this impossible, but the principle is to walk from downwind while remaining on the highest ground. Grouse which are alarmed but do not flush nearly always run uphill and then often squat on the crest or just over the top. Therefore call the dog in when you approach any rise giving you a short horizon or the birds will flush out of sight.

All this is a counsel of perfection and many compromises will be necessary, not least with time, for to work an area out perfectly could take longer than is justified. You will soon discover that walking-up grouse is much more complicated than just strolling over moors with a gun and dog. Alarmed grouse will often run a very considerable distance. If the scent is hot, but you cannot come to terms, retrace your steps to the starting point and cast the dog in the opposite direction – you may have been tracking where they came from earlier in the day. And, of course, they may be lying downwind of you. If baffled make a wide cast a couple of hundred yards downwind. Also remember the preference of grouse for old heather for shelter and look first among the taller growth. Peat hags are also a favourite sheltering area and as some can be higher than a man, one has to be particularly careful to preserve a clear view.

Eventually grouse will flush. From a culinary point of view you want young birds, but for the good of the stock you should try to select, and shoot, the adults. This is easier than might be expected for if the covey has flushed by design the first bird up will be an adult. Most double-barrel misses occur through the confusion and excitement caused by a number of highly sought after birds appearing where a fraction of a second before there was a barren moor. Concentrate on that first bird to the exclusion of all else. Then look for a bird which is both bigger and darker than the rest. There are no particular skills to shooting walked-up grouse. The problems come from a combination of fatigue, rough ground underfoot, and the unevenness of flight. They are not, I repeat, quite as easy as made out to be.

Single birds can be shot without hesitation, for they are usually old, past breeding successfully and, if cocks, a nuisance to younger breeding couples. If a covey of 'cheepers' rises, spare the parents for they have an important job still to do. If the covey rises out of range, or you miss with both barrels, I think it perfectly ethical to follow them up. No doubt some readers will observe I objected to following up snipe in like circumstances, but there is a difference. Snipe frequently settle quite close, can be easily marked and will be there when you arrive. Following up grouse, however, is a far harder task and if you can come to terms with them again you are entitled to a second chance. (Unless, that is, you have already scored, when they should be left.) It is rarely grouse will pitch within your sight, but note carefully the point at which they cross the horizon. It is surprising how often they will settle the instant you are out of view, and this applies particularly when the cut-off point is higher ground. I think this, and the tendency of alarmed grouse to run uphill, is explained by the instinctive desire to be in the best position to launch themselves into flight.

If you think you have hit a bird watch it until out of sight, which, on the hills, can often mean a mile or more. If it does drop, note the spot very carefully for, rest assured, the surroundings will look very different when you get there. Given a reasonable dog there is no reason why, if you are tenacious enough, you should not gather virtually every bird dropped. In the last four years my sons and I have walked-up and shot over two hundred brace of grouse and have only failed to retrieve two.

You are likely to hear the beautiful, liquid call of the golden plover before you spot the bird. It will rarely be alone, and the flocks will sometimes be substantial. These are frequently found on the higher, more barren ground and, if you are two Guns and the contours are favourable, one can hide and the other drive. The unusual reaction of 'goldies' to a gun report is to dive and a barrel fired when a flock is passing over out of range will often cause them to dive. Do, please, resist the temptation to brown the flock. They fly tightly packed and there is neither skill nor sportsmanship in bringing down half a dozen wounded birds.

At the level the golden plover favour, and higher, one meets ptarmigan. I have often hunted ptarmigan, but with a camera, and few I have encountered have been really wild. Most were content to eye me while I approached to within some twenty yards. No doubt when walked-up they provide difficult shots, and particularly in a wind, but I personally prefer to study them than shoot them.

On the low ground, whilst walking-up to the hills proper, you may find brown hares and on the higher ground, blue or mountain hares. Any man who shoots one while there is still more than half a mile to the finish is either a fool or remarkably keen.

Snipe we have already considered. Black game are enormous fun, combining speed of flight with a preference for the most attractive parts of the hills. At first acquaintance you will probably miss behind as their size deceives and they are moving faster than you think.

Lose no opportunity to shoot predators, not least because they may provide the only sport of the day! It is unlikely there will be any form of hunt and shooting a hill fox will make you a hero with the local shepherds. Sportsmanship will require, of course, that such a large animal is only shot at close quarters. Hooded crows are a most difficult adversary, with excellent eyesight and inborn caution. It is rare to get within range on an open moor, although chances improve greatly if you find a flock feeding on a sheep carcase. If time permits, and the hoodies go out of sight when you arrive, it is worth hiding and awaiting their return.

While on the subject of sheep, do keep an eye alert for sheep, or other stock, in difficulty. In some isolated areas it is the common practice to allow sheep to fend for themselves on the hills and no-one may visit them for weeks, or even months, at a time. Naturally the fatality rate is high and a major danger is that of getting bogged in the numerous soft spots found on most moors. The fleece prevents the sheep sinking and the poor animal is trapped until it dies of starvation. This would be bad enough, but once the hoodies and ravens spot an animal in trouble they peck out the eyes and tongue. This horrible fate even occurs to otherwise healthy ewes who have trouble giving birth and are temporarily unable to defend themselves. Even worse the birds attack the newly born lambs. Have no compunction about killing hoodies and if you spot a sheep in trouble detour to it. If merely trapped on its back it may need holding upright for a short time before it can stand on its own. Sometimes the condition of the sheep is so parlous you may judge it more humane to shoot it. This is a difficult decision, not least if you have later to justify it to the owner, but putting the welfare of the animal first must be the right course.

At the end of the day take precautions to protect the bag from flies for, at this time of the year, they will be active. It is sensible to check, before arrival, if there is a game larder and if not make a portable one in advance. A board suspended from a garage rafter, or similarly airy spot, with hooks under and surrounded by a muslin net works well.

Keep a close watch on the dog's feet, which may not stand up to many miles on coarse heather. Watch, also, for sheep ticks. They begin as miniature spiders running free over the dog and so small as to be very difficult to trace. The females then puncture the skin and sink their heads into the flesh. Once established they thrive on blood and rapidly swell to the size of an orange pip or larger. Attempting to pull them out usually leaves the head in and the wound festers. I find they can be removed by soaking, twice a day, in iodine until they die and fall off. Ticks are also partial to humans but they are unlikely to burrow far into your flesh before you discover their presence.

This is a very perfunctory review of high ground rough shooting. It is, I would stress, a hard sport and either loved or hated by those who have indulged. Success is never prolific and complete blanks not uncommon. Given good weather the scenery is almost too good for this world but, when the wind rises and the rain sheets in, the journey home can be misery.

I love it.

Chapter 9
Driven game

Of the various forms of driven game shooting the first to be practised in this country was driven pheasants, although quite when it began I cannot trace with certainty. The Reverend Daniel's *Rural Sports*, published in 1807, gives an account of an Italian nobleman shooting pheasants. Had driven pheasants been common at that time he would, by virtue of his social station, have shot them in this fashion, but the description of his lacerated legs and torn breeches and stockings make it plain he was walking through the coverts. Jonathan Ruffer in *The Big Shots*, places the beginning of driven shooting in the 1860s, but there is evidence of the practice well before then. Granted it takes the form of red-blooded Englishmen criticising what was a foreign introduction, but it is, nonetheless, evidence. In 1840, in his *The Moor and the Loch*, John Colquhoun quotes a periodical as saying, 'The battue is a bastard sport, an attempt to graft foreign customs on good English pastimes.' And by 1846, 'Craven', in his excellent *Recreations in Shooting*, could write, 'This new-fangled contrivance, the battue, has overrun the land with a plague of pheasants and hares, and transformed the gentleman preserver into an amateur poultry butcher.'

The ability to enjoy testing driven birds in great numbers and without undue physical effort, transformed the social status of shooting. In 1820 Bishop Latimer wrote, 'Hunting is a good exercise for men of rank, and shooting an amusement equally lawful and proper for inferior persons.' Within half a century an activity 'proper for inferior persons', became the major winter preoccupation for much of the cream of English society. Led by the Royal example at Sandringham, the great estates vied with one-another to produce the best shooting and the finest house parties, and although the common criticism that quality was disregarded for quantity was unfair to some of the more discriminating hosts, the prime aim was to achieve large bags. How well the landowners of Britain succeeded can be seen from some of the statistics. On the Prince of Wales' shoot at Sandringham, on 4th November 1896, 3114 pheasants were shot. Warter Priory, on 5th December 1909, bagged 3824, and Lord Burnham's home of Hall Barn, Bucks, topped this with 3937 on 18th December 1913.

Various writers have criticised the moral aspect of such mass slaughter and there is certainly something repugnant in the thought of so much money being spent, in an age of common poverty, and so many creatures being killed, simply to entertain a few very wealthy people. Whether, however, we can offer a complete defence by saying it is all a matter of degree and, as we are poorer people and shoot fewer, all is well, I am not entirely sure. However, as so often happens it was money rather than morals which dictated events, and the first shots of the Great War of 1914–18 signalled the intensification rather than the start, of the social changes which, principally through taxation, broke up or reduced the great estates.

The very circumstances which weighed ever more heavily on the private shoots created openings for the new concept of groups of men sharing the cost of the sport through syndicates. Although Richard Jefferies had mentioned syndicates in the later years of the nineteenth century, they played little part in the shooting scene until after the First World War. Even then their growth was modest when compared to the period following the 1939–45 War, and now the Game Conservancy tells me that no less than forty per cent of their members belong to syndicates.

Although the bags at driven pheasant shoots are but a shadow of the past, and the participants are drawn from a much wider social spectrum, the sport has not entirely thrown off the bad image of the early days. The fact that the general public equate driven pheasant shooting with rank and privilege is sad but understandable. What is, however, rather sadder and less understandable is the criticism sometimes voiced by other shooting men towards this branch of the sport. Much, no doubt, stems from envy, for to shoot driven game one has, undeniably, to be either at least moderately well-to-do or blessed with suitable friends. Whatever the motive the ill-will peeps out in a variety of ways. One is to suggest driven game is merely a test of marksmanship and requires neither a knowledge of the countryside nor physical fitness. This is largely true, but it by no means follows that the participants lack these qualities. Another attack brands syndicate members as men who appear, in expensive cars, on the shooting days only, and are never seen during the close season. This, again, is often true, but rather than repeating this criticism parrot-like it is only fair to consider why. Driven game shooting is expensive and, as I wrote earlier, a man has to be reasonably well-off to afford a Gun in a syndicate. Nowadays the majority of men who enjoy a good income work very hard to achieve it – they have to, for tax rates are so high. As a result free time is at a premium and there will be little to spare for wandering around the shoot in the summer months. This is not, I freely admit, a complete defence for all syndicate Guns, some of whom do not fit neatly into the country scene. We have all seen the brash, town-orientated Gun who talks down to the beaters, upsets the keeper, shoots low hens with utter indifference to the syndicate manager's feelings and generally harms the syndicate image. To get the matter in perspective one must remember the other unpleasant characters who can be encountered on a syndicate day – from the surly fellow driving the game cart to the walker on the public footpath who shouts abuse – but unpleasant behaviour from those who 'have' creates a much worse impression than from a 'have-not'. The argument as to whether syndicate Guns are or are not inferior sportsmen to the farming community and other who do not pay heavily for their sport will doubtless continue as long as syndicates exist but, whatever the truth, it is essential not to lose sight of the vital part syndicates play in the contemporary sporting scene. It is the money poured into their sport by enthusiastic syndicate members which assists shooting in a variety of ways. Without syndicates there would be far less driven pheasant shooting, therefore less rearing and therefore far fewer pheasants in the countryside generally. It is more than short-sighted for the rough shooter to pass the parked Jaguars and Mercedes in his five-year-old Ford, curse the affluent and, a few hours later, return from his little 'patch' with several pheasants reared by the syndicate's keeper some months earlier. Syndicates give employment to keepers and beaters, opportunities to pickers-up, yet more employment to gunsmiths, cartridge manufacturers and dozens of other occupations. They bring custom to the local pubs, hotels and garages, assist the funds of the Game Conservancy and other worthy organisations, and cause many pockets of cover to be preserved which would otherwise be ploughed under. In these, and many other ways, they are an asset to the sport and the countryside. Fellow sportsman should resist petty carping over trivial detail.

Having made this plea for tolerance towards syndicate members, it must be stated that sins of behaviour are not confined to syndicate members only and, as driven game shooting requires close human involvement, one bad performer can spoil the day for many. However, as most shooting men are fairly positive, no-nonsense characters, such problems are usually dealt with firmly and I can move on to a more pleasant observation. This is that the men who gain the most from a day's driven pheasant shooting are invariably those who both observe and participate to the full. Such men will remark that they see seven shades of brown in the wood before their peg; not only comment that the woodcock have moved on but venture a suggestion why; spot the roe deer which slipped into the rue, the sparrowhawk flitting over the firs and the prints of a rat in the mud. They are the men who, almost invariably, bring a dog; help the game cart driver carry a heavy load; remember, before the Landrovers move off, that the walking Gun has not turned up yet. They are the backbone of the shoot.

When, however, all the side issues are dispensed with, there remains the central issue of driven game shooting – marksmanship. The task of the organisation is to put birds over the Guns and the task of the Guns is to kill them cleanly and consistently. We have, of course, already considered marksmanship in chapter 3 and it is now a question of applying these general conclusions to the specialised targets of driven game.

Driven game shots have one great advantage enjoyed but rarely by exponents of other forms of the sport – advance knowledge. They know what to expect, where it is coming from, usually where it will be flying to and, roughly, when it will come. The wise man will make use of this information, and the time elapsing before action begins, to prepare himself thoroughly, both mentally and physically. This done, he can concentrate entirely on the target and absolute concentration is the first step to a clean kill. A good rule is to get to your peg in good time, and assess the position in detail. Start with the feet and ensure a good base. If on plough, stamp a flat area and move any stones, frozen clods or other obstacles. And on a steep hill moving a yard or two may provide a flat rather than sloping surface. Naturally safety will forbid one moving more than a very short distance but even a foot or two can be a great help. Examples are shooting in woodland when a trunk or branch is obscuring the obvious flight line and, conversely, moving to gain shelter from a low, dazzling sun by a trunk or branch. Having established my position I next make sure I know precisely where my neighbouring Guns are stationed and, equally important, that they are aware of me. Theoretically once the Guns have taken up positions they will remain there until the drive concludes but there is one commonsense variation well illustrated by an event on the very afternoon of the day I wrote this. I was shooting on the South Downs and the Guns were lining out in a valley cutting through a large wood. It was mid-January and a bitterly cold north wind was bringing flecks of snow. The beaters had a large block of covert to bring in and no action was likely for some twenty minutes, so, after advising my neighbours, I retired twenty yards to the edge of the wood at my back and sat snugly in the lee of an ivy clad bush. At first thought this is placing personal comfort before effectiveness but, in fact, both aspects are satisfied. Effectively I risked missing an (unlikely) early bird in return for being in better physical shape when the action really started. The same principal applies whenever weather conditions are severe – it is better for the Guns to shelter and risk losing the odd bird than stand for long periods in exposed conditions. Nor is it realistic to suggest that if the beaters can stand it so can the Guns for, usually, it is more comfortable to be keeping warm by moving inside the wood than standing still, exposed, outside it.

Given, however, that you are firmly on your peg and not skulking in the wood, the next, and very important, step is to settle safety angles. The object here is to emblazon on the brain the safe and unsafe segments, once again, to allow one's complete concentration on the shot without hesitating over detail which could have been settled earlier. The oft given advice to beware stops and pickers-up hidden by or in hedges is grossly misleading, for it implies that were these hazards not present, one would normally fire at face level. No sane man would do this even if confident there were no humans present and I am concerned with other safety angles. At a pheasant shoot any bird worth shooting will normally be at a safe angle through 360 degrees, but there are sometimes special dangers to watch. One is where the birds are being driven off higher ground and the normally safe angle is too close to the beating line. Another is where pellets, fired safely, will fall among residential buildings. They are not 'quite safe', for a host of possible accidents, such as the eyes of a baby lying face up in a pram, exist, and, at the least, the image of shooting is not helped by rattling pellets among the non-shooting public. If a bird is wounded, or a bird obviously wounded earlier comes through low, it is sometimes desirable to fire low to the rear. The Gun who has checked there is adequate open space behind, free from pickers-up, can do this with confidence.

Safety having been comfortably dealt with, more practical matters arise. Dogs of doubtful stability are best secured, for single-minded shooting is never helped by keeping a wary eye groundwards. And do start with ample cartridges. When I make this error I soon begin to assess whether I should carry on normally and hope supplies will last out, start picking my shoots, or ration them on a strict one per bird basis. As a result concentration goes and with it marksmanship. (The ability to borrow cartridges from neighbours is yet another reason for using a 12 bore rather than something smaller.)

Consider next the likely flight path of the birds. On a familiar shoot this will be known but on strange ground much can be deduced. The covert, or cover, from which the birds are to be flushed is usually obvious and if their destination is also in view then the flight line should be clear. This information is of little help where the birds can be seen several hundred yards before reaching you but there are positions, of which a stand in a narrow ride before the leaf is fully off is an example, where it is vital. On land which undulates pheasants will, provided it takes them in the general direction they wish to travel, take a downhill route to gain increased speed. Conversely they are reluctant to fly uphill, unless anxious to attain a particular spot. Wind will not turn pheasants and partridges away from their destination unless it is very strong, but it may change their route to it. Tall trees also affect flight paths, for birds will not climb over a narrow clump of trees when they can avoid them with a slight change of course. Such reasoning should suggest the most likely spot at which birds will appear and the good Gun will concentrate on this. This is not to say he will stare, for concentration will soon fade and other movement around the periphery may be missed. It is more a question of taking a relaxed and general view, but paying special attention to the favoured spot. Perhaps the greatest mistake of driven game shots is to become bored and allow attention to wander. Most of us would be delighted to enjoy a drive composed of those

Waiting for the grouse, with the gun at rest but in position, spare cartridges to hand and a steady gaze on the horizon.

birds we have missed over the years because our eyes and thoughts had drifted elsewhere!

Another useful preliminary is to assess the effect of the wind upon not just the flight path of the birds but their overall performance. A strong side wind will cause a pheasant approaching head-on to drift sideways, but the lack of fixed marks in the sky will make this difficult to spot. Assessing the fact beforehand and making a mental note to aim off is one more potential problem dealt with in advance. Birds with the wind in their tails will obviously need greater lead and birds flying into a strong wind can easily be missed in front.

A further important contribution towards an effective performance comes from ensuring one is properly dressed for the conditions, for no-one can shoot to their normal standard when cold or wet. Clothing has been covered fully in an earlier chapter, but driven game shots are inclined to forget how the long spells of enforced immobility, usually in open positions, exposes them to cold more than others. Closely observing my companions I note a tendency to wear much the same clothes through the season, which must mean being over-dressed on some occasions and under on others. Granted it is not easy to dress correctly for an entire day, for it is often freezing for the first drive, pleasantly warm just before lunch and freezing again as the day ends, but a flexible approach is both practical and possible. At very little inconvenience a game bag can be taken, holding a spare pullover, waterproof trousers, neckscarf and – luxury on a raw day! – a flask of coffee. (Beware the nips of whisky or rum which draw the heat to the skin, warm for a brief interval and leave one colder than before.) Mittens give warmth to the hands without loss of finger sensitivity and a silk scarf gives surprising warmth to the neck. All these items offer the flexibility of removal if the day warms, and early in the season it is sensible to avoid clothing which cannot be discarded; for example, a heavily padded shooting jacket or thick underwear. Later in the season, when the forecast is for severe weather, flexibility can be forgotten and it is sensible to start with a good layer of underclothes. It is now fashionable to laugh at 'long Johns', but, in an Angus grouse butt in October or the open face of the South Downs in January, I am content to feel the smug evidence of my decadence while others turn blue proving their fortitude. In fact, my favourite garment for driven game and wildfowling – equally cold activities – is a one-piece, Churchillian, combined vest and long pants, from wrists to ankles.

One snare for formal shoot participants is the shooting suit, which undeniably looks excellent but lacks the ability of more mundane clothing to keep out prolonged rain. I accept that sartorially a suit raises a man above the common herd, but I will forgo this in return for the ability to snap a hood onto my Barbour and turn my back to driving rain slanting in at 45 degrees.

The most important contribution towards keeping warm also contains the added advantage of stirring up the body and senses but, surprisingly, few people seem to make use of it. Cold is such a problem at driven shoots because the Guns spend most of their time standing still. Why, therefore, not walk between drives rather than climbing stiffly into a cold vehicle and riding? Sometimes, of course, distance and time make walking impossible, but very often a brisk five minute walk will raise both temperature and spirits. Try it.

Finally, in this summary of preparations and precautions, I will touch on a subject almost never mentioned – spectacles. Given the presence of a suspected dangerous shot, a shield of glass or plastic in front of the eyes is reassuring, but this minor advantage is more than off-set by the problems of shooting in rain or drizzle. Spectacle wearers of long standing will have evolved their own solutions, but for new-comers some advice will help. The first essential is a really wide-brimmed hat to keep the rain drops from the lenses. Much depends on whether the rain is falling vertically or slanting in on a strong wind. If the former a conventional cap or fore and aft will do, but the latter conditions require greater protection. A golfer's cap with a very wide sunshade brim, dyed to a sombre colour, is excellent and surplus Army stores sometimes have fatigue caps of a similar design. They look hideous and provide material for the shoot wag but they do keep rain off glasses. Equally they stop you seeing birds overhead but this is the lesser of two evils. In really heavy rain it is best to ask your neighbours to shout when a bird is approaching and then keep the glasses clear by looking away from the weather. In practice, you will find that however bad vision appears beforehand, the eyes, when a target appears, will disregard the blur of water and focus on it. Up to a certain level it is possible to shoot normally with vision interference but, eventually, the lenses must be cleaned. Naturally, a clean, dry handkerchief is essential and where the forecast is wet it is sensible to bring several. (For that matter it is also sensible to bring a change of exterior clothing, for it is a luxury to don a dry jacket, trousers and hat after lunch when all around people are struggling into well soaked clothing.)

Essentially the message of the last few hundred words is that good shooting at driven game is not entirely dependent on marksmanship. A man of only medium ability as a shot, who makes the best of the chances which come his way, can achieve at least as good a percentage of kills to cartridges as the excellent marksman who is lazy and muddled in his preparations and application.

Generalities dealt with, we can be specific, and, as the driven game season begins with grouse, start with the problems of this most testing quarry. There are many differences between driven pheasant and grouse but one liable to catch the newcomer unawares, and which is rarely mentioned, is the problem of distance. On low ground extra cartridges or dry clothes are rarely far away but the time taken to reach a moor can make a return journey impractical. Therefore make a check list of all you will need, ensure it is packed and if in doubt take extra. This applies with particular force to clothing, for men with no hill experience underestimate the severe weather conditions which can be encountered, even in August. Conversely the hot days can be very hot indeed and ample drink is needed. *Also take a tube of fly repellent*. Do not, at your peril, disregard this as trivial advice and forget it or the day may come when the midges are out and you have no defence. I have never met weather conditions which have caused me discomfort approaching that of the common midge.

A shooting stick is almost essential for many drives involve a long wait. Additionally some butts are too low and, as concealment requires one to hide as much as possible, the lack of a shooting stick imposes a tiring stoop. Interest is added to the day by enquiring, before each drive, the plan of operations and, given a butt with a good view, it is fascinating to watch the operation unfold. The extreme contrasts of the views from different butts is another aspect which will impress the low ground man. On one drive the horizon can be several miles and on another twenty yards, giving, or so it appears, an impossible instant of time in which to shoot. In fact, butt sitings have usually been established over many years and the apparently 'impossible' would not be there if they were. The real drawback to the short horizon butt is the utter boredom of staring at the same small patch of heather for what seems hours.

It is sensible to move into the butts in good time, for the beaters will sometimes flush grouse while walking to their starting positions. If your host, or another Gun with a knowledge of the ground, is to hand, ask for the likely flight lines. Grouse are very much birds of habit over flight and fore-knowledge of where they will appear saves a valuable moment of time. Without this guidance you should assume the first birds through are following the normal route and concentrate on this segment of the horizon.

Once in the butt follow the practice of careful preparation. Locate the neighbouring butts and, if there are no warning sticks, and you are a grouse novice, put your gun sleeve, cartridge bag or other impedimenta on the butt wall to remind you of safety angles. If an end Gun, the organiser should have warned you of any flankers, but keep an eye open if he has not. Consider your horizon, for it may be irregular with a much longer range of vision on one side than the other. If so, concentrate rather more on the short horizon, at least until the first arrivals give a clue to the line. Check there are no awkward clumps of heather on the butt parapet and trim any that are. Test the base for levelness and firmness. If muddy find some stone or, failing this, heather. Concealment is important, for grouse will often turn from a butt with an obvious occupant. (Light coloured shifts, scarves, and lady companions dressed for effect not camouflage, should be avoided.) The ideal parapet height is that over which one can just shoot horizontally when standing upright. If it is lower than this, and there is time to spare, build the level up with heather clumps. Unless you are shooting double guns, lay several cartridges on the parapet, bases towards you, for rapid reloading. This is better than having a lady hold them, as the parapet does not jump up and down shouting, 'Look, there's another lot coming', while you try to wrest cartridges from it. Now do the unusual thing and take a good look behind, something most Guns do as the first covey streaks over. You may find the horizon is so short that the birds will be out of view before a shot can be taken behind and it is pointless to turn round. Or this limitation may apply to only one flank.

Consider, now, the wind and whether the grouse will be drifting. And the sun. If it blinds to the left, and birds split either side of the butt, then your fore-knowledge will tell you to turn away from it. Almost certainly you will have been instructed on when to cease shooting forward, but if not consider whether you will see the beaters before they are dangerously near and, if not, what you propose to do about it.

You are now ready, and, if this is your first attempt at driven grouse, likely to suffer some humiliation. Grouse, being brown birds flying low over a brown background, are difficult to spot. Additionally, flat moors are never flat and hilly ones are very hilly. As a result a covey is likely to burst upon you totally unexpected. This lack of awareness is intensified by two further factors. Firstly, grouse drives often take a long time and concentration wanes. Secondly, grouse fly fast and with a wind behind them, devilishly so. I certainly do not hold myself out to be an expert driven grouse shot but I have evolved two rules which are essential for solving the problems – they are to keep a constant, but relaxed watch on one's front no matter how long the drive takes, and to shoot fast with the intention of taking both shots in front. The first rule is obvious, but the second requires some explanation. Grouse fly at such speed that the time taken to turn round sees them well behind and the second barrel is rarely effective. While it is often difficult to get off two barrels in front the prospects of a kill with the second barrel are usually greater than an attempt behind. Of course, every case varies and some situations may make it better, or even essential, to take the second barrel behind. However, all things being equal, it is usually far better to take both barrels in front. Here the driven pheasant man is at a disadvantage, for all his experience encourages him to leave the first shot too late. Forty yards is quite close enough, for by the time the shot and target meet the range will be several yards closer. One sensible but difficult discipline is to fire the choke barrel first, reserving the more open barrel for what will be a closer target.

Advising a relative newcomer to the sport of shooting to fire two rapid shots would invite two wild misses, but you, my readers, are experienced men. We know that some of our best shots are made when there is no time for any deliberation and forcing oneself to fire quickly may have beneficial results. Alternatively it may be disastrous, in which event it is best to slow to normal pace and take one, hopefully effective, shot per covey and then speed up as confidence returns.

For most of us opportunities to shoot driven grouse are limited by money and distance. Sadly, sport with that other superb quarry, the partridge, has also been restricted for many years through the decline in numbers. This, as we know through the researches of the Game Conservancy, is essentially due to modern farming practices, which have created unfavourable conditions in several ways. However, some modest compromises, coupled with luck with the weather at critical times in the breeding cycles of not only partridges but insects, can produce a shootable surplus. Additionally, and with less element of chance, the techniques of rearing partridges have been much improved and the numbers reared grow steadily each year. Many regret that red-legs have proved more suitable for this, particularly for 'holding' after release, but experience with driving red-legs has largely overcome the old criticism of their tendency to fly poorly.

The driven pheasant man trying his hand at partridges for the first time will encounter fewer problems than with grouse, for the general format of surroundings, driving methods and much else follows the familiar pattern of a pheasant shoot. Regrettably partridge shooting is not what it was, and not only in quantity but performance. Grouse moor keepers have always looked down on pheasant shooting – in this season I heard an Angus keeper, on learning the afternoon was to be devoted to pheasants, say, 'Och, weel, so we are going to be shooting the poultry' – but in the old days partridge beat keepers had similar feelings of superiority. Certainly it is harder to drive partridges just where you want them than it is pheasants, although I have seen it done to perfection at Sutton Scotney.

Understandably in the days when partridge shooting played a larger part in the season, much more money and effort was devoted to them. Crop planning was done with sport very much in mind and hedges were allowed to grow higher. In fact it was common for tenant farmers to have a clause in their lease expressly forbidding the trimming of hedge tops. A short experience of driven partridge shooting will soon demonstrate the wisdom of this. Given a low hedge, birds can spot the Guns and veer off in sufficient time, but with high hedges and tree belts the birds are almost over the Guns before seeing them. Not only does high cover 'commit' the partridges to crossing the line, it also forces them to fly high and height, from the Gun's viewpoint, usually means more time. Firstly, he enjoys earlier warning as high birds can often be spotted through gaps in the cover. Secondly, the second barrel can be taken straight down the line, rather than raising the barrels to a safe angle, while low birds cross, and taking the second shot behind.

One of the signs of an experienced partridge man is where he positions himself in relation to the cover or, if the host, where he positions his Guns. The optimum is far enough back to give maximum shooting time without being so far as to allow the birds to spot the Gun in time and swing. It is not possible to give firm guidance in terms of X yards back for every foot height of the cover, for other factors are involved. On falling ground the Guns can stand further back; on rising ground nearer. When the birds come with the wind, and therefore faster, the Guns can stand further back and equally so when the sun is at their backs and in the eyes of the partridges. Conversely with either of these factors reversed the Guns must stand nearer.

Silence is very important, for once a single covey of birds has been frightened back, or to the flanks, others may follow. Avoid firing at pigeons for the same reason.

The main problem over successful marksmanship at partridges is precisely the same as grouse – it all happens too quickly. One moment the sky is empty, an instant later it is dotted with a confusion of brown birds and

Confident that he has killed cleanly, the Gun is already looking for the next bird.

immediately it is empty again. Once again the rule is to spend the early stages in general preparation, and then decide where the birds will show and concentrate on that area. In general, the possible flight lines for the partridges are more restricted than for grouse and, usually, the flanks can be ignored until shots from the neighbours sound a warning. Partridges are reluctant to fly higher than forced to by obstacles, and if the cover in front has obvious low gaps these are the places to watch.

Both grouse and partridge give the impression of moving very fast, giving little time to shoot. With grouse this is painfully true, but with partridge there is usually more time than appears. Provided your eyes pick them up as they first appear, there should be ample time for two barrels, indeed, many of the great shots of old thought little of taking four birds from one covey when shooting double guns. Here the man who prefers to shoot deliberately and slowly is at a disadvantage and maximum success goes to the instinctive shot who fires 'at' the bird the instant the butt beds. A further complication for the slower shot, who is used to following and overtaking pheasants with the barrels, is the reluctance of startled partridges to fly in a straight line. Like fragments from a bursting shell they hurtle in all directions and the Gun who hesitates is lost.

And so to the mainstay of driven shooting – pheasants. Around the turn of the century a poll was held among the top shots of the country to ascertain the most difficult shot and, by an overwhelming majority, the pheasant won. Opinions varied as to the precise form of pheasant. Some were foxed by curlers, others by dropping birds on still wings and yet more by sheer height, but the details do not matter so much as the declared supremacy of the pheasant. In fact, I cannot accept this without qualifications. Firstly the jury were simply the best shots known to the enquirer and they, for social reasons, had far more experience of pheasants than other quarries. Secondly, they were not commenting on the average pheasant, which is not difficult, but the most difficult shots presented by pheasants. A poll conducted on the most difficult bird, judged on the *average* shot presented, would certainly place grouse first and, probably, coastal duck before the pheasant.

I have already dealt with the importance of adequate preparation, leaving the Gun free to concentrate mind and body on marksmanship and, this done, I am reluctant to hold forth too positively on precisely how driven pheasants should be shot. As I explained in chapter 3, everyone has his own style and peculiarities and unless some aspect is blatantly wrong, trying to alter the style of an experienced shooting man, developed over some years, may do more harm than good. This said, however, some particular aspects warrant attention. As a start I make the categorical statement that most Guns leave the shot too late. Hit well in front pheasants require less lead and, if missed, there is time for a measured second barrel. But stand as an end Gun and look up the line – see how many men delay their first barrel until the bird is almost overhead and then have to rush the second or turn round. Ideally the bodies should fall around the pegs but usually they are well behind.

For many Guns, and I am one, the bird both quartering and rising presents unusual difficulty. The cowardly answer is to turn through 90 degrees and take it as a simple crosser. Always provided, that is, your neighbour does not grow impatient and take it first! Which leads to that vexed question of poaching, one of the major sources of irritation in driven game shooting. Nothing I write here will cure the problem of the greedy Gun who knowingly shoots the birds of others. The oft-proffered solution is to poach his birds, but it is a poor remedy. I know, for I have tried it. One raises one's gun to poach, feels guilty, fails to swing correctly and misses. At this the sinner then shoots the bird, his own by right, and feels morally free to poach yours for the rest of the day.

Fortunately deliberate poachers are few and the greater problem comes from the many situations in which fair Guns are in doubt. The extreme points of view vary between the man who believes he has a perfect right to shoot at any bird within range to the strict principle that a bird should only be shot by the Gun to whom it is heading. The argument that any bird in range is legitimate is soon destroyed. Consider a line of Guns facing a covert. A pheasant rises opposite number four, flies towards him until forty yards away, then swings downhill at an angle, climbing as it progresses. It was in range of four, but a low, slow shot. Obviously he should not fire. The bird is now heading directly for number seven, but will pass five and six within range. If we apply the opposite extreme, that birds should be shot by the Gun they cross, five and six will not shoot. But as the pheasant sweeps past them it makes a more testing target than for seven, to whom it is a straightforward oncomer – has not number five a right to shoot? But it will be faster and higher by the time it passes six – should not five leave it for six? There are endless permutations of men, pheasants and angles and it is difficult to form a clear and straightforward rule. Personally, I believe one can shoot those birds which are nearer to oneself than anyone else, always provided that, if left, they would not have made more testing birds for a companion. This definition includes crossing birds heading elsewhere and, as I realise this practice will offend some, when on a strange shoot I always play safe and leave questionable birds until discovering the local standards. (One exception is the wounded bird, for example, one with a leg down or a slow, weak flyer. Here any Gun in range should fire, for the priority is humaneness rather than courtesy.)

Naturally a good sportsman will not always apply the local rule without regard to the circumstances. Various occasions come to mind when birds, although legitimate shots, should be allowed through; for example, when the recipient has drawn badly and seen little sport for some time, or is a youngster who shoots as many in a season as you in a good day. A practice which I find annoying is the Gun who waits until his neighbour has had his first barrel and then fires. If a bird is 'yours', you are entitled to take two barrels without interruption. Then, and only then, may others join in, although there is a strong moral argument that one man only is entitled to try to kill a bird and if he fails it should go free.

The extremes of difficulty in shooting driven pheasants vary considerably, with the easy end sometimes very easy. Conversely, wind or height makes pheasants very difficult and a combination of both sometimes well-nigh impossible. It is common to read that no pheasant every flies so high as to be out of shot, but I doubt this. My good fortune takes me to several shoots where the best drives produce very high pheasants. I believe a pheasant looks the same size whether fifty yards high or fifty yards sideways; indeed, viewed from below it should look bigger. Many of the birds at which I shoot are fifty yards high and, on some drives, practically all are over forty. Nearly a century ago Payne-Gallwey carried out various experiments, from which he concluded that only one pheasant in six would be killed if struck overhead, in the centre of the pattern, at forty yards. Correspondence I conducted with Messrs. Eley's raises questions over the soundness of Payne-Gallwey's research, but I am sure many really high birds are missed not through ineptitude but the sheer ballistic impossibility of killing consistently at these ranges. The fact that every so often someone kills an absolute angel and the assembly choruses, 'There you are – it can be done', leaves me unconvinced. A post-mortem would almost certainly show a single pellet in the head or heart plus one or two in relatively harmless positions. Had the one pellet been half an inch either way it would have been another apparent miss.

This point made, however, there is no denying the ability of *experienced* good shots to kill reasonably high birds consistently, and I stress experienced, for there is as much a knack in killing high pheasants as shooting driven grouse. In practice, although people talk of the difficulties of high pheasants, I believe the problem comes not from the height but the distance. The complexities of shooting moving targets are such that few shots will be perfectly aimed, and as a mis-aimed shot travels further from the gun, so the distance the centre of the pattern moves away from the correct flight path will increase. Within normal ranges this will not matter over-much, for as distance increases so the shot pattern widens to compensate for minor errors. However, at long ranges the outer rim of the pattern has opened up to such a degree that the pellet density is too sporadic to ensure a kill, or even a hit with a single pellet, and only birds well centred in the pattern will be killed. In other words the accuracy of aim called for in distant shots is greater than with medium ranges and it is not height but range that defeats us. Indeed, I believe a bird forty yards high is easier than a low bird or rabbit forty yards wide, for the high target stands out clearly.

Apart from the paramount need for accuracy the other most common reason for missing high birds is insufficient lead and, surprisingly, this failing often occurs with men who have considerable experience at driven pheasants, shown at modest heights. The explanation lies in the technique of shooting 'at' birds and letting instinct look after lead. This works well at the closer ranges but when more distant shots are taken a perceptible lead is necessary and this is more easily applied by a slow and deliberate shot. Certainly, when I am failing at high pheasants the decision to miss the next one in front often provides a cure.

Comparatively few shots nowadays shoot with double Guns, and many sportsmen will never have enjoyed this, literally, high powered form of the sport. If you happen to be a single gun owner and receive an invitation including this requirement, have no hesitation in accepting and borrowing a second gun. Even ignoring the fact that double guns imply much sport, the very act of shooting doubles is an experience not to be missed. Having found the spare gun you next need a loader and while a local keeper is best almost any sensible man can learn the knack in minutes. Failing this one's wife will doubtless perform very well, although a telephone call to the host is wise to ensure there is no objection.

It is essential to have a brief practice session with the loader beforehand. The technique of changing guns is simple, but a few rules need following. Both Gun and loader should hand guns over with the safety catch in the safe position and with the barrels vertical. The loader looks at the guns and the Gun continues to look ahead for targets. The Gun holds the gun he is passing back with his right hand and holds his left hand open to receive the replacement, while the loader takes the empty gun by the fore-end with his left hand and, holding the loaded gun with his right hand, places the fore-end in the Gun's open left hand.

In practice, unless targets are prolific the possession of a spare gun does not enable one to fire a great many more shots. At first thought this sounds a controversial statement, but if you go through a season considering just how many extra shots could have been taken with a second gun, the answer is surprisingly few. Apart from the occasional 'bouquet', there is usually time to reload between pheasants and, all too frequently, there is little enough time to get off both barrels at grouse or partridge, let alone change guns. To my mind the real advantage of double guns is not increased fire power, but relaxation and vigilance. With a single gun one's concentration is broken by the need to reload and in a hot corner the complexities of spotting, shooting and reloading lead to pressure, fumbling and, eventually, loss of rhythm and form. Given double guns and a loader the panic disappears and one can concentrate on spotting and shooting. Double guns provide not just an opportunity to fire more cartridges but to shoot better.

Chapter 10
Shoot management

Many experienced shooting men find that willingly or otherwise they become involved in shoot management. Two truths emerge rapidly – it is a far more complex job than first appears and most aspects boil down to money. (I am sorry to bring money into our sport, but it is unavoidable and, this being so, we must strive to operate as economically as possible.) Shoots, and consequently the task of running them, vary considerably, but this chapter is concerned principally with the type of shoot responsible for the majority of low ground sport in Britain – a driven shoot of eight to ten Guns operating as a syndicate and bagging mainly pheasants. Either side of this norm lie the extremes, ranging from the private shoot where the Guns are guests, to the modest enterprise where the members do their own keepering and alternate between beating and standing on shooting days. The next chapter is devoted to this latter form. Private shoots are nearly always operated by the owner or tenant of the ground and, for reasons irrelevant to this book, financial burdens weigh less heavily on them than syndicates. As this chapter never wanders far from the pressure of money, it will offer less to such fortunates but there may be the odd straw of wisdom for them.

Chapter 6 included advice on finding, assessing and leasing ground, so I will start from the presumption that the ground is in hand. In broad terms the task falls into three areas: setting up the structure of the shoot; planning and managing all the operations necessary to ensure an adequate stock of game; shooting it efficiently, safely and enjoyably.

The first step is to resolve your own personal position as the shoot manager – are you doing the job for pleasure or to derive a benefit? Unquestionably there is a strong case for seeking a reward in some form. A shoot manager's responsibilities last the year round; his shooting days are never entirely free for enjoyment; all problems come to rest on his back and if the season is a failure, he carries the blame. Not unreasonably some managers expect to receive a free Gun, or at least pay a reduced subscription, in return. Unfortunately any such concession tends to engender ill-feeling – as soon as a manager accepts a reward he also attracts a heavier obligation and criticisms are voiced which would previously have been stillborn. My own view is that if one does not want to manage the shoot for the pleasure of being involved in all the activities, and doing an interesting job well, then it is better just to pay the sub and be an ordinary Gun.

It is essential to form a clear picture at the beginning of the form of shoot you wish to build. Unless a shoot is properly balanced in all respects, major problems are inevitable. To give simple examples, if your intended fellow Guns have only limited money available for their subscriptions, then no time need be wasted contemplating a lease of 2000 plus acres and employing a keeper and assistant. And plans to rear 4000–5000 birds a year will not fit with a lease of only a few hundred acres. Most new shoots begin because a man of initiative, which all shoot managers are, has either ground or members in view and it is wise to start with a large sheet of clean paper, list the known factors at the top and plan the structure.

Basically you are concerned with how much sport the shoot will have to provide, what this will cost and how much the Guns will be willing to pay. Unless these three factors all make sense you would be unwise to proceed. Some simple arithmetic quickly demonstrates the size of the task. Guns in driven game shoots want to shoot driven game – on the face of it a ridiculously simple statement, but one easily overlooked by organisers. In every other form of shooting, particularly normal rough shooting, the participants have much to occupy them. With driven game most of the day is spent standing still waiting for a target and unless targets appear at not too infrequent intervals, boredom and dissatisfaction develops. Nine Guns is enough for most driven shoots and although it is impossible to say how much sport each man needs to keep him happy, a reasonable average is probably around fifteen pheasants a day. This figure is based on seven drives a day, four before and three after lunch, which gives about two birds per drive – not generous, but enough. With nine Guns this means a daily bag of 135, and if there are eight main days shooting, a total of 1080. Allowing for a couple of boundary days takes the annual bag to about 1200. How many birds must be reared to provide this will vary considerably with the ground – in East Anglia a couple of thousand or less would do, but in Sussex or Dorset it could run as high as four thousand.

There is, you will discover, little real scope for financial flexibility in running a good driven shoot for each step directs you inescapably towards the next and all lead upward. If, as I have just reasoned, even modest sport requires a bag of a thousand plus, then a full-time keeper is essential. (There are, of course, shoots that manage without and still top a thousand birds, but a detailed examination will always reveal an exceptional reason. It may be surrounded by keepered shoots, who rear heavily, or run by the resident farmer whose personal involvement, plus that of staff with an hour or so to spare regularly, adds up to virtually a full-time man.) As a base, therefore, you must start with an adequate acreage and a full-time man.

The man, and no doubt a family, must live somewhere. If you are lucky

In the final reckoning all that really matters is whether the Guns enjoyed the day.

he will already live locally; if not the shoot must house him and while a cottage may well go with the ground, so will the obligation to maintain it. A keeper will expect a vehicle. (He might conceivably be a better keeper with just a tractor and trailer, but that is another story.) There are sporting rates to be paid and a team of beaters every shooting day. These and many other outgoings add up to a formidable total, but I will not give actual figures, for they will be out of date before this book is even published.

It is at this point that many shoot organisers make the grave error of attempting to economise. The essential point of all the items I have listed so far is that they are inescapable and, except in exceptional circumstances, cannot be pruned. The remaining items can be pruned and after assessing the level to which the annual cost has risen, many men feel concern and restrict the rearing. The temptation is considerable for whether the birds are hatched from caught up stock, from day-olds or bought as poults, the cost is in direct proportion to numbers. Nor is the position helped by statistics on the lines of, 'the average cost per bird bagged is £11', or whatever the current rate may be. The vital point that is so often overlooked is that the basic overheads have to be paid whether ten pheasants or ten thousand are released, and once these are met the cost *per extra pheasant* is very low. Consider a shoot where an economy conscious manager has released two thousand birds and calculated the subs accordingly. With the basics already met the cost of extra birds is no more than the price of the eggs or chicks, plus some heat and food – it costs no more in keepering, rent of ground, beaters or anything else. In fact, the price for which the extra birds can be sold when bagged, even allowing for the fact that possibly only one in three will be bagged, will probably be little less than their cost. It comes down to maximum utilisation of equipment and labour and, in terms of driven pheasant shooting, the sensible course is never to rear the minimum required to give sufficient sport but to rear the maximum that the man and the ground can cope with.

The reasoning makes sense for the individual Gun as well. The cost of his shooting goes well beyond the annual subscription. It involves the use of a car to travel to the shoot, the maintenance of a dog or dogs, a gun or guns, insurance, possibly hotel accommodation. Not least it requires that most precious commodity for busy men – time. All these are basic overheads which are constant whatever the bag. How much better to pay a relatively small increase in the subscription and see substantially more sport.

If the money available simply will not run to a shoot on the scale so far envisaged, then you will not, for the reasons just outlined, achieve a significant saving by reducing the numbers reared. The answer is the more fundamental one of altering the concept of the shoot by dispensing with a full-time keeper.

For many shooting men accustomed to large, formal shoots this may sound a ridiculous suggestion but, organised properly, a respectable bag can be achieved with a part-timer, as will be demonstrated in the next chapter. The secret is to use his limited time to the maximum effect, which means some careful thinking to get the priorities right. One of the most time-consuming tasks on well keepered ground is predator control, and no doubt to the horror of some readers, I suggest this can be largely abandoned to allow a part-timer to concentrate on rearing, and later, feeding. The fact, so often forgotten, is that jays, magpies, rats, stoats and other so-called villains do not harm well grown poults and mature pheasants. The only real danger to adult pheasants is foxes and neither they nor minor predators harm pheasant chicks and young poults during rearing if properly protected. Provided the rearing principles I set out shortly are followed, poults are not at risk until they are at least seven weeks old and even then the exposure is low. Given proper care for the reared birds, the real purpose of predator control is to assist the wild pheasants and partridges to breed, but if there is simply not enough money for all aspects of the job, the concentration must go on rearing. This policy must make economic sense, particularly in those areas which do not naturally favour game, and where the wild population would not produce a good stock even if well keepered. Nor, in advocating this policy, am I forgetting those areas which are claimed to carry a high 'natural' head of game. What this usually means is that it is good shooting country and large numbers are reared over a wide area. Stop all rearing and see what happens to the dense 'natural' stock within a couple of years.

There are more aspects of a keeper's work that must be neglected by a part-timer than just predator control and I am certainly not suggesting indifference to these short-comings. The essence of my advice is that if a shoot can only afford a part-timer then he cannot try to do everything or everything will be done badly – the priorities must be done well and the remainder either left or tackled when time permits. The essentials of a part-timer's year are to spend February and March making sure the rearing equipment and pens are in first-class order and doing predator control. From then on rearing will occupy all his available time until the birds are free in the coverts, when the priority is feeding. The only exception is fox control which, subject to local practice, is a year round activity.

In considering the more impecunious I must not lose sight of those affluent shoots able to afford more than one man. However, it does not follow that the money is best spent by employing an assistant the year through. In good areas the constant attention to predator control permitted by an extra man may mean a significant increase in wild stock but this should not be taken for granted. Adding up what the assistant costs will produce a formidable total and it may be the money is better spent in rearing more birds and employing extra help in the rearing season only. However, there may be local factors which make a full-time assistant more important than extra birds in the release pen. Poaching is one. There is little point in putting more birds into the woods if an over-stretched single-handed keeper cannot stop the locals taking them out a few months later.

So far I have written entirely for the shoot manager of a syndicate and ignored men operating shoots on ground they personally own or tenant as farmers. In practice such advice is rarely needed for most suitable ground has been run as a shoot for many years and the occupant moved into an established situation from the start. The shoot manager who is also the farmer has enormous advantages over we lesser beings in every respect. He can plan his crops with the shooting in mind, divert labour, obtain tail corn for feeding, leave odd corners for wild birds to breed, be home in a flash to change when wet – the list is endless. This is not to say that every shoot of this nature is perfectly run. There is a tendency to go on in the same way without taking an occasional deep look at whether improvements are possible. Whatever criticisms may be levelled at syndicates, their need to be money conscious has provided the stimulus for many improvements and economies in driven game shooting.

Few men wake up one morning with neither ground nor members and suddenly decide to form a syndicate – the process is more usually a slow development which is spurred by the arrival of one factor or the other. Even if you have a nucleus of tried and trusted shooting friends anxious to join with you, it will almost certainly be necessary to recruit some strangers. To fit well into the team they need to be safe shots, have at least some experience of driven game shooting and be pleasant people. Finding such paragons is time consuming, but resist the temptation to accept the first applicants and hope for the best. Of all the factors which spoil a day's shooting, nothing, neither rain, slovenly beaters, a paucity of birds nor any other misfortunate casts such gloom as an unsafe or unpleasant Gun. Even worse most problems can be solved quickly but getting rid of a bad Gun is an embarrassing matter. The safest course is to seek recruits from your shooting friends, widening the circle as necessary. This failing, one is driven to advertising and the wording should state positively that only safe and congenial men should respond. Such a statement of intent will attract rather than repel the good men and discourage the suspects. To avoid the embarrassment of telling a man he is unsuitable, proceed cautiously. Start with a box number, when some replies can be discarded at the start. Progress to a telephone chat, implying that a vacancy is expected depending on the business commitments of an existing member. Whilst untrue, it gives you flexibility and is kinder to the applicant than discussing a positive vacancy for which he may be refused. *Always* meet an applicant personally – it is far too hazardous to accept a Gun without. Quite naturally an applicant will wish to see the ground and this provides a good opportunity to meet in the countryside. However acceptable he may be as a person, the matter of safety will still be unresolved. The temptation to assume that an apparently sensible man is a safe shot is considerable but as a shoot manager you cannot opt to take a personal chance. The safety of other people is in your hands and your duty is to take all reasonable measures to check. If discreet questioning fails to reveal common friends where inquiry can be made, I think it entirely proper to ask the name of another shoot manager or owner who can be approached for a reference. Anyone who takes umbrage at such a reasonable precaution is unlikely to make a good syndicate member.

There is more to the matter of members but first we must look at a deeper aspect. So far I have written of the work of a shoot manager but not defined the position in detail. In some cases a manager is simply elected from a group of equals but in others his power is not just popular support but legal. There are advantages and disadvantages in both and those in a position to select their standing need to weigh the factors carefully. Broadly speaking he who holds the lease controls the shoot. If you find the ground you have the opportunity either to take it in your own name or in the name of the syndicate (with members giving individual guarantees). Becoming the sole legal tenant gives you absolute power to form and run the syndicate according to your own rules, including taking Guns on an annual basis, with the advantage of dropping those who prove unsafe or otherwise undesirable. However, as the sole tenant you are personally liable for the rent and for performing all the obligations of the lease. If, for any reason, your Guns resign you are left holding all the babies, not the smallest of which would be redundancy obligations to the keeper. Perhaps the best compromise is to spread the risk by taking the lease in the names of a few known friends and 'topping up' with annual Guns.

Because shooting is carried out for relaxation and pleasure many shoots are, foolishly, casual over the formalities. In fact, as the circumstances are favourable for not just commercial dispute but also injury and death, it is important to set out the responsibilities and obligations between the people involved. Sad though it may be, people sometimes get shot and the solicitor acting for the widow will lose no time in involving the shoot manager in the action for heavy compensation. At the best you will have a worrying and expensive time proving you were not negligent in your organisation and, at the worst, the man who pulled the trigger will shed a measure of blame onto you. It could cost tens of thousands and the plea that you were organising for the good of the members and not personal gain will be no defence. Insure. Insure not just yourself, but everybody involved in the shoot in any way against anything. One small example of the complex claims which can arise will demonstrate the point. Several years ago I was shooting in Sussex when a fellow Gun caught his foot in a fox wire, fell and broke the stock of his top quality London gun. He claimed the cost of re-stocking, several hundred pounds, from the shoot manager on the grounds that the keeper should have been instructed to lift all wires before a formal shooting day. The insurance company accepted the argument and paid.

Be careful what you promise new Guns, for you are entering into a form of contract, saying, in effect, 'Pay me so much money and I will give you sport'. There is, in legal terms, offer and acceptance. If you make the mistake of quantifying the amount of sport too closely, a dissatisfied Gun could bring an action for compensation. I am a great believer in confirming all arrangements in writing but, in this case, you will be wise not to make specific forecasts about how many birds will be reared or how many bagged. Some aspects can, indeed should, be spelt out carefully by letter. If it is a truly democratic shoot in which all are equal, then you should spell out that it is a condition of membership that all Guns are equally responsible for all problems, financial or otherwise. The same letter can deal with safety, preferably stating that a dangerous shot can be expelled without compensation. (In fairness it can be added that if a replacement can be found, the balance of his subscription will be refunded.)

You may wonder why I have left the matter of finding the keeper until now – as usual the answer is money. Taking on the lease of decent ground, either alone or with a few friends, rarely involves any great risk for it can always be relet. But taking on a keeper, one cannot personally afford, before finding the companions who will share the salary and other expenses, is unwise. Employing a keeper is not unlike buying a new gundog – an older, experienced one raises the question of why the present owner is letting him go, and a young, inexperienced one has no known vices but has yet to prove ability. In the past I have found the Game Conservancy a great help over keepers, for the staff cover the country and can often give either advice on a suitable man or an opinion on one who has already applied for the post. Most keepering appointments begin in February, as the old season ends, and advertisements start appearing in the sporting press several months beforehand. I would not presume to tell you how to conduct a personal interview but I would suggest two rules worth observing rigidly. The first is never to employ anyone you have not interviewed personally. The second is never to take anyone without obtaining a reference from his existing or previous employer. There will sometimes be convincing reasons advanced why you should not make such inquiries – the stronger the reasons the greater should be your determination to research. I always prefer to seek references by telephone, for men will usually speak more openly than they will write. Bear in mind that a good keeper is not just a skilled rural technician – he is also honest, tactful, a natural organiser and a 'self-starter' at work, for he will not normally be supervised. Modern rearing methods have taken much of the art from keepering and replaced it with science, and, personally, I would rather have an enthusiastic young man, short on experience but displaying common-sense, than an older, experienced man whom I suspected of idleness.

Once you have appointed your keeper, make it plain to the syndicate that his orders must only come through the shoot manager. Equally complaints or criticisms of the keeper's performance should be discussed with the manager and not made direct.

The application of Value Added Tax to shooting is complicated but I will try to give a personal interpretation in a few words. In general if a number of friends join together for the purpose of sharing the cost of their sport then VAT does not arise upon the contributions or subscriptions paid into the common fund. Their association is not a business activity nor is their motive that of making a profit.

There are, however, a number of instances in which VAT may arise. Landlords or tenants who have let the shooting rights of their ground are obliged to charge VAT on the rent if they are registered for VAT themselves.

Another clear cut case is the sporting agencies, selling shooting by the day or week, who are a business activity and, with certain exceptions, will have to charge VAT on their fees. The question of a private, non-profit making shoot, which has had a good rearing season, finding itself with a surplus of birds, and then selling a day's shooting either to an individual or to a full team of Guns with the purpose of getting some money in the 'kitty', varies according to circumstances. As an occasional operation it is probably not necessary to charge VAT as the shoot would not be registered and the amount charged would fall well short of the £15,000 ceiling at which it is necessary to register for VAT.

Land-owners, with shooting in hand, are more vulnerable as a result of the action brought by H.M. Customs and Excise against Lord Fisher in 1977 and resolved in 1981. The Customs and Excise consider that subscriptions paid to such a shoot could be liable for VAT as the activity can be held to be part of the business of the estate. The judgement in the particular case went against them, after which the Customs and Excise issued a statement saying that they would regard subscriptions paid to a land-owner as exempt from VAT if the shoot complied with certain conditions. These are: (a) participation in the shoot is restricted to relatives and close friends of the land-owner (b) the land-owner himself makes a contribution to the cost of the shoot which is at least equal to the average contribution from each other participant (c) the land-owner neither seeks nor makes a profit from year to year by his shooting activities.

And so, with ground, Guns and keeper we move to phase two – ensuring the ground is well stocked. If you have so far failed to carry out your moral responsibility to the sport by joining the Game Conservancy, now is the time to repent and benefit both your conscience and the shoot. No matter how experienced you may be, it is unlikely that a few hours spent on the ground with one of the Conservancy's field staff will fail to produce valuable ideas, sometimes saving the fee several times over in the first season. There is another advantage less frequently aired. Most syndicate keepers have a firm conviction, albeit never voiced, that they know more about the job than the syndicate manager. In matters of detail they are usually right, which sometimes makes it difficult to obtain their co-operation on policy matters where the manager, seeing the wider picture, is more usually correct. The backing of a Game Conservancy advisor will give a stamp of authority to the manager over these difficulties.

In an earlier chapter I pointed out the need to have sufficient coverts to provide enough drives, and it is worth running through comparable arithmetic again. Most managers will agree it is undesirable to drive a covert more than three times in a season. (Cock days excluded.) Suppose you plan to shoot, outside days excluded, on eight days in the season and have eight drives per day. That is sixty-four drives, and at three per covert you need no less than twenty-one coverts. You will be exceptionally fortunate if the ground offers this and it may well be necessary to plant additional cover. What and where needs deciding in January, not June, for not only has it to be planted but farmers, owners or tenants have to be negotiated with.

I am strongly of the view, which I appreciate many will disagree with, that on a one keeper shoot the maximum effort should go into rearing. Encouraging wild birds is all very well but a prolonged spell of bad weather means a season ruined. Rearing a good stock of birds costs more but almost certainly ensures a good season. Once again it comes down to money and most shoot members would rather pay a higher subscription and be sure of sport than less and chance it. (A cynic might observe that by the time a man can afford to have a Gun in a driven game syndicate, he has not enough years left to risk a poor one.)

Keepers, quite properly, expect to live to a higher standard than their predecessors and we, quite properly, are entitled to use their services as efficiently as possible. Many keepers would prefer to spend from February onwards trapping predators and other traditional activities, arguing that the best plan is to buy in day-old chicks or even six/seven week poults later. In fact, it is much more economic to carry out the whole rearing process, with one exception, on the ground starting with catching-up an adequate stock for laying pens. The exception is hatching and there is a good case for sending the eggs away for incubation, partly because the cost is relatively low and partly to give the keeper time to renovate release pens and other work neglected through the season. It is worth considering whether the laying-

With labour costs so high it is now imperative to rear intensively.

pen operation can be expanded to give a substantial egg surplus. If so these might be used to pay for the incubating service. In considering the economics of rearing, remember that the keeper is a fixed overhead anyway and if one starts with caught up birds, which cost nothing, the main expense of the whole operation is food; in the early stages for laying birds and later for chicks and poults.

A good keeper will know more about rearing pheasants, his way, than the average shoot manager, but the emphasis is on 'his way', which is not necessarily best. The famous green booklets of the Game Conservancy cover the whole business of pheasant rearing so thoroughly that I believe a complete novice, blessed with commonsense, could succeed, and any man who obtains and studies these can meet his keeper with an inner confidence. Descriptions of rearing fields in the old days painted a delightful pastoral scene but with labour so expensive we must benefit from modern techniques and go in for mass production. The minimum capacity for brooder houses should be 250 and 500 is better. If there is electricity available it is more convenient as a heat source but bottled gas has the major advantage of not suffering unexpected cuts. A recent trend has been the intensive rearing of pheasants indoors, usually in dim light to reduce feather picking. Not having done it I cannot write with authority, but my instincts are against it for two reasons. Firstly, I cannot believe that chicks in a closed atmosphere and poor light can develop as well as those outdoors – the country saying that all livestock does better 'with the sun on their backs' has a solid ring of truth. Secondly, one of the largest hurdles for poults is the first few days after transfer to the release pen and unless 'indoor' birds go through a hardening process beforehand, they must be very vulnerable.

One of the major problems of intensive rearing, feather picking, has now been overcome by the introduction of 'bits'. However, it is important to ensure all bits are removed when the birds are transferred to the rearing pen for, if not, they can cause beak deformities.

Up to the moment of reaching the release pens pheasants have usually led a relatively sheltered and safe life. Strangely many shoots now lower their guard a little, and this at a critical stage. Hundreds of part-grown, vulnerable, innocent poults are taken from their brooder units and turned into pens which should be veritable fortresses against the only real threat – foxes. In practice, they are frequently simple enclosures, formed of posts and wire netting, five or six feet high. Any self-respecting fox would expect to be over the top in under thirty seconds or to have tunnelled under in ten minutes. By this age – six to seven weeks – poults are worth as much as they will fetch when sold to the game dealer in a few months' time and it is very foolish not to spend adequate time and money on their protection. A good pen should have eighteen inches of wire projecting vertically outwards at the top and not less than a foot projecting outwards at the base and buried several inches. Provided the height is not less than five feet this should suffice but for little more cost complete protection is available. An electric fence consisting of two strands positioned one above the other and about eighteen inches from the netting at the base, with a single strand just outside the overhanging wire at the top, will keep out any fox. Even more it stops foxes patrolling around the perimeter looking for weak spots and frightening the poults in the process.

It is surprising how many shoots do not wing clip their poults before putting them into the release pens. Not to so do means that within a few days, possibly a few hours, they will be over the top, easy prey for a fox or likely to wander off into dense summer undergrowth and lose the security of the pen. When invited to explain, many shoot managers say it allows the birds to escape if a fox should enter the pen, but the right approach is to keep poults in and foxes out from the start.

Building really good pens at a time when the keeper is not busy saves him time when he is. A major reason for having a larger number of smaller pens rather than a lesser number of large ones was to minimise the kill if a fox got in. Fox-proof pens make it practical to contain large numbers of birds in a pen and the task of feeding and watering can be completed far quicker. Large pens are also cheaper to build, for with as few as a hundred birds the perimeter needs to be a yard per bird. This ratio decreases as the size increases and for a thousand birds or more falls to three birds per yard.

Of course, there is a very great deal more to release pens; one can discourse for hours on the proportion of thick cover, thin cover and sunning areas; the best types of re-entry tunnels and when and how to feed, but all these details are covered adequately by the Game Conservancy publications and others. My concern is to emphasise the need for thorough fox-proofing and the advantages of really large release pens.

Before we leave foxes let us look the position squarely in the eyes. We are all concerned with maintaining good relationships between the various field sports and some limited investigations have been made to prove that foxes and pheasants can co-exist on the same ground. Once the pheasants are older and more wary it is certainly true that a fox cannot carry out the mass slaughter which would have been possible a few months earlier in a release pen. However, the fact is that pheasants do not eat foxes but foxes most assuredly do eat pheasants. If your ground holds foxes then they will co-exist with your pheasants, but eating some in the process. This is a price you will doubtless pay willingly for the good of your local Hunt, but do not be under any illusions. If there is no Hunt then wage war on the foxes for it will unquestionably save you birds.

The moment of catching up the poults for transfer to the release pens provides an opportunity for that invaluable, but rarely performed practice of tagging. Far too many shoots are content to turn loose several thousand pounds worth of pheasants and harvest an unknown percentage of them several months later. 'But', you cry, 'we do know – we bag about forty percent'. With respect, you do not know – all you know is that the number you shoot equals forty percent of the number put down, but you have no idea how these are divided between your birds, wild birds, last year's reared birds and birds reared by your neighbours. You may respond that as long as the percentage is reasonable you do not greatly care, but this is short-sighted. Gaining a clear picture of what happens to the reared birds and how the bag is formed enables a shoot manager to adjust his management plans to give optimum results.

To give accurate results a tagging programme needs to be done carefully. Every bird should be tagged with individually numbered tags and a record kept of the rearing batch, the pen into which the bird was released and the date. When shooting begins, at the end of each drive have the tags removed and placed in a numbered bag. At the end of the day plot on a large scale map where each bird was shot and note its release pen. By the end of the season several important facts will emerge. Firstly, you will know precisely how many reared birds of the year have been shot. If they represent a large proportion of the bag then it shows how much the shoot depends on rearing, but if a considerable number are untagged, then perhaps a change of policy may be needed. Certainly if no other birds are reared in the area then the balance must be wild birds and putting more effort into old fashioned keepering may pay off. How much is owed to reared birds from previous years cannot be told until a tagging programme has been carried on for several seasons, but my own experience is that very few birds figure in the bag in the second season after release. (My record was a hen, shot five and a half years after release and only a few hundred yards from the pen.) Operating a tagging system which shows the release pen for individual birds makes it a simple matter to calculate the percentage recovered from each pen, and if one or more are well below average, a remedy must be sought. Again from personal experience I have made the not surprising discovery that pens near the centre of a shoot give a better return than those near the perimeter. (Birds from the latter are more likely just to walk off the ground.) However, the answer is not always so simple and one often finds birds will tend to move down a valley or use a wide hedge as a highway. Only tagging will show a clear picture of 'drift' and enable it to be utilised if favourable and cured if not.

One lesson I have learnt from my own tagging experiments is that if tagging is to be done at all it is worth doing well. Simply finding the percentage of reared birds shot only tells whether the recovery is satisfactory or not, but if not, only a more detailed inquiry will point the way to the remedy, or more probably, remedies, for poor results are usually a combination of causes. It is rarely possible to tag for one season only, for the first season's results will lead to changes in management and the outcome of these will need checking next season. For those readers keen to learn more about their birds, but reluctant to become too scientific, there is a compromise. Allocate a colour to each release pen and tag the birds with their appropriate colour. Without too much effort this will give the result of each pen, and 'drift' tendencies can be roughly observed. However, the system lacks the sophistication of being able to observe the history of each bird, when it is often possible to learn from a situation which had not even been suspected.

For example, if unseasonal cold, wet weather arrives shortly after several batches of poults are transferred to the release pens, the subsequent recovery figures may show considerable discrepancies between the different batches. An inquiry into the history of the worst performers could reveal a different hardening off procedure, a sub-standard game farm, indifferent keepering, or some other reason capable of remedy.

There is one other reason in favour of tagging – it is immensely interesting. It is only when we cease to regard our quarries as mere targets and look at their natural history that we taste the full flavour of our sport.

Ever since shooting men began to concentrate large numbers of valuable birds into small areas, poaching has been a problem. The conditions of poverty which led men to poach in the last century have disappeared but need has turned to greed and the nuisance persists. Doubtless it always will, for however much we sportsmen may class poaching as common stealing, the general public do not see it that way and poachers care for the attitude of their friends and neighbours rather than sportsmen. Economics have moved against us, for while science has made it easier to rear large numbers of birds, inflation has made it impossible to employ adequate staff to protect them. Fortunately science has recently come to our aid with various forms of electronic security and while these are something of a novelty now, I am sure they will be essential equipment before many years. Once the main poaching threat only occurred when the pheasants were mature, that is to say, dead and marketable as food. Now they are also at risk in rearing and release pens, for young, live pheasants are readily saleable. Birds are particularly vulnerable to theft when young as they are concentrated closely together, but, fortunately, the same conditions make their protection simpler. There are several basic forms of electronic intruder detection. One consists of an infra-red ray beamed from one point and received by another, and when the ray is broken, the alarm is activated. Although highly effective, it is expensive, has to stand clear of undergrowth, is inflexible, and generally unsuitable for our needs.

Another, and more practical system consists of pressure pads which activate the alarm when trodden on. Because of the work involved in installing the pads only limited areas can be guarded, but excellent protection can be given to such danger spots as the entrance gate to rearing pens or the main ride into a covert.

Possibly the best system for our needs consists of a circuit of fine wire which can be up to two miles in length. Covered in green or brown plastic it can be strung around a pen or the entire perimeter of a covert and is difficult to see in daylight let alone at night. It is inexpensive, simple to put down and retrieve and the alarm sounds immediately the wire is broken by an intruder walking through it.

Although all systems activate an alarm there are a variety of possible alarms. If the purpose is simply to scare poachers a siren can be positioned, out of reach, in a tree. However, most shoots will be more interested in catching the poachers and having the police prosecute, so an alarm which alerts the keeper but not the thieves is desired. The simplest, and cheapest form continues the circuit to the keeper's cottage, or nearest dwelling, and activates a bell. The more sophisticated set off a short wave radio transmitter and the receiving set can be carried in the keeper's vehicle when he is not at home. A further refinement is to alarm all the coverts and have each transmitter operating on a different frequency so the keeper knows where the poachers are.

It is possible that poachers will eventually develop counter-measures against electronic protection but this will only happen when such coverage is almost universal among all shoots with large pheasant populations. However, for the moment, once the word goes round that a shoot is protected, they will just leave it alone and concentrate on the rest. One shudders at the thought of the poaching pressure on the last major shoot in an area to go 'electronic'.

Having put the birds onto the shoot it is obviously critical to keep them there. Any good keeper will know the principles well enough, but when a keeper is new and untried a shoot manager will wish to keep an eye on his efforts. In the matter of keeping pheasants at home no other factor even approaches the importance of feeding them well; and as the year moves on and natural food becomes scarce, the drawing power of food increases. Where, when and how they are fed will vary with the numbers to be fed, the physical circumstances of the shoot and the labour available, but the shoot manager should be satisfied that the programme is the most practical and has not been devised for the convenience of the keeper.

Before leaving the question of stocking the shoot, let me set out the case for partridges. Many shoots feel that their finances are limited and are better concentrated on pheasants, which they understand, than partridges, which they do not. This reasoning misses the critical point, for the object of partridges is not to add some variety and increase the bag, but to extend the season. While one can mess about with pheasants on the boundaries in the latter half of October, serious pheasant shooting cannot begin until early

Rearing partridges is an excellent, and relatively inexpensive, way of extending the season.

November, and in a late season, the middle of that month. Ten to twelve weeks later it is all over. Partridges add a new dimension – new problems to be solved, a different form of shooting and all this from early September until the pheasants are ready. They also add flavour to the early boundary days, which can become dull when too many Guns are working narrow boundaries, hedges and woods. The techniques of rearing and releasing red-legs, which have less wanderlust than greys, have been researched and improved in recent years and, properly done, the recovery rate will be at least equal to the pheasants. Once again the Game Conservancy is the source of wisdom.

And so, at last, sport can begin. Wise shoot managers always write and confirm the date, time and venue of every shoot. The very wisest will also have a printed note for handing to guests which sets out important data, so familiar to the regular Guns that they assume everyone else will know it. This will include clear instructions on reaching the meeting place, whether to bring a picnic, the attitude of the shoot to dogs and ladies (not necessarily in that order), whether it is done to shoot ground game (including foxes) and many other points helpful to a stranger.

A sure sign of a competent shoot manager is that the day keeps moving. The fact, mentioned earlier, but easily overlooked by busy managers and keepers, is that in driven game shooting the Guns have little to do but shoot driven game. Long periods of inactivity create boredom and on cold days morale soon drops. Therefore, plan the day in advance and keep the tempo up. Everything depends on the example set by the manager and the first rule is to start punctually. Waiting for a Gun, particularly if he is habitually late, merely encourages everyone to be casual. Leave a message, or a beater, and start. It is surprising how missing the first drive sharpens up offenders.

Normal practice requires the Guns to be in position before the drive begins, but this only works smoothly when both Guns and beaters can move into their new positions immediately a drive is over. On those shoots, the majority, where the Guns pick-up with their own dogs, there is a built-in delay. Very often the manager will welcome this, either to give the beaters a breather or to use up time on days when he wants to keep the bag down. The important point is to be flexible and vary the pick-up time according to the circumstances. For example, in mid-winter, when days are short, it may be essential to get onto the next drive quickly. Or if one man has had most of the shooting, it is wrong to keep the rest of the team hanging about, getting cold, while his dog, possibly a poor performer, searches. Two rules emerge. Firstly, if the pick-up is to cease at the wish of the manager and not the whim of the Guns, there must be a recognised signal at which Guns must assemble or risk being left. Secondly, if Guns may be called off before gathering all their birds there must be several competent pickers-up in attendance who can be left to complete the job.

Efficient picking-up is just one of the many aspects of a well-run shoot.

There are some drives, possibly involving blanking in adjoining cover, which take a long time to carry out. Here there is a strong case for breaking the rule of positioning the Guns before the start. With only a few exceptions such drives rarely put more than the odd bird or two over the Guns in the early stages, and it is questionable whether it is worth condemning the Guns possibly to three-quarters of an hour's sentry duty, in what may be an exposed position, just for the slight chance of a shot. Better to let the Guns complete the pick-up, or even 'coffee-house' out of the wind, while the beaters carry out the initial stages of the drive.

A shoot manager should always bear in mind the comfort of the Guns, not all of whom are necessarily young, fit and able to withstand unlimited cold, rain and wind. On days of severe weather it is often possible to let some of the Guns stand in shelter close to their pegs and only signal them out when action is imminent. Other acts of mercy can be performed. If an elderly Gun has a long trudge to his peg across sticky plough, a lift in a handy vehicle may put him nearer. Alternatively, a younger Gun may be willing to swap numbers for the drive. Nor are the Guns always best treated by saving them from walking. In really cold weather, and particularly for the first hour or so of the day, or after a long stand, it is best to suggest they walk to the next drive. It is nonsense to grow cold standing and then miss the opportunity to warm up by walking.

All well run shoots have clear signals to indicate the start and finish of each drive and there must be a rigid rule against shooting before or after these. On those drives where the beaters eventually arrive at a point well above the level of the Guns, it is wise to have a third signal which forbids taking further shots in front.

Never leave the programme for the day to be decided by the keeper. Not the least of the problems of running a shoot is that the keeper usually knows more about it than the manager and, as any man concerned with man-management knows, this puts one at a grave disadvantage. However, the conduct of the day is one area in which a manager with some experience and commonsense can speak with decision and authority, not least because he will look beyond the straightforward issues of the day to broader issues, such as averaging out the bag over the season. Be discreet, however, when over-ruling the keeper, for it is he who executes the plans and if you make decisions against his advice then the plans will assuredly fail. A little low cunning is permissible. For instance, where the keeper suggests a risky manoeuvre, never rule it out, but agree after expressing misgivings. If it goes well you deserve credit for allowing him the chance and if it fails – well!

One reason for planning the drives well before the day is to allow the keeper to feed birds into (or sometimes out of) the coverts to be beaten. However, it is a mistake to be inflexible. A sudden snap of cold weather will sometimes empty a covert exposed to a particular direction and concentrate the birds in another. Or a very strong wind will make it difficult to drive birds in the usual direction. Flexibility allows one to take advantage of special conditions rather than be defeated by them.

It is, in my view, a mistake for shooting authors to give too much specific advice on how to drive pheasants. With every covert birds have their own fixed ideas on where and how they are going to flush, and whence they intend to fly. The art is not to try to make the birds change their natural inclinations but to so plan each drive that you take advantage of them. Of course, every manager will start with the knowledge that birds always fly better towards home and the object is to entice them away from home by feeding, and then drive them back over the Guns. Ideally one will feed birds onto high ground so they invariably cross the Guns at a good height. But all these are ideals and the danger of written words is that earnest managers strive too hard to follow them. Experiment by all means, but with the object of improving the birds' natural flight rather than altering it. Once again the Game Conservancy's publications contain many wise words on this complex subject.

So far as possible every detail of the day that can be settled in advance should be. If this is done there is more time available to cope with the unexpected or even to enjoy shooting. The position of stops, pickers-up, who drives the game-cart, sewelling, putting out the number pegs – the list is long.

Numbering brings me to the warning – always have the Guns draw for position and never attempt to allocate Guns in the belief that you can share the sport rather than expose the Guns to the cruelty of chance. You will assuredly fail and the more frantically you place the deprived Gun or Guns in the best positions, the more will fate send the birds elsewhere. No man ever made friends by personally placing Guns.

As an aside I would mention that the conventional system of moving up two places is sometimes unfair. Depending on the sequence of the drives it is possible for a Gun to find that when he is on the flanks few birds come his way, and when he is central it is for the least prolific drives. Conversely, the man in the middle for the best drives may have the flank numbers where these are good. On those shoots where the drives usually follow a set sequence, it is quite practical to produce a card for each Gun on which his numbers are selected to give a fair proportion of good and less good stands.

A good shoot manager will try to provide an adequate volume of sport throughout the season. At first thought the ideal would be to average the bag out so that each day's total was about the same. In practice this is impossible, undesirable and unnecessary. At the start of the season the birds are usually not fully grown and certainly not strong fliers. There is a strong case for arguing that no pheasant should be shot until the first of November and preferably the middle of that month. In fact, there is a stronger case against, which is that the shooting season for pheasants is short enough and it is better to enjoy the bulk of it at the price of some less good birds rather than concentrate it into a shorter time of better birds. Fortunately at the start of the season most men are happy just to be out with a gun once more and modest bags are acceptable. However, this euphoria will not last long and if a shoot is favoured with a drive or two which invariably shows good birds, it is sensible to use these at the season's start rather than stick exclusively to the outside coverts and hedges, which will show little sport. (If they hold many birds the keeper has failed.) In other words, there is no objection to shooting October pheasants provided they can be shown reasonably well.

Come November and mature, stronger pheasants, it is a mistake to pursue them with maximum effort or, inevitably, the bag will soon shrink. There is certainly a case for arguing that January pheasants fly so well that quality compensates for fewer birds, but this only goes so far. There comes a point where the highest pheasants in Britain will not make up for long, blank spells. It is surprising how many shoots overlook the simple fact that you can only shoot a pheasant once and hammer away in November as if the season finished on the 30th. The sensible plan is to estimate how many are to be shot each month, and regulate the days to this pattern. Some readers may feel this is difficult, or even impossible, but with care it can be done with fair accuracy. (Consider the examples of the top class shoots which sell days on the basis of an expected bag of so many hundred birds. It is rare for the bag either to fall short or exceed by much.)

If a stock for later shoots is to be conserved, then positive steps must be taken to keep the bag down. One is to start the beaters half way through the coverts. Another, with the attraction of saving money, is to use fewer beaters than are necessary and consequently fail to flush all the birds. Where local conditions permit, the best system is continually to shoot the coverts that produce the best birds and leave the rest untouched. This has the advantage of not only keeping the bag down, but, by leaving some coverts in peace, the birds are less inclined to leave the shoot through overall disturbance. Obviously the feeding programme has to be carefully designed to draw sufficient birds back into the 'shooting' coverts, and even this may not suffice after several days' shooting. Some of the 'reservoir' coverts can then be shot both to bring the bag level up and move birds into the 'shooting' coverts for the next day. Of course, the best laid plans of mice and shoot managers gang oft awry, and things will rarely work out precisely. However, perseverance, commonsense and a readiness to vary plans to meet changed circumstances should produce balanced sport through the season.

One factor which causes some frustration in January is the common rule of 'cocks only' after Christmas. On shoots which rely on wild birds for much of their stock this is good sense, but on ground where wild birds never do well the only reason for preserving hens is to have them available for catching-up. As there is no guarantee how many birds are left and how effective the catch-up will be, a blanket veto is applied to all hens and frequently there is a surplus which is not needed for laying. It is highly questionable whether the insignificant numbers that these hens will produce next summer justify the reduction in January sport which results from sparing them. Personally I favour starting the catch-up in mid-December and, provided the numbers are achieved, shooting both cocks and hens through to the season's end. Some readers will, I know, feel this is a grave error, believing that a good stock of wild hens in February is a priceless asset. In East Anglia I would wholeheartedly agree, but only those with experience of poor game country appreciate how low survival rates of adult birds are, let alone their prospects of breeding. I have personal experience of a Sussex shoot which released and tagged five thousand pheasants one summer. In the second subsequent shooting season only eighteen were shot – in other words after a year had elapsed only a handful survived.

Taking a broader view of the manager's task I suggest one should not be too obsessed by the oft repeated maxim that the size of the bag is of far less importance than the quality of the birds shown; a view usually expressed over lunch as, 'I'd rather shoot one really high bird than a dozen ordinary ones.' Fine though this declaration sounds, it is rarely true – let the speaker finish the day having shot three, high birds in eight drives, while his neighbour has bagged thirty-six and listen to his comments on returning home. Once again we are back to the fact that in driven game shooting the day can be deadly dull if it is mainly spent standing and waiting. However, this is not quite the point, which is that the higher and faster the birds the better. I will commit the heresy of querying this. Driven pheasants of normal height and speed are not easy for normal shots. This is not to say most are missed, but certainly it is a rare shoot where more than fifty to sixty percent of the pheasants seen are bagged. Now if the birds are shown higher and faster, how many will be killed? Certainly not one in three. Possibly one in four, but it could well be one in five or six – or worse! Given this low kill rate two issues arise. Firstly, and of least importance, I suspect many men would not enjoy such testing targets as a permanence. We all prefer to succeed rather than fail and the pleasure soon fades in striving for the unattainable. Secondly, and of much more importance, come humane considerations. At the range at which really good birds cross the line the pattern spread is considerable. Men who kill the majority of the normal pheasants at which they shoot will not miss the higher ones by a large margin, and the percentage of pricked high birds will be higher than the normal fliers. Quite how many are pricked, and how severely, we do not know, but this element presents a very strong case for not putting large numbers of difficult birds over a team of average shots.

We frequently come across writers insisting that we should not take 'unsporting' low and slow shots. This is nonsense for, from the quarry's angle, these are the very shots we should take, ensuring, as they do, an instant and painless death. It is the 'sporting', that is to say, difficult, shots which are more likely to wound. I am not, let me stress, advocating concentrating on easy targets and foregoing the testing ones – merely pointing out that some of our attitudes were formulated in days when little or no consideration was given to the quarry.

There are many other aspects of a day's shooting which call for the shoot manager's attention. Some may feel I have ignored the welfare of the beaters. This is partly deliberate as the beaters are well able to look after themselves. Certainly more thought is needed for men required to stand motionless outside a wood in mid-winter than for those able to move about freely inside it. It is also true that the circumstances and attitudes of beaters have changed vastly. Once members of a deprived class, principally concerned with money, most beaters now arrive in their own car and the majority could earn more by spending the day at a different task. Although it might be difficult to gain many admissions, I suspect most beaters, particularly those who do not work in the country, enjoy the job. We should take this change of emphasis into account in our dealings with them and both the shoot manager and the keeper should keep the beating team informed of the broader aspects of the shoot's activities. The beaters are a vital part of the operation and will respond better if treated accordingly and in most cases their interest will run much deeper than just a list of the day's drives. Where it is felt that the beaters have done a good job through the season it is a pleasant, and not very expensive gesture, to hold a beaters' supper.

Turning back to the welfare of the Guns, we can consider lunch, a subject which raises a surprising degree of argument. The extremes vary between those who favour a sandwich, snatched in the lee of a barn, and the trenchermen who spend an hour plus round a well stocked table near a roaring fire. The former argue that they are there to shoot and luxury is out of place. The latter believe shooting is as much concerned with companionship as sport. I will not pronounce on either view, nor advocate a middle course. Each to his own and when anyone is so kind as to ask me shooting, I gladly fall in with his custom. There is, however, one practice I dislike, which, when first introduced, appeared to offer advantages. The winter days, the reasoning went, are short, therefore shoot without a break until the early afternoon, finish for the day and have a leisurely late lunch. Attractively simple and logical, but it ignores the need for a break from even such a pleasurable activity as shooting. After three hours or so food and relaxation are not essential but certainly very acceptable, and one restarts mentally and physically refreshed – not least the unfortunate who has shot badly and has used the break to relax and rebuild his morale.

Advice on shoot management usually includes the admonishment to make proper arrangements for transporting dead game rather than trampling it underfoot on the floor of a Landrover. This sound advice is justified on the grounds of both appearance and saleability but there is a further reason. We should, I submit, show proper respect for our quarries. Only a short time before they were superb living creatures, better specimens of their race than most of us of ours. Even in death they each have their special beauty and to treat them as so many items of dead meat shows an insensitivity out of keeping with an all-round sportsman.

Sensible managers will, of course, see that gift braces of birds go to appropriate homes at appropriate intervals and the land owner, if he is not a member of the syndicate, and any tenant farmers, will come high on the list.

Lastly comes the problem not of shooting but of not shooting – that is, when to cancel because of rain. Whenever the problem is discussed there is no shortage of authoritative voices declaring the wisdom of a decisive cancellation rather than shooting in the rain. But come the day, with everyone huddled in the barn door looking at the raindrops in the puddles, it is not so easy. Of course, if everyone could come back tomorrow it would be simple but they cannot. The Guns will be busy men who have reserved the day weeks in advance, and some may have travelled long distances. If you send everyone home the sun will break through in an hour and if you play the optimist and start, sodden Guns and beaters will curse you ere lunch. Do not guess – telephone the nearest Meteorological Office, who really are very good on local weather. If they predict hours of rain then cancel at once. However, if a clearance is forecast by, say, midday, it is better to make a firm pronouncement that shooting will begin at twelve o'clock and allow local residents to get on with other things rather than keep a large team assembled under a cloud of boredom.

There are many other aspects of running a shoot which space prevents me mentioning, but these are covered in my earlier book *Game Shooting: Management and Economics*. If, however, I am to finish the subject with this skimpy coverage, I would advance one vital principle. I touched earlier on the maxim that the quality of the birds shown is more important than the quantity. As a truism of the sport this points in the right direction, but does not go far enough, leaving, as it does, the implication that the object is testing marksmanship rather than numbers killed. The object is not killing game, difficult or otherwise, but for a group of people to enjoy a day's sport in the countryside. The shoot manager who consistently sends home a bunch of happy people has succeeded irrespective of how many birds hang in the game larder, or how high they flew.

Chapter 11
Self-help shoots

To judge by literature written before the last war, shooting could be divided into two well defined groups – driven and rough. Driven was carried out as it had been for many decades, is now, and doubtless will be in the future. Rough shooting was a sport for a man on his own or, at the most, two or three friends. Rarely was mention made of any middle course, nor was there any good reason why one should exist. If a man had the money and the desire he shot driven game. If he lacked money or preferred to hunt for his sport, he rented a rough shoot. In 1938 Julian Tennyson wrote *Rough Shooting*, and devoted a chapter to taking a rough shoot. In this he commented that farmers needed stirring up. He had, he wrote, advertised for four successive weeks for a rough shoot in the local paper and received no replies, yet, when he called on them he found that more than half had shooting to let. Even around London, he wrote, 'There are still quiet districts which can be successfully explored for good shooting.'

Now, of course, the situation is totally changed. Many more men have the money, the leisure and the transport to take up shooting and this increased pressure falls on substantially less ground. Much has been eaten up for towns, factories, motorways, airports and other development. That which is left is intensively farmed, producing pressures on wildlife that range from larger fields and less cover to a much greater use of pesticide and herbicides. As a result the rent of all forms of ground has risen to the point where it is unrealistic for a single man, or two friends, to take a rough shoot of any size. Without quoting figures which will rapidly outdate, but thinking in proportional terms which should remain constant, the rent a man will have to pay for a rough shoot of five hundred acres or so will buy him a Gun in a decent syndicate – and this before he pays any sporting rates, stocking costs, winter feed or other expenses of the rough shoot which, if not essential, are certainly desirable.

Men who have the money, and no great desire to rough shoot, turn to syndicate driven game shooting, but the more impecunious, that is to say the majority, have no alternative but to share the rent of a rough shoot with several friends. The euphoria of possessing shooting rights has rapidly faded before the reality that while a sparsely stocked rough shoot – and ground let for rough shooting is rarely the best – may be great fun for a couple of Guns, it is rarely so for four or five (or more). Something, it is quickly evident, has to be done, and so another self-help shoot is born. (I coined the phrase 'self-help shoot' in 1974 for my book on management and economics, written when the worst recession since 1929 was biting. It is not an entirely satisfactory title but a better has yet to appear.)

From the decision to act, matters progress logically. Firstly it is obvious that the ground must contain more quarries to allow a reasonable amount of sport for each Gun. Secondly, it is agreed the cost of this operation must be kept to an absolute minimum. Thirdly, it is soon found that the number of Guns makes many of the conventional rough shooting techniques, for example hedge walking, both over-crowded and dangerous. The decision is made that, where possible, game will be driven.

And so, step by step, what was once a small rough shoot producing a modest annual bag for a man or two has inexorably become a mini-driven game shoot. What follows is advice on how best to achieve this.

It is harder to give advice on the formation and structure of a self help shoot than a normal driven shoot, for the very essence of the former is its flexibility. Such a shoot is essentially a compromise by men of initiative making the best of restricted circumstances, and, as there will be less money involved to grease the wheels, the job of the organiser will be harder in some respects. This need occurs at the very start, for in choosing one's fellow Guns they will need an extra characteristic above the qualities sought in a formal driven shoot – they must be natural workers. In an arrangement where effort is required instead of cash, idleness has no place. Here again there is no fixed formula. In some shoots (the term 'self help' will now be dropped for most of this chapter), all the work will be done by the members and expenditure kept to a minimum; in others, part-time labour will be employed, a good stock of birds put down and the annual subscription may be not greatly below that of a formal driven shoot.

Age is no bar to members. An older man may not be productive when building release pens but can be far more reliable than the young bulls of the summer when it comes to rising early for a cold routine of winter feeding.

All my previous observations on finding and securing ground apply, as also do those on ensuring prospective members are safe, insurance and, indeed, all other aspects except money. Even here some principles apply, not least my conviction that, as many overheads are constant, as many birds should be put down as the ground can hold or the members can afford.

However good the ground, it is most unlikely that the quality and quantity of the shooting cannot be improved. In practice any ground which escapes the net of the larger, wealthier, formal shoots will range between average and very poor and an effort by the shoot can be taken for granted. There are three major steps to be taken, and local conditions will determine how much emphasis should go into each. These are improving the habitat – stocking – and feeding. (It is purely commonsense – if the ground is to hold game there have to be areas which give shelter and security, there must be food, and the natural stock needs supplementing.)

Of these three factors habitat is the one over which the shoot will probably have least control, for the rent is unlikely to be *relatively* high and their power to change the nature of the ground will be limited. Improvement will divide into making the best of that which is already there and providing new cover. Ideally one would like a number of small woods, well-maintained and dotted evenly over the shoot. In practice they will probably be in the wrong places and too large. Woods cannot be moved and only rarely reduced, but some improvements are usually possible, provided the owner will give permission. Stocking will normally centre on pheasants and it must be remembered that pheasants are birds of the woodland fringes. They are not to be found in the centre of large gloomy woods where a thick overhead

Self-help shoots, having less financial muscle, frequently operate on ground with inadequate cover. Cover crops, such as this maize, can transform the holding power of the ground.

canopy has killed off ground cover. What is needed is sky windows. Cut down enough timber, with permission, of course, to form a small clearing into which light and air can enter. After a spring and summer ground cover will emerge, a feed point can be established and an area holding birds will have been created where previously it was barren. This treatment should be repeated as frequently as is both necessary and possible, although whether consent will be forthcoming will vary with the type of woods and their condition.

This leads to one important principle. It is a great help if the man from whom the ground is rented is a member of the shoot. If he is many blessings will flow – consent for work such as 'sky windows' will be more easily obtained, equipment loaned, tractors and trailers are available, farm workers with an hour to spare get diverted onto pen building, tail corn becomes available without charge; the list is long. In many cases the farm owner or tenant may be the shoot organiser who has brought in other Guns to provide labour and cash. In others he may not have the time for the shoot or, less likely, the know-how. But, whatever the reason, involving the owner in the shoot is usually for the best, even if he plays no part and is just invited as the guest of the shoot occasionally.

While woods with a thick overhead canopy have no ground cover, young woodland or open coppice usually suffers from an excess, and usually of bramble. This would be difficult to beat, even with a full team of beaters, and it is essential to thin it prior to the season. Cutting by hand is very slow work and it is well worth borrowing or hiring a tractor and flail to cut out manageable areas.

The test of good cover is not whether it holds birds in the early autumn but whether they are still there in December and January with the wind from the north-east. Ideally a wood will have thick, low level growth around the perimeter to act as a wind break. If not, the correct solution of planting a suitable hedge is both too long term and too expensive for a shoot on a short lease. However, some worthwhile improvement can often be made by building a low wall of unwanted straw bales which, as bramble and other undergrowth laces through it, will last for a surprisingly long time.

Beating large expanses of wood with relatively few people is difficult and the drives should be rehearsed well before the start of the season. If necessary old rides should be opened up to create manageable blocks and, wherever possible, the plan should be to drive large areas towards the edge of the wood and into sections which narrow. Driving towards Guns standing in narrow rides is hopeless as most birds will just spring across and those that do fly will be low.

So far we have dealt with making the most of existing cover, but there is also the alternative of creating new cover either for shooting or simply nesting cover for wild birds. Nesting and general cover can be small in area and almost all farms have corners which can be excluded from the farming operations and allowed to grow rough. Alternatively these can be roughly cultivated and sown with a game mixture. These areas can provide permanent sanctuary, but larger areas of temporary crops can be sown specifically to provide shooting. Provided the shoot's wishes fall in with the farm's programme, it is often possible to sow strips of kale, mustard, or other suitable crops in strategic positions which will allow birds to be shown to the best advantage. However, if the farmer, quite reasonably, expects to be reimbursed for the cost of preparing the ground, seed and sowing, fertilising and the loss of profit, from the ground used, the cost to those shoots particularly concerned with money can be prohibitive. Where the money problem can be overcome temporary cover crops can be very effective.

There are severe physical limitations on what can be done with habitat improvement; money apart there are none on stocking. Now this is the point at which keepers, and others, will wax indignant on the nonsense of releasing young birds onto ground crawling with predators – a 'waste of time and money'. There are, I cheerfully admit, problems but they can be overcome and if the predators are going to wipe out reared birds the wild stock will stand no chance. For the reasons I gave in the previous chapter, if poults are fully protected until seven weeks and then turned out in a really good release pen, their only threat comes from foxes. If the shoot concentrates its limited efforts on foxes, the prospects of reared birds surviving is good, even if the natural wild stock has been largely wiped out, at the various stages from the egg onwards by hordes of crows, magpies, rats, weasels, stoats, cats, etc. The operation of a self help shoot is a continuing exercise in determining priorities – almost nothing can be done perfectly for want of money and labour. Of course, the percentage of reared birds recovered will be less than on a fully keepered shoot but one thing is sure – if nothing is put in very little will come out. Some years ago I ran just such a shoot in a not very suitable part of Surrey, but we still managed a return of 26.8 percent on reared birds. Have no truck with the pessimists and proceed boldly.

So far as is practical, members should do their best to control predators. Both the targets and the methods will be known to most readers, and there is ample literature for those in doubt. The wise manager will not allow his members to expend all their enthusiasm on this aspect but will channel some energies into really first-class release pens, renovating feeding points, etc. Much thought needs to be given to the rearing programme and the details will mainly be determined by the available labour. More affluent shoots may have a part-time keeper, the ideal being a retired keeper, and then can rear on the ground in the normal way. The greater problem comes for the shoot operating entirely with its own labour. Once again there can be no set rules, for circumstances will vary greatly between shoots. One of the most important factors is the location of the shoot in relation to the members, for this will determine whether rearing can be done on the ground. The distance must be such that one or more members can make several inspections each day, for if pheasant chicks are left alone for long spells, all manner of disasters can strike. If rearing on the ground is impractical, it is perfectly possible to rear quite large numbers of birds in one's garden, for, at least in the early stages, little space is needed. Home rearing has the great advantage that any reasonable wife will gladly neglect her children and home to make frequent inspections of the chicks, particularly during sudden showers.

Although by the standards of a large, formal shoot the numbers reared will be small, the rearing policy needs careful thought if the maximum benefit is to be made of the funds available. Buying six or seven week poults overcomes all the labour problems but will halve the birds obtained for a given sum. At the other extreme, catching-up and using a laying-pen means a great deal of work over a long period. Nor can a small shoot easily find the cost of an incubator and if eggs have to be sent away for hatching, much of the saving in catching-up disappears. In planning a rearing policy it is wise to remember it is easier to turn a day-old chick into a poult than an egg into a chick. For most self help shoots the best compromise of money and labour is to purchase day-olds. As an example, any handyman can make a brooder house, but building incubators is more difficult. Modern techniques and pellet foods have made pheasant rearing a very straightforward operation and even the complete beginner should have no difficulty if he follows the advice in the Game Conservancy booklets. However, these were written with conventional facilities in mind and men trying to rear pheasants as an extra activity in an already full day need to beware of various pitfalls. Perhaps the most important rule with very young birds is to keep them warm and, for the first few days, they need frequent checking. Long before they die of cold they trample themselves to death by huddling together for warmth. They are also masters at drowning themselves in the drinking bowls and escaping from the brooder house through holes which would defeat a bumble bee. Nor are the times at which they are released into the run in the morning and herded back to the brooder house in the afternoon constant, but need to be varied with the weather conditions. (Yes, I know they should return indoors to the heat when they feel cold, but the idiots don't – they huddle together outdoors and commit suicide.)

It is this need for constant supervision which makes it unwise to attempt to rear on the shoot unless a member can, without fail, make frequent visits. Home rearing usually works very well, but in situations bordering on built-up areas foxes can be a major problem, for urban foxes have fewer enemies than their country brethren. Cats are also a threat, not least because the owners are quite possibly your neighbours and friends! While the chicks are in the brooder house and its adjacent run there is no real problem, but as they grow and have to be allowed into a larger pen they become very vulnerable. The conventional pen of light weight panels affords little protection and a more substantial structure is essential. I have used a permanent pen with the lowest level of wire of $\frac{1}{2}$ inch diameter mesh and dug well in at the base. Prior to using this small mesh I sometimes had young birds inside the pen killed by either cats or foxes from outside. These predators presumably lay in wait then clamp the poult to the wire with a paw, for I would find headless corpses lying close to the perimeter. Even a fine mesh wire does not prevent disturbance by foxes and cats prowling around the perimeter looking for weak spots and the only answer is an electric fence. Properly positioned and maintained this is a complete solution. While a permanent pen can be made entirely predator proof it carries the disadvantage of a disease risk from constantly rearing birds on the same ground, and a careful watch should be kept.

Rearing birds close at hand makes it possible to commence the hardening-off process in good time, for the decision whether to let them jug out in the rearing pen or shut them away can be deferred until the last possible moment each night. Personally I am strongly in favour of having birds jug out as soon as possible, for this encourages feather growth and generally increases their chances of survival when moved to the release pen. In drought conditions spray birds daily to encourage feather growth or a sudden change to cold, wet weather could produce many deaths.

It is a mistake to think that wing tagging is a scientific activity only practised by big shoots. All the reasons for tagging to find out the subsequent movements of the birds, and what percentage are shot, apply just as much to a small shoot – perhaps moreso as less is likely to be known from past experience. When birds are tagged it is sensible to advise adjoining shoots of the type of tag and ask if they will return any recovered. If your neighbours are large shoots you will gain more than information. Most large shoots are convinced their smaller neighbours feed frantically to lure their birds over the boundary. The discovery that they are actually shooting birds put down by their minor neighbours will do much for goodwill. As with large shoots, if tagging is to be done at all it takes very little more trouble to do it thoroughly and produces a great deal more information. Tagging should, of course, be done when birds are caught up for the release pen, and wing clipping can be done at the same time.

I have already covered the importance of building really adequate release pens in the previous chapter. This is a job well within the scope of the members and the reward for a good job is the ability to sleep soundly and not dream of foxes. With well positioned re-entry tunnels and members walking poults in each evening, the transition from the shelter of the pen to living entirely in the harsh outside world should be slow. The wing clipping will stop any bird leaving the pen until it is ten weeks or so and many will still be spending the nights in the pen when several months old.

Which brings us to the third stage – feeding. Most shoots are far better at rearing birds than they are at keeping them on the ground, although in most cases the shoot knows only that they have disappeared but not where. Even on the best shoots the research of the Game Conservancy shows that about a third of reared birds have gone by the start of shooting, but the proportions which are lost to predators, disease and other causes are not known. Unkeepered shoots are particularly vulnerable to high losses at the time the birds begin to leave the release pen, for it is all too easy for them to wander into dense undergrowth, and never to return to the pen. Apart from predators these birds are also at risk from starvation for they have never had to fend for themselves. With a full-time keeper the risk would be minimised for he would dog the surrounding areas and drive birds back like errant sheep. It is certainly well worth while calling for a major effort from the members at this time to 'police' the pen.

There will, however, come a time when rapidly maturing pheasants will only stay in an area if cajoled rather than forced. Three principal factors will achieve this: peace and quiet, good habitat (which is partly the same thing), and ample and regular food. Growing pheasants have large appetites. Feed them well and they stay; fail and they wander off to forage elsewhere. Nothing keeps pheasants at home so much as the old fashioned straw ride, hand fed at regular times by the keeper. Only a few months ago I stood in a ride of a wood on the Sussex Downs. A couple of dozen pheasants were in view, pecking disinterestedly at the ground. 'Watch this', said the keeper, filling his bucket with corn. He moved down the ride, whistled and begun to distribute supper. It was an amazing sight. Pheasants came galloping from every quarter, packing the pathways and converging on the central ride until it became a river of bustling, brown bodies. Within a minute a thousand and more pheasants were at table and obviously all would be back the next evening.

Some self help shoots will be able to organise a rota for hand feeding, but the majority will have to accept imperfection. An excellent alternative is a number of strategically placed automatic feeders. (Most readers will know of this invention which, for the benefit of the few, is a food hopper capable of hurling pellets or corn in a circle when a time clock operates the mechanism. It is battery operated and also sounds a bell to tell the birds the meal is served.) Automatic feeders are very effective but have the major disadvantage for an impecunious shoot of being relatively expensive – particularly when several are needed. An excellent substitute, if available, is an elderly local resident prepared to hand feed in return for a modest payment and the occasional brace of pheasants.

Finally, there are static feed hoppers, in a legion of designs. Nothing has yet beaten, for economy and effectiveness, the metal five gallon oil drum, suitably slit and inverted. The corn saved by fitting the sparrow guards, sold by the Game Conservancy, will more than pay for the guards in the first season. Remember the important principle that birds which have to work for their food are more likely to stay at home than those to whom it comes easily. Hoppers are best placed under a cover of some description – corrugated iron does well – and a good depth of straw strewn around. Here pheasants can scratch happily in dry straw for hours. Such feed points should be placed in protected positions but, even so, a wind break of straw bales makes them even more attractive.

There are other variations of feed hoppers but all good ones offer food at all times and straw. It is sense to feed the young poults in the release pen from whatever form of hopper they will encounter outside, for they will then instantly recognise a food point in the vital first few hours and days. The more feed points, within reason, the better, for pheasants dislike being crowded. Take care over their position and aim for quiet, protected spots in cover, yet open enough to catch any sun. Pheasants like to feel secure and instead of placing hoppers in an open ride, cut small 'lay-bys', which will give the birds cover on three sides. In siting feed points in the summer bear in mind the need to reach them in winter mud. If suitably large metal containers are available, it is sensible to build up central storage points in advance.

In most respects a self help shoot follows just the same general principles as a large, formal shoot and this applies when, at last, the season opens. It is unlikely that any serious pheasant shooting can be done until well into October, but as the members will be content with far smaller bags than their grander neighbours, the outside days can be both more frequent and more extensive in scope. Nor need they have pheasants as the only quarry and the resulting forays at anything from pigeons to rabbits will, if properly planned, do much to push the pheasants away from the perimeter.

Once serious pheasant shooting begins the question of procedure arises. Ideally all the members would like to stand while high quality pheasants were driven over them, but the high cost of a team of beaters will almost certainly prohibit this – indeed, if the shoot can afford this, then the money should have been spent on putting down more birds. The normal procedure is for the members to take it in turn to beat and shoot and, given reasonable cover, this usually works well. However, in large, thick woods a beating team with a maximum of four or five will make little impression and re-inforcements are needed. If finances permit, the employment of a few beaters will often pay for itself in the value of the extra game bagged. Other solutions are available to the nimble mind, and dogs come high on the list. An energetic dog equals at least half a dozen humans in thick cover and the only reason dogs are not used extensively on large shoots is their uncontrollability

Experienced working dogs play an important role in many self-help shoots.

when compared to the human beaters. A well disciplined team of beaters will dispatch the great majority of the birds in the right direction and, equally important, regulate their departure and avoid large flushes, whereas dogs are likely to flush birds in any direction and any quantity. However, this irregular performance is not a serious drawback when beaters are also Guns and, in any event, it is better to flush birds irregularly with dogs rather than walk over them with insufficient beaters. It will have already occurred to the opportunists that it is not essential to have only the most obedient dogs and it may well be possible to find enthusiastic dog owners who will grasp the chance to work their particular beast without thought of reward.

Wives, fianceés and girl friends who enjoy the countryside can play a very useful part in the shoot and this extends to beating. Naturally the ladies will be kept clear of the thickest cover and spared shoulder-deep wet kale. Nor, no matter how dark your suspicions, should they be accused of heading a bird and directing it to their own man! Finally, there are youngsters. Most rural areas have a crop of boys keen to follow tradition and beat, but too young for the formal shoots. They can be surprisingly good, but restrict the numbers or discipline collapses.

One of the problems of this form of beating and driving is the question of who shoots what. In theory the walking Guns take anything going sideways or back and leave birds going forward to the standing Guns. In practice, and particularly when sport is very sparse, the walking Guns tend to bend the rules, the standing Guns bend them even more when next they walk, and everyone feels rather testy. One solution, which has much to commend it at the start of the season when the need is to keep the bag down, is to have the walking Guns operate as beaters only and leave their guns in a safe cache.

My previous recommendation to rear partridges applies equally to self help shoots; perhaps more so as the members are unlikely to enjoy grouse or other early shooting, and the season has been open a long time before pheasants are mature enough to shoot. The price of six to seven week old partridges has been falling towards the level of pheasants this last year or so, but rearing them from day-olds will naturally save money. Have no reservations about doing this for they are easier and more enjoyable than pheasants. Not only are they more manageable, but partridge chicks are delightful little creatures and their musical murmur at dusk on a summer evening has a special appeal. Partridges had a bad reputation for straying and this is still true for greys. Frenchmen, however, can produce a yield at least as good as pheasants *if* the correct releasing techniques are followed. As usual the Game Conservancy gives chapter and verse and an essay into partridges should be very well worth while.

Self help shoots are essentially a communal activity and the calibre of the members determines the degree of success or failure in all aspects of the exercise.

Chapter 12
Wildfowling

With one exception, experience in any form of shooting teaches a sportsman enough for him to adapt to other forms very quickly. The exception is wild-fowling, where the problems posed by conditions below the high water mark call for a long apprenticeship, even for a well experienced inland shooter. For this reason I feel able to give more basic advice in this chapter than others.

Strictly speaking, true wildfowling takes place below the high water mark on our coasts and estuaries and, thereby, takes the wildfowler to many remote, wild and eerily beautiful places. Fowling above the high tide mark is simply inland shooting, usually on freshwater marshes, and although conditions can be severe they are rarely so harsh as those encountered out on the saltings, mud and sand. Apart from exposure to cold, wet and wind, wildfowling is also dangerous, and it is a rare year passes without at least one drowning. However, the degree of danger is exactly related to the common-sense with which one approaches the sport, and very few deaths have occurred to provident men with a proper respect for the sea.

To avoid disappointment it is necessary to form a realistic picture of wild-fowling in advance, and this will not be obtained from the extensive des-criptive literature on the subject. Wildfowling appeals to the manner of men who climb mountains, fly gliders, canoe down wild rivers, sail, and generally love battling with the elements and physical exertion. Such men are grapplers with life and given to extremes of behaviour and description. As a result books on the sport emphasise the excitements of crashing seas, fiery skies and skeins of fowl. They do not dwell on long boring spells spent crouched in a muddy gutter, growing steadily colder, while gazing at an empty grey sky. Results in terms of fowl bagged are usually very sparse and many recruits to wildfowling give the sport up within a season or two. Those who remain loyal are a special breed of shooting men; the hunters *par excellence*, who have an affinity with the broad horizons and the lonely places.

The story of man's pursuit of wildfowl since the early ages is a fascinating one. I know, for I devoted most of my spare time for two years, and in the process read nearly ninety books, mostly old and rare, to trace the history of the sport from 30,000 B.C. to the present day. The result is *The History of Wildfowling*, and I commend readers to this, not for reasons of self-interest but because the growth of the different aspects of wildfowling is so very interesting. The development of punts and punt-gunning justifies a book on its own and there is a rich harvest of related information ranging from the discovery of duck decoys made of mud and feathers in Egyptian tombs to the enormous numbers of duck taken annually in the decoys which once dotted this country.

The part played by the famous Colonel Peter Hawker in the development of the sport is often misunderstood. He did not, as many believe, invent wildfowling in its modern form, but he did, in his superb *Instructions to Young Sportsmen* (1814), introduce it to a wider public and, also, make it an activity socially acceptable for gentlemen gunners. There is clear evidence that some purely sporting wildfowlers existed in the eighteenth century, but the majority were market gunners; fishermen and other coastal dwellers who shot to sell the bag. Hawker changed this, and brought many more inland sportsmen to the coast, although it remained the case that throughout the nineteenth century many of the gentlemen did their wildfowling floating in a gun-punt and the others squelched through the mud.

No introduction to wildfowling would be complete without reference to WAGBI – the Wildfowlers' Association of Great Britain and Ireland, founded in 1908 by Stanley Duncan with a handful of members and now one of the largest shooting organisations in the world. The story of its growth is a heartening example of what can be achieved by ordinary sportsmen, prepared to give their time and energies voluntarily for a cause they believe in, and it receives a full chapter in *The History of Wildfowling*.

It is impossible to deal with all aspects of this most complex form of the sport in one chapter, but I will cover the main principles. For readers seeking a more thorough treatment I recommend my book, *The Practical Wildfowler*.

The legitimate quarries of the wildfowler are included in the Schedule III list of The Protection of Birds' Act of 1954, (Revised 1967). Part II of Schedule I lists other quarries which are included in a different schedule as they enjoy special protection during the close season. The whole question of what one may, and may not, shoot is complicated and every responsible shooting man, being at heart also a conservationist, will wish to comply with the law. On first studying the list of shootable and non-shootable fowl it appears an impossible problem, short of spending months by the water improving one's ability to distinguish between birds which, particularly in poor light, look almost indistinguishable. Ideally you should never shoot anything you have not identified but, at least for ducks and geese, such a strict discipline is unnecessary. It is sufficient, and far simpler, to learn what you must not shoot. The protected ducks are eider, smew, shelduck, goosander and red-breasted merganser, none of which are likely to be confused with unprotected species by anyone with even a rudimentary knowledge. Learn these, and shoot the other duck with a light heart. Geese are even easier – you shoot the grey and leave the black. To elaborate, the greylag, whitefront, pinkfoot and bean geese vary from grey-brown to brown-grey and are all quarry species. The protected geese are brent and barnacles, which are basically black. There are two exceptions, namely that barnacles can be shot in a few specific areas in Scotland and that Canada geese are also mainly black but can be shot. However, Canadas will not be encountered in a true wildfowler's territory, so the principle of shooting the greys and leaving the blacks is sound.

Curlew are easily identified, but I confess I find their call so beautiful that I must be desperately short of sport before I shoot one. For the same reasons I rarely, if ever, shoot waders and he who would has much swotting up to do on his identifications.

In chapter 2 I dealt at some length with the question of the best gun for wildfowling, narrowing the choice to a standard twelve bore and a magnum twelve capable of firing a heavy shot charge, although I stressed the weight disadvantage of the heavier gun only gave a maximum increased range of less than ten yards. There is no easy solution to this choice, for different conditions call for different guns. For the novice wildfowler it is wisest to stick to a standard twelve bore, the more so if he expects to walk any considerable distances. After a few expeditions he will suffer the disease all new fowlers go through as certainly as children catch measles – a craving for a very large gun firing a very heavy charge. Resist it, for it will soon pass and it is an expensive indulgence.

I have already touched briefly on finding suitable fowling grounds. The man who is intent upon really serious wildfowling will do best to join a coastal club, although membership does not ensure one's fellow members will willingly divulge the local knowledge built up over many years.

The first major consideration for a novice wildfowler is not how to bag wildfowl but how to survive. Men unfamiliar with the sea almost always underestimate its potential to kill and extreme care is essential. There are a variety of ways in which a wildfowler can drown himself, but far and away the most common is to get cut off by a rising tide. The extent of the rise and fall of the tide varies at different places on the coast, but can be as great as thirty feet. On a steeply shelving shore the distance between high and low water marks is small, possibly tens of yards, but on a near flat estuary of mud or sand it can be several miles. Once the tide begins to flow it can advance faster than a man, heavily laden and in thigh waders, can progress and, as the flats will be criss-crossed with deep creeks and gutters, it will be appreciated how the inexperienced can be cut-off and drowned even in daylight and good weather. In the dark and a gale the odds are heavier still.

The author's third son proceeding with proper caution.

By far the safest course is not to venture out without an experienced companion. Do not, however, make the error of thinking that men who have spent some time wildfowling are always safe. Doing is not necessarily learning. Whether with a companion or not *always* observe certain precautions. The most important is to know the time and height of high tide, which statement calls for a very brief explanation of tides. Twice each twenty-four hours the tide flows and ebbs and, due to the variations in gravitational forces caused by the changing positions of the earth, moon and sun, this gigantic movement of water varies, giving different tide heights. The highest tides, called springs, occur twice each lunar month, at the time of the new and full moons. During the first and last quarter of the moon the lowest tides occur, and these are called neaps. It is suicidal to enter a marsh without knowing when the tide will start to flow, when it will be full and its height. (It is also bad tactics, for the movement of the tide affects the behaviour of the fowl.)

In general terms the nearer you are to the edge of the sea the more likely you are to encounter wildfowl. Given suitable ground it is possible to hide at the tide edge and retreat as it advances, but 'suitable ground' is rare. The main danger is the tide creeping up the gutters and channels until you find your retreat cut off by a deep creek. If this should happen never try to cross fully dressed and wearing equipment such as a cartridge belt, rucksack and a gun in a sling. Carry this loosely so that it can be dropped if you get into trouble. However, the vital rule is not to get out of trouble but to avoid getting into it in the first place. Caution dictates that your first few expeditions should concentrate not so much on pursuing fowl as learning the marsh; in fact, the wisest course is to explore it in mild weather without a gun. Discover which areas flood and which do not at various heights of the tide, and which routes across the marsh involve only minor gutter crossings which can be jumped. Given this information you will then be relatively safe – until, that is, you either try to come off in the dark or are trapped by a heavy mist. Always include in your standard equipment a compass and torch. You should also be aware that the heights given in the tide tables are approximate only and will vary with the atmospheric pressure and the wind direction – a combination of extreme conditions can produce a variation of several feet.

On several previous occasions I have reasoned against carrying equipment which is not essential but in wildfowling it is often hard to judge for or against. Walking is usually arduous and it is sensible to avoid weight, but some items have a strong claim in that they are not just convenient but potential life savers. One such is a wading stick, an invaluable aid to testing not just water depth but mud. Mud is more than an obstacle – it is a major danger and you should never attempt to fight through deep mud, particularly if it is covered with water. Mud is one of the reasons for having a companion, for a fowler trapped in deep mud when the tide is rising has little hope without outside help. You will quickly learn to spot the different appearance of hard and soft mud, and also to walk on it, rather than in it, by quick sliding movements. When lifting the foot, rock it forward onto the toes, semi-straighten the foot in line with the leg and lift through the hole created. This breaks the suction which would occur with a straight lift.

Other worthwhile equipment includes a first-aid kit, for help is rarely close at hand on a marsh. Also, I carry the space-blanket and pocket flares mentioned in the chapter on high ground rough shooting. Unless you expect a shot, the gun is better carried in a sleeve, and slung over one shoulder. This keeps it clean and leaves the hands free. A recognised distress signal is three shots fired in quick succession, a pause, followed by three more, and so on.

So far we have concentrated on survival; now we will look at the less vital but still important question of comfort. I dealt with the problems of keeping warm and dry in chapter 5, and most experienced shooting men will have their own personal wrinkles. However, wildfowling imposes exceptional conditions and additional precautions are necessary. The major variation from inland shooting is footwear, for thigh waders are essential, but not, as some novices believe, for wading through deep water or mud. This would be too risky and the main need for waders is to allow one to kneel and stay dry. The lack of cover forces the wildfowler to spend much time in contact with mud or sand and unless your whole exterior clothing is waterproof, a wetting is inevitable. A waterproof exterior jacket is essential and to cover the gap between this and the wader tops I recommend a pair of old waterproof trousers cut off at the knee. While a hood is useful for the inland sportsman, it is essential for the wildfowler and, given this complete outfit in good condition, it is possible to sit out the severest of storms and stay bone dry. Staying warm is, however, another matter, for it is often necessary to stay in one position for several hours and inland sportsmen rarely appreciate how much heat is generated by moving even slowly. The obvious answer is to wear plenty of warm underclothing, but this presents the counter-problem of becoming excessively warm when walking onto, or off the marsh. Written simply this may sound trivial, but a two mile walk across heavy mud, over-dressed and sweating profusely, is unpleasant. There is no complete solution, but I minimise the problem by taking a rucksack and carrying pullovers and other items in this until needed. Buy waders large enough to wear two pairs of socks, remember a silk scarf for the neck, and protection for the hands. I wear gloves when not shooting and change to mittens once the gun comes out. One of the patent hand-warmers keeps the fingers supple on a very cold day. In the worst conditions a woollen balaclava is the best form of headgear, but it does muffle one's hearing.

A rucksack provides space for the safety equipment mentioned earlier,

The conflict between useful equipment and the desirability of travelling light poses problems.

plus other accessories. One useful item is a length of old towelling with which to wipe water and mud from hands and gun. Another is sustenance. For high ground rough shooting I advised against carrying food on the grounds of weight, but the circumstances of wildfowling are different. The weight is there, of course, but you will be carrying so much that the extra is insignificant and eating, if nothing else, does wonders for morale. The greatest benefit comes from a flask of hot soup. Do provide for your dog. The towelling also serves to wipe it down after a water retrieve on very cold days and it will appreciate food as much as you. A small square of plastic sheet makes a waterproof base for sitting on wet mud, for both you and the dog, and takes no space. Although cartridges can be carried in a conventional belt, they easily gather mud and are a danger if you fall in deep water. I prefer a handful in a pocket and the rest in the rucksack. Obviously they should be plastic cased.

The newcomer to wildfowling does not appreciate just how difficult it is to move and shoot in mud. Inevitably it will cover you and your equipment and you should not take anything new or valuable. Guns are particularly vulnerable, for the sea-water will cause discolouration and corrosion. You would be ill-advised to take a valuable game gun below the sea wall.

The novice wildfowler has now been warned of the dangers, properly armed and clothed, and instructed as to the tides. It is time to pursue the wildfowl.

Engrave on your mind the cardinal principle of the sport – the art of wildfowling is getting in range of the fowl. Consider the problems. Short of actually entering the water, you, a mere man, could not be operating in worse conditions. Mud is underfoot and all around, progress is painfully slow and you cannot walk any distance without encountering a muddy or water-filled creek. Creeks and gutters apart, the ground is flat and almost devoid of cover and to the wary and sharp-eyed fowl you are visible long before they fly into range. Lying flat on the marsh surface may gain the cover of the short marsh grasses, but makes it difficult to see over a wide arc and impossible to shoot quickly. Taking cover in the creeks often leaves you struggling for a toe-hold on a slippery, sloping bank and once the tide makes you are flooded out.

Ideally you need to resolve the problems to the point where you are, so far as possible, concealed, comfortable and able to shoot quickly from a convenient position. In practice, this is impossible but the good wildfowler will inspect the immediate area, pick the best spot and compromise as far as he can. We will shortly look more thoroughly into this aspect.

If the art of wildfowling is getting in range of the fowl, the question is how? In view of the lack of cover it is rarely possible to approach the fowl and they must come to you. To achieve this calls for two skills – firstly waiting in the right place and, secondly, concealing yourself successfully. The first requirement calls for considerable knowledge of the ways of the fowl. The second calls only for commonsense and yet it is surprising how many experienced wildfowlers are weak on this aspect and can frequently be seen, either sitting proud of the marsh surface, or even walking about aimlessly. The fowl need only watch the line of their flight path, but the wildfowler has to scan a full 360 degrees. He is also far larger than the wildfowl and consequently more obvious to them at any given distance than the reverse. Even if he spots the fowl before they spot him, the movement of crouching attracts their attention, and keeping still – the better course – still leaves him as prominent as a lighthouse. As a first principle, absorb and practise the rule of remaining concealed at all times that it is not actually necessary to change position. You would never dream of waiting for an opportunity with an empty gun, but this would be no more ridiculous than remaining in an obvious position. The fact that nothing has happened for the last couple of hours is irrelevant – wildfowling rarely presents more than the occasional chance.

The classic solutions to flat mud or sand are a grave or pit. Both consist of holes, the first being shallow and long enough to lie in, and the second deeper and designed to sit in. In both cases the excavated material is heaped in a rounded mound on the side from which the fowl are expected to arrive. The grave leaves you in an impossible position to take a quick shot and the pit is a major physical task. Both are likely to fill with water and ooze. On the right occasions they are very useful but you should be very sure you need to be in such a difficult spot before beginning the labour. Another important factor is whether ethical considerations should exclude you from the place, for bare, flat areas are frequently used for roosting and it is now regarded as wrong to disturb such sanctuaries.

Cover improves as one moves nearer to the high water mark, for large creeks split up into even smaller water courses and the marsh grasses grow in greater abundance. Wide creeks are rarely suitable, for the sides shelve and fowl can see into the bottoms while still at long range. Small creeks and gutters, being narrower, are better, but are shallow and one is forced to kneel. They also only occur at the higher levels and at low tide you will probably wish to operate near the water's edge in the large creeks. The solution is a garden trowel; simple, light but highly effective. With this dig a horseshoe shaped indentation into the lip of a creek wall which runs parallel to the direction you wish to face. Make the depth such that you can kneel in the horseshoe, rest your chest and arms on the marsh surface, and place your rucksack in front of your face for concealment. Finally, slope the flat 'table' on which your knees will rest slightly inwards so you will slip into the cavity rather than out. This simple tactic gives excellent concealment from behind as well as in front, for, provided you are still, the rear view will not alarm fowl. Additionally the position is comfortable, for the weight is well spread between knees, body and arms and, finally, it offers as good a shooting position as is possible, short of standing up.

Obviously the man who has previously shot only from a standing position will find marksmanship when kneeling difficult. Shots over a narrow arc in front are fairly simple, but it is awkward to swing properly as the limit of movement to either side is reached. Where you can stand upright at the moment of shooting this is obviously best, but it is essential to be able to spring up quickly or what is gained by standing will be lost by the distance the quarry will have flown on seeing you. At twilight or dusk it is in order to find a firm base and enjoy the luxury of shooting upright. When kneeling, lying or in any way firing from a cramped position, you must estimate the path of the fowl and the position in which you expect to take the shot. Then manoeuvre your body into the right position to ensure maximum flexibility at the moment of swinging. One of the secrets of good marksmanship on the marsh is to spot approaching quarry well in advance. You then have ample time to sink down into maximum concealment and adjust the body position, and properly done, the first warning the quarry will have of your presence is the shot. This delayed warning is also a great help with the second barrel for duck flare violently when alarmed.

Dogs need concealing just as much as wildfowlers, particularly if yellow labs or springers. It is essential to have an obedient dog which will lie quietly and can be covered with marsh grasses or a small square of camouflage net. Whenever possible sit a dog out of the wind.

Crouching in creeks and gutters is only possible when the tide is low and, once it flows, you will be driven onto the marsh surface. You can, of course, retreat to the higher levels where the channels are only part filled but, normally, one wants to stay as far out as safety permits. In daylight you must either lie in the grasses or build a hide. The former allows you to change position instantly, but makes concealment, observation and shooting difficult and a simple, portable hide is better. A short length of wire netting is effective, for it is light to carry and can be woven with grasses. This, however, takes time and my own preference is for a length of camouflage netting and a few bamboo canes. At the simplest level this system can be restricted to two small canes, suspending a short curtain of netting only a foot or so high. Even this primitive arrangement is effective, for it can be knelt behind and breaks up the outline of a human figure. If you plan to stay in one spot until the tide drops off, a more elaborate hide can be built by forming a three foot square with four posts and draping the netting around the perimeter. Keep the height down to about two feet and dig a foot hole about fifteen inches square against the side you wish to look over. Form a seat with the excavated mud and you will be concealed and moderately comfortable. Finally, weave grasses into the top edge so you can peer through them rather than showing your head over a straight top.

Having advised on how to conceal oneself, the next question is where? Wildfowl spend only a small proportion of their day in the air and divide the time mainly between resting and feeding. Our problem is to anticipate both the resting and feeding areas, forecast the routes they will take from one to the other, and lie in wait beneath them. In fact, there are other opportunities of coming to terms, but it is these major flights which provide the bulk of a wildfowler's chances.

Put in the simplest terms, the pattern of duck behaviour is to rest on the sea or saltings during daylight, to fly inland to feed at dusk, and to flight back to the safety of the coast at dawn. Geese do the reverse, spending the night on their coastal roosts and flying inland to feed during the day. This explanation is merely a general statement and local conditions will cause many variations – for example, where there are large, quiet, inland lakes or reservoirs wildfowl will frequently use them as daytime roosts. And during moonlight nights geese usually flight to the coast at dusk, rest, then return to their inland feeding grounds under the moon. The whole question of wildfowl movement is very complex and the only certain thing is that when wildfowl flight, or alternatively do not flight, there is a reason.

Weather plays a major part – for example, heavy rain may attract large numbers of coastal duck inland to flooded water meadows, but a hard frost will send the entire inland population out to the coast, where the salt prevents freezing. Wind, obviously, has a major effect, altering not just the height at which the duck flight, but the rest areas they select. On nights of good moons the absence of cloud at dusk will encourage duck to delay their flight, whereas moonless nights see the entire population flighting in good time.

These are merely a few examples and when one considers the permutations of tide, wind, light, changing feeding areas, moon, shooting pressures and other factors, it is readily understood that successful wildfowling calls for extensive local experience plus luck. Much, however, can be achieved by observation and commonsense. One is also helped by the desire of duck to follow water courses and, failing other more inspired ideas, it is always worth waiting by a main channel or a major creek. Generations of duck will follow the same principal flight lines, varying slightly according to conditions, and one can sometimes learn more by looking for empty cartridge cases than observing wildfowl.

Evening flight offers more scope for success than morning flight. At dawn the light is improving, there is no pressing hurry for duck to leave their feeding grounds, and they tend to drift off over an extended period. At dusk the light is failing and, except when there is a moon, they must flight promptly. Equally important for the wildfowler, at dusk the duck are concentrating towards small feeding areas and are more easily intercepted than at dawn when they disperse over wider areas. One further, important factor favours evening flight – it is not necessary to rise early from a warm bed into a cold, dark, winter morning.

Not all duck will flight inland, particularly in freezing conditions and a reconnaissance of the marsh in daylight may reveal feathers and droppings where duck have been 'working' the saltings. The state of the droppings will show whether they are old or fresh from the previous night and, if the latter, this is an excellent spot to take evening flight.

When selecting a position to wait under a flight line at dusk, the main considerations are a firm base underfoot and some modest cover for the early stages before the light dims. However, waiting where you expect the fowl actually to pitch needs rather more thought. Obviously the duck will approach into the wind and you must be upwind of the spot or they will land before reaching you. This may not matter at the start, but if you are to see the fowl in bad light you must place yourself so they cross your vision above the horizon. If at all possible place yourself with your back to the east, thereby facing west and, hopefully, silhouetting the duck against the brighter western sky. Judging range is often difficult in fading light, but the tendency is to think duck are further than they are and you will frequently be surprised at how close apparently distant duck are found to lie when retrieved. Once it is almost dark you can assume any duck near enough to see is also near enough to shoot. Some writers recommend placing a blob of mud on the foresight to help see the position of the barrels. Personally I have not found this necessary, for if I can see duck some distance away, there is no problem about seeing the barrels at a couple of feet.

Most novice wildfowlers make the mistake of leaving evening flight too soon. There comes a moment when the world is poised between day and night; a moment which has an eerie, magical quality, which I cannot fully describe, but you will recognise if you wait for flight in a wild and lonely spot. It is then that the duck come, responding to the urgent need to feed under the cover of night. When the moment passes – and you will know it has – the main chance is over, but experienced wildfowlers will stay on for there are often late-comers, frequently fowl which have been driven off their original destination by another gunner.

Morning flight follows the same general pattern, but do remember you will be attempting to reach your place on the marsh in the dark. At the best it will take longer than in daylight and, at the worst, you may not find it at all.

Many wildfowlers, both experienced and novices, suffer the twin drawbacks of time and distance. The best bags are nearly always made in hard weather and bliss for a wildfowler is a full gale that does not carry rain. Unfortunately most of us have to work, and combining spare time with the right weather is difficult. Additionally, the ideal conditions of weather, tide and fowl movements usually occur without much warning and rarely last long. This gives the fortunate few who live near the marshes a great advantage over the majority who, in living some distance away, not only fail to make the journey in time but frequently never even knew the conditions existed. Sad though this may be, there is little we can do about it but, when we have snatched a day and driven some distance, it is a pity to restrict the sport to the brief time of a single flight. Nor need we for day flighting can sometimes provide good sport and even when it does not the keen naturalist wildfowler can enjoy a full day.

Some of the best day flighting occurs in very rough weather, for duck will not tolerate prolonged buffeting in open water and will flight into the marshes for shelter. When, therefore, there is a forecast of heavy winds, make time, and head for the marsh. These are very much occasions for flexibility. Do not arrive with a set plan, but sit down with your binoculars, observe events and use your initiative.

When, as is usually my lot, I have to select a day in advance, I pick one where the tide is out by late morning and then flowing to its peak by about the time of evening flight. Arriving by mid-morning I can move onto the marsh and review the position. With luck duck may be spotted in a position which will allow a stalk down a convenient creek, but failing this diversification, plans can be laid for the tide flight to come. Quite why duck flight as extensively as they do when the tide makes I cannot tell. In theory they simply move from the flooding rest areas of mud and sand into the shelter of the marsh but, usually, the degree of movement is far greater than is necessary to achieve this simple objective. The same happens with wind for, as I mentioned on the subject of pigeons, it encourages birds to fly for no apparent reason. Perhaps it is that wild creatures are, of necessity, healthy and in good condition and healthy bodies enjoy flashes of physical effort.

Whatever the reason, duck flight when the tide floods and usually into the marsh. The wildfowler who knows where they are likely to head, and who also knows where he can wait with safety, should have some chances. These will be increased if he makes use of decoys for, like pigeons, duck are tempted to join their fellows already alighted. Decoying is quite an art and, on occasions, can be highly successful. The more decoys set out the greater their drawing power, but the physical problem of carrying them imposes a limit of about half a dozen. 'Blow-up' rubber decoys are available, but do not survive the rigours of marsh life for long. Plastic decoys are far stronger, but bulky. Whatever tethering arrangement you devise, arrange matters so the decoys can be retrieved at any state of the tide, otherwise you will one day abandon your decoys as you flee, prematurely, before a pending storm. I set out a main anchor line, with loops at intervals, by attaching it to a short stick and pushing this into the mud on the opposite bank of a creek. Pairs of decoys can then be tethered to the individual loops. Take care, however, to consider the flow of the incoming water in the creek and the direction of the wind, or a dreadful tangle will result. Dogs, also, need teaching not to retrieve decoys.

The position you choose to wait should be selected after taking into account the direction from which fowl are likely to appear and the wind. As with pigeon decoying the ideal is to have them crossing your front on a steady path whilst on their way into the decoys. There is, however, an additional factor which does not enter into pigeon decoying – retrieving. As decoying is mainly done on a flowing tide there is usually plenty of water about and your position should be such that retrieving duck is made easier rather than the reverse. Always try to shoot duck where they will fall on land rather than water. If, as if often the case, this is difficult to contrive, position yourself downwind of the anticipated flight line. Duck falling on the water will then be blown to you rather than away. In the same fashion, try to have the tide helping rather than hindering a retrieve. If you drop a wounded duck onto water, kill if at once, for few dogs are consistent retrievers of wounded duck in an element which favours the quarry. In fact, it is surprisingly difficult to kill a wounded duck on water and, if it is at long range and has been shot without actually seeing you clearly, the best plan is to remain concealed. The duck will then swim to land to find cover and the retrieve should be simple.

Geese are not only a most romantic quarry but, on closer acquaintance, highly likeable creatures. They illustrate vividly the contradiction of those shooting men who both love the quarries and yet strive to kill them. The fundamental principles of shooting them are the same as with duck; that is, finding the feeding and roosting areas and lying in ambush in between. There are, however, strong ethical considerations which have been developed by the more responsible wildfowlers and need observing, namely, that it is wrong to disturb geese on either their feeding or roosting areas. In practice, some flexibility exists over feeding areas, for where the geese have been 'working' a small area in large numbers, the crop damage can be serious and restrained shooting can serve the twin purposes of giving sport and moving the geese on. It has, however, to be restrained and not a free-for-all slaughter.

Where the geese winter in large numbers their habits are rather more predictable than duck and it is not too difficult, particularly with local help, to get under the flight line. The geese, being great survivors, have responded by flying high over areas of known danger and it is fascinating to see them gain height as they approach a sea wall or line of dunes in the popular wildfowling areas. Their passage often attracts fire at ridiculous ranges, for men who have journeyed far cannot resist the temptation. Doubtless you, as a responsible sportsman, will.

There is only one answer to the problem of successful goose shooting, and it lies beyond our power, for it is wind. Not just strong wind, which the geese ignore, but roaring gales, when even they are forced to descend to make progress against it. Again we come back to the problem of long distance fowling, for the occasions when a gale blows at the right time, from the right quarter, are so few, and last so briefly, that a man at a distance has little hope of benefiting. Wildfowlers living on the coast, and free to come and go as they choose, should not be held in awe for bagging geese each season.

An occasional exception to the rule of no gale, no geese in the bag, is moonlight flighting, when the geese will sometimes flight at realistic heights. Given the right conditions of moon, intermittent cloud, and distant goose talk, it is one of the most exciting and romantic forms of shooting. Conversely if the night clouds over and it starts to drizzle, it is also one of the dreariest!

Duck can also be flighted very successfully on moonlit nights, but some backcloth of cloud is necessary if they are to be seen. Such expeditions depend very much on the right combination of conditions and, even then, luck plays a major part. For all that is spoken and written about night flighting, you will find few wildfowlers who are consistently regular followers of this form of the sport.

I have just mentioned the ethics of shooting, or rather not shooting, geese on their feeding and roosting grounds and there are other questions of moral responsibility to be weighed by the wildfowler. Long range shooting is one aspect where self-discipline is called for. One can frequently spend hours without a chance and the temptation to fire at excessively long ranges, in the hope of pulling off a fluke, is strong. The danger of magnums and large bore guns is that they ease one's conscience for, having acquired a long range weapon, is it not justifiable to use it at long ranges? Yes, but, 'longer', not 'long'; and longer, as we saw in chapter 2, is not more than ten yards extra. In my view sixty yards is the maximum one should fire at duck, irrespective of the size of the gun, and, with geese, this should be reduced to forty-five yards. No doubt, duck have been killed at eighty yards, or even a hundred, but it is an achievement to be ashamed of rather than proud.

'Browning' is another temptation to avoid, particularly with teal which fly so closely. However, I am not against shooting a sitting duck, provided it is close enough to be reasonably sure of a clean kill. This apparent ethical anomaly stems from the view that before a sportsman kills a quarry he must give himself a test of skill. With a driven pheasant it is one of marksmanship, and getting in range of a sitting, or more probably floating duck on a marsh will call for fieldcraft.

Do not commit the sin of making an excessive bag. Very, very occasionally everything may slot together and you will have the chance to kill a lot of wildfowl. By all means take a decent bag – you are entitled to after possibly years of disappointment – but avoid wanton greediness. Prolonged hard weather puts the wildfowl at our mercy. They grow thin and weak and can often be shot without difficulty. On such occasions Section 7 of the Protection of Birds' Act, 1967, makes provision for the temporary suspension of wildfowling but, during the severe weather of the first quarter of 1979, there was a sharp difference of opinion between the field sports' organisations and The Royal Society for the Protection of Birds over whether an official ban on shooting should be declared. With the great good sense which has characterised discussions between the shooting world and conservationists over the last decade or so, it was quickly accepted that public squabbling helped no-one, least of all the wildfowl, and a working party, under the Chairmanship of the Nature Conservancy Council, was formed to arrive at a simple objective system to determine when a ban was really necessary. The arrangement now agreed is that wildfowlers will be called on to exercise restraint after seven days of continuous freezing or ten days of freezing interspersed with one or two-day thaws. (Thaws not to contribute to the total of ten days.) After fourteen days a statutory ban will be invoked, but after a thaw or thaws of three or more days, then the earlier period of freezing will be disregarded. Essentially the machinery for recommending the Department of the Environment to operate a ban will function through the Nature Conservancy Council.

It is, however, up to every wildfowler to stop, without waiting for a ban, whenever he considers local conditions require it. I have, naturally, assumed no man would wildfowl without a dog, for few wounded duck would be retrieved without one.

A budding wildfowler should be aware of his responsibilities to other sportsmen. Do not arrive late on the marsh and spoil the flight for others by moving about at the critical time. Avoid flashing a torch in the twilight, moving to retrieve when duck are heading for another man, or taking a long shot at a fowl which will give a closer shot to another. Do not take up a position close to a wildfowler already established, and, in particular, do not settle between him and the direction from which the fowl are expected.

If you leave the marsh in severe conditions and do not return home immediately, do let someone know you are safe. This will prevent an unnecessary search being made. If you shoot a ringed fowl, do advise the address provided.

On leaving the marsh you will, no doubt, dry the dog thoroughly and see it lies on something warm and dry. It is well worth giving the gun a preliminary wipe off with an absorbent paper towel and then a liberal spray with one of the anti-moisture oils, for the quicker the corrosive salt can be removed the better. Naturally the normal, thorough cleaning should be given as soon as possible, and if the gun has got very wet it is best to leave it in a warm spot for a few days. Non-wildfowlers rarely appreciate how rapidly the saltings can damage a gun.

With care it is possible to avoid making the interior of one's car look like a creek bottom. Take two large plastic or paper sacks. Bundle the thigh boots into one and all exterior clothing into the other. Insist that companions, who, not owning the car will be less conscientious, do likewise. If, as a shooting man, you have been so improvident as not to acquire an estate car, make dogs lie on the floor on thick layers of newspaper.

At the end of each season all equipment needs overhauling, as many weaknesses, for example rusting metal buckles or rotting decoy strings, will develop. Exterior clothing of the oiled cotton varieties, which includes Barbours, will need re-dressing, for the action of mud and water soon removes the dressing and destroys the waterproof qualities.

Chapter 13
A mixed bag

In this chapter I deal with various aspects of the sport not touched on previously.

First let us take that most pleasurable duty of teaching the young shooting (which is a much wider discipline than simply teaching them to shoot). Some of my happiest shooting hours have come from teaching my three sons shooting, but I began with the advantage that all three were keen to learn. Beware of assuming an automatic interest, for boys dragged unwillingly into a father's interests may turn against a sport they would otherwise have grown into.

The question of how old to start a boy shooting is not easily answered and, if he is enthusiastic, you will come under great pressure for an early beginning. Various factors have to be considered, but one is over-riding, namely that guns kill and it is better to err on the cautious side. An experienced shooting man is likely to have involved his son in the sport from an early age, (my wife was decoying pigeons over a Cambridgeshire pea field a fortnight before our first son was born), and many of the rules of safety and behaviour will have been absorbed. This will not remove the need for detailed instruction on all aspects, but it will enable the youngster to comprehend faster. An important consideration is the character of the individual, for some youngsters are responsible before their teens and others still immature when they leave them.

There is an excellent theoretical argument for not letting any youngster shoot before fifteen or sixteen, but it is a very strong father who will withstand pressure until this age. Nor, in my view, is the age a youngster starts to shoot so important as how. The main problem, in a nutshell, is to stop him shooting either others or himself. You will, of course, lecture him on the dangers and how they are to be avoided, but such self-disciplines do not come easily to young males and, sooner or later, he will grow careless, or over-excited, and do something silly. Given that this is almost inevitable, common sense suggests the closer the supervision he receives and the fewer people there are about, the less the chance of error turning into disaster.

When, then, and where to begin? From the time the boy first starts to accompany you, explain what you are doing and why, but do not overstretch him, either mentally or physically. In the physical context, the young have surprising stamina provided they are interested and not hungry. Never go out without ample snacks, for no healthy young male appears to be able to last more than two hours without nourishment. At about eleven acquire an air rifle and, always under your supervision, teach the basics of aiming, firing and safety. Do not let him use the gun alone at this stage.

Next acquire a double-barrel .410, with conventional top lever opening and safety catch. Disregard the advice of friends who say a .410 is not a practical gun and the lad will be hard pressed to kill things with it. They are absolutely right and it is a major reason for my recommending it. No matter how careful you may be, this is a dangerous stage for a young shot and if he does make a mistake it is best that he is using the lightest possible charge. Another, far less important reason is that he must not develop the habit of flinching when firing and even a very light youngster will not suffer from recoil with a .410. No matter what the financial attractions of alternatives, do buy a double-barrel which is, in every respect, a miniature of a conventional twelve bore. A single-barrel, bolt action, .410 will be much cheaper, but if the boy is to be trained to use a second barrel quickly, to empty his gun when crossing a fence, reload after firing one barrel, wait until he raises the gun before taking off the safety catch, and all the other essential procedures, then he must begin with a replica of the real thing.

A final advantage of the .410 is weight. From the start it is important to have the novice adopting the correct posture with his body and mounting the gun correctly. If the gun is heavy a youngster counteracts this by leaning backwards and gets into the bad habit of shooting off his back foot rather than the front. Weight also matters from the simple aspect of carrying, for most of the boy's shooting will involve walking and an extra pound or two bears more heavily on a boy than a man.

So at what age? Reluctantly I state that my boys were all shooting, within strict limitations, by the time they were twelve. I say reluctantly because I think twelve is too young, but I am not good at resisting the sparkle of enthusiasm in young eyes. Begin with our old friend the pigeon. Take the boy decoying, sit behind him in the hide and let him bang away. The advantages, from a safety angle, are obvious. He is stationary, and cannot stumble or fall, and the hide imposes a restricted arc of fire which you will have ensured is safe. You can watch every move, including his safety catch drill, and pounce on such crimes as wanting to lean a loaded gun in a corner while he sets up dead pigeons. It is also a good opportunity to instruct in marksmanship, and correct such faults as putting the butt to the shoulder prematurely or poking.

So far you will observe I have given priority to safety, for there is no rush for him to learn to hit the target. This is not to say that marksmanship is unimportant – rather that *how* he does things is more important than

Even the most natural young shot will benefit by occasional coaching to eradicate bad habits at an early stage.

marksmanship at this stage. Gun fitting is a major problem with teenagers, for no gun will fit correctly for more than a year or so, but if left to shoot with a badly fitting gun, the efforts made to compensate can develop into a bad technique. This is another advantage of a .410, for most are intended for youngsters and have a short stock. Where it is too long you can have it cut down, for by the time the boy grows out of the stock he will also have grown out of a .410.

Once he has had enough shooting to have some basic idea, take him to a shooting school. Nowadays this is an expensive exercise, but it is essential to groove him into the right technique from the start. Watch and listen to the instructor, for much of what he says will be forgotten by the boy and you can correct the particular faults when they reappear. If you can afford regular lessons, these will obviously be a great help but, if not, it is better to have the occasional lesson as he develops rather than a complete course at the start and nothing more for years.

Do not worry if he shows little ability as a marksman. Many youngsters simply do not develop their powers of co-ordination and timing for some years and then it comes in a rush. My own experience was that a boy would finish one season as a very indifferent shot, not touch a gun for months, then begin the next season as a much improved shot. It is very important that we do not lose our sense of proportion in teaching young shots – always remember the object is for them to enjoy themselves and, provided they do this, the issues that would make or mar our day are unimportant.

When you move on from the pigeon hide, or some other form of static shooting, under no circumstances have the boy shoot with several companions. This is unfair both to the boy and the other Guns. While he is a raw novice you should be the only person with him and you should always walk to the right – the safer side. Our good fortune in having rough shooting in the Hebrides provided an ideal training ground for youngsters, for one can see for miles and there is no risk of shooting anyone through a foolish shot into a hedge. Over the years I have walked hundreds of miles with the boys and each of them has made his errors without risk to anyone.

At the beginning make a firm rule that if you shout 'No!', the boy immediately takes the gun from his shoulder without hesitation or question. Only in this way can you be sure of bringing matters to a halt if you see a dangerous situation developing.

Readers may feel I accept the prospect of safety errors too complacently, but it is an attitude based on reality rather than idealism. Naturally in one's attitude to the youngster both the prospect and the fact of an infringement of safety are treated very seriously, but you cannot expect a flawless performance. Nor am I a disciple of the much vaunted practice of sending a boy home or taking his gun away for several months if he makes a mistake. Obviously acts of unthinking stupidity or irresponsibility must mean a temporary end to shooting but understandable errors and omissions should be discussed on the basis that, the mistake having revealed the danger, it will never be repeated. One would not set about teaching a youngster to drive and then refuse to give him or her any more lessons for a month because they stalled the engine.

You will recall I advocated starting with a .410 because it was the least dangerous, practical gun. Once the boy has become competent and reasonably safe there comes the problem of the next gun. If he is well developed physically and strong (which two factors do not always occur at once), he may be able to go into a twelve bore. In theory, this offends the principle of only letting him move up to a shot charge large enough to give a reasonable prospect of consistent kills, but this can be overcome by restricting him to the Eley two inch, or the one ounce Impax. However, while this limits the power of the cartridge, the lad still has the weight of a standard twelve bore to cope with, and worse, it will almost certainly be too long in the stock. Our own solution was a twenty bore with a relatively short stock and this worked so well that, in turn, each of the boys was reluctant eventually to move on to a twelve and lingered with the twenty for a season or so. A twenty bore really is an excellent size for youngsters and lady shots, combining light weight and modest recoil with a heavy enough charge to cope adequately with all normal close and medium range shooting.

As time passes you will observe the boy gradually imposing his own disciplines. Lose no opportunity to commend any positive act of safety, such as withholding fire at a rabbit because of a dog, or letting a walked-up grouse go to avoid firing at a rather close skyline. I also found it useful to encourage the boys to challenge me over any unsafe act on my part, explaining that errors were not limited to novices. It was a suggestion accepted with enthusiasm and led to me tightening up my own performance. (Try explaining to a youngster why it was sufficient merely to break the gun, but not remove the cartridges, because the dilapidated wire fence could be stepped over easily!).

Eventually your son will shoot in the company of others and it is as well to warn him that he will be viewed with apprehension by most and, human nature being what it is, particularly by the least safe Guns.

Naturally a boy must be required to treat the gun he uses carefully and clean it well at the end of each day. Never let a youngster have possession of a gun other than when shooting – there is no point in this and there is potential danger. Personally I keep all guns locked in a security cabinet and store cartridges in another part of the house.

Mention of the need to require a youngster to clean his gun well leads neatly to the matter of how we care for our own equipment. I can advance a strong argument for conscientious maintenance, namely that well-maintained equipment will avoid such inconveniences as a jammed gun or a leaking jacket, but many readers will doubtless agree with me that caring for possessions should be done as a matter of principle first and function second.

Considering how much they now cost, and how long they last if well cared for, it is surprising how badly some men treat guns. When assembling or dismantling a gun it only takes a few seconds longer to do the job with care. Work over a soft surface, grass or a car seat, rather than a hard drive or gravel, and if a component is dropped no damage will occur. And it wounds my instinctive sympathy for mechanical things to hear a man clash his barrels onto the action – why can he not unite them gently? A gun is a fine example of design and craftsmanship and demands proper respect. It is foolish not to carry a gun, on formal shoots, in a well padded sleeve. As it will not be used between one drive and the next, there is no point in having it ready to hand and virtually all damage to game guns occurs not when actually shooting but in travelling about the shoot. How frequently one sees a man climb into a Landrover with an exposed gun, place the butt on a wet, muddy floor and place his dirty boots either side of the stock. It hurts.

Even when a gun is well sleeved, always hold it vertically when in a vehicle. If you lay it down, or lean it against a seat, the heaviest dog or man will sit or fall on it. Sleeving a gun also helps prevent water seeping into the action on wet days and shielding it with the body when waiting in rain is also good sense.

Considering my enthusiasm for gun care, readers may be surprised to learn that I do not necessarily clean my gun at the end of every day. The arrival of non-corrosive cartridge caps removed the danger of barrel pitting by chemical deposits from the ignition of the powder and cap. The problem now is not the deposits but their tendency to attract and hold damp in wet weather. Consequently when I am shooting on successive days in dry weather I simply follow my standard practice of a squirt of anti-moisture oil down each barrel, but no more. On occasions I have left the barrels uncleaned for a week or more without the slightest ill effect. However, it is important to clean the barrel flats and action faces at the end of the day for powder fragments and particles of dirt will hasten the time when the action will need tightening. Even though I may be shooting again within a few hours I always dismantle and case a gun, rather than leave it in a sleeve, where it is more vulnerable.

The practice of spraying the barrels immediately shooting ceases not only stops corrosion through damp, but makes the subsequent cleaning far easier. During the interval before cleaning, the oil soaks into the barrel fouling and softens it. A ball formed from a paper tissue, pushed through by the cleaning rod, will then do ninety per cent of the cleaning and a good scrub with an oiled patch on a jag will do the rest. I only use a phosphor bronze brush if really necessary. On wet days it is wise to spray the entire gun liberally with oil, which will creep under the moisture and allow it to run off. The oil layer can subsequently be wiped off and, after cleaning, the gun needs to be left in a warm spot to dry any internal moisture.

Clay shooters, I am told, make a practice of firing a shot through each barrel at the start of each day, believing the oil deposit will spoil the pattern. Whether this is really necessary I cannot say, but I never notice other sportsmen performing this fad of perfection.

I suspect far too many men either do not insure their guns at all or have them under-insured. Which is a good moment to mention the wisdom of personal insurance against shooting others or being shot. The cost is so little, and the impact of a major award against one so crippling if, for example, one cut down a brilliant young surgeon approaching his prime, that not to be covered is foolish. Membership of WAGBI now automatically carries insurance against shooting accidents. However, additional cover is advisable to cover gun, as distinct from human damage.

Clothing is an item we tend to take for granted until a cold, clammy feeling reveals a flaw. Some forms have a natural life and then must be replaced, but Barbours, and other makes based on waxed cotton material remain waterproof until they literally wear out provided they are re-proofed regularly. Garments can either be returned to the manufacturer or treated personally with a tin of proprietary wax. It is a simple and quick task and takes little more time than the alternative of packing and posting the garment. Sewing up minor tears prevents them becoming major ones.

As one of the prime objects of shooting is to cast off our cares and relax in the countryside, most shooting men are not very interested in the various laws affecting the sport. However, the more responsible sportsmen will wish to know their legal obligations and the following review of some important aspects may reveal the occasional area of ignorance.

Provided our smooth bore guns have barrels of not less than twenty-four inches we escape the need to have a Firearms' Certificate and, instead, require the more easily obtained Shot Gun Certificate. There are certain exceptions, of which the only one likely to be of use to us is the right to borrow a shot gun from the occupier of private premises and use it on the premises in the presence of the occupier. In other words, if you have a friend to stay, who has no Certificate, you may lend him a gun to shoot on your ground provided you accompany him.

The grounds upon which a Chief Constable may refuse to issue a Certificate are very limited and it is unlikely that any readers will have experienced difficulty. However, the law is somewhat vague, stating the Chief Constable will issue a Certificate unless he has reason to believe the individual cannot be permitted to possess a shot gun without danger to the public safety or to the peace. This was intended to cope with cases where the police had reason to suspect an intent to poach, or similar 'disturbances of good order', but some Chief Constables have interpreted this as grounds for refusing a Certificate where the applicant cannot show he has land upon which to shoot. When these cases come to light the representatives of the shooting community object strongly and usually obtain a Certificate for the individual. If I did not feel these refusals were the thin end of a very thick wedge, I would not support these efforts to gain freedom for all to shoot whatever their circumstances. It is unfortunate but true that much of the irresponsible shooting and poaching comes from town-based youngsters who buy a gun and then look for somewhere to fire it.

One area of the law which readers may be forced to explore is that which relates to youngsters and shot guns. I first applied for a Shot Gun Certificate for each of my boys as they reached the age of eleven and, on each occasion I had to explain to a very courteous policeman that there is no minimum age for a Shot Gun Certificate. The law severely curtails the rights of a youngster preventing him from buying or hiring a shot gun, or ammunition, when under the age of seventeen. Between the ages of fifteen and seventeen he may be given a shot gun, or ammunition, and at less than fifteen he may not own a gun or ammunition, no matter how it has come into his possession. Furthermore, unless the gun is in a securely fastened gun cover, he cannot have an assembled shot gun with him unless he is under the supervision of someone at least twenty-one years old.

Formidable though all this sounds, it actually imposes no unreasonable restriction at all. Even if the law was silent few parents would be happy to let a boy of less than fifteen shoot unsupervised. And it is a simple matter for a grandfather to leave his Holland or Churchill in trust for a fortunate grandson when he reaches the age of fifteen.

I suspect there are a not inconsiderable number of otherwise law abiding citizens who should take out an annual Game Licence but do not. In idle moments, at some fairly high-powered formal shoots, I look around me at all the men of standing and consequence and speculate on what would happen if the village Bobby appeared and asked to see everyone's Game Licence. Fortunately, perhaps, even rural police are not clear on the law. Once, in Norfolk of all places, I was walking off a freshwater marsh with a mallard when a constable asked for my Game Licence. In fact, there are several Acts of Parliament dealing with shooting game and, together, they produce some complexities. For example, shooting at, but missing, a pheasant in the summer is not an offence (you have not killed it), but missing one on Christmas Day is (you have tried to kill it and, on Christmas Day, that is enough). It is also an offence, if you do not hold a Game Licence, accidentally to knock down a pheasant with your car and then take it away.

Contrary to much popular belief, a Game Licence is needed to kill rabbits, but with an exemption for the tenant of the land or by anyone acting with his direction or permission. Regrettably the prospect of support in high places for a reduction in the Licence fee is diminished by the exemption of any member of the Royal Family. Were it not for a specific exemption, the various assistants in the shooting scene, the beaters, loaders, pickers-up and others, would need a Game Licence and, even with this, the dividing line between correct and incorrect practice is thin. For example, a picker-up must not lend his, or her dog to anyone else.

One useful snippet is that if you hold a Game Licence you are legally entitled to ask anyone you see killing game to show his Licence to you. This could be a very effective way to quieten down a neighbouring Gun who has been poaching your pheasants all morning.

In spite of various cases over the years, the law is still not entirely clear over the question of standing on your ground and shooting game over your neighbour's. Certainly if you flush game on your ground and shoot it over his, then the carcase is yours, but if you go and pick it up without permission you are guilty of trespass. If, however, your dog crosses into your neighbour's ground and flushes game which you shoot, then the carcase belongs to your neighbour. Not only the courts, but generations of shooting men, have argued the various permutations of these boundary arguments. It is doubtful whether the time and thought devoted to them are justified by the few occasions when disputes actually occur.

It is, of course, pointless to dwell on the penalties for poaching, for no reader of this book would be guilty of so heinous a crime. However, circumstances could make you appear guilty and you should know that a policeman has the power to search you, in any public place, if he has cause to suspect you of poaching, or of the possession of game unlawfully obtained.

The Protection of Birds' Act, 1954, is, not surprisingly, complex, but I imagine most readers will know those aspects dealing with shooting. One point to watch is the restriction against using a mechanically propelled boat in immediate pursuit of a wild bird. This will allow wildfowlers to use a boat with an engine to reach the area they wish to shoot in, but not to approach fowl with the object of taking a shot. The critical words are 'immediate pursuit'.

Walking on a public road with a loaded gun creates an offence, even if all one has done is to move from peg 5 in the stubble, to cross the road to peg 7 in the sugar-beet. In so doing you have had with you in a public place a loaded shot gun, which is an offence unless you can satisfy the Court you had a reasonable excuse. Serves you right for not unloading between drives. Of greater relevance is the law about shooting on or near the highway. Only last October my Norfolk host placed me behind a roadside hedge to await the partridge coveys. Granted in rural Norfolk the farmers regard the roads as their own, but I felt some apprehension. In fact, in spite of the belief that one cannot shoot within fifty feet of the centre of a highway, the law does not actually say this. What it does forbid is discharging a firearm within fifty feet from the centre of a highway as a consequence of which the highway is damaged or a user of the highway is injured, interrupted or endangered. The implication is that provided you do none of these things, no offence is committed, although common sense will prohibit one from firing when a vehicle or pedestrian is anywhere near.

Hopefully the attitude of the law to your sport will remain of only academic interest to you, but if you should need to investigate any aspect I commend you to *Gun Law*, by Godfrey Sandys-Winsch.

One aspect of shooting in which some experienced shots are lacking is first-aid. Bearing in mind the sometimes rough ground in which we operate, the constant presence of powerful guns, and the time lag which would usually occur before help arrived, we should all have some basic knowledge of how to cope. The most likely problem is severe bleeding caused by a gunshot wound, and this must be stopped. The once almost standard method of applying a tourniquet has now given way to the practice of stopping the bleeding by covering the wound with a pad. For this to be successful the pad must be really thick, cover a large area around the wound and be held firmly in place. Under no circumstances remove the pad, for the object is not to soak up blood, but to stop the flow. If blood soaks through simply add more padding. Keep the patient warm, do *not* give him alcohol and get him to a doctor or hospital.

Severe bleeding is very serious but at least the treatment open to the layman is simple. Broken limbs, although less of a threat to life, are more complicated. If an arm, contrive a sling, bind the arm to the body to minimise movement and help the patient walk slowly to safety. Legs are far more difficult, for moving the patient could cause more damage. If skilled help can be summoned quickly, it is better to call it and merely keep the patient warm. Again, no alcohol, but any form of hot drink, and, of course, all available coats and pullovers piled under, round and on. If you are forced to move the patient, then first construct a splint from whatever material is at hand. In the unlikely event of there being nothing, tie the damaged leg to the sound leg. Carry the patient across one shoulder with the legs dangling down your back. However, it is far better to take longer to get the patient to safety, but to do so properly and comfortably on a stretcher. (Never underestimate the advantages of joining a syndicate which includes a doctor and/or a surgeon!)

It is virtually impossible to read an instructional book on shooting without eventually reading an exhortation to join the various organising bodies of the sport. This is mine, and stated in unequivocable terms. It is a disgrace that such a relatively small percentage of the shooting community in this country supports BFSS, The Game Conservancy, and WAGBI. These bodies exist because for many years a large number of selfless individuals have given time, energy and money to furthering the interests of the sport. Not everyone has the time to help, but very few shooting men are unable to afford an annual subscription to at least one, but preferably all of the three bodies. It is the old, depressing story of human apathy, with people only stirring to defend their interests when it is almost too late. In the main I will be preaching to the converted, but if you are one of the minority please feel guilty and do something about it now.

It has always seemed a little unrealistic to me that everyone, members or not, have access to the famous green booklets published by the Game Conservancy. In these pages can be found the compounded wisdom of generations of scientists, gamekeepers and others on a wide range of topics to do with game, their rearing, habitat and diseases. A card to the Conservancy at Fordingbridge, Hapmshire will bring a list of the current booklets and the price asked for their contents is one of the few examples of excellent value for money left in this country.

Up to now I have had little to say on the subject of dogs; an omission which will be but partly remedied, for I do not feel justified in writing authoritatively. Like most keen shooting men I am very attached to my dogs, but pressures of time make it impossible both to train them to a high standard and, almost equally difficult, to maintain them there. At one time this shortcoming troubled me, but I have developed a philosophy of simply enjoying the companionship of my dogs, and not expecting too much. I was once attracted to a headline, dealing with the problems of America's President, which said, 'We must not compare Carter to God, but the alternatives'. Equally we should not judge our dogs by how much they fall short of perfection, but how they rank against the next man's, and on this basis, my spaniels, which are far from angels, do not come out too badly. 'God', for our comparison, is a Field Trial Champion, or, to be more realistic, its trainer. Now this gifted man or woman devotes his or her life to training, investigating in the process various dogs and retaining only the most promising. These receive highly skilled and very regular training under ideal conditions. You and I, on the other hand, are often forced to go days on end without being able to find any training time at all. And this for a young dog selected for no really sound reason, from a litter never previously seen and cannot now get rid of because it has made its mark on the family. Take heart, not least in the fact that in the course of a season one sees very, very few really good dogs. This is not a cry of defeat, or a suggestion that it is hardly worth bothering. Obviously there is both utility and satisfaction in training one's dog to the highest possible standard. But the operative word is 'possible' and there is no point in fretting over that which is not feasible.

Some years of training my own dogs have led me to a few basic conclusions which I pass on. There is a marked similarity between raising children and training dogs, in that both have inborn objection to discipline and both will be as disobedient as their parents/trainer permits. Both species also vary widely in trainability, ranging from the tractable to the near uncontrollable. Finally comes the complication that the more high-spirited and difficult often possess the brightest and most lovable personalities. In both cases results only come from patient, tenacious, and firm insistence upon adherence to certain standards and the moment you accept defeat and relax a requirement, so will the subject eagerly take up the new freedom. As an example, at the puppy stage it is a nuisance to insist that, once off the lead a dog walks strictly to heel but, a few years later, this spells the difference between a dog always close by and the familiar sight of a wide ranging beast with an owner constantly calling it back.

Among those men, and for that matter pickers-up, who are only concerned with retrieving at formal shoots, there is often a lack of appreciation of the much greater difficulty of training a dog for the various forms of rough shooting. Consider the training of a dog required entirely for formal shooting. It has to be a good retriever, which performance requires it to

A young springer, bred by the author and trained by his wife.

follow a scent, pick up the quarry and deliver it to its handler. There is no difficulty in teaching a dog to follow a scent – it is a basic, inborn instinct, and it is not so much a question of teaching it as just allowing it to follow its wishes. Nor is there any problem in teaching most dogs to retrieve to hand, or to stand by a peg while firing is in progress. Obviously the latter discipline takes time, but the immediate proximity of the owner exerts a powerful influence. Even when the dog is sent to retrieve at the end of the drive there is no need to impose limitations on the distance it travels. No such freedom can be granted to the rough shooter's dog which, if it is to do its job properly, must never work beyond easy range of its master. Now if you read the various instructional books on dog training this is the point at which they are weakest. Even H. W. Carlton in his classic of 1915, *Spaniels: Their Breaking for Sport and Field Trials*, said that to prevent a dog working too far out he relied mostly upon showing it that the handler was helping it to find game. Doubtless this works with a dog which feels in need of help, but few of them do. None of the others have anything constructive to offer and my experience has been that this is far the most difficult aspect of dog training, particularly with spaniels. Whatever the books may say, if you are working a young spaniel bursting with fitness, in thick cover, and it gets onto the scent of a rabbit or fast travelling cock pheasant, nothing on this earth will stop it. It cannot see you, would not stop to look for instructions if it could, and nor can you see it. As a result in a few seconds it is eighty yards away. Although frowned upon by some experts, I have had some success in open country by working a youngster on a check cord, but once this is discarded it needs constant vigilance to prevent the dog working out of range.

Probably the most common fault of the shooting man setting out to train his own dog is to start too soon and advance too quickly. By all means have a dog walking to heel and carrying out simple retrieves at six months or so, but do not confuse this with real training – this begins when you and the dog are both determined it will do different things, which takes us back to the great gulf between letting a labrador follow the scent of a wounded bird and requiring an enthusiastic spaniel to remain within twenty-five yards. There is just no comparison in the degree of difficulty.

Obviously it is good sense for a young dog to be out with you in the country on every possible occasion, always provided it is kept under firm control. This is a major reason why gamekeepers are good trainers, for their dogs can be with them for hours each day. By the time we have learnt how to be good parents to our children it is too late, for the opportunity has gone, but with dogs we are permitted several opportunities. One error I have seen perpetrated many times is the foolishness of letting a dog take an active part when attending its first shoot. X will turn up, proud of his new dog, on whose training he has worked hard all summer. The dog, whose experience to date consists of hearing a starting pistol and retrieving several cold pigeons, is surrounded by a welter of other dogs, many people, and a profusion of exciting smells. Half an hour later it hears a crescendo of noise, watches birds flying in all directions and bodies crashing to the ground. It is the equivalent of expecting an extrovert seventeen year old boy, home from a long term at boarding school, to go to a party with plenty of girls, unlimited drink, no parental supervision, and to behave like a monk. To the surprise of no-one but X the dog is excited and uncontrollable and several months' hard work disappears in ten minutes. I favour taking young dogs shooting, but as observers only. There are many small lessons which can be given without allowing the dog out of control. The lesson of not entering or leaving a vehicle without command can be instilled, dead pheasants can be sniffed, and even, in a quiet moment and a quiet spot, a carcase concealed for a short distance retrieve.

Done sensibly and slowly the process of bringing on a young dog should be a pleasure and not a worry. The ideal rule would be never to give an instruction to a dog which you cannot enforce if it disobeys and, with this in mind, it is true to say that when you reach the stage where the dog will sit obediently when you blow the stop whistle, then you are at least three-quarters of the way to success.

When, however, we have finished with the mechanics of training, what matters is the relationship between dog and man. There are not many really unpleasant shooting men, but it is noticeable that those who are either lack a dog altogether or pay little regard to it. Conversely, the better a man treats his dog the better companion he makes, and I will regard it as a good start if my young daughters eventually find suitors who are by nature keen dog men.

In a book in which there has been, of necessity, a concentration on factual instruction, the relationship between dogs and people is a good point to conclude. The countryside would be a poorer place without shooting men and their dogs and I very much hope that, generations on, both will still be playing their parts.

Index

Also by John Marchington

Photographing Wildlife
Shooting – A Complete Guide for Beginners
An Introduction to Bird and Wildlife Photography (with Anthony Clay, ARPS)
Sportsman's Bag
Game Shooting – Management and Economics
The Practical Wildfowler
Pugs and Drummers
A Portrait of Shooting (anthology)
The History of Wildfowling
The Natural History of Game

TEN COMMANDMENTS FOR THE COMPLETE SHOT

One

Be at all times safe

Two

Strive to achieve clean kills—avoid long-range shooting

Three

Retrieve and dispatch wounded game immediately

Four

Place the well-being of your dog before your own

Five

Study to be quiet